By Matthew Stover

IRON DAWN

JERICHO MOON

HEROES DIE

BLADE OF TYSHALLE

STAR WARS: THE NEW JEDI ORDER: TRAITOR

STAR WARS: SHATTERPOINT

STAR WARS: EPISODE III REVENGE OF THE SITH

EPISODE III

REVENGE OF THE SITH™

STAR WARS®

EPISODE III
REVENGE OF THE SITH™

MATTHEW STOVER

BASED ON THE STORY AND SCREENPLAY BY
GEORGE LUCAS

LUCAS BOOKS

THE RANDOM HOUSE PUBLISHING GROUP
NEW YORK

Star Wars: Episode III *Revenge of the Sith* is a work of fiction. Names, characters, places, and incidents are the products of the author's imagination or are used fictitiously. Any resemblance to actual events, locales, or persons, living or dead, is entirely coincidental.

Copyright © 2005 by Lucasfilm Ltd., & ® or ™ where indicated.
All Rights Reserved. Used Under Authorization.

Published in the United States by Del Rey Books, an imprint of The Random House Publishing Group, a division of Random House, Inc., New York.

Del Rey is a registered trademark and the Del Rey colophon is a trademark of Random House, Inc.

The Cataloging-in-Publication Data for this title is available from the publisher.

Printed in the United States of America

www.starwars.com
www.starwarskids.com
Del Rey Books website address: www.delreybooks.com

2   4   6   8   9   7   5   3   1

First Edition

the author respectfully dedicates this adaptation

To George Lucas

with gratitude for the dreams of a generation,
and of generations to come,
for twenty-eight years, and counting . . .

thank you, sir.

A LONG TIME AGO IN A GALAXY FAR, FAR AWAY. . . .

This story happened a long time ago in a galaxy far, far away. It is already over. Nothing can be done to change it.

 It is a story of love and loss, brotherhood and betrayal, courage and sacrifice and the death of dreams. It is a story of the blurred line between our best and our worst.

 It is the story of the end of an age.

 A strange thing about stories—

 Though this all happened so long ago and so far away that words cannot describe the time or the distance, it is also happening right now. Right here.

 It is happening as you read these words.

 This is how twenty-five millennia come to a close. Corruption and treachery have crushed a thousand years of peace. This is not just the end of a republic; night is falling on civilization itself.

 This is the twilight of the Jedi.

 The end starts now.

INTRODUCTION

THE AGE OF HEROES

The skies of Coruscant blaze with war.

The artificial daylight spread by the capital's orbital mirrors is sliced by intersecting flames of ion drives and punctuated by starburst explosions; contrails of debris raining into the atmosphere become tangled ribbons of cloud. The nightside sky is an infinite lattice of shining hairlines that interlock planetoids and track erratic spirals of glowing gnats. Beings watching from rooftops of Coruscant's endless cityscape can find it beautiful.

From the inside, it's different.

The gnats are drive-glows of starfighters. The shining hairlines are light-scatter from turbolaser bolts powerful enough to vaporize a small town. The planetoids are capital ships.

The battle from the inside is a storm of confusion and panic, of galvened particle beams flashing past your starfighter so close that your cockpit rings like a broken annunciator, of the boot-sole shock of concussion missiles that blast into your cruiser, killing beings you have trained with and eaten with and played and laughed and bickered with. From the inside, the battle is desperation and terror and the stomach-churning certainty that the whole galaxy is trying to kill you.

Across the remnants of the Republic, stunned beings watch in horror as the battle unfolds live on the HoloNet. Everyone knows the war has been going badly. Everyone knows that more Jedi are killed or captured every day, that the Grand Army of the Republic has been pushed out of system after system, but this—

A strike at the very heart of the Republic?

An *invasion* of *Coruscant itself*?

How can this *happen*?

It's a nightmare, and no one can wake up.

Live via HoloNet, beings watch the Separatist droid army flood the government district. The coverage is filled with images of overmatched clone troopers cut down by remorselessly powerful destroyer droids in the halls of the Galactic Senate itself.

A gasp of relief: the troopers seem to beat back the attack. There are hugs and even some quiet cheers in living rooms across the galaxy as the Separatist forces retreat to their landers and streak for orbit—

We won! beings tell each other. *We held them off!*

But then new reports trickle in—only rumors at first—that the attack wasn't an invasion at all. That the Separatists weren't trying to take the planet. That this was a lightning raid on the Senate itself.

The nightmare gets worse: the Supreme Chancellor is missing.

Palpatine of Naboo, the most admired man in the galaxy, whose unmatched political skills have held the Republic together. Whose personal integrity and courage prove that the Separatist propaganda of corruption in the Senate is nothing but lies. Whose charismatic leadership gives the whole Republic the will to fight on.

Palpatine is more than respected. He is loved.

Even the rumor of his disappearance strikes a dagger to the heart of every friend of the Republic. Every one of them knows it in her heart, in his gut, in its very bones—

Without Palpatine, the Republic will fall.

And now confirmation comes through, and the news is worse than anyone could have imagined. Supreme Chancellor Palpatine has been captured by the Separatists—and not just the Separatists.

He's in the hands of General Grievous.

Grievous is not like other leaders of the Separatists. Nute Gunray is treacherous and venal, but he's Neimoidian: venality and treachery are expected, and in the Chancellor of the Trade Federation they're even virtues. Poggle the Lesser is Archduke of the weapon masters of Geonosis, where the war began: he is analytical and pitiless, but also pragmatic. Reasonable. The political heart of the Separatist Confederacy, Count Dooku, is known for his integrity, his principled stand against what he sees as corruption in the Senate. Though they believe he's wrong, many respect him for the courage of his mistaken convictions.

These are hard beings. Dangerous beings. Ruthless and aggressive.

General Grievous, though—

Grievous is a *monster.*

The Separatist Supreme Commander is an abomination of nature, a fusion of flesh and droid—and his droid parts have more compassion than what remains of his alien flesh. This half-living creature is a slaughterer of billions. Whole planets have burned at his command. He is the evil genius of the Confederacy. The architect of their victories.

The author of their atrocities.

And his durasteel grip has closed upon Palpatine. He confirms the capture personally in a wideband transmission from his command cruiser in the midst of the orbital battle. Beings across the galaxy watch, and shudder, and pray that they might wake up from this awful dream.

Because they know that what they're watching, live on the HoloNet, is the death of the Republic.

Many among these beings break into tears; many more reach out to comfort their husbands or wives, their crèche-mates or kin-triads, and their younglings of all descriptions, from children to cubs to spawn-fry.

But here is a strange thing: few of the younglings *need* comfort. It is instead the younglings who offer comfort to their elders. Across the Republic—in words or pheromones, in magnetic pulses, tentacle-braids, or mental telepathy—the message from the younglings is the same: *Don't worry. It'll be all right.*

Anakin and Obi-Wan will be there any minute.

They say this as though these names can conjure miracles.

Anakin and Obi-Wan. Kenobi and Skywalker. From the beginning of the Clone Wars, the phrase *Kenobi and Skywalker* has become a single word. They are everywhere. HoloNet features of their operations against the Separatist enemy have made them the most famous Jedi in the galaxy.

Younglings across the galaxy know their names, know everything about them, follow their exploits as though they are sports heroes instead of warriors in a desperate battle to save civilization. Even grown-ups are not immune; it's not uncommon for an exasperated parent to ask, when faced with offspring who have just tried to pull off one of the spectacularly dangerous bits of foolishness that are the stock-in-trade of high-spirited younglings everywhere, *So which were you supposed to be, Kenobi or Skywalker?*

Kenobi would rather talk than fight, but when there is fighting to be done, few can match him. Skywalker is the master of audacity; his intensity, boldness, and sheer jaw-dropping luck are the perfect complement to Kenobi's deliberate, balanced steadiness. Together, they are a Jedi hammer that has crushed Separatist infestations on scores of worlds.

All the younglings watching the battle in Coruscant's sky know it: when Anakin and Obi-Wan get there, those dirty Seppers are going to wish they'd stayed in bed today.

The adults know better, of course. That's part of what being a grown-up is: understanding that heroes are created by the HoloNet, and that the real-life Kenobi and Skywalker are only human beings, after all.

Even if they really are everything the legends say they are, who's to say they'll show up in time? Who knows where they are right now? They might be trapped on some Separatist backwater. They might be captured, or wounded. Even dead.

Some of the adults even whisper to themselves, *They might have fallen.*

Because the stories are out there. Not on the HoloNet, of course—the HoloNet news is under the control of the Office of the Supreme Chancellor, and not even Palpatine's renowned candor would allow tales like these to be told—but people hear whispers. Whispers of names that the Jedi would like to pretend never existed.

Sora Bulq. Depa Billaba. Jedi who have fallen to the dark. Who have joined the Separatists, or worse: who have massacred civilians, or even murdered their comrades. The adults have a sickening suspicion that Jedi cannot be trusted. Not anymore. That even the greatest of them can suddenly just . . . snap.

The adults know that legendary heroes are merely legends, and not heroes at all.

These adults can take no comfort from their younglings. Palpatine is captured. Grievous will escape. The Republic will fall. No mere human beings can turn this tide. No mere human beings would even try. Not even Kenobi and Skywalker.

And so it is that these adults across the galaxy watch the HoloNet with ashes where their hearts should be.

Ashes because they can't see two prismatic bursts of realspace reversion, far out beyond the planet's gravity well; because they can't see a pair of starfighters crisply jettison hyperdrive rings and streak into the storm of Separatist vulture fighters with all guns blazing.

A pair of starfighters. Jedi starfighters. Only two.

Two is enough.

Two is enough because the adults are wrong, and their younglings are right.

Though this is the end of the age of heroes, it has saved its best for last.

PART ONE

VICTORY

The dark is generous.

Its first gift is concealment: our true faces lie in the dark beneath our skins, our true hearts remain shadowed deeper still. But the greatest concealment lies not in protecting our secret truths, but in hiding from us the truths of others.

The dark protects us from what we dare not know.

Its second gift is comforting illusion: the ease of gentle dreams in night's embrace, the beauty that imagination brings to what would repel in day's harsh light. But the greatest of its comforts is the illusion that the dark is temporary: that every night brings a new day. Because it is day that is temporary.

Day is the illusion.

Its third gift is the light itself: as days are defined by the nights that divide them, as stars are defined by the infinite black through which they wheel, the dark embraces the light, and brings it forth from the center of its own self.

With each victory of the light, it is the dark that wins.

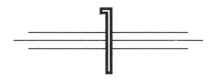

ANAKIN AND OBI-WAN

Antifighter flak flashed on all sides. Even louder than the clatter of shrapnel and the snarl of his sublight drives, his cockpit hummed and rang with near hits from the turbolaser fire of the capital ships crowding space around him. Sometimes his whirling spinning dive through the cloud of battle skimmed bursts so closely that the energy-scatter would slam his starfighter hard enough to bounce his head off the supports of his pilot's chair.

Right now Obi-Wan Kenobi envied the clones: at least they had helmets.

"Arfour," he said on internal comm, "can't you do something with the inertials?"

The droid ganged into the socket on his starfighter's left wing whistled something that sounded suspiciously like a human apology. Obi-Wan's frown deepened. R4-P17 had been spending too much time with Anakin's eccentric astromech; it was picking up R2-D2's bad habits.

New bursts of flak bracketed his path. He reached into the Force, feeling for a safe channel through the swarms of shrapnel and sizzling nets of particle beams.

There wasn't one.

He locked a snarl behind his teeth, twisting his starfighter around another explosion that could have peeled its armor like an overripe Ithorian starfruit. He hated this part. *Hated* it.

Flying's for droids.

His cockpit speakers crackled. *"There isn't a droid made that can outfly you, Master."*

He could still be surprised by the new depth of that voice. The calm confidence. The maturity. It seemed that only last week Anakin had been a ten-year-old who wouldn't stop pestering him about Form I lightsaber combat.

"Sorry," he muttered, kicking into a dive that slipped a turbo-laser burst by no more than a meter. "Was that out loud?"

"Wouldn't matter if it wasn't. I know what you're thinking."

"Do you?" He looked up through the cockpit canopy to find his onetime Padawan flying inverted, mirroring him so closely that but for the transparisteel between them, they might have shaken hands. Obi-Wan smiled up at him. "Some new gift of the Force?"

"Not the Force, Master. Experience. That's what you're always thinking."

Obi-Wan kept hoping to hear some of Anakin's old cocky grin in his tone, but he never did. Not since Jabiim. Perhaps not since Geonosis.

The war had burned it out of him.

Obi-Wan still tried, now and again, to spark a real smile in his former Padawan. And Anakin still tried to answer.

They both still tried to pretend the war hadn't changed them.

"Ah." Obi-Wan took a hand from the starfighter's control yoke to direct his upside-down friend's attention forward. Dead ahead, a blue-white point of light splintered into four laser-straight trails of ion drives. "And what does experience tell you we should do about those incoming tri-fighters?"

*"That we should break—*right*!"*

Obi-Wan was already making that exact move as Anakin spoke. But they were inverted to each other: breaking right shot him one way while Anakin whipped the other. The tri-fighters' cannons ripped space between them, tracking faster than their starfighters could slip.

His onboard threat display chimed a warning: two of the droids had remote sensor locks on him. The others must have lit up his partner. "Anakin! Slip-jaws!"

"My thought exactly."

They blew past the tri-fighters, looping in evasive spirals. The droid ships wrenched themselves into pursuit maneuvers that would have killed any living pilot.

The slip-jaws maneuver was named for the scissorlike mandibles of the Kashyyyk slash-spider. Droids closing rapidly on their tails, cannonfire stitching space on all sides, the two Jedi pulled their ships through perfectly mirrored rolls that sent them streaking head-on for each other from opposite ends of a vast Republic cruiser.

For merely human pilots, this would be suicide. By the time you can see your partner's starfighter streaking toward you at a respectable fraction of lightspeed, it's already too late for your merely human reflexes to react.

But these particular pilots were far from merely human.

The Force nudged hands on control yokes and the Jedi starfighters twisted and flashed past each other belly-to-belly, close enough to scorch each other's paint. Tri-fighters were the Trade Federation's latest space-superiority droid. But even the electronic reflexes of the tri-fighters' droid brains were too slow for this: one of his pursuers met one of Anakin's head-on. Both vanished in a blossom of flame.

The shock wave of debris and expanding gas rocked Obi-Wan; he fought the control yoke, barely keeping his starfighter out of a tumble that would have smeared him across the cruiser's ventral hull. Before he could straighten out, his threat display chimed again.

"Oh, marvelous," he muttered under his breath. Anakin's surviving pursuer had switched targets. "Why is it always me?"

"Perfect." Through the cockpit speakers, Anakin's voice carried grim satisfaction. *"Both of them are on your tail."*

"Perfect is *not* the word I'd use." Obi-Wan twisted his yoke, juking madly as space around him flared scarlet. "We have to split them up!"

"Break left." Anakin sounded calm as a stone. *"The turbolaser tower off your port bow: thread its guns. I'll take things from there."*

"Easy for you to say." Obi-Wan whipped sideways along the cruiser's superstructure. Fire from the pursuing tri-fighters blasted burning chunks from the cruiser's armor. "Why am I always the bait?"

"I'm right behind you. Artoo, lock on."

Obi-Wan spun his starfighter between the recoiling turbocannons close enough that energy-scatter made his cockpit clang like a gong, but still cannonfire flashed past him from the tri-fighters behind. "Anakin, they're all over me!"

"Dead ahead. Move right to clear my shot. Now!"

Obi-Wan flared his port jets and the starfighter kicked to the right. One of the tri-fighters behind him decided it couldn't follow and went for a ventral slip that took it directly into the blasts from Anakin's cannons.

It vanished in a boil of superheated gas.

"Good shooting, Artoo." Anakin's dry chuckle in the cockpit's speakers vanished behind the clang of lasers blasting ablative shielding off Obi-Wan's left wing.

"I'm running out of *tricks* here—"

Clearing the vast Republic cruiser put him on course for the curving hull of one of the Trade Federation's battleships; space between the two capital ships blazed with turbolaser exchanges.

Some of those flashing energy blasts were as big around as his entire ship; the merest graze would blow him to atoms.

Obi-Wan dived right in.

He had the Force to guide him through, and the tri-fighter had only its electronic reflexes—but those electronic reflexes operated at roughly the speed of light. It stayed on his tail as if he were dragging it by a tow cable.

When Obi-Wan went left and Anakin right, the tri-fighter would swing halfway through the difference. The same with up and down. It was averaging his movements with Anakin's; somehow its droid brain had realized that as long as it stayed between the two Jedi, Anakin couldn't fire on it without hitting his partner. The tri-fighter was under no similiar restraint: Obi-Wan flew through a storm of scarlet needles.

"No wonder we're losing the war," he muttered. "They're getting *smarter.*"

"What was that, Master? I didn't copy."

Obi-Wan kicked his starfighter into a tight spiral toward the Federation cruiser. "I'm taking the deck!"

"Good idea. I need some room to maneuver."

Cannonfire tracked closer. Obi-Wan's cockpit speakers buzzed. *"Cut right, Obi-Wan! Hard right! Don't let him get a handle on you! Artoo, lock on!"*

Obi-Wan's starfighter streaked along the curve of the Separatist cruiser's dorsal hull. Antifighter flak burst on all sides as the cruiser's guns tried to pick him up. He rolled a right wingover into the service trench that stretched the length of the cruiser's hull. This low and close to the deck, the cruiser's antifighter guns couldn't depress their angle of fire enough to get a shot, but the tri-fighter stayed right on his tail.

At the far end of the service trench, the massive support buttresses of the cruiser's towering bridge left no room for even Obi-Wan's small craft. He kicked his starfighter into a half roll that whipped him out of the trench and shot him straight up the tower's angled leading edge. One burst of his underjets jerked him past the forward viewports of the bridge with only meters to spare—and the tri-fighter followed his path exactly.

"Of course," he muttered. "That would have been too easy. Anakin, where *are* you?"

One of the control surfaces on his left wing shattered in a burst of plasma. It felt like being shot in the arm. He toggled switches, fighting the yoke. R4-P17 shrilled at him. Obi-Wan keyed internal comm. "Don't try to fix it, Arfour. I've shut it down."

"I have the lock!" Anakin said. *"Go! Firing—now!"*

Obi-Wan hit maximum drag on his intact wing, and his starfighter shot into a barely controlled arc high and right as Anakin's cannons vaporized the last tri-fighter.

Obi-Wan fired retros to stall his starfighter in the blind spot behind the Separatist cruiser's bridge. He hung there for a few seconds to get his breathing and heart under control. "Thanks, Anakin. That was—thanks. That's all."

"Don't thank me. It was Artoo's shooting."

"Yes. I suppose, if you like, you can thank your droid for me as well. And, Anakin—?"

"Yes, Master?"

"Next time, *you're* the bait."

This is Obi-Wan Kenobi:

A phenomenal pilot who doesn't like to fly. A devastating warrior who'd rather not fight. A negotiator without peer who frankly prefers to sit alone in a quiet cave and meditate.

Jedi Master. General in the Grand Army of the Republic. Member of the Jedi Council. And yet, inside, he feels like he's none of these things.

Inside, he still feels like a Padawan.

It is a truism of the Jedi Order that a Jedi Knight's education truly begins only when he becomes a Master: that everything important about being a Master is learned from one's student. Obi-Wan feels the truth of this every day.

He sometimes dreams of when he was a Padawan in fact as well as feeling; he dreams that his own Master, Qui-Gon Jinn, did not die at the plasma-fueled generator core in Theed. He dreams that his Master's wise guiding hand is still with him. But Qui-Gon's death is an old pain, one with which he long ago came to terms.

A Jedi does not cling to the past.

And Obi-Wan Kenobi knows, too, that to have lived his life without being Master to Anakin Skywalker would have left him a different man. A lesser man.

Anakin has taught him so much.

Obi-Wan sees so much of Qui-Gon in Anakin that sometimes it hurts his heart; at the very least, Anakin mirrors Qui-Gon's flair for the dramatic, and his casual disregard for rules. Training Anakin—and fighting beside him, all these years—has unlocked something inside Obi-Wan. It's as though Anakin has rubbed off on him a bit, and has loosened that clenched-jaw insistence on absolute correctness that Qui-Gon always said was his greatest flaw.

Obi-Wan Kenobi has learned to relax.

He smiles now, and sometimes even jokes, and has become known for the wisdom gentle humor can provide. Though he does not know it, his relationship with Anakin has molded him into the great Jedi Qui-Gon always said he might someday be.

It is characteristic of Obi-Wan that he is entirely unaware of this.

Being named to the Council came as a complete surprise; even now, he is sometimes astonished by the faith the Jedi Council has in his abilities, and the credit they give to his wisdom. Greatness was never his ambition. He wants only to perform whatever task he is given to the best of his ability.

He is respected throughout the Jedi Order for his insight as well as his warrior skill. He has become the hero of the next generation of Padawans; he is the Jedi their Masters hold up as a model. He is the being that the Council assigns to their most important missions. He is modest, centered, and always kind.

He is the ultimate Jedi.

And he is proud to be Anakin Skywalker's best friend.

"Artoo, where's that signal?"

From its socket beside the cockpit, R2-D2 whistled and beeped. A translation spidered across Anakin's console readout: SCANNING. LOTS OF ECM SIGNAL JAMMING.

"Keep on it." He glanced at Obi-Wan's starfighter limping through the battle, a hundred meters off his left wing. "I can feel his jitters from all the way over here."

A tootle: A JEDI IS ALWAYS CALM.

"He won't think it's funny. Neither do I. Less joking, more scanning."

For Anakin Skywalker, starfighter battles were usually as close to fun as he ever came.

This one wasn't.

Not because of the overwhelming odds, or the danger he was in; he didn't care about odds, and he didn't think of himself as being in any particular danger. A few wings of droid fighters didn't much scare a man who'd been a Podracer since he was six, and had won the Boonta Cup at nine. Who was, in fact, the only human to ever *finish* a Podrace, let alone win one.

In those days he had used the Force without knowing it; he'd thought the Force was something inside him, just a feeling, an

instinct, a string of lucky guesses that led him through maneuvers other pilots wouldn't dare attempt. Now, though . . .

Now—

Now he could reach into the Force and feel the engagement
throughout Coruscant space as though the whole battle were
happening inside his head.

His vehicle became his body. The pulses of its engines were
the beat of his own heart. Flying, he could forget about his slavery, about his mother, about Geonosis and Jabiim, Aargonar and
Muunilinst and all the catastrophes of this brutal war. About
everything that had been done to him.

And everything he had done.

He could even put aside, for as long as the battle roared
around him, the starfire of his love for the woman who waited for
him on the world below. The woman whose breath was his only
air, whose heartbeat was his only music, whose face was the only
beauty his eyes would ever see.

He could put all this aside because he was a Jedi. Because it
was time to do a Jedi's work.

But today was different.

Today wasn't about dodging lasers and blasting droids.
Today was about the life of the man who might as well have been
his father: a man who could die if the Jedi didn't reach him in
time.

Anakin had been late once before.

Obi-Wan's voice came over the cockpit speakers, flat and
tight. *"Does your droid have anything? Arfour's hopeless. I think
that last cannon hit cooked his motivator."*

Anakin could see exactly the look on his former Master's
face: a mask of calm belied by a jaw so tight that when he spoke
his mouth barely moved. "Don't worry, Master. If his beacon's
working, Artoo'll find it. Have you thought about how we'll find
the Chancellor if—"

"No." Obi-Wan sounded absolutely certain. *"There's no need*

to consider it. Until the possible becomes actual, it is only a distraction. Be mindful of what is, not what might be."

Anakin had to stop himself from reminding Obi-Wan that he wasn't a Padawan anymore. "I should have been here," he said through his teeth. "I *told* you. I should have *been* here."

"Anakin, he was defended by Stass Allie and Shaak Ti. If two Masters could not prevent this, do you think you could? Stass Allie is clever and valiant, and Shaak Ti is the most cunning Jedi I've ever met. She's even taught me a few tricks."

Anakin assumed he was supposed to be impressed. "But General Grievous—"

"Master Ti had faced him before, Anakin. After Muunilinst. She is not only subtle and experienced, but very capable indeed. Seats on the Jedi Council aren't handed out as party favors."

"I've noticed." He let it drop. The middle of a space battle was no place to get into this particular sore subject.

If only *he'd* been here, instead of Shaak Ti and Stass Allie, Council members or not. If he had been here, Chancellor Palpatine would be home and safe already. Instead, Anakin had been stuck running around the Outer Rim for months like some useless Padawan, and all Palpatine had for protectors were Jedi who were *clever* and *subtle*.

Clever and subtle. He could whip any ten *clever and subtle* Jedi with his lightsaber tied behind his back.

But he knew better than to say so.

"Put yourself in the moment, Anakin. Focus."

"Copy that, Master," Anakin said dryly. "Focusing now."

R2-D2 twittered, and Anakin checked his console readout. "We've got him, Master. The cruiser dead ahead. That's Grievous's flagship—*Invisible Hand*."

"Anakin, there are dozens *of cruisers dead ahead!"*

"It's the one crawling with vulture fighters."

The vulture fighters clinging to the long curves of the Trade Federation cruiser indicated by Palpatine's beacon gave it eerily life-like ripples, like some metallic marine predator bristling with Alderaanian walking barnacles.

"Oh. That one." He could practically hear Obi-Wan's stomach dropping. *"Oh, this should be easy . . ."*

Now some of them stripped themselves from the cruiser, ignited their drives, and came looping toward the two Jedi.

"Easy? No. But it might be fun." Sometimes a little teasing was the only way to get Obi-Wan to loosen up. "Lunch at Dex's says I'll blast two for each of yours. Artoo can keep score."

"Anakin—"

"All right, dinner. And I promise this time I won't let Artoo cheat."

"No games, Anakin. There's too much at stake." There, that was the tone Anakin had been looking for: a slightly scolding, schoolmasterish edge. Obi-Wan was back on form. *"Have your droid tight-beam a report to the Temple. And send out a call for any Jedi in starfighters. We'll come at it from all sides."*

"Way ahead of you." But when he checked his comm readout, he shook his head. "There's still too much ECM. Artoo can't raise the Temple. I think the only reason we can even talk to each other is that we're practically side by side."

"And Jedi beacons?"

"No joy, Master." Anakin's stomach clenched, but he fought the tension out of his voice. "We may be the only two Jedi out here."

"Then we will have to be enough. Switching to clone fighter channel."

Anakin spun his comm dial to the new frequency in time to hear Obi-Wan say, *"Oddball, do you copy? We need help."*

The clone captain's helmet speaker flattened the humanity out of his voice. *"Copy, Red Leader."*

"Mark my position and form your squad behind me. We're going in."

"On our way."

The droid fighters had lost themselves against the background of the battle, but R2-D2 was tracking them on scan. Anakin shifted his grip on his starfighter's control yoke. "Ten vultures inbound, high and left to my orientation. More on the way."

"I have them. Anakin, wait—the cruiser's bay shields have dropped! I'm reading four, no, six ships incoming." Obi-Wan's voice rose. *"Tri-fighters! Coming in fast!"*

Anakin's smile tightened. This was about to get interesting.

"Tri-fighters first, Master. The vultures can wait."

"Agreed. Slip back and right, swing behind me. We'll take them on the slant."

Let Obi-Wan go first? With a blown left control surface and a half-crippled R-unit? With Palpatine's *life* at stake?

Not likely.

"Negative," Anakin said. "I'm going head-to-head. See you on the far side."

"Take it easy. Wait for Oddball and Squad Seven. Anakin—"

He could hear the frustration in Obi-Wan's voice as he kicked his starfighter's sublights and surged past; his former Master still hadn't gotten used to not being able to order Anakin around.

Not that Anakin had ever been much for following orders. Obi-Wan's, or anyone else's.

"Sorry we're late." The digitized voice of the clone whose call sign was Oddball sounded as calm as if he were ordering dinner. *"We're on your right, Red Leader. Where's Red Five?"*

"Anakin, form up!"

But Anakin was already streaking to meet the Trade Federation fighters. "Incoming!"

Obi-Wan's familiar sigh came clearly over the comm; Anakin knew exactly what the Jedi Master was thinking. The same thing he was *always* thinking.

He still has much to learn.

Anakin's smile thinned to a grim straight line as enemy

starfighters swarmed around him. And he thought the same thing *he* always thought.

We'll see about that.

He gave himself to the battle, and his starfighter whirled and his cannons hammered, and droids on all sides began to burst into clouds of debris and superheated gas.

This was how *he* relaxed.

This is Anakin Skywalker:

The most powerful Jedi of his generation. Perhaps of any generation. The fastest. The strongest. An unbeatable pilot. An unstoppable warrior. On the ground, in the air or sea or space, there is no one even close. He has not just power, not just skill, but *dash:* that rare, invaluable combination of boldness and grace.

He is the best there is at what he does. The best there has ever been. And he knows it.

HoloNet features call him the Hero With No Fear. And why not? What should he be afraid of?

Except—

Fear lives inside him anyway, chewing away the firewalls around his heart.

Anakin sometimes thinks of the dread that eats at his heart as a dragon. Children on Tatooine tell each other of the dragons that live inside the suns; smaller cousins of the sun-dragons are supposed to live inside the fusion furnaces that power everything from starships to Podracers.

But Anakin's fear is another kind of dragon. A cold kind. A dead kind.

Not nearly dead enough.

Not long after he became Obi-Wan's Padawan, all those years ago, a minor mission had brought them to a dead system: one so immeasurably old that its star had long ago turned to a frigid dwarf of hypercompacted trace metals, hovering a quantum fraction of a degree above absolute zero. Anakin couldn't even remember what the mission might have been, but he'd never forgotten that dead star.

It had scared him.

"*Stars* can *die*—?"

"It is the way of the universe, which is another manner of saying that it is the will of the Force," Obi-Wan had told him. "Everything dies. In time, even stars burn out. This is why Jedi form no attachments: all things pass. To hold on to something— or someone—beyond its time is to set your selfish desires against the Force. That is a path of misery, Anakin; the Jedi do not walk it."

That is the kind of fear that lives inside Anakin Skywalker: the dragon of that dead star. It is an ancient, cold dead voice within his heart that whispers *all things die* . . .

In bright day he can't hear it; battle, a mission, even a report before the Jedi Council, can make him forget it's even there. But at night—

At night, the walls he has built sometimes start to frost over. Sometimes they start to crack.

At night, the dead-star dragon sometimes sneaks through the cracks and crawls up into his brain and chews at the inside of his skull. The dragon whispers of what Anakin has lost. And what he will lose.

The dragon reminds him, every night, of how he held his dying mother in his arms, of how she had spent her last strength to say *I knew you would come for me, Anakin* . . .

The dragon reminds him, every night, that someday he will lose Obi-Wan. He will lose Padmé. Or they will lose him.

All things die, Anakin Skywalker. Even stars burn out . . .

And the only answers he ever has for these dead cold whispers are his memories of Obi-Wan's voice, or Yoda's.

But sometimes he can't quite remember them.

all things die . . .

He can barely even think about it.

But right now he doesn't have a choice: the man he flies to rescue is a closer friend than he'd ever hoped to have. That's what puts the edge in his voice when he tries to make a joke; that's what flattens his mouth and tightens the burn-scar high on his right cheek.

The Supreme Chancellor has been family to Anakin: always there, always caring, always free with advice and unstinting aid. A sympathetic ear and a kindly, loving, unconditional acceptance of Anakin exactly as he is—the sort of acceptance Anakin could never get from another Jedi. Not even from Obi-Wan. He can tell Palpatine things he could never share with his Master.

He can tell Palpatine things he can't even tell Padmé.

Now the Supreme Chancellor is in the worst kind of danger. And Anakin is on his way despite the dread boiling through his blood. That's what makes him a real hero. Not the way the HoloNet labels him; not without fear, but *stronger* than fear.

He looks the dragon in the eye and doesn't even slow down.

If anyone can save Palpatine, Anakin will. Because he's already the best, and he's still getting better. But locked away behind the walls of his heart, the dragon that is his fear coils and squirms and hisses.

Because his real fear, in a universe where even stars can die, is that being the best will never be quite good enough.

Obi-Wan's starfighter jolted sideways. Anakin whipped by him and used his forward attitude jets to kick himself into a skew-flip: facing backward to blast the last of the tri-fighters on his tail. Now there were only vulture droids left.

A *lot* of vulture droids.

"Did you like that one, Master?"

"Very pretty." Obi-Wan's cannons stitched plasma across the hull of a swooping vulture fighter until the droid exploded. "But we're not through yet."

"Watch this." Anakin flipped his starfighter again and dived, spinning, directly through the flock of vulture droids. Their drives blazed as they came around. He led them streaking for the upper deck of a laser-scarred Separatist cruiser. *"I'm going to lead them through the needle."*

"Don't lead them anywhere." Obi-Wan's threat display tallied the vultures on Anakin's tail. Twelve of them. *Twelve.* "First Jedi principle of combat: survive."

"No choice." Anakin slipped his starfighter through the storm of cannonfire. *"Come down and thin them out a little."*

Obi-Wan slammed his control yoke forward as though jamming it against its impact-rest would push his battered fighter faster in pursuit. "Nothing fancy, Arfour." As though the damaged droid were even capable of anything fancy. "Just hold me steady."

He reached into the Force and felt for his shot. "On my mark, break left—*now!*" The shutdown control surface of his left wing turned the left break into a tight overhead spiral that traversed Obi-Wan's guns across the paths of four vultures—

flash flash flash flash

—and all four were gone.

He flew on through the clouds of glowing plasma. He couldn't waste time going around; Anakin still had eight of them on his tail.

And what was this? Obi-Wan frowned.

The cruiser looked familiar.

The needle? he thought. *Oh, please say you're kidding.*

Anakin's starfighter skimmed only meters above the cruiser's dorsal hull. Cannon misses from the vulture fighters swooping toward him blasted chunks out of the cruiser's armor.

"Okay, Artoo. Where's that trench?"

His forward screen lit with a topograph of the cruiser's hull. Just ahead lay the trench that Obi-Wan had led the tri-fighter into. Anakin flipped his starfighter through a razor-sharp wingover down past the rim. The walls of the service trench flashed past him as he streaked for the bridge tower at the far end. From here, he couldn't even see the minuscule slit between its support struts.

With eight vulture droids in pursuit, he'd never pull off a slant up the tower's leading edge as Obi-Wan had. But that was all right.

He wasn't planning to.

His cockpit comm buzzed. *Don't try it, Anakin. It's too tight.*

Too tight for you, maybe. "I'll get through."

R2-D2 whistled nervous agreement with Obi-Wan.

"Easy, Artoo," Anakin said. "We've done this before."

Cannonfire blazed past him, impacting on the support struts ahead. Too late to change his mind now: he was committed. He would bring his ship through, or he would die.

Right now, strangely, he didn't actually care which.

"Use the Force." Obi-Wan sounded worried. *"Think yourself through, and the ship will follow."*

"What do you expect me to do? Close my eyes and whistle?" Anakin muttered under his breath, then said aloud, "Copy that. Thinking now."

R2-D2's squeal was as close to terrified as a droid can sound. Glowing letters spidered across Anakin's readout: ABORT! ABORT ABORT!

Anakin smiled. "Wrong thought."

Obi-Wan could only stare openmouthed as Anakin's starfighter snapped onto its side and scraped through the slit with centimeters to spare. He fully expected one of the struts to knock R2's dome off.

The vulture droids tried to follow . . . but they were just a hair too big.

When the first two impacted, Obi-Wan triggered his cannons in a downward sweep. The evasion maneuvers preprogrammed into the vulture fighters' droid brains sent them diving away from Obi-Wan's lasers—straight into the fireball expanding from the front of the struts.

Obi-Wan looked up to find Anakin soaring straight out from the cruiser with a quick snap-roll of victory. Obi-Wan matched his course—without the flourish.

"I'll give you the first four," Anakin said over the comm, *"but the other eight are mine."*

"Anakin—"

"All right, we'll split them."

As they left the cruiser behind, their sensors showed Squad Seven dead ahead. The clone pilots were fully engaged, looping through a dogfight so tight that their ion trails looked like a glowing ball of string.

"Oddball's in trouble. I'm going to help him out."

"Don't. He's doing his job. We need to do ours."

"Master, they're getting eaten alive over—"

"Every one of them would gladly trade his life for Palpatine's. Will you trade Palpatine's life for theirs?"

"No—no, of course not, but—"

"Anakin, I understand: you want to save everyone. You always do. But you *can't.*"

Anakin's voice went tight. *"Don't remind me."*

"Head for the command ship." Without waiting for a reply, Obi-Wan targeted the command cruiser and shot away at maximum thrust.

The cross of burn-scar beside Anakin's eye went pale as he turned his starfighter in pursuit. Obi-Wan was right. He almost always was.

You can't save everyone
His mother's body, broken and bloody in his arms—
Her battered eyes struggling to open—
The touch of her smashed lips—
I knew you would come to me . . . I missed you so much . . .
That's what it was to be not quite good enough.

It could happen anytime. Anyplace. If he was a few minutes late. If he let his attention drift for a single second. If he was a whisker too weak.

Anyplace. Anytime.

But not here, and not now.

He forced his mother's face back down below the surface of his consciousness.

Time to get to work.

They flashed through the battle, dodging flak and turbolaser bolts, slipping around cruisers to eclipse themselves from the sensors of droid fighters. They were only a few dozen kilometers from the command cruiser when a pair of tri-fighters whipped across their path, firing on the deflection.

Anakin's sensor board lit up and R2-D2 shrilled a warning. "Missiles!"

He wasn't worried for himself: the two on his tail were coming at him in perfect tandem. Missiles lack the sophisticated brains of droid fighters; to keep them from colliding on their inbound vectors, one of them would lock onto his fighter's left drive, the other onto his right. A quick snap-roll would make those vectors intersect.

Which they did in a silent blossom of flame.

Obi-Wan wasn't so lucky. The pair of missiles locked onto his sublights weren't precisely side by side; a snap-roll would be worse than useless. Instead he fired retros and kicked his dorsal jets to halve his velocity and knock him a few meters planetward. The lead missile overshot and spiraled off into the orbital battle.

The trailing missile came close enough to trigger its proximity sensors, and detonated in a spray of glowing shrapnel. Obi-Wan's starfighter flew through the debris—and the shrapnel *tracked* him.

Little silver spheres flipped themselves into his path and latched onto the starfighter's skin, then split and sprouted spidery arrays of jointed arms that pried up hull plates, exposing the starfighter's internal works to multiple circular whirls of blade like ancient mechanical bone saws.

This was a problem.

"I'm hit." Obi-Wan sounded more irritated than concerned. *"I'm hit."*

"I have visual." Anakin swung his starfighter into closer pursuit. "Buzz droids. I count five."

"Get out of here, Anakin. There's nothing you can do."

"I'm not leaving you, Master."

Cascades of sparks fountained into space from the buzz droids' saws. *"Anakin, the mission! Get to the command ship! Get the Chancellor!"*

"Not without you," Anakin said through his teeth.

One of the buzz droids crouched beside the cockpit, silvery arms grappling with R4; another worked on the starfighter's nose, while a third skittered toward the ventral hydraulics. The last two of the aggressive little mechs had spidered to Obi-Wan's left wing, working on that damaged control surface.

"You can't help me." Obi-Wan still maintained his Jedi calm. *"They're shutting down the controls."*

"I can fix that . . ." Anakin brought his starfighter into line only a couple of meters off Obi-Wan's wing. "Steady . . . ," he muttered, "steady . . . ," and triggered a single burst of his right-side cannon that blasted the two buzz droids into gouts of molten metal.

Along with most of Obi-Wan's left wing.

Anakin said, "Whoops."

The starfighter bucked hard enough to knock Obi-Wan's skull against the transparisteel canopy. A gust of stinging smoke filled the cockpit. Obi-Wan fought the yoke to keep his starfighter out of an uncontrolled tumble. "Anakin, that's not *helping.*"

"You're right, bad idea. Here, let's try this—move left and swing under—easy . . ."

"Anakin, you're too close! Wait—" Obi-Wan stared in disbelief as Anakin's starfighter edged closer and with a dip of its wing physically slammed a buzz droid into a smear of metal. The impact jolted Obi-Wan again, pounded a deep streak of dent into his starfighter's hull, and shattered the forward control surface of Anakin's wing.

Anakin had forgotten the first principle of combat. Again. As usual.

"You're going to get us both killed!"

His atmospheric scrubbers drained smoke from the cockpit, but now the droid on the forward control surface of Obi-Wan's starfighter's right wing had peeled away enough of the hull plates that its jointed saw arms could get deep inside. Sparks flared into space, along with an expanding fountain of gas that instantly crystallized in the hard vacuum. Velocity identical to Obi-Wan's, the shimmering gas hung on his starfighter's nose like a cloud of fog. "Blast," Obi-Wan muttered. "I can't see. My controls are going."

"You're doing fine. Stay on my wing."

Easier said than done. "I have to accelerate out of this."

"I'm with you. Go."

Obi-Wan eased power to his thrusters, and his starfighter parted the cloud, but new vapor boiled out to replace it as he went. "Is that last one still on my nose? Arfour, can you do anything?"

The only response he got came from Anakin. *"That's a negative on Arfour. Buzz droid got him."*

"It," Obi-Wan corrected automatically. "Wait—they attacked *Arfour*?"

"Not just Arfour. One of them jumped over when we hit."

Blast, Obi-Wan thought. *They* are *getting smarter.*

Through a gap torn in the cloud by the curve of his cockpit, Obi-Wan could see R2-D2 grappling with a buzz droid hand-to-hand. Well: saw-arm-to-saw-arm. Even flying blind and nearly out of control through the middle of a space battle, Obi-Wan could not avoid a second of disbelief at the bewildering variety of auxiliary tools and aftermarket behaviors Anakin had tinkered onto his starfighter's astromech, even beyond the sophisticated upgrades performed by the Royal Engineers of Naboo. The little device was virtually a partner in its own right.

R2's saw cut through one of the buzz droid's grapplers, sending the jointed arm flipping lazily off into space. Then it did the same to another. Then a panel opened in R2-D2's side and its datajack arm stabbed out and smacked the crippled buzz droid right off Anakin's hull. The buzz droid spun aft until it was caught in the blast wash of Anakin's sublights then blew away faster than even Obi-Wan's eye could follow.

Obi-Wan reflected that the Separatist droids weren't the only ones that were getting smarter.

The datajack retracted and a different panel opened, this time in R2-D2's dome. A claw-cable shot from it into the cloud of gas that still billowed from Obi-Wan's right forward wing, and pulled back out dragging a struggling buzz droid. The silver droid twisted and squirmed and its grapplers took hold of the cable, climbing back along it, saw arms waving, until Anakin popped the starfighter's underjets and R2 cut the cable and the buzz droid dropped away, tumbling helplessly through the battle.

"You know," Obi-Wan said, "I begin to understand why you speak of Artoo as though he's a living creature."

"Do you?" He could hear Anakin's smile. *"Don't you mean, it?"*

"Ah, yes." He frowned. "Yes, of course. It. Erm, thank it for me, will you?"

"Thank him yourself."

"Ah—yes. Thanks, Artoo."

The whistle that came back over the comm had a clear flavor of *you're welcome.*

Then the last of the fog finally dispersed, and the sky ahead was full of ship.

More than one kilometer from end to end, the vast command cruiser filled his visual field. At this range, all he could see were savannas of sand-colored hull studded with turbolaser mountains that lit up space with thunderbolts of disintegrating energy.

And that immense ship was getting bigger.

Fast.

"Anakin! We're going to collide!"

"That's the plan. Head for the hangar."

"That's not—"

"I know: first Jedi principle of—"

"No. It's not going to *work.* Not for me."

"What?"

"My controls are gone. I can't head for *anything.*"

"Oh. Well. All right, no problem."

"No *problem?*"

Then his starfighter clanged as if he'd crashed into a ship-sized gong.

Obi-Wan jerked and twisted his head around to find the other starfighter just above his tail. Literally just above: Anakin's left lead control surface was barely a hand span from Obi-Wan's sublight thrusters.

Anakin had *hit* him. On *purpose.*

Then he did it again.

CLANG

"What are you *doing?*"

"Just giving you . . ." Anakin's voice came slow, tight with concentration. *". . . a little help with your steering . . ."*

Obi-Wan shook his head. This was completely impossible. No other pilot would even attempt it. But for Anakin Skywalker, the completely impossible had an eerie way of being merely difficult.

He reflected that he should be used to it by now.

While these thoughts chased each other aimlessly through his mind, he had been staring bleakly at a blue shimmer of energy filling the yawning hangar bay ahead. Belatedly, he registered what he was looking at.

He thought, *Oh, this is bad.*

"Anakin—" Obi-Wan began. He tried rerouting control paths through his yoke. No luck.

Anakin drew up and tipped his forward surfaces down behind the sparking scrap that used to be Arfour.

"Anakin—!"

"Give me . . . just a second, Master." Anakin's voice had gone even tighter. A muffled thump, then another. Louder. And a scrape and a squeal of ripping metal. *"This isn't quite . . . as easy as it looks . . ."*

"Anakin!"

"What?"

"The hangar bay—"

"What about it?"

"Have you noticed that the *shield's still up?*"

"Really?"

"Really." Not to mention so close that Obi-Wan could practically *taste* it—

"Oh. Sorry. I've been busy."

Obi-Wan closed his eyes.

Reaching into the Force, his mind followed the starfighter's mangled circuitry to locate and activate the sublight engines' manual test board. With a slight push, he triggered a command normally used only in bench tests: full reverse.

The cometary tail of glowing debris shed by his disintegrating starfighter shot past him and evaporated in a cascade of miniature starbursts on contact with the hangar shield. Which was exactly what was about to happen to him.

The only effect of full reverse from his failing engines was to give him more time to see it coming.

Then Anakin's starfighter swooped in front of him, crossing left to right at a steep deflection. Energy flared from his cannons, and the shield emitters at the right side of the hangar door exploded into scrap. The blue shimmer of the bay shield flickered, faded, and vanished just as Obi-Wan came spinning across the threshold and slammed along the deck, trailing sparks and a scream of tortured metal.

His entire starfighter—what was left of it—vibrated with the roar of atmosphere howling out from the unshielded bay. Massive blast doors ground together like jaws. Another Force-touch on the manual test board cut power to his engines, but he couldn't trigger the explosive bolts on his cockpit canopy, and he had a bad feeling that those canopy bolts were the only thing on his craft that *weren't* about to explode.

His lightsaber found his hand and blue energy flared. One swipe and the canopy burst away, ripped into space by the hurricane of escaping air. Obi-Wan flipped himself up into the stunningly cold gale and let it blow him tumbling away as the remnants of his battered craft finally exploded.

He rode the shock wave while he let the Force right him in the air. He landed catfooted on the blackened streak—still hot enough to scorch his boots—that his landing had gouged into the deck.

The hangar was full of battle droids.

His shoulders dropped and his knees bent and his lightsaber

came up to angle in front of his face. There were far too many for him to fight alone, but he didn't mind.

At least he was out of that blasted starfighter.

Anakin slipped his craft toward the hangar through a fountain of junk and flash-frozen gas. One last touch of the yoke twisted his starfighter through the closing teeth of the blast doors just as Obi-Wan's canopy went the other way.

Obi-Wan's ship was a hunk of glowing scrap punctuating a long smoking skid mark. Obi-Wan himself, beard rimed with frost, lightsaber out and flaming, stood in a tightening ring of battle droids.

Anakin slewed his starfighter into a landing that scattered droids with the particle blast from his sublight thrusters and for one second he was nine years old again, behind the controls of a starfighter in the Theed royal hangar, his first touch of a real ship's real cannons blasting battle droids—

He'd have done the same right here, except that Palpatine was somewhere on this ship. They just might need one of the light shuttles in this hangar to get the Chancellor safely to the surface; a few dozen cannon blasts bouncing around in here could wreck them all.

This he'd have to do by hand.

One touch blew his canopy and he sprang from the cockpit, flipping upward to stand on the wing. Battle droids opened fire instantly, and Anakin's lightsaber flashed. "Artoo, locate a computer link."

The little droid whistled at him, and Anakin allowed himself a tight smile. Sometimes he thought he could almost understand the droid's electrosonic code. "Don't worry about us. Find Palpatine. Go on, I'll cover you."

R2 popped out of its socket and bounced to the deck. Anakin jumped ahead of it into a cascade of blasterfire and let the Force direct his blade. Battle droids began to spark and collapse.

"Get to that link!" Anakin had to shout above the whine of blasters and the roar of exploding droids. "I'm going for Obi-Wan!"

"No need."

Anakin whirled to find Obi-Wan right behind him in the act of slicing neatly through the braincase of a battle droid.

"I appreciate the thought, Anakin," the Jedi Master said with a gentle smile. "But I've already come for you."

This, then, is Obi-Wan and Anakin:

They are closer than friends. Closer than brothers. Though Obi-Wan is sixteen standard years Anakin's elder, they have become men together. Neither can imagine life without the other. The war has forged their two lives into one.

The war that has done this is not the Clone Wars; Obi-Wan and Anakin's war began on Naboo, when Qui-Gon Jinn died at the hand of a Sith Lord. Master and Padawan and Jedi Knights together, they have fought this war for thirteen years. Their war is their life.

And their life is a weapon.

Say what you will about the wisdom of ancient Master Yoda, or the deadly skill of grim Mace Windu, the courage of Ki-Adi-Mundi, or the subtle wiles of Shaak Ti; the greatness of all these Jedi is unquestioned, but it pales next to the legend that has grown around Kenobi and Skywalker.

They stand alone.

Together, they are unstoppable. Unbeatable. They are the ultimate go-to guys of the Jedi Order. When the Good Guys absolutely, positively have to *win,* the call goes out.

Obi-Wan and Anakin always answer.

Whether Obi-Wan's legendary cleverness might beat Anakin's raw power, straight up, no rules, is the subject of schoolyard fistfights, crèche-pool wriggle-matches, and pod-chamber stinkwars across the Republic. These struggles always end, somehow, with the combatants on both sides admitting that it doesn't matter.

Anakin and Obi-Wan would never fight each other.

They couldn't.

They're a team. They're *the* team.

And both of them are sure they always will be.

DOOKU

The storm of blasterfire ricocheting through the hangar bay suddenly ceased. Clusters of battle droids withdrew behind ships and slipped out hatchways.

Obi-Wan's familiar grimace showed past his blade as he let it shrink away. "I hate it when they do that."

Anakin's lightsaber was already back on his belt. "When they do what?"

"Disengage and fall back for no reason."

"There's always a reason, Master."

Obi-Wan nodded. "That's why I hate it."

Anakin looked at the litter of smoking droid parts scattered throughout the hangar bay, shrugged, and snugged his black glove. "Artoo, where's the Chancellor?"

The little droid's datajack rotated in the wall socket. Its holoprojector eye swiveled and the blue scanning laser built a ghostly image near Anakin's boot: Palpatine shackled into a large swivel chair. Even in the tiny translucent blur, he looked exhausted and in pain—but alive.

Anakin's heart thumped once, painfully, against his ribs. He wasn't too late. Not this time.

He dropped to one knee and squinted at the image. Palpatine looked as if he'd aged ten years since Anakin had last seen him. Muscle bulged along the young Jedi's jaw. If Grievous had hurt the Chancellor—had so much as *touched* him—

The hand of jointed durasteel inside his black glove clenched so hard that electronic feedback made his shoulder ache.

Obi-Wan spoke from over that shoulder. "Do you have a location?"

The image rippled and twisted into a schematic map of the cruiser. Far up at the top of the conning spire R2 showed a pulsar of brighter blue.

"In the General's Quarters." Obi-Wan scowled. "Any sign of Grievous himself?"

The pulsar shifted to the cruiser's bridge.

"Hmm. And guards?"

The holoimage rippled again, and transformed into an image of the cruiser's General's Quarters once more. Palpatine appeared to be alone: the chair sat in the center of an arc of empty floor, facing a huge curved viewing wall.

Anakin muttered, "That doesn't make *sense*."

"Of course it does. It's a trap."

Anakin barely heard him. He stared down at his black-gloved fist. He opened his fist, closed it, opened it again. The ache from his shoulder flowed down to the middle of his bicep—

And didn't stop.

His elbow sizzled, and his forearm; his wrist had been packed with red-hot gravel, and his hand—

His hand was on *fire*.

But it wasn't *his* hand. Or his wrist, or his forearm, or his elbow. It was a creation of jointed durasteel and electrodrivers.

"Anakin?"

Anakin's lips drew back from his teeth. "It hurts."

"What, your replacement arm? When did you have it equipped with pain sensors?"

"I *didn't*. That's the *point*."

"The pain is in your mind, Anakin—"

"No." Anakin's heart froze over. His voice went cold as space. "I can feel him."

"Him?"

"Dooku. He's here. Here on this ship."

"Ah." Obi-Wan nodded. "I'm sure he is."

"You *knew*?"

"I guessed. Do you think Grievous couldn't have found Palpatine's beacon? It can hardly be accident that through all the ECM, the Chancellor's homing signal was in the clear. This is a trap. A Jedi trap." Obi-Wan laid a warm hand upon Anakin's shoulder, and his face was as grim as Anakin had ever seen it. "Possibly a trap set for us. Personally."

Anakin's jaw tightened. "You're thinking of how he tried to recruit you on Geonosis. Before he sent you down for execution."

"It's not impossible that we will again face that choice."

"It's not a choice." Anakin rose. His durasteel hand clenched and stayed that way, a centimeter from his lightsaber. "Let him ask. My answer is right here on my belt."

"Be mindful, Anakin. The Chancellor's safety is our only priority."

"Yes—yes, of course." The ice in Anakin's chest thawed. "All right, it's a trap. Next move?"

Obi-Wan allowed himself a bit of a smile of his own as he headed for the nearest exit from the hangar bay. "Same as always, my young friend: we spring it."

"I can work with this plan." Anakin turned to his astromech. "You stay here, Artoo—"

The little droid interrupted him with a wheedling whirr.

"No arguments. Stay. I mean it."

R2-D2's whistling reply had a distinctly sulky tone.

"Listen, Artoo, someone has to maintain computer contact; do you see a datajack anywhere on *me*?"

The droid seemed to acquiesce, but not before wheeping what sounded like it might have been a suggestion where to look.

Waiting by the open hatchway, Obi-Wan shook his head. "Honestly, the way you talk to that thing."

Anakin started toward him. "Careful, Master, you'll hurt his feelings—" He stopped in his tracks, a curious look on his face as if he was trying to frown and to smile at the same time.

"Anakin?"

He didn't answer. He couldn't answer. He was looking at an image inside his head. Not an image. A reality.

A memory of something that hadn't happened yet.

He saw Count Dooku on his knees. He saw lightsabers crossed at the Count's throat.

Clouds lifted from his heart: clouds of Jabiim, of Aargonar, of Kamino, of even the Tusken camp. For the first time in too many years he felt young: as young as he really was.

Young, and free, and full of light.

"Master . . ." His voice seemed to be coming from someone else. Someone who hadn't seen what he'd seen. Hadn't done what he'd done. "Master, right here—right now—you and I . . ."

"Yes?"

He blinked. "I think we're about to win the war."

The vast semisphere of the view wall bloomed with battle. Sophisticated sensor algorithms compressed the combat that sprawled throughout the galactic capital's orbit to a view the naked eye could enjoy: cruisers hundreds of kilometers apart, exchanging fire at near lightspeed, appeared to be practically hull-to-hull, joined by pulsing cables of flame. Turbolaser blasts became swift shafts of light that shattered into prismatic splinters against shields, or bloomed into miniature supernovae that swallowed ships whole. The invisible gnat-clouds of starfighter dogfights became a gleaming dance of shadowmoths at the end of Coruscant's brief spring.

Within that immense curve of computer-filtered carnage, the only furnishing was one lone chair, centered in an expanse of empty floor. This was called the General's Chair, just as this apartment atop the flagship's conning spire was called the General's Quarters.

With his back to that chair and to the man shackled within it, hands folded behind him beneath his cloak of silken armorweave, stood Count Dooku.

Stood Darth Tyranus, Lord of the Sith.

He looked upon his Master's handiwork, and it was good.

More than good. It was *magnificent.*

Even the occasional tremor of the deck beneath his boots, as the entire ship shuddered under enemy torpedo and turbolaser blasts, felt to him like applause.

Behind him sounded the initiating hum of the intraship holocomm, which crackled into a voice both electronic and oddly expressive: as though a man spoke through a droid's electrosonic vocabulator. *"Lord Tyranus, Kenobi and Skywalker have arrived."*

"Yes." Dooku had felt them both in the Force. "Drive them toward me."

"My lord, I must express once more my objections—"

Dooku turned. From his commanding height, he stared down at the blue-scanned holoimage of *Invisible Hand*'s commander. "Your objections have been noted already, General. Leave the Jedi to me."

"But driving them to you also sends them directly toward the Chancellor himself! Why does he remain on this ship at all? He should be hidden. He should be guarded. We should have had him outsystem hours ago!"

"Matters are so," Count Dooku said, "because Lord Sidious

wishes them so; should you desire to press your objections, please feel at liberty to take them up with *him*."

"*I, ah, don't believe that will be necessary . . .*"

"Very well, then. Confine your efforts to preventing support troops from boarding. Without their pet clones to back them up, no Jedi is a danger to me."

The deck shuddered again, more sharply, followed by a sudden shift in the vector of the cruiser's artificial gravity that would have sent a lesser man stumbling; with the Force to maintain the dignified solidity of his posture, the effect on Dooku was confined to the lift of one eyebrow. "And may I suggest that you devote some attention to protecting this ship? Having it destroyed with both you and me aboard might put something of a cramp in the war effort, don't you think?"

"*It is already being done, my lord. Does my lord wish to observe the progress of the Jedi? I can feed the security monitors onto this channel.*"

"Thank you, General. That will be welcome."

"*Gracious as ever, my lord. Grievous out.*"

Count Dooku allowed himself a near-invisible smile. His inviolable courtesy—the hallmark of a true aristocrat—was effortless, yet somehow it seemed always to impress the common rabble. As well as those with the intellect of common rabble, regardless of accomplishment or station: like, for example, that repulsive cyborg Grievous.

He sighed. Grievous had his uses; not only was he an able field commander, but he would soon make a marvelous scapegoat upon whom to hang every atrocity of this sadly necessary war. Someone had to take that particular fall, and Grievous was just the creature for the job. It certainly would not be Dooku.

This was, in fact, one purpose of the cataclysmic battle outside.

But not the only one.

The blue-scanned image before him now became miniatures

of Kenobi and Skywalker as he had seen them so many times be-fore: shoulder-to-shoulder, lightsabers whirling as they enthusi-astically dismantled droid after droid after droid. Feeling as if they were winning, while in truth they were being chivvied ex-actly where the Lords of the Sith wanted them to go.

Such children they were. Dooku shook his head.

It was almost too easy.

This is Dooku, Darth Tyranus, Count of Serenno:

Once a great Jedi Master, now an even greater Lord of the Sith, Dooku is a dark colossus bestriding the galaxy. Nemesis of the corrupt Republic, oriflamme of the principled Confederacy of Independent Systems, he is the very personification of shock and awe.

He was one of the most respected and powerful Jedi in the Order's twenty-five-thousand-year history, yet at the age of sev-enty Dooku's principles would no longer allow him to serve a Republic in which political power was for sale to the highest bid-der. He'd said farewell to his former Padawan, Qui-Gon Jinn, now a legendary Master in his own right; he'd said farewell to his close friends on the Jedi Council, Mace Windu and the ancient Master Yoda; he'd said farewell to the Jedi Order itself.

He is numbered among the Lost: the Jedi who renounced their fealty to the Order and resigned their commissions of Jedi Knighthood in service of ideals higher than even the Order itself professed. The Lost Twenty, as they have been known since Dooku joined their number, are remembered with both honor and regret among the Jedi; their images, sculpted from bronz-ium, stand enshrined in the Temple archives.

These bronzium images serve as melancholy reminders that some Jedi have needs the Order cannot satisfy.

Dooku had retired to his family estate, the planetary system of Serenno. Assuming his hereditary title as its Count made him one of the wealthiest beings in the galaxy. Amid the unabashed corruption endemic to the Republic, his immense wealth could have bought the allegiance of any given number of Senators; he could, perhaps, have bought control of the Republic itself.

But a man of such heritage, such principle, could never stoop to be lord of a garbage heap, chief of a horde of scavengers squabbling over scraps; the Republic, to him, was nothing more than this.

Instead, he used all the great power of his family fortune—and the vastly greater power of his unquestioned integrity—to begin the cleansing of the galaxy from the fester of this so-called democracy.

He is the icon of the Separatist movement, its public face. He is to the Confederacy of Independent Systems what Palpatine is to the Republic: the living symbol of the justice of its cause.

This is the public story.

This is the story that even Dooku, in his weaker moments, almost believes.

The truth is more complicated.

Dooku is . . . different.

He doesn't remember quite when he discovered this; it may have been when he was a young Padawan, betrayed by another learner who had claimed to be his friend. Lorian Nod had said it to his face: "You don't know what friendship is."

And he didn't.

He had been angry, certainly; furious that his reputation had been put at risk. And he had been angry at himself, for his error in judgment: trusting as an ally one who was in fact an enemy. The most astonishing part of the whole affair had been that even after turning on him before the Jedi, the other boy had expected him to participate in a lie, in the name of their "friendship."

It had been all so preposterous that he hadn't known how to reply.

In fact, he has never been entirely sure what beings mean when they speak of friendship. Love, hate, joy, anger—even when he can feel the energy of these emotions in others, they translate in his perception to other kinds of feelings.

The kinds that make sense.

Jealousy he understands, and possessiveness: he is fierce when any being encroaches on what is rightfully his.

Intolerance, at the intractability of the universe, and at the undisciplined lives of its inhabitants: this is his normal state.

Spite is a recreation: he takes considerable pleasure from the suffering of his enemies.

Pride is a virtue in an aristocrat, and indignation his inalienable right: when any dare to impugn his integrity, his honor, or his rightful place atop the natural hierarchy of authority.

And moral outrage makes perfect sense to him: when the incorrigibly untidy affairs of ordinary beings refuse to conform to the plainly obvious structure of How Society Ought To Be.

He is entirely incapable of caring what any given creature might feel for him. He cares only what that creature might do for him. Or to him.

Very possibly, he is what he is because other beings just aren't very . . . interesting.

Or even, in a sense, entirely real.

For Dooku, other beings are mostly abstractions, simple schematic sketches who fall into two essential categories. The first category is Assets: beings who can be used to serve his various interests. Such as—for most of his life, and to some extent even now—the Jedi, particularly Mace Windu and Yoda, both of whom had regarded him as their friend for so long that it had effectively blinded them to the truth of his activities. And of course—for now—the Trade Federation, and the InterGalactic

Banking Clan, the Techno Union, the Corporate Alliance, and the weapon lords of Geonosis. And even the common rabble of the galaxy, who exist largely to provide an audience of sufficient size to do justice to his grandeur.

The other category is Threats. In this second set, he numbers every sentient being he cannot include in the first.

There is no third category.

Someday there may be not even a second; being considered a Threat by Count Dooku is a death sentence. A death sentence he plans to pronounce, for example, on his current allies: the heads of the aforementioned Trade Federation, InterGalactic Banking Clan, Techno Union, and Corporate Alliance, and Geonosian weaponeers.

Treachery is the way of the Sith.

Count Dooku watched with clinical distaste as the blue-scanned images of Kenobi and Skywalker engaged in a preposterous farce-chase, pursued by destroyer droids into and out of turbolift pods that shot upward and downward and even sideways.

"It will be," he said slowly, meditatively, as though he spoke only to himself, "an embarrassment to be captured by him."

The voice that answered him was so familiar that sometimes his very thoughts spoke in it, instead of in his own. "An embarrassment you can survive, Lord Tyranus. After all, he is the greatest Jedi alive, is he not? And have we not ensured that all the galaxy shares this opinion?"

"Quite so, my Master. Quite so." Again, Dooku sighed. Today he felt every hour of his eighty-three years. "It is . . . fatiguing, to play the villain for so long, Master. I find myself looking forward to an honorable captivity."

A captivity that would allow him to sit out the rest of the war in comfort; a captivity that would allow him to forswear his former allegiances—when he would conveniently appear to finally discover the true extent of the Separatists' crimes against civilization—and bind himself to the *new* government with his reputation for integrity and idealism fully intact.

The new government . . .

This had been their star of destiny for lo, these many years.

A government clean, pure, direct: none of the messy scramble for the favor of ignorant rabble and subhuman creatures that made up the Republic he so despised. The government he would serve would be Authority personified.

Human authority.

It was no accident that the primary powers of the Confederacy of Independent Systems were Neimoidian, Skakoan, Quarren and Aqualish, Muun and Gossam, Sy Myrthian and Koorivar and Geonosian. At war's end the aliens would be crushed, stripped of all they possessed, and their systems and their wealth would be given into the hands of the only beings who could be trusted with them.

Human beings.

Dooku would serve an Empire of Man.

And he would serve it as only he could. As he was *born* to. He would smash the Jedi Order to create it anew: not shackled by the corrupt, narcissistic, shabby little beings who called themselves politicians, but free to bring true authority and true peace to a galaxy that so badly needed both.

An Order that would not negotiate. Would not mediate.

An Order that would *enforce*.

The survivors of the Jedi Order would become the Sith Army.

The Fist of the Empire.

And that Fist would become a power beyond any Jedi's darkest dreams. The Jedi were not the only users of the Force in the galaxy; from Hapes to Haruun Kal, from Kiffu to Dathomir, powerful Force-capable humans and near-humans had long refused to surrender their children to lifelong bound servitude in the Jedi Order. They would not so refuse the Sith Army.

They would not have the choice.

Dooku frowned down at the holoimage. Kenobi and Skywalker were going through more low-comedy business with another balky turbolift—possibly Grievous having some fun with the shaft controls—while battle droids haplessly pursued.

Really, it was all so . . .

Undignified.

"May I suggest, Master, that we give Kenobi one last chance? The support of a Jedi of his integrity would be invaluable in establishing the political legitimacy of our Empire."

"Ah, yes. Kenobi." His Master's voice went silken. "You have long been interested in Kenobi, haven't you?"

"Of course. His Master was my Padawan; in a sense, he's practically my grandson—"

"He is too old. Too indoctrinated. Irretrievably poisoned by Jedi fables. We established that on Geonosis, did we not? In his mind, he serves the Force itself; reality is nothing in the face of such conviction."

Dooku sighed. He should, he supposed, have no difficulty with this, having ordered the Jedi Master's death once already. "True enough, I suppose; how fortunate we are that I never labored under any such illusions."

"Kenobi must die. Today. At your hand. His death may be the code key of the final lock that will seal Skywalker to us forever."

Dooku understood: not only would the death of his mentor tip Skywalker's already unstable emotional balance down the darkest of slopes, but it would also remove the greatest obstacle to Skywalker's successful conversion. As long as Kenobi was alive, Skywalker would never be securely in the camp of the Sith; Kenobi's unshakable faith in the values of the Jedi would keep the Jedi blindfold on Skywalker's eyes and the Jedi shackles on the young man's true power.

Still, though, Dooku had some reservations. This had all come about too quickly; had Sidious thought through all the implications of this operation? "But I must ask, my Master: is Skywalker truly the man we want?"

"He is powerful. Potentially more powerful than even myself."

"Which is precisely," Dooku said meditatively, "why it might be best if I were to kill *him*, instead."

"Are you so certain that you can?"

"Please. Of what use is power unstructured by discipline? The boy is as much a danger to himself as he is to his enemies. And that mechanical arm—" Dooku's lip curled with cultivated distaste. "Revolting."

"Then perhaps you should have spared his real arm."

"Hmp. A gentleman would have learned to fight one-handed." Dooku flicked a dismissive wave. "He's no longer even entirely human. With Grievous, the use of these bio-droid devices is almost forgivable; he was such a disgusting creature already that his mechanical parts are clearly an improvement. But a blend of droid and *human*? Appalling. The depths of bad taste. How are we to justify associating with him?"

"How fortunate I am"—the silk in his Master's voice softened further—"to have an apprentice who feels it is appropriate to *lecture* me."

Dooku lifted an eyebrow. "I have overstepped, my Master," he said with his customary grace. "I am only observing, not arguing. Not at all."

"Skywalker's arm makes him, for our purposes, even better. It is the permanent symbol of the sacrifices he has made in the name of peace and justice. It is a badge of heroism that he must publicly wear for the rest of his life; no one can ever look at him and doubt his honor, his courage, his integrity. He is perfect, just as he is. *Perfect.* The only question that remains is whether he is capable of transcending the artificial limitations of his Jedi indoctrination. And that, my lord Count, is precisely what today's operation is designed to discover."

Dooku could not argue. Not only had the Dark Lord introduced Dooku to realms of power beyond his most spectacular fantasies, but Sidious was also a political manipulator so subtle that his abilities might be considered to dwarf even the power of the dark side itself. It was said that whenever the Force closes a hatch, it opens a viewport . . . and every viewport that had so much as cracked in this past thirteen standard years had found a Dark Lord of the Sith already at the rim, peering in, calculating how best to slip through.

Improving upon his Master's plan was near to impossible; his own idea, of substituting Kenobi for Skywalker, he had to admit was only the product of a certain misplaced sentimentality. Skywalker was almost certainly the man for the job.

He should be; Darth Sidious had spent a considerable number of years making him so.

Today's test would remove the *almost.*

He had no doubt that Skywalker would fall. Dooku understood that this was more than a test for Skywalker; though Sidious had never said so directly, Dooku was certain that he himself was being tested as well. Success today would show his Master that he was worthy of the mantle of Mastery himself: by the end of the coming battle, he would have initiated Skywalker into the manifold glories of the dark side, just as Sidious had initiated him.

He gave no thought to failure. Why should he?

"But—forgive me, Master. But Kenobi having fallen to my blade, are you certain Skywalker will ever accept my orders? You must admit that his biography offers little confidence that he is capable of obedience at all."

"Skywalker's power brings with it more than mere obedi-

ence. It brings creativity, and luck; we need never concern ourselves with the sort of instruction that Grievous, for example, requires. Even the blind fools on the Jedi Council see clearly
enough to understand this; even they no longer try to tell him
how, they merely tell him *what*. And he finds a way. He always
has."

Dooku nodded. For the first time since Sidious had revealed
the true subtlety of this masterpiece, Dooku allowed himself to
relax enough to imagine the outcome.

With his heroic capture of Count Dooku, Anakin Skywalker
will become the ultimate hero: the greatest hero in the history of
the Republic, perhaps of the Jedi Order itself. The loss of his
beloved partner will add just exactly the correct spice of tragedy
to give melancholy weight to his every word, when he gives his
HoloNet interviews denouncing the Senate's corruption as im-
peding the war effort, when he delicately—oh, so delicately, not
to mention *reluctantly*—insinuates that corruption in the Jedi
Order prolonged the war as well.

When he announces the creation of a new order of Force-
using warriors.

He will be the perfect commanding general for the Sith
Army.

Dooku could only shake his head in awe. And to think that
only days earlier, the Jedi had seemed so close to uncovering,
even destroying, all he and his Master had worked for. But he
should never have feared. His Master never lost. He would never
lose. He was the definition of unbeatable.

How can one defeat an enemy one thinks is a friend?

And now, with a single brilliant stroke, his Master would turn
the Jedi Order back upon itself like an Ethrani ourobouros de-
vouring its own tail.

This was the day. The hour.

The death of Obi-Wan Kenobi would be the death of the Republic.

Today would see the birth of the Empire.

"Tyranus? Are you well?"

"Am I . . ." Dooku realized that his eyes had misted. "Yes, my Master. I am beyond well. Today, the climax—the grand finale—the culmination of all your decades of work . . . I find myself somewhat overcome."

"Compose yourself, Tyranus. Kenobi and Skywalker are nearly at the door. Play your part, my apprentice, and the galaxy is ours."

Dooku straightened and for the first time looked his Master in the eyes.

Darth Sidious, Dark Lord of the Sith, sat in the General's Chair, shackled to it at the wrist and ankle.

Dooku bowed to him. "Thank you, Chancellor."

Palpatine of Naboo, Supreme Chancellor of the Republic, replied, "Withdraw. They are here."

THE WAY OF THE SITH

The turbolift's door whished open. Anakin pressed himself against the wall, a litter of saber-sliced droid parts around his feet. Beyond appeared to be a perfectly ordinary lift lobby: pale and bare and empty.

Made it. At last.

Anakin's whole body hummed to the tune of his blue-hot blade.

"Anakin."

Obi-Wan stood against the opposite wall. He looked calm in a way Anakin could barely understand. He gave a significant stare down at the lightsaber in Anakin's hand. "Anakin, rescue," he said softly. "Not mayhem."

Anakin kept his weapon right where it was. "And Dooku?"

"Once the Chancellor is safe," Obi-Wan said with a ghost of a smile, "we can blow up the ship."

Anakin's mechanical fingers tightened until the grip of his lightsaber creaked. "I'd rather do it by hand."

Obi-Wan slipped cautiously through the turbolift's door. Nothing shot at him. He beckoned. "I know this is difficult,

Anakin. I know it's personal for you on many levels. You must take extra care to be mindful of your training here—and not only your *combat* training."

Heat rose in Anakin's cheeks. "I am *not*—" *your Padawan anymore* snarled inside his head, but that was adrenaline talking; he bit back the words and said instead, "—going to let you down, Master. Or Chancellor Palpatine."

"I have no doubt of that. Just remember that Dooku is no mere Dark Jedi like that Ventress woman; he is a Lord of the Sith. The jaws of this trap are about to snap shut, and there may be danger here beyond the merely physical."

"Yes." Anakin let his blade shrink away and moved past Obi-Wan into the turbolift lobby. Distant concussions boomed throughout the ship, and the floor rocked like a raft on a river in flood; he barely noticed. "I just—there has been so much—what he's *done*—not just to the Jedi, but to the *galaxy*—"

"Anakin . . . ," Obi-Wan began warningly.

"Don't worry. I'm not angry, and I'm not looking for revenge. I'm just—" He lifted his lightsaber. "I'm just looking forward to ending it."

"Anticipation—"

"Is distraction. I know. And I know that hope is as hollow as fear." Anakin let himself smile, just a bit. "And I know everything else you're dying to tell me right now."

Obi-Wan's slightly rueful bow of acknowledgment was as affectionate as a hug. "I suppose at some point I will eventually have to stop trying to train you."

Anakin's smile broadened toward a soft chuckle. "I think that's the first time you've ever admitted it."

They stopped at the the door to the General's Quarters: a huge oval of opalescent iridiite chased with gold. Anakin stared at his ghostly almost-reflection while he reached into the room beyond with the Force, and let the Force reach into him. "I'm ready, Master."

"I know you are."

They stood a moment, side by side.

Anakin didn't look at him; he stared into the door, through the door, searching in its shimmering depths for a hint of an unguessable future.

He couldn't imagine not being at war.

"Anakin." Obi-Wan's voice had gone soft, and his hand was warm on Anakin's arm. "There is no other Jedi I would rather have at my side right now. No other man."

Anakin turned, and found within Obi-Wan's eyes a depth of feeling he had only rarely glimpsed in all their years together; and the pure uncomplicated love that rose up within him then felt like a promise from the Force itself.

"I . . . wouldn't have it any other way, Master."

"I believe," his onetime Master said with a gently humorous look of astonishment at the words coming out of his mouth, "that you should get used to calling me Obi-Wan."

"Obi-Wan," Anakin said, "let's go get the Chancellor."

"Yes," Obi-Wan said. "Let's."

Inside a turbolift pod, Dooku watched hologrammic images of Kenobi and Skywalker cautiously pick their way down the curving stairs from the entrance balcony to the main level of the General's Quarters, moving slowly to stay braced against the pitching of the cruiser. The ship shuddered and bucked with multiple torpedo bursts, and the lights went out again; lighting was always the first to fail as power was diverted from life support to damage control.

"*My lord.*" On the intraship comm, Grievous sounded actively concerned. "*Damage to this ship is becoming severe. Thirty percent of automated weapons systems are down, and we may soon lose hyperspace capability.*"

Dooku nodded judiciously to himself, frowning down at the translucent blue ghosts slinking toward Palpatine. "Sound the retreat for the entire strike force, General, and prepare the ship for jump. Once the Jedi are dead, I will join you on the bridge."

"As my lord commands. Grievous out."

"Indeed you are, you vile creature," Dooku muttered to the dead comlink. "Out of luck, and out of time."

He cast the comlink aside and ignored its clatter across the deck. He had no further use for it. Let it be destroyed along with Grievous, those repulsive bodyguards of his, and the rest of the cruiser, once he was safely captured and away.

He nodded to the two hulking super battle droids that flanked him. One opened the lift door and they marched through, pivoting to take positions on either side.

Dooku straightened his cloak of shimmering armorweave and strode grandly into the half-dark lift lobby. In the pale emergency lighting, the door to the General's Quarters still smoldered where those two idiotic peasants had lightsabered it; to pick his way through the hole would risk getting his trousers scorched. Dooku sighed and gestured, and the opalescent wreckage of the door silently slid itself out of his way.

He certainly did not intend to fight two Jedi with his pants on fire.

Anakin slid along the bank of chairs on one side of the immense situation table that dominated the center of the General's Quarters' main room; Obi-Wan mirrored him on the opposite side. Silent lightning flashed and flared: the room's sole illumination came from the huge curving view wall at its far end, a storm of turbolaser blasts and flak bursts and the miniature supernovae that were the deaths of entire ships.

A stark shadow against that backdrop of carnage: the silhouette of one tall chair.

Anakin caught Obi-Wan's eye across the table and nodded toward the dark shape ahead. Obi-Wan replied with the Jedi hand signal for *approach with caution,* and added the signal for *be ready for action.*

Anakin's mouth compressed. Like he needed to be told. After all the trouble they'd had with the turbolifts, anything could be up here by now. The place could be full of droidekas, for all they knew.

The lights came back on.

Anakin froze.

The dark figure in the chair—it *was* Chancellor Palpatine, it was, and there were no droids to be seen, and his heart should have leapt within his chest, but—

Palpatine looked bad.

The Chancellor looked beyond old, looked ancient like Yoda was ancient: possessed of incomprehensible age. And exhausted, and in pain. And worse—

Anakin saw in the Chancellor's face something he'd never dreamed he'd find there, and it squeezed breath from his lungs and wiped words from his brain.

Palpatine looked *frightened.*

Anakin didn't know what to say. He couldn't *imagine* what to say. All he could imagine was what Grievous and Dooku must have done to put fear on the face of this brave good man—

And that imagining ignited a sizzle in his blood that drew his face tight and clouded his heart and started again the low roll of thunder in his ears: thunder from Aargonar. From Jabiim.

Thunder from the Tusken camp.

If Obi-Wan was struck by any similar distress, it was invisible. With his customary grave courtesy, the Jedi Master inclined his head. "Chancellor," he said, a calmly respectful greeting as though they had met by chance on the Grand Concourse of the Galactic Senate.

Palpatine's only response was a tight murmur. "Anakin, *behind* you—!"

Anakin didn't turn. He didn't have to. It wasn't just the clack of boot heels and clank of magnapeds crossing the threshold of the entrance balcony; the Force gathered within him and around him in a sudden clench like the fists of a startled man.

In the Force, he could feel the focus of Palpatine's eyes: the source of the fear that rolled off him in billows like vapor down a block of frozen air. And he could feel the even colder wave of power, colder than the frost on a mynock's mouth, that slid into the room behind him like an ice dagger into his back.

Funny, he thought. *After Ventress, somehow I always expect the dark side to be hot . . .*

Something unlocked in his chest. The thunder in his ears dissolved into red smoke that coiled at the base of his spine. His lightsaber found his hand, and his lips peeled off his teeth in a smile that a krayt dragon would have recognized.

That trouble he was having with talking went away.

"This," he murmured to Palpatine, and to himself, "is not a problem."

The voice that spoke from the entrance balcony was an elegant basso with undernotes of oily resonance like a kriin-oak cavernhorn.

Count Dooku's voice.

"General Kenobi. Anakin Skywalker. Gentlemen—a term I use in its loosest possible sense—you are my prisoners."

Now Anakin didn't have any troubles at all.

The entrance balcony provided an appropriate angle—far above the Jedi, looking down upon them—for Dooku to make final assessments before beginning the farce.

Like all true farce, the coming denouement would proceed with remorseless logic from its ridiculous premise: that Dooku could ever be overcome by mere Jedi. Any Jedi. What a pity his old friend Mace couldn't have joined them today; he had no doubt the Korun Master would have enjoyed the coming show.

Dooku had always preferred an educated audience.

At least Palpatine was here, shackled within the great chair at the far end of the room, the space battle whirling upon the view wall behind him as though his stark silhouette spread great wings of war. But Palpatine was less audience than he was author.

Not at all the same thing.

Skywalker gave Dooku only his back, but his blade was already out and his tall, lean frame stood frozen with anticipation: so motionless he almost seemed to shiver. Pathetic. It was an insult to call this boy a Jedi at all.

Kenobi, now—he was something else entirely: a classic of his obsolete kind. He simply stood gazing calmly up at Dooku and the super battle droids that flanked him, hands open, utterly relaxed, on his face only an expression of mild interest.

Dooku derived a certain melancholy satisfaction—a pleasurably lonely contemplation of his own unrecognized greatness—from a brief reflection that Skywalker would never understand how much thought and planning, how much *work*, Lord Sidious had invested in so hastily orchestrating his sham victory. Nor would he ever understand the artistry, the true mastery, that Dooku would wield in his own defeat.

But thus was life. Sacrifices must be made, for the greater good.

There was a war on, after all.

He called upon the Force, gathering it to himself and wrapping himself within it. He breathed it in and held it whirling inside his heart, clenching down upon it until he could feel the spin of the galaxy around him.

Until he became the axis of the Universe.

This was the real power of the dark side, the power he had suspected even as a boy, had sought through his long life until Darth Sidious had shown him that it had been his all along. The dark side didn't bring him to the center of the universe. It *made* him the center.

He drew power into his innermost being until the Force it-self existed only to serve his will.

Now the scene below subtly altered, though to the physical eye there was no change. Powered by the dark side, Dooku's perception took the measure of those below him with exhilarating precision.

Kenobi was luminous, a transparent being, a window onto a sunlit meadow of the Force.

Skywalker was a storm cloud, flickering with dangerous lightning, building the rotation that threatens a tornado.

And then there was Palpatine, of course: he was beyond power. He showed nothing of what might be within. Though seen with the eyes of the dark side itself, Palpatine was an event horizon. Beneath his entirely ordinary surface was absolute, perfect nothingness. Darkness beyond darkness.

A black hole of the Force.

And he played his helpless-hostage role perfectly.

"Get help!" The edge of panic in his hoarse half whisper sounded real even to Dooku. "You *must* get help. Neither of you is any match for a Sith Lord!"

Now Skywalker turned, meeting Dooku's direct gaze for the first time since the abandoned hangar on Geonosis. His reply was clearly intended as much for Dooku as for Palpatine. "Tell that to the one Obi-Wan left in pieces on Naboo."

Hmp. Empty bravado. Maul had been an animal. A skilled animal, but a beast nonetheless.

"Anakin—" In the Force, Dooku could feel Kenobi's disapproval of Skywalker's boasting; and he could also feel Kenobi's effortless self-restraint in focusing on the matter at hand. "This time, we do it *together.*"

Dooku's sharp eye picked up the tightening of Skywalker's droid hand on his lightsaber's grip. "I was about to say exactly that."

Fine, then. Time to move this little comedy along.

Dooku leaned forward, and his cloak of armorweave spread like wings; he lifted gently into the air and descended to the main level in a slow, dignified Force-glide. Touching down at the head of the situation table, he regarded the two Jedi from under a lifted brow.

"Your weapons, please, gentlemen. Let's not make a mess of this in front of the Chancellor."

Obi-Wan lifted his lightsaber into the balanced two-handed guard of Ataro: Qui-Gon's style, and Yoda's. His blade crackled into existence, and the air smelled of lightning. "You won't escape us this time, Dooku."

"Escape you? Please." Dooku allowed his customary mild smile to spread. "Do you think I orchestrated this entire operation with the intent to *escape*? I could have taken the Chancellor outsystem hours ago. But I have better things to do with my life than to babysit him while I wait for the pair of you to attempt a rescue."

Skywalker brought his lightsaber to a Shien ready: hand of black-gloved durasteel cocked high at his shoulder, blade angling upward and away. "This is a little more than an attempt."

"And a little less than a rescue."

With a flourish, Dooku cast his cloak back from his right shoulder, clearing his sword arm—which he used to gesture idly at the pair of super battle droids still on the entrance balcony above. "Now please, gentlemen. Must I order the droids to open fire? That becomes so untidy, what with blaster bolts bouncing about at random. Little danger to the three of us, of course, but I should certainly hate for any harm to come to the Chancellor."

Kenobi moved toward him with a slow, hypnotic grace, as though he floated on an invisible repulsor plate. "Why do I find that difficult to believe?"

Skywalker mirrored him, swinging wide toward Dooku's flank. "You weren't so particular about bloodshed on Geonosis."

"Ah." Dooku's smile spread even farther. "And how *is* Senator Amidala?"

"Don't—" The thunderstorm that was Skywalker in the Force boiled with sudden power. "Don't even speak her name."

Dooku waved this aside. The lad's personal issues were too tiresome to pursue; he knew far too much already about Skywalker's messy private life. "I bear Chancellor Palpatine no ill will, foolish boy. He is neither soldier nor spy, whereas you and your friend here are both. It is only an unfortunate accident of history that he has chosen to defend a corrupt Republic against my endeavor to reform it."

"You mean *destroy* it."

"The Chancellor is a civilian. You and General Kenobi, on the other hand, are legitimate military targets. It is up to you whether you will accompany me as captives—" A twitch of the Force brought his lightsaber to his hand with invisible speed, its brilliant scarlet blade angled downward at his side. "—or as *corpses.*"

"Now, there's a coincidence," Kenobi replied dryly as he swung around Dooku to place the Count precisely between Skywalker and himself. "You face the identical choice."

Dooku regarded each of them in turn with impregnable calm. He lifted his blade in the Makashi salute and swept it again to a low guard. "Just because there are two of you, do not presume you have the advantage."

"Oh, we know," Skywalker said. "Because there are two of *you.*"

Dooku barely managed to restrain a jolt of surprise.

"Or maybe I should say, *were* two of you," the young Jedi went on. "We're on to your partner *Sidious;* we tracked him all over the galaxy. He's probably in Jedi custody right now."

"Is he?" Dooku relaxed. He was terribly, terribly tempted to wink at Palpatine, but of course that would never do. "How fortunate for you."

Quite simple, in the end, he thought. *Isolate Skywalker, slaughter Kenobi.* Beyond that, it would be merely a matter of spinning Skywalker up into enough of a frenzy to break through his Jedi restraint and reveal the infinite vista of Sith power.

Lord Sidious would take it from there.

"Surrender." Kenobi's voice deepened into finality. "You will be given no further chance."

Dooku lifted an eyebrow. "Unless one of you happens to be carrying Yoda in his pocket, I hardly think I shall need one."

The Force crackled between them, and the ship pitched and bucked under a new turbolaser barrage, and Dooku decided that the time had come. He flicked a false glance over his shoulder—a hint of distraction to draw the attack—

And all three of them moved at once.

The ship shuddered and the red smoke surged from Anakin's spine into his arms and legs and head and when Dooku gave the slightest glance of concern over his shoulder, distracted for half an instant, Anakin just couldn't wait anymore.

He sprang, lightsaber angled for the kill.

Obi-Wan leapt from Dooku's far side in perfect coordination—and they met in midair, for the Sith Lord was no longer between them.

Anakin looked up just in time to glimpse the bottom of Dooku's rancor-leather boot as it came down on his face and smacked him tumbling toward the floor; he reached into the Force to effortlessly right himself and touched down in perfect balance to spring again toward the lightning flares, scarlet against sky blue, that sprayed from clashing lightsabers as Dooku pressed Obi-Wan away with a succession of weaving, flourishing thrusts that drove the Jedi's blade out of line while they reached for his heart.

Anakin launched himself at Dooku's back—and the Count half turned, gesturing casually while holding Obi-Wan at bay with an elegant one-handed bind. Chairs leapt up from the situation table and whirled toward Anakin's head. He slashed the first one in half contemptuously, but the second caught him across the knees and the third battered his shoulder and knocked him down.

He snarled to himself and reached through the Force to pick up some chairs of his own—and the situation table itself slammed into him and drove him back to crush him against the wall. His lightsaber came loose from his slackening fingers and clattered across the tabletop to drop to the floor on the far side.

And Dooku barely even seemed to be paying attention to him.

Pinned, breathless, half stunned, Anakin thought, *If this keeps up, I am going to get mad.*

While effortlessly deflecting a rain of blue-streaking cuts from Kenobi, Dooku felt the Force shove the situation table away from the wall and send it hurtling toward his back with astonishing speed; he barely managed to lift himself enough that he could backroll over it instead of having it shatter his spine.

"My my," he said, chuckling. "The boy has some power after all."

His backroll brought him to his feet directly in front of the lad, who was charging, headlong and unarmed, after the table he had tossed, and was already thoroughly red in the face.

"I'm *twice* the Jedi I was last time!"

Ah, Dooku thought. *Such a fragile little ego. Sidious will have to help him with that. But until then—*

The grip of Skywalker's blade whistled through the air to meet his hand in perfect synchrony with a sweeping slash. "My powers have *doubled* since we last met—"

"How lovely for you." Dooku neatly sidestepped, cutting at the boy's leg, yet Skywalker's blade met the cut as he passed and he managed to sweep his blade behind his head to slap aside the casual thrust Dooku aimed at the back of his neck—but his clumsy charge had put him in Kenobi's path, so that the Jedi Master had to Force-roll over his partner's head.

Directly at Dooku's upraised blade.

Kenobi drove a slash at the scarlet blade while he pivoted in the air, and again Dooku sidestepped so that now it was Kenobi in Skywalker's way.

"Really," Dooku said, "this is pathetic."

Oh, they were certainly energetic enough, leaping and whirling, raining blows almost at random, cutting chairs to pieces and Force-hurling them in every conceivable direction, while Dooku continued, in his gracefully methodical way, to out-maneuver them so thoroughly it was all he could to do keep from laughing out loud.

It was a simple matter of countering their tactics, which were depressingly straightforward; Skywalker was the swift one, whooshing here and there like a spastic hawk-bat—attempting a Jedi variant of neek-in-the-middle so they could come at him from both sides—while Kenobi came on in a measured Shii-Cho cadence, deliberate as a lumberdroid, moving step by step, cutting off the angles, clumsy but relentlessly dogged as he tried to chivvy Dooku into a corner.

Whereas all Dooku need do was to slip from one side to another—and occasionally flip over a head here and there—so that he could fight each of them in turn, rather than both of them at the same time. He supposed that in their own milieu, they might actually prove reasonably effective; it was clear that their style had been developed by fighting as a team against large numbers of opponents. They were not prepared to fight together against a single Force-user, certainly not one of Dooku's power; he, on the other hand, had always fought alone. It was laughably easy to keep the Jedi tripping and stumbling and getting in each other's way.

They didn't even comprehend how utterly he dominated the

combat. Because they fought as they had been trained, by releasing all desire and allowing the Force to flow through them, they
had no hope of countering Dooku's mastery of Sith techniques.
They had learned nothing since he had bested them on Geonosis.

They allowed the Force to direct them; Dooku directed the
Force.

He drew their strikes to his parries, and drove his own ri-
postes with thrusts of dark power that subtly altered the Jedi's
balance and disrupted their timing. He could have slaughtered
both of them as casually as that creature Maul had destroyed the
vigos of the Black Sun.

However, only one death was in his plan, and this dumb-
show was becoming tiresome. Not to mention tiring. The dark
power that served him went only so far, and he was, after all, not
a young man.

He leaned into a thrust at Kenobi's gut that the Jedi Master
deflected with a rising parry, bringing them chest-to-chest,
blades flaring, locked together a handbreadth from each other's
throats. "Your moves are too slow, Kenobi. Too predictable.
You'll have to do better."

Kenobi's response to this friendly word was to regard him
with a twinkle of gentle amusement in his eye.

"Very well, then," the Jedi said, and shot straight upward
over Dooku's head so fast it seemed he'd vanished.

And in the space where Kenobi's chest had been was now
only the blue lightning of Skywalker's blade driving straight for
Dooku's heart.

Only a desperate whirl to one side made what would have
been a smoking hole in his chest into a line of scorch through his
armorweave cloak.

Dooku thought, *What?*

He threw himself spinning up and away from the two Jedi to
land on the situation table, disengaging for a moment to recover

his composure—that had been *entirely* too close—but by the time his boots touched down Kenobi was there to meet him, blade weaving through a defensive velocity so bewilderingly fast that Dooku dared not even try a strike; he threw a feint toward Kenobi's face, then dropped and spun in a reverse ankle-sweep—

But not only did Kenobi easily overleap this attack, Dooku nearly lost his *own* foot to a slash from *Skywalker* who had again come out of *nowhere* and now carved through the table so that it collapsed under Dooku's weight and dumped the Sith Lord unceremoniously to the floor.

This was *not* in the plan.

Skywalker slammed his following strike down so hard that the shock of deflecting it buckled Dooku's elbows. Dooku threw himself into a backroll that brought him to his feet—and Kenobi's blade was there to meet his neck. Only a desperate whirling slash-block, coupled with a wheel kick that caught Kenobi on the thigh, bought him enough time to leap away again, and when he touched down—

Skywalker was already there.

The first overhand chop of Skywalker's blade slid off Dooku's instinctive guard. The second bent Dooku's wrist. The third flash of blue forced Dooku's scarlet blade so far to the inside that his own lightsaber scorched his shoulder, and Dooku was forced to give ground.

Dooku felt himself blanch. Where had *this* come from?

Skywalker came on, mechanically inexorable, impossibly powerful, a destroyer droid with a lightsaber: each step a blow and each blow a step. Dooku backed away as fast as he dared; Skywalker stayed right on top of him. Dooku's breath went short and hard. He no longer tried to block Skywalker's strikes but only to guide them slanting away; he could not meet Skywalker strength-to-strength—not only did the boy wield tremendous reserves of Force energy, but his sheer physical power was astonishing—

And only then did Dooku understand that he'd been suckered.

Skywalker's Shien ready-stance had been a ruse, as had his Ataro gymmnastics; the boy was a Djem So stylist, and as fine a one as Dooku had ever seen. His own elegant Makashi simply did not generate the kinetic power to meet Djem So head-to-head. Especially not while also defending against a second attacker.

It was time to alter his own tactics.

He dropped low and spun into another reverse ankle-sweep—the weakness of Djem So was its lack of mobility—that slapped Skywalker's boot sharply enough to throw the young Jedi off balance, giving Dooku the opportunity to leap away—

Only to find himself again facing the wheel of blue lightning that was Kenobi's blade.

Dooku decided that the comedy had ended.

Now it was time to kill.

Kenobi's Master had been Qui-Gon Jinn, Dooku's own Padawan; Dooku had fenced Qui-Gon thousands of times, and he knew every weakness of the Ataro form, with its ridiculous acrobatics. He drove a series of flashing thrusts toward Kenobi's legs to draw the Jedi Master into a flipping overhead leap so that Dooku could burn through his spine from kidneys to shoulder blades—and this image, this plan, was so clear in Dooku's mind that he almost failed to notice that Kenobi met every one of his thrusts without so much as moving his feet, staying perfectly centered, perfectly balanced, blade never moving a millimeter more than was necessary, deflecting without effort, riposting with flickering strikes and stabs swifter than the tongue of a Garollian ghost viper, and when Dooku felt Skywalker regain his feet and stride once more toward his back, he finally registered the source of that blinding defensive velocity Kenobi had used a moment ago, and only then, belatedly, did he understand that Kenobi's Ataro and Shii-Cho had been ploys, as well.

Kenobi had become a master of Soresu.

Dooku found himself having a sudden, unexpected, over-powering, and entirely distressing *bad feeling* about this . . .

His farce had suddenly, inexplicably, spun from humorous to deadly serious and was tumbling rapidly toward terrifying. Realization burst through Dooku's consciousness like the blossoming fireballs of dying ships outside: this pair of Jedi fools had somehow managed to become entirely dangerous.

These clowns might—just possibly—actually be able to *beat* him.

No sense taking chances; even his Master would agree with that. Lord Sidious could come up with a new plan more easily than a new apprentice.

He gathered the Force once more in a single indrawn breath that summoned power from throughout the universe; the slightest whipcrack of that power, negligent as a flick of his wrist, sent Kenobi flying backward to crash hard against the wall, but Dooku didn't have time to enjoy it.

Skywalker was all over him.

The shining blue lightsaber whirled and spat and every over-hand chop crashed against Dooku's defense with the unstoppable power of a meteor strike; the Sith Lord spent lavishly of his reserve of the Force merely to meet these attacks without being cut in half, and Skywalker—

Skywalker was getting *stronger.*

Each parry cost Dooku more power than he'd used to throw Kenobi across the room; each block aged him a decade.

He decided he'd best revise his strategy once again.

He no longer even tried to strike back. Force exhaustion began to close down his perceptions, drawing his consciousness back down to his physical form, trapping him within his own skull until he could barely even feel the contours of the room around him; he dimly sensed stairs at his back, stairs that led up to the entrance balcony. He retreated up them, using the higher ground for leverage, but Skywalker just kept on coming, tirelessly ferocious.

That blue blade was everywhere, flashing and whirling faster and faster until Dooku saw the room through an electric haze, and now *Kenobi* was back in the picture: with a shout of the Force, he shot like a torpedo up the stairs behind Skywalker, and Dooku decided that under these rather extreme circumstances, it was at least arguably permissible for a gentleman to cheat.

"Guards!" he said to the pair of super battle droids that still stood at attention to either side of the entrance. "Open fire!"

Instantly the two droids sprang forward and lifted their hands. Energy hammered out from the heavy blasters built into their arms; Skywalker whirled and his blade batted every blast back at the droids, whose mirror-polished carapace armor deflected the bolts again. Galvened particle beams screeched through the room in blinding ricochets.

Kenobi reached the top of the stairs and a single slash of his lightsaber dismantled both droids. Before their pieces could even hit the floor Dooku was in motion, landing a spinning sidestamp that folded Skywalker in half; he used his last burst of dark power to continue his spin into a blindingly fast wheel-kick that brought his heel against the point of Kenobi's chin with a *crack* like the report of a huge-bore slugthrower, knocking the Jedi Master back down the stairs. Sounded like he'd broken his neck.

Wouldn't that be lovely?

There was no sense in taking chances, however.

While Kenobi's bonelessly limp body was still tumbling toward the floor far below, Dooku sent a surge of energy through the Force. Kenobi's fall suddenly accelerated like a missile burning the last of its drives before impact. The Jedi Master struck the floor at a steep angle, skidded along it, and slammed into the wall so hard the hydrofoamed permacrete buckled and collapsed onto him.

This Dooku found exceedingly gratifying.

Now, as for Skywalker—

Which was as far as Dooku got, because by the time his attention returned to the younger Jedi, his vision was rather completely obstructed by the sole of a boot approaching his face with something resembling terminal velocity.

The impact was a blast of white fire, and there was a second impact against his back that was the balcony rail, and then the room turned upside down and he fell toward the ceiling, but not really, of course: it only felt that way because he had flipped over the rail and he was falling headfirst toward the floor, and neither his arms nor his legs were paying any attention to what he was trying to make them do. The Force seemed to be busy elsewhere, and really, the whole process was entirely mortifying.

He was barely able to summon a last surge of dark power before what would have been a disabling impact. The Force cradled him, cushioning his fall and setting him on his feet.

He dusted himself off and fixed a supercilious gaze on Skywalker, who now stood upon the balcony looking down at him—and Dooku couldn't hold the stare; he found this reversal of their original positions oddly unsettling.

There was something troublingly *appropriate* about it.

Seeing Skywalker standing where Dooku himself had stood only moments ago . . . it was as though he was trying to remember a dream he'd never actually had . . .

He pushed this aside, drawing once more upon the certain knowledge of his personal invincibility to open a channel to the Force. Power flowed into him, and the weight of his years dropped away.

He lifted his blade, and beckoned.

Skywalker leapt from the balcony. Even as the boy hurtled downward, Dooku felt a new twist in the currents of the Force between them, and he finally understood.

He understood how Skywalker was getting stronger. Why he no longer spoke. How he had become a machine of battle. He understood why Sidious had been so interested in him for so long.

Skywalker was a natural.

There was a thermonuclear furnace where his heart should be, and it was burning through the firewalls of his Jedi training. He held the Force in the clench of a white-hot fist. He was half Sith already, and he didn't even know it.

This boy had the gift of fury.

And even now, he was holding himself back; even now, as he landed at Dooku's flank and rained blows upon the Sith Lord's defenses, even as he drove Dooku backward step after step, Dooku could feel how Skywalker kept his fury banked behind walls of will: walls that were hardened by some uncontrollable dread.

Dread, Dooku surmised, of himself. Of what might happen if he should ever allow that furnace he used for a heart to go supercritical.

Dooku slipped aside from an overhand chop and sprang backward. "I sense great fear in you. You are consumed by it. Hero With No Fear, indeed. You're a *fraud*, Skywalker. You are nothing but a posturing child."

He pointed his lightsaber at the young Jedi like an accusing finger. "Aren't you a little old to be afraid of the dark?"

Skywalker leapt for him again, and this time Dooku met the boy's charge easily. They stood nearly toe-to-toe, blades flashing faster than the eye could see, but Skywalker had lost his edge: a simple taunt was all that had been required to shift the focus of his attention from winning the fight to controlling his own emotions. The angrier he got, the more afraid he became, and the fear fed his anger in turn; like the proverbial Corellian multipede, now that he had started *thinking* about what he was doing, he could no longer walk.

Dooku allowed himself to relax; he felt that spirit of playfulness coming over him again as he and Skywalker spun 'round each other in their lethal dance. Whatever fun was to be had, he should enjoy while he could.

Then Sidious, for some reason, decided to intervene.

"Don't fear what you're feeling, Anakin, *use* it!" he barked in Palpatine's voice. "Call upon your fury. Focus it, and he cannot stand against you. *Rage* is your weapon. Strike now! *Strike! Kill* him!"

Dooku thought blankly, *Kill me?*

He and Skywalker paused for one single, final instant, blades locked together, staring at each other past a sizzling cross of scarlet against blue, and in that instant Dooku found himself wondering in bewildered astonishment if Sidious had suddenly lost his mind. Didn't he understand the advice he'd just given?

Whose side was he on, anyway?

And through the cross of their blades he saw in Skywalker's eyes the promise of hell, and he felt a sickening presentiment that he already knew the answer to that question.

Treachery is the way of the Sith.

JEDI TRAP

This is the death of Count Dooku:

A starburst of clarity blossoms within Anakin Skywalker's mind, when he says to himself *Oh. I get it, now* and discovers that the fear within his heart can be a weapon, too.

It is that simple, and that complex.

And it is final.

Dooku is dead already. The rest is mere detail.

The play is still on; the comedy of lightsabers flashes and snaps and hisses. Dooku & Skywalker, a one-time-only command performance, for an audience of one. Jedi and Sith and Sith and Jedi, spinning, whirling, crashing together, slashing and chopping, parrying, binding, slipping and whipping and ripping the air around them with snarls of power.

And all for nothing, because a nuclear flame has consumed Anakin Skywalker's Jedi restraint, and fear becomes fury without effort, and fury is a blade that makes his lightsaber into a toy.

The play goes on, but the suspense is over. It has become mere pantomime, as intricate and as meaningless as the space–time curves that guide galactic clusters through a measureless cosmos.

Dooku's decades of combat experience are irrelevant. His mastery of swordplay is useless. His vast wealth, his political influence, impeccable breeding, immaculate manners, exquisite taste—all the pursuits and points of pride to which he has devoted so much of his time and attention over the long, long years of his life—are now chains hung upon his spirit, bending his neck before the ax.

Even his knowledge of the Force has become a joke.

It is this knowledge that shows him his death, makes him handle it, turn it this way and that in his mind, examine it in detail like a black gemstone so cold it burns. Dooku's elegant farce has degenerated into bathetic melodrama, and not one shed tear will mark the passing of its hero.

But for Anakin, in the fight there is only terror, and rage.

Only he stands between death and the two men he loves best in all the world, and he can no longer afford to hold anything back. That imaginary dead-star dragon tries its best to freeze away his strength, to whisper him that Dooku has beaten him before, that Dooku has all the power of the darkness, to remind him how Dooku took his hand, how Dooku could strike down even Obi-Wan himself seemingly without effort and now Anakin is all alone and he will never be a match for any Lord of the Sith—

But Palpatine's words *rage is your weapon* have given Anakin permission to unseal the shielding around his furnace heart, and all his fears and all his doubts shrivel in its flame.

When Count Dooku flies at him, blade flashing, Watto's fist cracks out from Anakin's childhood to knock the Sith Lord tumbling back.

When with all the power that the dark side can draw from throughout the universe, Dooku hurls a jagged fragment of the durasteel table, Shmi Skywalker's gentle murmur *I knew you would come for me, Anakin* smashes it aside.

His head has been filled with the smoke from his smothered

heart for far too long; it has been the thunder that darkens his mind. On Aargonar, on Jabiim, in the Tusken camp on Tatooine, that smoke had clouded his mind, had blinded him and left him flailing in the dark, a mindless machine of slaughter; but here, now, within this ship, this microscopic cell of life in the infinite sterile desert of space, his firewalls have opened so that the terror and the rage are *out there*, in the fight instead of in his head, and Anakin's mind is clear as a crystal bell.

In that pristine clarity, there is only one thing he must do.

Decide.

So he does.

He decides to *win*.

He decides that Dooku should lose the same hand he took. Decision is reality, here: his blade moves simultaneously with his will and blue fire vaporizes black Corellian nanosilk and disintegrates flesh and shears bone, and away falls a Sith Lord's lightsaber hand, trailing smoke that tastes of charred meat and burned hair. The hand falls with a bar of scarlet blaze still extending from its spastic death grip, and Anakin's heart sings for the fall of that red blade.

He reaches out and the Force catches it for him.

And then Anakin takes Dooku's other hand as well.

Dooku crumples to his knees, face blank, mouth slack, and his weapon whirs through the air to the victor's hand, and Anakin finds his vision of the future happening before his eyes: two blades at Count Dooku's throat.

But here, now, the truth belies the dream. Both lightsabers are in *his* hands, and the one in his hand of flesh flares with the synthetic bloodshine of a Sith blade.

Dooku, cringing, shrinking with dread, still finds some hope in his heart that he is wrong, that Palpatine has not betrayed him, that this has all been proceeding according to plan—

Until he hears "Good, Anakin! Good! I *knew* you could do it!" and registers this is Palpatine's voice and feels within the darkest depths of all he is the approach of the words that are to come next.

"Kill him," Palpatine says. "Kill him now."

In Skywalker's eyes he sees only flames.

"Chancellor, please!" he gasps, desperate and helpless, his aristocratic demeanor invisible, his courage only a bitter memory. He is reduced to begging for his life, as so many of his victims have. "Please, you promised me *immunity*! We had a *deal*! *Help* me!"

And his begging gains him a share of mercy equal to that which he has dispensed.

"A deal only if you released me," Palpatine replies, cold as intergalactic space. "Not if you used me as bait to kill my friends."

And he knows, then, that all has indeed been going according to plan. Sidious's plan, not his own. This had been a Jedi trap indeed, but Jedi were not the quarry.

They were the bait.

"Anakin," Palpatine says quietly. "Finish him."

Years of Jedi training make Anakin hesitate; he looks down upon Dooku and sees not a Lord of the Sith but a beaten, broken, cringing old man.

"I shouldn't—"

But when Palpatine barks, "Do it! Now!" Anakin realizes that this isn't actually an order. That it is, in fact, nothing more than what he's been waiting for his whole life.

Permission.

And Dooku—

As he looks up into the eyes of Anakin Skywalker for the final time, Count Dooku knows that he has been deceived not just today, but for many, many years. That he has never been the true apprentice. That he has never been the heir to the power of the Sith. He has been only a tool.

His whole life—all his victories, all his struggles, all his heritage, all his principles and his sacrifices, everything he's done, everything he owns, everything he's been, all his dreams and grand vision for the future Empire and the Army of Sith—have been only a pathetic sham, because all of them, all of *him,* add up only to this.

He has existed only for this.

This.

To be the victim of Anakin Skywalker's first cold-blooded murder.

First but not, he knows, the last.

Then the blades crossed at his throat uncross like scissors.

Snip.

And all of him becomes nothing at all.

Murderer and murdered each stared blindly.

But only the murderer blinked.

I did that.

The severed head's stare was fixed on something beyond living sight. The desperate plea frozen in place on its lips echoed silence. The headless torso collapsed with a slowly fading sigh from the cauterized gape of its trachea, folding forward at the waist as though making obeisance before the power that had ripped away its life.

The murderer blinked again.

Who am *I?*

Was he the slave boy on a desert planet, valued for his astonishing gift with machines? Was he the legendary Podracer, the only human to survive that deadly sport? Was he the unruly, high-spirited, trouble-prone student of a great Jedi Master? The star pilot? The hero? The lover? The Jedi?

Could he be all these things—could he be *any* of them—and still have done what he has done?

He was already discovering the answer at the same time that he finally realized that he needed to ask the question.

The deck bucked as the cruiser absorbed a new barrage of torpedoes and turbolaser fire. Dooku's severed staring head bounced along the deck and rolled away, and Anakin woke up.

"What—?"

He'd been having a dream. He'd been flying, and fighting, and fighting again, and somehow, in the dream, he could do whatever he wanted. In the dream, whatever he did was the right thing to do simply because he wanted to do it. In the dream there were no rules, there was only power.

And the power was his.

Now he stood over a headless corpse that he couldn't bear to see but he couldn't make himself look away, and he knew it hadn't been a dream at all, that he'd really *done* this, the blades were still in his hands and the ocean of wrong he'd dived into had closed over his head.

And he was drowning.

The dead man's lightsaber tumbled from his loosening fingers. "I—I couldn't stop myself . . ."

And before the words left his lips he heard how hollow and obvious was the lie.

"You did well, Anakin." Palpatine's voice was warm as an arm around Anakin's shoulders. "You did not only well, but *right*. He was too dangerous to leave alive."

From the Chancellor this sounded true, but when Anakin repeated it inside his head he knew that Palpatine's truth would be one he could never make himself believe. A tremor that began between his shoulder blades threatened to expand into a full case of the shakes. "He was an unarmed *prisoner* . . ."

That, now—that simple unbearable fact—*that* was truth. Though it burned him like his own lightsaber, truth was something he could hang on to. And somehow it made him feel a little better. A little stronger. He tried another truth: not that he couldn't have stopped himself, but—

"I shouldn't have done that," he said, and now his voice came out solid, and simple, and final. Now he could look down at the corpse at his feet. He could look at the severed head.

He could see them for what they were.

A crime.

He'd become a war criminal.

Guilt hit him like a fist. He *felt* it—a punch to his heart that smacked breath from his lungs and buckled his knees. It hung on his shoulders like a yoke of collapsium: an invisible weight beyond his mortal strength, crushing his life.

There were no words in him for this. All he could say was, "It was wrong."

And that was the sum of it, right there.

It was wrong.

"Nonsense. Disarming him was nothing; he had powers beyond your imagination."

Anakin shook his head. "That doesn't matter. It's not the Jedi way."

The ship shuddered again, and the lights went out.

"Have you never noticed that the Jedi way," Palpatine said, invisible now within the stark shadow of the General's Chair, "is not always the *right* way?"

Anakin looked toward the shadow. "You don't understand. You're not a Jedi. You *can't* understand."

"Anakin, listen to me. How many lives have you just saved with this stroke of a lightsaber? Can you count them?"

"But—"

"It wasn't wrong, Anakin. It may be *not the Jedi way,* but it was *right.* Perfectly natural—he took your hand; you wanted revenge. And your revenge was *justice.*"

"Revenge is never just. It *can't* be—"

"Don't be childish, Anakin. Revenge is the *foundation* of justice. Justice began with revenge, and revenge is still the only justice some beings can ever hope for. After all, this is hardly your first time, is it? Did Dooku deserve mercy more than did the Sand People who tortured your mother to death?"

"That was *different*."

In the Tusken camp he had lost his mind; he had become a force of nature, indiscriminate, killing with no more thought or intention than a sand gale. The Tuskens had been killed, slaughtered, massacred—but that had been beyond his control, and now it seemed to him as if it had been done by someone else: like a story he had heard that had little to do with him at all.

But Dooku—

Dooku had been murdered.

By him.

On purpose.

Here in the General's Quarters, he had looked into the eyes of a living being and coldly decided to end that life. He could have chosen the right way. He could have chosen the Jedi way.

But instead—

He stared down at Dooku's severed head.

He could never unchoose this choice. He could never take it back. As Master Windu liked to say, there is no such thing as a second chance.

And he wasn't even sure he wanted one.

He couldn't let himself think about this. Just as he didn't let himself think about the dead on Tatooine. He put his hand to his eyes, trying to rub away the memory. "You promised we would never talk about that again."

"And we won't. Just as we need never speak of what has happened here today." It was as though the shadow itself spoke kindly. "I have always kept your secrets, have I not?"

"Yes—yes, of course, Chancellor, but—" Anakin wanted to crawl away into a corner somewhere; he felt sure that if things would just *stop* for a while—an hour, a minute—he could pull himself together and find some way to keep moving forward. He had to keep moving forward. Moving forward was all he could do.

Especially when he couldn't stand to look back.

The view wall behind the General's Chair blossomed with looping ion spirals of inbound missiles. The shuddering of the ship built itself into a continuous quake, gathering magnitude with each hit.

"Anakin, my restraints, please," the shadow said. "I'm afraid this ship is breaking up. I don't think we should be aboard when it does."

In the Force, the field-signatures of the magnetic locks on the Chancellor's shackles were as clear as text saying UNLOCK ME LIKE THIS; a simple twist of Anakin's mind popped them open. The shadow grew a head, then shoulders, then underwent a sudden mitosis that left the General's Chair standing behind and turned its other half into the Supreme Chancellor.

Palpatine picked his way through the debris that littered the gloom-shrouded room, moving surprisingly quickly toward the stairs. "Come along, Anakin. There is very little time."

The view wall flared white with the missiles' impacts, and one of them must have damaged the gravity generators: the ship seemed to heel over, forcing Palpatine to clutch desperately at the banister and sending Anakin skidding down a floor that had suddenly become a forty-five-degree ramp.

He rolled hard into a pile of rubble: shattered permacrete, hydrofoamed to reduce weight. "Obi-Wan—!"

He sprang to his feet and waved away the debris that had buried the body of his friend. Obi-Wan lay entirely still, eyes closed, dust-caked blood matting his hair where his scalp had split.

Bad as Obi-Wan looked, Anakin had stood over the bodies of too many friends on too many battlefields to be panicked by a little blood. One touch to Obi-Wan's throat confirmed the strength of his pulse, and that touch also let Anakin's Force perception flow through the whole body of his friend. His breathing was strong and regular, and no bones were broken: this was a concussion, no more.

Apparently Obi-Wan's head was somewhat harder than the cruiser's interior walls.

"Leave him, Anakin. There is no time." Palpatine was half hanging from the banister, both arms wrapped around a stanchion. "This whole spire may be about to break free—"

"Then we'll all be adrift together." Anakin glanced up at the Supreme Chancellor and for that instant he didn't like the man at all—but then he reminded himself that brave as Palpatine was, his was the courage of conviction; the man was no soldier. He had no way of truly comprehending what he was asking Anakin to do.

"His fate," he said in case Palpatine had not understood, "will be the same as ours."

With Obi-Wan unconscious and Palpatine waiting above, with responsibility for the lives of his two closest friends squarely upon him, Anakin found that he had recovered his inner balance. Under pressure, in crisis, with no one to call upon for help, he could focus again. He had to.

This was what he'd been born for: saving people.

The Force brought Obi-Wan's lightsaber to his hand and he clipped it to his friend's belt, then hoisted the limp body over his shoulder and let the Force help him run lightly up the steeply canted floor to Palpatine's side.

"Impressive," Palpatine said, but then he cast a significant gaze up the staircase, which the vector of the artificial gravity had made into a vertical cliff. "But what now?"

Before Anakin could answer, the erratic gravity swung like a pendulum; while they both clung to the railing, the room seemed to roll around them. All the broken chairs and table fragments and hunks of rubble slid toward the opposite side, and now instead of a cliff the staircase had become merely a corrugated stretch of floor.

"People say"—Anakin nodded toward the door to the turbolift lobby—"when the Force closes a hatch, it opens a viewport. After you?"

GRIEVOUS

The ARC-170s of Squad Seven had joined the V-wings of Squad Four in swarming the remaining vulture fighters that had screened the immense Trade Federation flagship, *Invisible Hand*. Clone pilots destroyed droid after droid with machine-like precision of their own. When the last of the vultures had been converted to an expanding globe of superheated gas, the clone fighters peeled away, leaving *Invisible Hand* exposed to the full fire of Home Fleet Strike Group Five: three *Carrack*-class light cruisers—*Integrity*, *Indomitable*, and *Perseverance*—in support of the Dreadnaught *Mas Ramdar*.

Strike Group Five had deployed in a triangle around *Mas Ramdar*, maintaining a higher orbit to pin *Invisible Hand* deep in Coruscant's gravity well. Turbolasers blasted against *Invisible Hand*'s faltering shields, but the flagship was giving as good as it got: *Mas Ramdar* had sustained so much damage already that it was little more than a target to absorb the *Hand*'s return fire, and *Indomitable* was only a shell, most of its crew dead or evacuated, being run remotely by its commander and bridge crew; it swung unsteadily through the *Hand*'s vector cone of escape routes to block any attempt to run up toward jump.

As its shields finally failed, *Invisible Hand* began to roll, whirling like a bullet from a rifled slugthrower, trailing spiral jets of crystallizing gas that gushed from multiple hull ruptures. The rolling picked up speed, breaking the targeting locks of the ship's Republic adversaries. Unable to pound the same point again and again, their turbolasers weren't powerful enough to breach the *Hand*'s heavy armor directly; their tracking points became rings that circled the ship, chewing gradually into the hull in tightening garrotes of fire.

On the *Hand*'s bridge, overheated Neimoidians were strapped into their battle stations in full crash webbing. The air reeked of burning metal and the funk of reptilian stress hormones, and the erratically shifting gravity threatened to add a sharper stench: the faces of several of the bridge officers had already paled from healthy gray-green to nauseated pink.

The sole being on the bridge who was not strapped into a chair stalked from one side to the other, floor-length cape draped over shoulders angular as exposed bone. He ignored the jolts of impact and was unaffected by the swirl of unpredictable gravity as he paced the deck with metal-on-metal clanks; he walked on taloned creations of magnetized duranium, jointed to grab and crush like the feet of a Vratixan blood eagle.

His expression could not be read—his face was a mask of bleached ceramic armorplast stylized to evoke a humanoid skull—but the pure venom in the voice that hissed through the mask's electrosonic vocabulator made up for it.

"Either get the gravity generators calibrated or disable them altogether," he snarled at a blue-scanned image of a cringing Neimoidian engineer. "If this continues, you won't live long enough to be killed by the Republic."

"But, but, but sir—it's really up to the repair droids—"

"And because they *are* droids, it's useless to threaten them. So I am threatening *you*. Understand?"

He turned away before the stammering engineer could summon a reply. The hand he extended toward the forward viewscreen wore a jointed gauntlet of armorplast fused to its bones of duranium alloy. "Concentrate fire on *Indomitable*," he told the senior gunnery officer. "All batteries at maximum. Fire for effect. Blast that hulk out of space, and we'll make a hyperspace jump through its wreckage."

"But—the forward towers are already *overloading*, sir." The officer's voice trembled on the edge of panic. "They'll be at critical failure in less than a *minute*—"

"Burn them out."

"But sir, once they're gone—"

The rest of the senior gunnery officer's objection was lost in the wetly final crunching sound his face made under the impact of an armorplast fist. That same fist opened, seized the collar of the officer's uniform, and yanked his corpse out of the chair, ripping the crash webbing free along with it.

An expressionless skull-face turned toward the junior gunnery officer. "Congratulations on your promotion. Take your post."

"Y-y-yes, sir." The newly promoted senior gunnery officer's hands shook so badly he could barely unbuckle his crash web, and his face had gone deathly pink.

"Do you understand your orders?"

"Y-y-y—"

"Do you have any objections?"

"N-n-n—"

"Very well, then," General Grievous said with flat, impenetrable calm. "Carry on."

This is General Grievous:

Durasteel. Ceramic armorplast-plated duranium. Electro-drivers and crystal circuitry.

Within them: the remnants of a living being.

He doesn't breathe. He doesn't eat. He cannot laugh, and he does not cry.

A lifetime ago he was an organic sentient being. A lifetime ago he had friends, a family, an occupation; a lifetime ago he had things to love, and things to fear. Now he has none of these.

Instead, he has *purpose*.

It's built into him.

He is built to intimidate. The resemblance to a human skeleton melded with limbs styled after the legendary Krath war droids is entirely intentional. It is a face and form born of childhood's infinite nightmares.

He is built to dominate. The ceramic armorplast plates protecting limbs and torso and face can stop a burst from a starfighter's laser cannon. Those indestructible arms are ten times stronger than human, and move with the blurring speed of electronic reflexes.

He is built to eradicate. Those human-sized hands have human-sized fingers for exactly one reason: to hold a lightsaber.

Four of them hang inside his cloak.

He has never constructed a lightsaber. He has never bought one, nor has he recovered one that was lost. Each and all, he has taken from the dead hands of Jedi he has killed.

Personally.

He has many, many such trophies; the four he carries with him are his particular favorites. One belonged to the interminable K'Kruhk, whom he had bested at Hypori; another to the Viraanntesse Jedi Jmmaar, who'd fallen at Vandos; the other two had been created by Puroth and Nystammall, whom Grievous had slaughtered together on the flame-grass plains of Tovarskl so that each would know the other's death, as well as their own;

these are murders he recalls with so much pleasure that touching these souvenirs with his hands of armorplast and durasteel brings him something resembling joy.

But only resembling.

He remembers joy. He remembers anger, and frustration. He remembers grief and sorrow.

He doesn't actually feel any of them. Not anymore.

He's not designed for it.

───

White-hot sparks zipped and crackled through the smoke that billowed across the turbolift lobby. Over Anakin's shoulder, the unconscious Jedi Master wheezed faintly. Beside his other shoulder, Palpatine coughed harshly into the sleeve of his robe, held over his face for protection from caustic combustion products of the overloading circuitry.

"Artoo?" Anakin shook his comlink sharply. The blasted thing had been on the blink ever since Obi-Wan had stepped on it during one of the turbolift fights.

"Artoo, do you copy? I need you to activate—" The smoke was so thick he could barely make out the numerals on the code plate. "—elevator three-two-two-four. *Three-two-two-four*, do you copy?"

The comlink emitted a fading *fwheep* that might have been an acknowledgment, and the doors slid apart, but before Anakin could carry Obi-Wan through, the turbolift pod shot upward and the artificial gravity vector shifted again, throwing him and his partner into a heap next to Palpatine in the lobby's opposite corner.

Palpatine was struggling to rise, still coughing, sounding weak. Anakin let the Force lift Obi-Wan back to his shoulder, then picked himself up. "Perhaps you should stay down, sir," he said to the Chancellor. "The gravity swings are getting worse."

Palpatine nodded. "But, Anakin—"

Anakin looked up. The turbolift doors still stood open. "Wait here, sir."

He opened himself more fully to the Force and in his mind placed himself and Obi-Wan balanced on the edge of the open doorway above. Holding this image, he leapt, and the Force made his intention into reality: his leap carried him and the unconscious Jedi Master precisely to the rim.

The altered gravitic vector had made the turbolift shaft into a horizontal hallway of unlit durasteel, laser-straight, shrinking into darkness. Anakin was familiar with the specs for Trade Federation command cruisers; the angled conning spire was some three hundred meters long. As it stood, they could walk it in two or three minutes. But if the wrong gravity shift were to catch them inside the shaft . . .

He shook his head, grimly calculating the odds. "We'll have to be fast."

He glanced back over his shoulder, down at Palpatine, who still huddled below. "Are you all right, Chancellor? Are you well enough to run?"

The Supreme Chancellor finally rose, patting his robes in a futile attempt to dust them off. "I haven't run since I was a boy on Naboo."

"It's never too late to start getting into shape." Anakin reached through the Force to give Palpatine a little help in clambering up to the open doorway. "There are light shuttles on the hangar deck. We can be there in five minutes."

Once Palpatine was safely within the shaft-hall, Anakin said, "Follow me," and turned to go, but the Chancellor stopped him with a hand on his arm.

"Anakin, wait. We need to get to the bridge."

Through an entire shipful of combat droids? Not likely. "The hangar deck's right below—well, *beside* us, now. It's our best chance."

"But the bridge—*Grievous* is there."

Now Anakin did stop. Grievous. The most prolific slaughterer of Jedi since Durge. In all the excitement, Anakin had entirely forgotten that the bio-droid general was aboard.

"You've defeated Dooku," Palpatine said. "Capture Grievous, and you will have dealt a wound from which the Separatists may never recover."

Anakin thought blankly: *I could do it.*

He had dreamed of capturing Grievous ever since Muunilinst—and now the general was close. So close Anakin could practically *smell* him . . . and Anakin had never felt so powerful. The Force was with him today in ways more potent than he had ever experienced.

"Think of it, Anakin." Palpatine stood close by his shoulder, opposite to Obi-Wan, so close he needed only to whisper. "You have destroyed their political head. Take their military commander, and you will have practically won the war. *Singlehanded*. Who else could do that, Anakin? Yoda? Mace Windu? They couldn't even capture Dooku. Who would have a chance against Grievous, if not Anakin Skywalker? The Jedi have never faced a crisis like the Clone Wars—but also they have never had a hero like *you*. You can save them. You can save *everyone*."

Anakin jerked, startled. He turned a sharp glance toward Palpatine. The way he had said that . . .

Like a voice out of his dreams.

"That's—" Anakin tried to laugh; it came out a little shaky. "That's not what Obi-Wan keeps telling me."

"Forget Obi-Wan," Palpatine said. "He has no idea how powerful you truly are. *Use* your power, Anakin. Save the Republic."

Anakin could see it, vivid as a HoloNet feature: arriving at the Senate with Grievous in electrobonds, standing modestly aside as Palpatine announced the end of the war, returning to the Temple, to the Council Chamber, where finally, after all this time, there would be a chair waiting, just for him.

They could hardly refuse him Mastership now, after he had won the war for them . . .

But then Obi-Wan shifted on his shoulder, moaning faintly, and Anakin snapped back to reality.

"No," he said. "Sorry, Chancellor. My orders are clear. This is a rescue mission; your safety is my only priority."

"I will never be safe while Grievous lives," Palpatine countered. "Master Kenobi will recover at any moment. Leave him here with me; he can see me safely to the hangar deck. Go for the general."

"I—I *would* like to, sir, but—"

"I can make it an order, Anakin."

"With respect, sir: no. You can't. My orders come from the Jedi Council, and the Council's orders come from the Senate. You have no direct authority."

The Chancellor's face darkened. "That may change."

Anakin nodded. "And perhaps it should, sir. But until it does, we'll do things my way. Let's go."

"Sir?" The thin voice of the comm officer interrupted Grievous's pacing. "We are being hailed by *Integrity*, sir. They propose a cease-fire."

Dark yellow eyes squinted through the skull-mask at the tactical displays. A pause in the combat would allow *Invisible Hand*'s turbolaser batteries to cool, and give the engineers a chance to get the gravity generators under control. "Acknowledge receipt of transmission. Stand by to cease fire."

"Standing by, sir." The gunnery officer was still shaking.

"Cease fire."

The lances of energy that had joined the *Hand* to the Home Fleet Strike Force melted away.

"Further transmission, sir. It's *Integrity*'s commander."

Grievous nodded. "Initiate."

A ghostly image built itself above the bridge's ship-to-ship hologenerator: a young human male of distinctly average height and build, wearing the uniform of a lieutenant commander. The only thing distinctive about his otherwise rather bland features was the calm confidence in his eyes.

"General Grievous," the young man said briskly, *"I am Lieutenant Commander Lorth Needa of RSS* Integrity. *At my request, my superiors have consented to offer you the chance to surrender your ship, sir."*

"Surrender?" Grievous's vocabulator produced a very creditable reproduction of a snort. "Preposterous."

"Please give this offer careful deliberation, General, as it will not be repeated. Consider the lives of your crew."

Grievous cast an icy glance around his bridge full of craven Neimoidians. "Why should I?"

The young man did not look surprised, though he did show a trace of sadness. *"Is this your reply, then?"*

"Not at all." Grievous drew himself up; by straightening the angles of his levered joints, he could add half a meter to his already imposing height. "I have a counteroffer. Maintain your cease-fire, move that hulk *Indomitable* out of my way, and withdraw to a minimum range of fifty kilometers until this ship achieves hyperspace jump."

"If I may use your word, sir: preposterous."

"Tell these superiors of yours that if my demands are not met within ten minutes, I will personally disembowel Supreme Chancellor Palpatine, live on the HoloNet. Am I understood?"

The young officer took this without a blink. *"Ah. The Chancellor is aboard your ship, then."*

"He is. Your pathetic Jedi so-called heroes have failed. They are dead, and Palpatine remains in my hands."

"Ah," the young officer repeated. *"So you will, of course, allow me to speak with him. To, ah, reassure my superiors that you are not simply—well, to put it charitably—bluffing?"*

"I would not lower myself to lie to the likes of you." Grievous turned to the comm officer. "Patch in Count Dooku."

The comm officer stroked his screen, then shook his head. "He's not responding, sir."

Grievous shook his head disgustedly. "Just *show* the Chancellor, then. Bring up my quarters on the security screen."

The security officer stroked his own screen, and made a choking sound. "Hrm, sir?"

"What are you *waiting* for? Bring it up!"

He'd gone as pink as the gunner. "Perhaps you should have a look *first*, sir?"

The plain urgency in his tone brought Grievous to his side without another word. The general bent over the screen that showed the view inside his quarters and found himself looking at jumbled piles of energy-sheared wreckage surrounding the empty shape of the General's Chair.

And that—that there—that looked like it could have been a body . . .

Draped in a cape of armorweave.

Grievous turned back toward the intership holocomm. "The Chancellor is—indisposed."

"Ah. I see."

Grievous suspected that the young officer saw entirely too well. "I *assure* you—"

"I do not require your assurance, General. You have the same amount of time you offered us. Ten minutes from now, I will have either your surrender, or confirmation that Supreme Chancellor Palpatine is alive, unharmed—and present—or Invisible Hand *will be destroyed."*

"Wait—you can't simply—"

"Ten minutes, General. Needa out."

When Grievous turned to the bridge security officer, his mask was blankly expressionless as ever, but he made up for it with the open murder in his voice.

"Dooku is dead and the Jedi are loose. They have the Chancellor. Find them and bring them to me."

His armorplast fingers curled into a fist that crashed down on the security console so hard the entire thing collapsed into a sparking, smoking ruin.

"*Find* them!"

RESCUE

Anakin counted paces as he trotted along the turbolift shaft, Obi-Wan over his shoulder and Palpatine at his side. He'd reached 102—only a third of the way along the conning spire—when he felt the gravity begin to shift.

Exactly the wrong way: changing the rest of the long, long shaft from *ahead* to *down*.

He put out his free arm to stop the Chancellor. "This is a problem. Find something to hang on to while I get us out of here."

One of the turbolift doors was nearby, seemingly lying on its side. Anakin's lightsaber found his hand and its sizzling blade burned open the door controls, but before he could even move aside the sparking wires, the gravitic vector lurched toward vertical and he fell, skidding along the wall, free hand grabbing desperately at a loop of cable, catching it, hanging from it—

And the turbolift doors opened.

Inviting. Safe. And mockingly out of reach: a meter above his outstretched arm—

And his other arm was the only thing holding Obi-Wan above a two-hundred-meter drop down which his lightsaber's handgrip now clanked and clattered, fading toward infinity. For half a second Anakin was actually glad Obi-Wan was unconscious, because he wasn't in the mood for another lecture about hanging on to his lightsaber right now, and that thought blew away and vanished because something *had grabbed on to his leg*—

He looked down.

It was Palpatine.

The Chancellor hugged Anakin's ankle with improbable strength, peering fearfully into the darkness below. "Anakin, do something! You have to *do* something!"

I'm open to suggestions, he thought, but he said, "Don't panic. Just hang on."

"I don't think I can . . ." The Chancellor turned his anguished face upward imploringly. "Anakin, I'm slipping. Give me your hand—you have to *give* me your *hand*!"

And drop Obi-Wan? Not in this millennium.

"Don't *panic*," Anakin repeated. The Chancellor had clearly lost his head. "I can get us out of this."

He wished he were as confident as he sounded. He had been counting on the artificial gravity to continue to swing until the shaft turned back into a hallway, but instead it seemed to have stopped where it was.

This would be an especially lousy time for the generators to start working right.

He fixed a measuring glance on the open lift doorway above; perhaps the Force could give him enough of a boost to carry all three of them to safety.

But that was an exceedingly large *perhaps.*

Obi-Wan, old buddy old pal, he thought, *this would be a really good time to wake up.*

Obi-Wan Kenobi opened his eyes to find himself staring at what he strongly suspected was Anakin's butt.

It *looked* like Anakin's butt—well, his pants, anyway—though it was thoroughly impossible for Obi-Wan to be certain, since he had never before had occasion to examine Anakin's butt upside down, which it currently appeared to be, nor from this rather uncomfortably close range.

And how he might have arrived at this angle and this range was entirely baffling.

He said, "Um, have I missed something?"

"Hang on," he heard Anakin say. "We're in a bit of a situation here."

So it *was* Anakin's butt after all. He supposed he might take a modicum of comfort from that. Looking up, he discovered Anakin's legs, and his boots—and a somewhat astonishing close-up view of the Supreme Chancellor, as Palpatine seemingly balanced overhead, supported only by a white-knuckled death-grip on Anakin's ankle.

"Oh, hello, Chancellor," he said mildly. "Are you well?"

The Chancellor cast a distressed glance over his shoulder. "I *hope* so . . ."

Obi-Wan followed the Chancellor's gaze; above Palpatine rose a long, long vertical shaft—

Which was when he finally realized that he wasn't looking *up* at all.

This must be what Anakin had meant by *a bit of a situation*.

"Ah," Obi-Wan said. At least he was finally coming to understand where he stood.

Well, lay. Hung. Whatever.

"And Count Dooku?"

Anakin said, "Dead."

"Pity." Obi-Wan sighed. "Alive, he might have been a help to us."

"Obi-Wan—"

"Not in this particular situation, granted, but nonetheless—"

"Can we discuss this *later*? The ship's breaking apart."

"Ah."

A familiar electrosonic *feroo-wheep* came thinly through someone's comlink. "Was that Artoo? What does he want?"

"I asked him to activate the elevator," Anakin said.

From the distant darkness above came a *clank*, and a *shirr*, and a *clonk*, all of which evoked in Obi-Wan's still-somewhat-addled brain the image of turbolift brakes unlocking. The accuracy of his imagination was swiftly confirmed by a sudden downdraft that smelled strongly of burning oil, followed closely by the bottom of a turbolift pod hurtling down the shaft like a meteorite down a well.

Obi-Wan said, "Oh."

"It seemed like a good idea at the time—"

"No need to get defensive."

"Artoo!" Anakin shouted. "Shut it down!"

"No time for that," Obi-Wan said. "Jump."

"Jump?" Palpatine asked with a shaky laugh. "Don't you mean, *fall?*"

"Um, actually, yes. Anakin—?"

Anakin let go.

They fell.

And fell. The sides of the turboshaft blurred.

And fell some more, until the gravitic vector finally eased a couple of degrees and they found themselves sliding along the side of the shaft, which was quickly turning into the bottom of the shaft, and the lift pod was still shrieking toward them faster than they could possibly run until Anakin finally got the comlink working and shouted, "Artoo, open the doors! All of them! All floors!"

One door opened just as they skidded onto it and all three of them tumbled through. They landed in a heap on a turbolift lobby's opposite wall as the pod shot past overhead.

They gradually managed to untangle themselves. "Are . . . all of your rescues so . . ." Palpatine gasped breathlessly. ". . . *entertaining?*"

Obi-Wan gave Anakin a thoughtful frown.

Anakin returned it with a shrug.

"Actually, now that you mention it," Obi-Wan said, "yes."

Anakin stared into the tangled masses of wreckage that littered the hangar bay, trying to pick out anything that still even
resembled a ship. This place looked as if it had taken a direct hit;
wind howled against his back through the open hatchway where
Obi-Wan stood with Chancellor Palpatine, and scraps of debris
whirled into the air, blown toward space through gaps in the
scorched and buckled blast doors.

"None of those ships will get us anywhere!" Palpatine
shouted above the wind, and Anakin had to agree. "What are we
going to do?"

Anakin shook his head. He didn't know, and the Force wasn't
offering any clues. "Obi-Wan?"

"How should I know?" Obi-Wan said, bracing himself in the
doorway, robe whipping in the wind. "You're the hero, I'm just
a Master!"

Past Obi-Wan's shoulder Anakin saw a cadre of super battle
droids marching around a corner into the corridor. "Master! Behind you!"

Obi-Wan whirled, lightsaber flaring to meet a barrage of
blaster bolts. "Protect the Chancellor!"

And let you have all the fun? Anakin pulled the Chancellor
into the hangar bay and pressed him against the wall beside the
hatch. "Stay under cover until we handle the droids!"

He was about to jump out beside Obi-Wan when he remembered that he had dropped his lightsaber down the turboshaft;
fighting super battle droids without it would be a bit tricky. Not
to mention that Obi-Wan would never let him hear the end of it.

"Droids are not our only problem!" Palpatine pointed across
the hangar bay. "Look!"

On the far side of the bay, masses of wreckage were shifting,
sliding toward the wall against which Anakin and Palpatine

stood. Then debris closer to them began to slide, followed by piles closer still. An invisible wave-front was passing through the hangar bay; behind it, the gravitic vector was rotated a full ninety degrees.

Gravity shear.

Anakin's jaw clenched. This just kept getting better and better.

He unspooled a length of his utility belt's safety cable and passed the end to Palpatine. The wind made it sing. "Cinch this around your waist. Things are about to get a little wild!"

"What's *happening*?"

"The gravity generators have desynchronized—they'll tear the ship apart!" Anakin grabbed one of the zero-g handles beside the hatchway, then leaned out into the firestorm of blaster bolts and saber flares and touched Obi-Wan's shoulder. "Time to go!"

"What?"

Explanation was obviated as the shear-front moved past them and the wall became the floor. Anakin grabbed the back of Obi-Wan's collar, but not to save him from falling; the torque of the gravity shear had buckled the blast doors—which were now overhead—and the hurricane of escaping air blasting from the corridor shaft blew the Jedi Master up through the hatch. Anakin dragged him out of the gale just as pieces of super battle droids began hurtling upward into the hangar bay like misfiring torpedoes.

Some of the super battle droids were still intact enough to open fire as they flew past. "Hang on to my belt!" Obi-Wan shouted and spun his lightsaber through an intricate flurry to deflect bolt after bolt. Anakin could do nothing but hold him braced against the gale; his grip on the zero-g handle was the only thing keeping him and Obi-Wan from being blown out into space and taking Palpatine with them.

"This is not the best plan we've ever had!" he shouted.

"This was a *plan*?" Palpatine sounded appalled.

"We'll make our way forward!" Obi-Wan shouted. "There are only droids back here! Once we hit live-crew areas, there will be escape pods!"

Only droids back here echoed inside Anakin's head. "Obi-Wan, *wait!*" he cried. "Artoo's still here somewhere! We can't leave him!"

"He's probably been destroyed, or blown into space!" Obi-Wan deflected blaster bursts from the last two gale-blown droids. They tumbled up to the gap in the blast doors and vanished into the infinite void. Obi-Wan put away his lightsaber and fought his way back to a grip beside Anakin's. "We can't afford the time to search for him. I'm sorry, Anakin. I know how much he meant to you."

Anakin desperately fished out his comlink. "Artoo! Artoo, come in!" He shook it, and shook it again. Artoo couldn't have been destroyed. He just *couldn't*. "Artoo, do you copy? Where are you?"

"Anakin—" Obi-Wan's hand was on his arm, and the Jedi Master leaned so close that his low tone could be heard over the rising gale. "We must go. Being a Jedi means allowing things— even things we love—to pass out of our lives."

Anakin shook the comlink again. "Artoo!" He couldn't just leave him. He couldn't. And he didn't exactly have an explanation.

Not one he could ever give Obi-Wan, anyway.

There are so few things a Jedi ever owns; even his lightsaber is less a possession than an expression of his identity. To be a Jedi is to renounce possessions. And Anakin had tried so hard, tried for so long, to do just that.

Even on their wedding day, Anakin had had no devotion-gift for his new wife; he didn't actually *own* anything.

But love will find a way.

He had brought something like a gift to her apartments in Theed, still a little shy with her, still overwhelmed by finding the feelings in her he'd felt so long himself, not knowing quite how to give her a gift which wasn't really a gift. Nor was it his to give.

Without anything of his own to give except his love, all he could bring her was a friend.

"I didn't have many friends when I was a kid," he'd told her, "so I built one."

And C-3PO had shuffled in behind him, gleaming as though he'd been plated with solid gold.

Padmé had lit up, her eyes gleaming, but she had at first tried to protest. "I can't accept him," she'd said. "I know how much he means to you."

Anakin had only laughed. What use is a protocol droid to a Jedi? Even one as upgraded as 3PO—Anakin had packed his creation with so many extra circuits and subprograms and heuristic algorithms that the droid was practically human.

"I'm not giving him to you," he'd told her. "He's not even really mine to give; when I built him, I was a slave, and everything I did belonged to Watto. Cliegg Lars bought him along with my mother; Owen gave him back to me, but I'm a Jedi. I have renounced possessions. I guess that means he's free now. What I'm really doing is asking you to look after him for me."

"Look after him?"

"Yes. Maybe even give him a job. He's a little fussy," he'd admitted, "and maybe I shouldn't have given him quite so much self-consciousness—he's a worrier—but he's very smart, and he might be a real help to a big-time diplomat . . . like, say, a Senator from Naboo?"

Padmé then had extended her hand and graciously invited C-3PO to join her staff, because on Naboo, high-functioning droids were respected as thinking beings, and 3PO had been so flustered at being treated like a sentient creature that he'd been barely able to speak, beyond muttering something about hoping he might make himself useful, because after all he was "fluent in over six million forms of communication." Then she had turned to Anakin and laid her soft, soft hand along his jawline to draw him down to kiss her, and that was all he had needed, all he had hoped for; he would give her everything he had, everything he was—

And there had come another day, two years later, a day that had meant nearly as much to him as the day they had wed: the day he had finally passed his trials.

The day he had become a Jedi Knight.

As soon as circumstances allowed he had slipped away, on his own now, no Master over his shoulder, no one to monitor his comings and his goings and so he could take himself to the vast Coruscant complex at 500 Republica where Naboo's senior Senator kept her spacious apartments.

And he had then, finally, two years late, a devotion-gift for her.

He had then one thing that he truly owned, that he had earned, that he was not required to renounce. One gift he could give her to celebrate their love.

The culmination of the Ceremony of Jedi Knighthood is the severing of the new Jedi Knight's Padawan braid. And it was this that he laid into Padmé's trembling hand.

One long, thin braid of his glossy hair: such a little thing, of no value at all.

Such a little thing, that meant the galaxy to him.

And she had kissed him then, and laid her soft cheek against his jaw, and she had whispered in his ear that she had something for him as well.

Out from her closet had whirred R2-D2.

Of course Anakin knew him; he had known him for years— the little droid was a decorated war hero himself, having saved

Padmé's life back when she had been Queen of Naboo, not to mention helping the nine-year-old Anakin destroy the Trade Federation's Droid Control Ship, breaking the blockade and saving the planet. The Royal Engineers of Naboo's aftermarket wizardry made their modified R-units the most sought after in the galaxy; he'd tried to protest, but she had silenced him with a soft finger against his lips and a gentle smile and a whisper of "After all, what does a politician need with an astromech?"

"But I'm a Jedi—"

"That's why I'm not giving him to you," she'd said with a smile. "I'm asking you to look after him. He's not really a gift. He's a friend."

All this flashed though Anakin's mind in the stretching second before his comlink finally crackled to life with a familiar *fwee-wheoo,* and his heart unclenched.

"Artoo, where are you? Come on, we have to get out of here!"

High above, on the wall that was supposed to be the floor, the lid of a battered durasteel storage locker shifted, pushed aside by a dome of silver and blue. The lid swung fully open and R2-D2 righted itself, deployed its booster rockets, and floated out from the locker, heading for the far exit.

Anakin gave Obi-Wan a fierce grin. Let someone he loves pass out of his life? Not likely. "What are we waiting for?" he said. "Let's go!"

From *Invisible Hand*'s bridge, the ship's spin made the vast curve of Coruscant's horizon appear to orbit the ship in a dizzying whirl. Each rotation also brought a view of the lazily tumbling wreckage of the conning spire, ripped from the ship and cast out of orbit by centripetal force, as it made the long burning fall toward the planetary city's surface.

General Grievous watched them both while his droid circuitry ticked off the seconds remaining in the life of his ship.

He had no fear for his own life; his specially designed escape module was preprogrammed to take him directly to a ship already primed for jump. Mere seconds after he sealed himself and the Chancellor within the module's heavily armored hull, they would be taken aboard the fleeing ship, which would then make a series of randomized microjumps to prevent being tracked before entering the final jump to the secret base on Utapau.

But he was not willing to go without the Chancellor. This operation had cost the Confederacy dearly in ships and personnel; to leave empty-handed would be an even graver cost in prestige. Winning this war was more than half a matter of propaganda: much of the weakness of the Republic grew from its citizens' superstitious dread of the Separatists' seemingly inevitable victory— a dread cultivated and nourished by the CIS shadowfeed that poisoned government propaganda on the HoloNet. The common masses of the Republic believed that the Republic was losing; to see the legendary Grievous himself beaten back and fleeing a battle would give them hope that the war might be won.

And hope was simply not to be allowed.

His built-in comlink buzzed in his left ear. He touched the sensor implant in the jaw of his mask. "Yes."

"The Jedi almost certainly escaped the conning spire, sir." The voice was that of one of his precious, custom-built IG 100-series MagnaGuards: prototype self-motivating humaniform combat droids designed, programmed, and armed specifically to fight Jedi. *"We recovered a lightsaber from the base of the turbolift shaft before the spire tore free."*

"Copy that. Stand by for instructions." One long stride put

Grievous next to the Neimoidian security officer. "Have you located them, or are you about to die?"

"I, ah, I ah—" The security officer's trembling finger pointed to a schematic of *Invisible Hand*'s hangar deck, where a bright blip slid slowly through Bay One.

"What is that?"

"It's, it's, it's the Chancellor's *beacon*, sir."

"What? The Jedi never deactivated it? Why not?"

"I, well, I can't actually—"

"Idiots." He looked down at the cringing security officer, considering killing the fool just for taking so long to figure this out.

The Neimoidian might as well have read Grievous's thought spelled out across his bone-colored mask. "If, if, if you hadn't—er, I mean, please recall my security console has been destroyed, and so I have been forced to reroute—"

"Silence." Grievous gave a mental shrug. The fool would be dead or captured soon enough regardless. "Order all combat droids to terminate their search algorithms and converge on the bridge. Wait, strike that: leave the battle droids. Useless things," he muttered into his mask. "A greater danger to us than to Jedi. Super battle droids and droidekas *only*, do you understand? We will take no chances."

As the security officer turned to his screens, Grievous again touched the sensor implant along the jaw of his mask. "IG-One-oh-one."

"Sir."

"Assemble a team of super battle droids and droidekas—as many as you can gather—and report to the hangar deck. I'll give you the exact coordinates as soon as they are available."

"Yes, sir."

"You will find at least one Jedi, possibly two, in the company of Chancellor Palpatine, imprisoned in a ray shield. They are to be considered extremely dangerous. Disarm them and deliver them to the bridge."

"If they are so dangerous, perhaps we should execute them on the spot."

"No. My orders are clear that the Chancellor is not to be harmed. And the Jedi—"

The general's right hand slipped beneath his cape to stroke the array of lightsabers clipped there.

"The Jedi, I will execute *personally.*"

A sheet of shimmering energy suddenly flared in front of them, blocking the corridor on the far side of the intersection they were trotting across, and Obi-Wan stopped so short that Anakin almost slammed into his back. He reached over and caught Palpatine by the arm. "Careful, sir," he said, low. "Better not touch it till we know what it is."

Obi-Wan unclipped his lightsaber, activated it, and cautiously extended its tip to touch the energy field; an explosive burst of power flared sparks and streaks in all directions, nearly knocking the weapon from his hands. "Ray shield," he said, more to himself than to the others. "We'll have to find a way around—"

But even as he spoke another sheet shimmered into existence across the mouth of the corridor they'd just left, and two more sizzled into place to seal the corridors to either side.

They were boxed in.

Caught.

Obi-Wan stood there for a second or two, blinking, then looked at Anakin and shook his head in disbelief. "I thought we were smarter than this."

"Apparently not. The oldest trap in the book, and we walked right into it." Anakin felt as embarrassed as Obi-Wan looked. "Well, *you* walked right into it. I was just trying to keep up."

"Oh, so now this is *my* fault?"

Anakin gave him a slightly wicked smile. "Hey, you're the Master. I'm just a hero."

"Joke some other time," Obi-Wan muttered. "It's the dark side—the shadow on the Force. Our instincts still can't be trusted. Don't you feel it?"

The dark side was the last thing Anakin wanted to think about right now. "Or, you know, it could be that knock on the head," he offered.

Obi-Wan didn't even smile. "No. All our choices keep going awry. How could they even locate us so precisely? Something is definitely wrong, here. Dooku's death should have lifted the shadow—"

"If you've a taste for mysteries, Master Kenobi," Palpatine interrupted pointedly, "perhaps you could solve the mystery of how we're going to *escape*."

Obi-Wan nodded, scowling darkly at the ray shield box as though seeing it for the first time; after a moment, he took out his lightsaber again, ignited it, and sank its tip into the deck at his feet. The blade burned through the durasteel plate almost without resistance—and then flared and bucked and spat lightning as it hit a shield in place in a gap below the plate, and almost threw Obi-Wan into the annihilating energy of the ray shield behind him.

"No doubt in the ceiling as well." He looked at the others and sighed. "Ideas?"

"Perhaps," Palpatine said thoughtfully, as though the idea had only just occurred to him, "we should simply surrender to General Grievous. With the death of Count Dooku, I'm sure that the two of you can . . ." He cast a significant sidelong glance at Anakin. ". . . *negotiate* our release."

He's persistent, I'll give him that, Anakin thought. He caught himself smiling as he recalled discussing "negotiation" with Padmé, on Naboo before the war; he came back to the present when he realized that undertaking "aggressive negotiations" could prove embarrassing under his current lightsaber-challenged circumstances.

"*I* say . . . ," he put in slowly, "patience."

"Patience?" Obi-Wan lifted an eyebrow. "That's a plan?"

"You know what Master Yoda says: *Patience you must have, until the mud settles and the water becomes clear.* So let's wait."

Obi-Wan looked skeptical. "Wait."

"For the security patrol. A couple of droids will be along in a moment or two; they'll have to drop the ray shield to take us into custody."

"And then?"

Anakin shrugged cheerfully. "And then we'll wipe them out."

"Brilliant as usual," Obi-Wan said dryly. "What if they turn out to be destroyer droids? Or something worse?"

"Oh, come on, Master. Worse than destroyers? Besides, security patrols are always those skinny useless little battle droids."

At that moment, four of those skinny useless battle droids came marching toward them, one along each corridor, clanking along with blaster rifles leveled. One of them triggered one of its preprogrammed security commands: *"Hand over your weapons!"* The other three chimed in with enthusiastic barks of *"Roger, roger!"* and a round of spastic head-bobbing.

"See?" Anakin said. "No problem."

Before Obi-Wan could reply, concealed doors in the corridor walls zipped suddenly aside. Through them rolled the massive bronzium wheels of destroyer droids, two into each corridor. The eight destroyers unrolled themselves behind the battle droids, haloed by sparkling energy shields, twin blaster cannons targeting the two Jedi's chests.

Obi-Wan sighed. "You were saying?"

"Okay, fine. It's the dark side. Or something." Anakin rolled his eyes. "I guess you're off the hook for the ray shield trap."

Through those same doorways marched sixteen super battle

droids to back up the destroyers, their arm cannons raised to fire over the destroyers' shields.

Behind the super battle droids came two droids of a type Anakin had never seen. He had an idea what they were, though.

And he was not happy about it.

Obi-Wan scowled at them as they approached. "You're the expert, Anakin. What are those things?"

"Remember what you were saying about *worse than destroyers?*" Anakin said grimly. "I think we're looking at them."

They walked side by side, their gait easy and straightforward, almost as smooth as a human's. In fact, they could have *been* human—humans who were two meters tall and made out of metal. They wore long swirling cloaks that had once been white, but now were stained with smoke and what Anakin strongly suspected was blood. They walked with the cloaks thrown back over one shoulder, to clear their left arms, where they held some unfamiliar staff-like weapon about two meters long—something like the force-pike of a Senate Guard, but shorter, and with an odd-looking discharge blade at each end.

They walked like they were made to fight, and they had clearly seen some battle. The chest plate of one bore a round shallow crater surrounded by a corona of scorch, a direct blaster hit that hadn't come close to penetrating; the other bore a scar from its cranial dome down through one dead photoreceptor—a scar that looked like it might have come from a lightsaber.

This droid looked like it had fought a Jedi, and survived.

The Jedi, he guessed, hadn't.

These two droids threaded between the super battle droids and destroyers and casually shoved aside one battle droid hard enough that it slammed into the wall and collapsed into a sparking heap of metal.

The one with the damaged photoreceptor pointed its staff at them, and the ray shields around them dropped. "He *said,* hand over your *weapons,* Jedi!"

This definitely wasn't a preprogrammed security command.

Anakin said softly, "I saw an Intel report on this; I think those are Grievous's personal bodyguard droids. Prototypes built to his specifications." He looked from Obi-Wan to Palpatine and back again. "To fight Jedi."

"Ah," Obi-Wan said. "Then under the circumstances, I suppose we need a Plan B."

Anakin nodded at Palpatine. "The Chancellor's idea is sounding pretty good right now."

Obi-Wan nodded thoughtfully.

When the Jedi Master turned away to offer his lightsaber to the bodyguard droid, Anakin leaned close to the Supreme Chancellor and murmured, "So you get your way, after all."

Palpatine answered with a slight, unreadable smile. "I frequently do."

As super battle droids came forward with electrobinders for their wrists and a restraining bolt for R2-D2, Obi-Wan cast one frowning look back over his shoulder.

"Oh, Anakin," he said, with the sort of quiet, pained resignation that would be recognized instantly by any parent exhausted by a trouble-prone child. *"Where* is your *lightsaber?"*

Anakin couldn't look at him. "It's not lost, if that's what you're thinking." This was the truth: Anakin could feel it in the Force, and he knew exactly where it was.

"No?"

"No."

"Where is it, then?"

"Can we talk about this later?"

"Without your lightsaber, you may not *have* a 'later.' "

"I don't need a lecture, okay? How many times have we had this talk?"

"Apparently, one time less than we needed to."

Anakin sighed. Obi-Wan could still make him feel about nine

years old. He gave a sullen nod toward one of the droid bodyguards. "He's got it."

"He does? And how did this happen?"

"I don't want to talk about it."

"Anakin—"

"Hey, he's got yours, too!"

"That's different—"

"This weapon is your *life,* Obi-Wan!" He did a credible-
enough Kenobi impression that Palpatine had to smother a
snort. "You must take *care* of it!"

"Perhaps," Obi-Wan said, as the droids clicked the binders
onto their wrists and led them all away, "we should talk about
this later."

Anakin intoned severely, "Without your *lightsaber,* you may
not *have* a—"

"All right, all right." The Jedi Master surrendered with a rueful smile. "You win."

Anakin grinned at him. "I'm sorry? What was that?" He
couldn't remember the last time he'd won an argument with
Obi-Wan. "Could you speak up a little?"

"It's not very Jedi to gloat, Anakin."

"I'm not gloating, Master," he said with a sidelong glance at
Palpatine. "I'm just . . . savoring the moment."

This is how it feels to be Anakin Skywalker, for now:

The Supreme Chancellor returns your look with a hint of
smile and a sliver of an approving nod, and for you, this tiny, trivial, comradely victory sparks a warmth and ease that relaxes the
dragon-grip of dread on your heart.

Forget that you are captured; you and Obi-Wan have been
captured before. Forget the deteriorating ship, forget the Jedi-

killing droids; you've faced worse. Forget General Grievous. What is he compared with Dooku? He can't even use the Force.

So now, here, for you, the situation comes down to this: you are walking between the two best friends you have ever had, with your precious droid friend faithfully whirring after your heels—

On your way to win the Clone Wars.

What you have done—what happened in the General's Quarters and, more important, *why* it happened—is all burning away in Coruscant's atmosphere along with Dooku's decapitated corpse. Already it seems as if it happened to somebody else, as if *you* were somebody else when you did it, and it seems as if that man—the dragon-haunted man with a furnace for a heart and a mind as cold as the surface of that dead star—had really only been an image reflected in Dooku's open staring eyes.

And by the time what's left of the conning spire crashes into the kilometers-thick crust of city that is the surface of Coruscant, those dead eyes will have burned away, and the dragon will burn with them.

And you, for the first time in your life, will truly be free.

This is how it feels to be Anakin Skywalker.

For now.

OBI-WAN AND ANAKIN 2

This is Obi-Wan Kenobi in the light:

As he is prodded onto the bridge along with Anakin and Chancellor Palpatine, he has no need to look around to see the banks of control consoles tended by terrified Neimoidians. He doesn't have to turn his head to count the droidekas and super battle droids, or to gauge the positions of the brutal droid body-guards. He doesn't bother to raise his eyes to meet the cold yellow stare fixed on him through a skull-mask of armorplast.

He doesn't even need to reach into the Force.

He has already let the Force reach into him.

The Force flows over him and around him as though he has stepped into a crystal-pure waterfall lost in the green coils of a forgotten rain forest; when he opens himself to that sparkling stream it flows into him and through him and out again without the slightest interference from his conscious will. The part of him that calls itself Obi-Wan Kenobi is no more than a ripple, an eddy in the pool into which he endlessly pours.

There are other parts of him here, as well; there is nothing here that is *not* a part of him, from the scuff mark on R2-D2's dome to the tattered hem of Palpatine's robe, from the spidering crack in one transparisteel panel of the curving view wall above to the great starships that still battle beyond it.

Because this is all part of the Force.

Somehow, mysteriously, the cloud that has darkened the Force for near to a decade and a half has lightened around him now, and he finds within himself the limpid clarity he recalls from his schooldays at the Jedi Temple, when the Force was pure, and clean, and perfect. It is as though the darkness has withdrawn, has coiled back upon itself, to allow him this moment of clarity, to return to him the full power of the light, if only for the moment; he does not know why, but he is incapable of even wondering. In the Force, he is beyond questions.

Why is meaningless; it is an echo of the past, or a whisper from the future. All that matters, for this infinite now, is *what,* and *where,* and *who.*

He is all sixteen of the super battle droids, gleaming in laser-reflective chrome, arms loaded with heavy blasters. He is those blasters and he is their targets. He is all eight destroyer droids waiting with electronic patience within their energy shields, and both bodyguards, and every single one of the shivering Neimoidians. He is their clothes, their boots, even each drop of reptile-scented moisture that rolls off them from the misting sprays they use to keep their internal temperatures down. He is the binders that cuff his hands, and he is the electrostaff in the hands of the bodyguard at his back.

He is both of the lightsabers that the other droid bodyguard marches forward to offer to General Grievous.

And he is the general himself.

He is the general's duranium ribs. He is the beating of Grievous's alien heart, and is the silent pulse of oxygen pumped through his alien veins. He is the weight of four lightsabers at the general's belt, and is the greedy anticipation the captured weapons sparked behind the general's eyes. He is even the plan for his own execution simmering within the general's brain.

He is all these things, but most importantly, he is still Obi-Wan Kenobi.

This is why he can simply stand. Why he can simply wait. He has no need to attack, or to defend. There will be battle here, but he is perfectly at ease, perfectly content to let the battle start when it will start, and let it end when it will end.

Just as he will let himself live, or let himself die.

This is how a great Jedi makes war.

General Grievous lifted the two lightsabers, one in each duranium hand, to admire them by the light of turbolaser blasts outside, and said, "Rare trophies, these: the weapon of Anakin Skywalker, and the weapon of General Kenobi. I look forward to adding them to my collection."

"That will not happen. I am in control here."

The reply came through Obi-Wan's lips, but it was not truly Obi-Wan who spoke. Obi-Wan was not in control; he had no need for control. He had the Force.

It was the Force that spoke through him.

Grievous stalked forward. Obi-Wan saw death in the cold yellow stare through the skull-mask's eyeholes, and it meant nothing to him at all.

There was no death. There was only the Force.

He didn't have to tell Anakin to subtly nudge Chancellor Palpatine out of the line of fire; part of him *was* Anakin, and was doing this already. He didn't have to tell R2-D2 to access its combat subprograms and divert power to its booster rockets, claw-arm, and cable-gun; the part of him that was the little astromech had seen to all these things before they had even entered the bridge.

Grievous towered over him. "So confident you are, Kenobi."

"Not confident, merely calm." From so close, Obi-Wan

could see the hairline cracks and pitting in the bone-pale mask, and could feel the resonance of the general's electrosonic voice humming in his chest. He remembered the Question of Master Jrul: *What is the good, if not the teacher of the bad? What is the bad, if not the task of the good?*

He said, "We can resolve this situation without further violence. I am willing to accept your surrender."

"I'm sure you are." The skull-mask tilted inquisitively. "Does this preposterous *I-will-accept-your-surrender* line of yours ever actually *work?*"

"Sometimes. When it doesn't, people get hurt. Sometimes they die." Obi-Wan's blue-gray eyes met squarely those of yellow behind the mask. "By *people,* in this case, you should understand that I mean *you.*"

"I understand enough. I understand that I will kill you." Grievous threw back his cloak and ignited both lightsabers. "Here. Now. With your own blade."

The Force replied through Obi-Wan's lips, "I don't think so."

The electrodrivers that powered Grievous's limbs could move them faster than the human eye can see; when he swung his arm, it and his fist and the lightsaber within it would literally vanish: wiped from existence by sheer mind-numbing speed, an imitation quantum event. No human being could move remotely as fast as Grievous, not even Obi-Wan—but he didn't have to.

In the Force, part of him was Grievous's intent to slaughter, and the surge from intent to action translated to Obi-Wan's response without thought. He had no need for a plan, no use for tactics.

He had the Force.

That sparkling waterfall coursed through him, washing away any thought of danger, or safety, of winning or losing. The Force, like water, takes on the shape of its container without effort, without thought. The water that was Obi-Wan poured itself into the container that was Grievous's attack, and while some materials might be water-tight, Obi-Wan had yet to encounter any that were entirely, as it were, *Force*-tight . . .

While the intent to swing was still forming in Grievous's mind, the part of the Force that was Obi-Wan was also the part of the Force that was R2-D2, as well as an internal fusion-welder Anakin had retrofitted into R2-D2's primary grappling arm, and so there was no need for actual communication between them; it was only Obi-Wan's personal sense of style that brought his customary gentle smile to his face and his customary gentle murmur to his lips.

"Artoo?"

Even as he opened his mouth, a panel was sliding aside in the little droid's fuselage; by the time the droid's nickname had left his lips, the fusion-welder had deployed and fired a blinding spray of sparks hot enough to melt duranium, and in the quarter of a second while even Grievous's electronically enhanced reflexes had him startled and distracted, the part of the Force that was Obi-Wan tried a little trick, a secret one that it had been saving up for just such an occasion as this.

Because all there on the bridge was one in the Force, from the gross structure of the ship itself to the quantum dance of the electron shells of individual atoms—and because, after all, the nerves and muscles of the bio-droid general were creations of electronics and duranium, not living tissue with will of its own— it was just barely possible that with exactly the right twist of his mind, in that one vulnerable quarter of a second while Grievous was distracted, flinching backward from a spray of flame hot enough to burn even his armored body, Obi-Wan might be able to temporarily reverse the polarity of the electrodrivers in the general's mechanical hands.

Which is exactly what he did.

Durasteel fingers sprang open, and two lightsabers fell free.

He reached through the Force and the Force reached through him; his blade flared to life while still in the air; it flipped toward him, and as he lifted his hands to meet it, its blue flame flashed between his wrists and severed the binders before the handgrip smacked solidly into his palm.

Obi-Wan was so deep in the Force that he wasn't even suprised it had worked.

He made a quarter turn to face Anakin, who was already in the air, having leapt simultaneously with Obi-Wan's gentle murmur because Obi-Wan and Anakin were, after all, two parts of the same thing; Anakin's flip carried him over Obi-Wan's head at the perfect range for Obi-Wan's blade to flick out and burn through his partner's binders, and while Grievous was still flinching away from the fountain of fusion fire, Anakin landed with his own hand extended; Obi-Wan felt a liquid surge in the waterfall that he was, and Anakin's lightsaber sang through the air and Anakin caught it, and so, one single second after Grievous had begun to summon the intent to swing, Obi-Wan Kenobi and Anakin Skywalker stood back-to-back in the center of the bridge, expressionlessly staring past the snarling blue energy of their lightsabers.

Obi-Wan regarded the general without emotion. "Perhaps you should reconsider my offer."

Grievous braced himself against a control console, its durasteel housing buckling under his grip. "This is my answer!"

He ripped the console wholly into the air, right out from under the hands of the astonished Neimoidian operator, raised it over his head, and hurled it at the Jedi. They split, rolling out of the console's way as it crashed to the deck, spitting smoke and sparks.

"Open *fire!*" Grievous shook his fists as though each held a Jedi's neck. "Kill them! *Kill them all!*"

For one more second there was only the scuttle of priming levers on dozens of blasters.

One second after that, the bridge exploded into a firestorm.

Grievous hung back, crouching, watching for a moment as his two MagnaGuards waded into the Jedi, electrostaffs whirling through the blinding hail of blasterfire that ricocheted around the bridge. Grievous had fought Jedi before, sometimes even in open battle, and he had found that fighting any one Jedi was much like fighting any other.

Kenobi, though—

The ease with which Kenobi had taken command of the situation was frightening. More frightening was the fact that of the two, Skywalker was reportedly the greater warrior. And even their *R2* unit could fight: the little astromech had some kind of aftermarket cable-gun it had used to entangle the legs of a super droid and yank it off its feet, and now was jerking the droid this way and that so that its arm cannons were blasting chunks off its squadmates instead of the Jedi.

Grievous was starting to think less about winning this particular encounter than about surviving it.

Let his MagnaGuards fight the Jedi; that's what they were designed for—and they were doing their jobs well. IG-101 had pressed Kenobi back against a console, lightning blazing from his electrostaff's energy shield where it pushed on Kenobi's blade; the Jedi general might have died then and there, except that one of the simple-minded super battle droids turned both arm cannons on his back, giving Kenobi the chance to duck and allow the hammering blaster bolts to slam 101 stumbling backward. Skywalker had stashed the Chancellor somewhere—that sniveling coward Palpatine was probably trembling under one of the control consoles—and had managed to sever both of 102's legs below the knee, which for some reason he apparently expected to end the fight; he seemed completely astonished when 102 whirled nimbly on one end of his electrostaff and used the stumps of his legs to thump Skywalker so soundly the Jedi went down skidding.

On the other hand, Grievous thought, *this might be salvageable after all.*

He tapped his internal comlink's jaw sensor to the general droid command frequency. "The Chancellor is hiding under one of the consoles. Squad Sixteen, find him, and deliver him to my escape pod immediately. Squad Eight, stay on mission. Kill the Jedi."

Then the ship bucked, sharper than it ever had, and the view wall panels whited out as radiation-scatter sleeted through the bridge. Alarm klaxons blared. The nav console flared sparks into the face of a Neimoidian pilot, setting his uniform on fire and adding his screams to the din, and another console exploded, ripping the newly promoted senior gunnery officer into a pile of shredded meat.

Ah, Grievous thought. In all the excitement, he had entirely forgotten about Lieutenant Commander Needa and *Integrity.*

The other pilot—the one who wasn't shrieking and slapping at the flames on his uniform until his own hands caught fire— leaned as far away from his screaming partner as his crash webbing would allow and shouted, "General, that shot destroyed the last of the aft control cells! The ship is *deorbiting!* We're going to burn!"

"Very well," Grievous said calmly. "Stay on course." Now it no longer mattered whether his bodyguards could overpower the Jedi or not: they would all burn together.

He tapped his jaw sensor to the control frequency for the escape pods; one coded order ensured that his personal pod would be waiting for him with engines hot and systems checks complete.

When he looked back to the fight, all he could see of IG-102 was one arm, the saber-cut joint still white hot. Skywalker was pursuing two super battle droids that had Palpatine by the arms. While Skywalker dismantled the droids with swift cuts, Kenobi was in the process of doing the same to IG-101—the MagnaGuard was hopping on its one remaining leg, whirling its electrostaff with its one remaining arm, and screeching some improbable threat regarding its staff and Kenobi's body cavities—and after Kenobi cut off the arm, 101 went hopping after him, still screeching. The droid actually managed to land one glancing kick before the Jedi casually severed its other leg, after which 101's limbless torso continued to writhe on the deck, howling.

With both MagnaGuards down, all eight destroyers opened up, dual cannons erupting gouts of galvened particle beams. The two Jedi leapt together to screen the Chancellor, and before Grievous could command the destroyers to cease fire, the Jedi had deflected enough of the bolts to blow apart three-quarters of the remaining super battle droids and send the survivors scurrying for cover beside what was left of the cringing Neimoidians.

The destroyers began to close in, hosing down the Jedi with heavy fire, advancing step by step, cannons against lightsabers; the Jedi caught every blast and sent them back against the destroyers' shields that flared in spherical haloes as they absorbed the reflected bolts. The destroyers might very well have prevailed over the Jedi, except for one unexpected difficulty—

Gravity shear.

All eight of them suddenly seemed, inexplicably, to leap into the air, followed by Skywalker, and Palpatine, and chairs and pieces of MagnaGuards and everything else on the bridge that was not bolted to the deck, except for Kenobi, who managed to grab a control console and now was hanging by one hand, upside down, still effortlessly deflecting blaster bolts.

The surviving Neimoidian pilot was screaming orders for the droids to magnetize, then started howling that the ship was breaking up, and managed to make so much annoying noise that

Grievous smashed his skull out of simple irritation. Then he looked around and realized he'd just killed the last of his crew: all the bridge crew he hadn't slain personally had sucked up the bulk of the random blaster ricochets.

Grievous shook the pilot's brains off his fist. Disgusting creatures, Neimoidians.

The invisible plane of altered gravity passed over the bio-droid general without effect—his talons of magnetized duranium kept him right where he was—and as one of the MagnaGuards' electrostaffs fell past him, his invisibly fast hand snatched it from the air. When another plane of gravity shear swept through the bridge, droids, Chancellor, and Jedi all fell back to the floor.

Though the droideka, also known as the destroyer droid, was the most powerful infantry combat droid in general production, it had one major design flaw. The energy shield that was so effective in stopping blasters, slugs, shrapnel, and even lightsabers was precisely tuned to englobe the droid in a standing position; if the droid was no longer standing—say, if it was knocked down, or thrown into a wall—the shield generator could not distinguish a floor or a wall from a weapon, and would keep ramping up power to disintegrate this perceived threat until the generator shorted itself out.

Between falling to the ceiling, bouncing off it, and falling back to the floor, the sum total output of all the shield generators of Squad Eight was, currently, one large cloud of black smoke.

It was impossible to say which one of them opened fire on the Jedi, and it didn't matter; inside of two seconds, eight droidekas had become eight piles of smoking scrap, and two Jedi, entirely unscathed, walked out of the smoke side by side.

Without a word, they parted to bracket the general.

Grievous clicked the electrostaff's power setting to overload; it spat lightning around him as he lifted it to combat ready. "I am sorry I don't have time to fight you—it would have been an interesting match—but I have an appointment with an escape pod. And you . . ."

He pointed at the transparisteel view wall and triggered his own concealed cable-gun, not unlike the one that fancy astromech of theirs had; the cable shot out and its grappling claw buried itself in one of the panel supports.

"You," he said, "have appointments with death."

The Jedi leapt, and Grievous hurled the overloading electrostaff—but not at the Jedi.

He threw it at a window.

One of the transparisteel panels of the view wall had cracked under a glancing hit from a starfighter's cannon; when the sparking electrostaff hit it squarely and exploded like a proton grenade, the whole panel blew out into space.

A hurricane roared to life, raging through the bridge, seizing Neimoidian corpses and pieces of droids and wreckage and hurling them out through the gap along with a white fountain of flash-frozen air. Grievous sprang straight up into the instant hurricane, narrowly avoiding the two Jedi, whose leaps had become frantic tumbles as they tried to avoid being sucked through along with him. Grievous, though, had no need to breathe, nor had he any fear of his body fluids boiling in the vacuum—the pressurized synthflesh that enclosed the living parts within his droid exoskeleton saw to that—so he simply rode the storm right out into space until he reached the end of the cable and it snapped tight and swung him whipping back toward *Invisible Hand*'s hull.

He cast off the cable. His hands and feet of magnetized duranium let him scramble along the hull without difficulty, the light-spidered curve of Coruscant's nightside whirling around him. He clambered over to the external locks of the bridge escape pods and punched in a command code. Looking back over his shoulder, he experienced a certain chilly satisfaction as he watched empty escape pods blast free of the *Hand*'s bridge and streak away.

All of them.

Well: all but one.

No trick of the Force would spring Kenobi and Skywalker out of this one. It was a shame he didn't have a spy probe handy to leave on the bridge; he would have enjoyed watching the Republic's greatest heroes burn.

The ion streaks of the escape pods spiraled through the battle that still flashed and flared silently in the void, pursued by starfighters and armed retrieval ships. Grievous nodded to himself; that should occupy them long enough for his command pod to make the run to his escape ship.

As he entered his customized pod, he reflected that he was, for the first time in his career, violating orders: though he was under strict orders to leave the Chancellor unharmed, Palpatine was about to die alongside his precious Jedi.

Then Grievous shrugged, and sighed. What more could he have done? There was a war on, after all.

He was sure Lord Sidious would forgive him.

On the bridge, a blast shield had closed over the destroyed transparisteel window, and every last surviving combat-model droid had been cut to pieces even before the atmosphere had had a chance to stabilize.

But there was a more serious problem.

The bucking of the ship had become continuous. White-hot sparks outside streamed backward past the view wall windows. Those sparks, according to the three different kinds of alarms that were all screaming through the bridge at once, were what was left of the ablative shielding on the nose of the disabled cruiser.

Anakin stared grimly down at a console readout. "All the escape pods are gone. Not one left on the whole ship." He looked up at Obi-Wan. "We're trapped."

Obi-Wan appeared more interested than actually concerned. "Well. Here's a chance to display your legendary piloting skills, my young friend. You can fly this cruiser, can't you?"

"Flying's no problem. The trick is *landing,* which, ah . . ." Anakin gave a slightly shaky laugh. "Which, you know, this cruiser is not exactly designed to do. Even when it's in *one* piece."

Obi-Wan looked unimpressed. "And so?"

Anakin unsnapped the crash webbing that held the pilot's corpse and pulled the body from its chair. "And so you'd better strap in," he said, settling into the chair, his fingers sliding over the unfamiliar controls.

The cruiser bounced even harder, and its attitude began to skew as a new klaxon joined the blare of the other alarms. "That wasn't me!" Anakin jerked his hands away from the board. "I haven't even *done* anything yet!"

"It certainly wasn't." Palpatine's voice was unnaturally calm. "It seems someone is shooting at us."

"Wonderful," Anakin muttered. "Could this day get any better?"

"Perhaps we can talk with them." Obi-Wan moved over to the comm station and began working the screen. "Let them know we've captured the ship."

"All right, take the comm," Anakin said. He pointed at the copilot's station. "Artoo: second chair. Chancellor?"

"Yes?"

"Strap in. Now. We're going in hot." Anakin grimaced at the scraps of burning hull flashing past the view wall. "In more ways than one."

The vast space battle that had ripped and battered Coruscant space all this long, long day, finally began to flicker out.

The shimmering canopy of ion trails and turbolaser bursts was fading into streaks of ships achieving jump as the Separatist strike force fled in full retreat. The light of Coruscant's distant star splintered through iridescent clouds of gas crystals that were the remains of starfighters, and of pilots. Damaged cruisers limped toward spaceyards, passing shattered hulks that hung dead in the infinite day that is interplanetary space. Prize crews took command of surrendered ships, imprisoning the living among their crews and affixing restraining bolts to the droids.

The dayside surface of the capital planet was shrouded in smoke from a million fires touched off by meteorite impacts of ship fragments; far too many had fallen to be tracked and destroyed by the planet's surface-defense umbrella. The nightside's sheet of artificial lights faded behind the red-white glow from craters of burning steel; each impact left a caldera of unimaginable death. In the skies of Coruscant now, the important vessels were no longer warships, but were instead the fire-suppression and rescue craft that crisscrossed the planet.

Now one last fragmentary ship screamed into the atmosphere, coming in too fast, too steep, pieces breaking off to spread apart and stream their own contrails of superheated vapor; banks of turbolasers on the surface-defense towers isolated their signature, and starfighters whipped onto interception courses to thin out whatever fragments the SD towers might miss, and far above, beyond the atmosphere, on the bridge of RSS *Integrity*, Lieutenant Commander Lorth Needa spoke urgently to a knee-high blue ghost scanned into existence by the phased-array lasers in a holocomm: an alien in Jedi robes, with bulging eyes set in a wrinkled face and long, pointed, oddly flexible ears.

"You have to stand down the surface-defense system, sir! It's General Kenobi!" Needa insisted. "His code verifies, Skywalker is with him—and *they have Chancellor Palpatine!*"

"Heard and understood this is," the Jedi responded calmly. *"Tell me what they require."*

Needa glanced down at the boil of hull plating that was burning off the falling cruiser, and even as he looked, the ship broke in half at the hangar deck; the rear half tumbled, exploding in sections, but whoever was flying the front half must have been one of the greatest pilots Needa had ever even *heard* of: the front half wobbled and slewed but somehow righted itself using nothing but a bank of thrusters and its atmospheric drag fins.

"First, a flight of fireships," Needa said, more calmly now. "If they don't get the burnoff under control, there won't be enough hull left to make the surface. And a hardened docking platform, the strongest available; they won't be able to set it down. This won't be a landing, it will be a controlled crash. Repeat: a controlled crash."

"Heard and understood this is," the hologrammic Jedi repeated. *"Crossload their transponder signature."* When this was done, the Jedi nodded grave approval. *"Thank you, Lieutenant Commander. Valiant service for the Republic you have done today—and the gratitude of the Jedi Order you have earned. Yoda out."*

On the bridge of *Integrity,* Lorth Needa now could only stand, and watch, hands clasped behind his back. Military discipline kept him expressionless, but pale bands began at his knuckles and spread whiteness nearly to his wrists.

Every bone in his body ached with helplessness.

Because he knew: that fragment of a ship was a death trap. No one could land such a hulk, not even Skywalker. Each second that passed before its final breakup and burn was a miracle in itself, a testament to the gifts of a pilot who was justly legendary—but when each second is a miracle, how many of them can be strung together in a row?

Lorth Needa was not religious, nor was he a philosopher or

metaphysician; he knew of the Force only by reputation, but nonetheless now he found himself asking the Force, in his heart, that when the fiery end came for the men in that scrap of a ship, it might as least come quickly.

His eyes stung. The irony of it burned the back of his throat. The Home Fleet had fought brilliantly, and the Jedi had done their superhuman part; against all odds, the Republic had won the day.

Yet this battle had been fought to save Supreme Chancellor Palpatine.

They had won the battle, but now, as Needa stood watching helplessly, he couldn't help feeling that they were about to lose the war.

This is Anakin Skywalker's masterpiece:

Many people say he is the best star pilot in the galaxy, but that's merely talk, born of the constant HoloNet references to his unmatched string of kills in starfighter combat. Blowing up vulture droids and tri-fighters is simply a matter of superior reflexes and trust in the Force; he has spent so many hours in the cockpit that he wears a Jedi starfighter like clothes. It's his own body, with thrusters for legs and cannons for fists.

What he is doing right now transcends mere flying the way Jedi combat transcends a schoolyard scuffle.

He sits in a blood-spattered, blaster-chopped chair behind a console he's never seen before, a console with controls designed for alien fingers. The ship he's in is not only bucking like a maddened dewback through brutal coils of clear-air turbulence, it's on fire and breaking up like a comet ripping apart as it crashes into a gas giant. He has only seconds to learn how to maneuver an alien craft that not only has no aft control cells, but has no *aft* at all.

This is, put simply, impossible. It can't be done.

He's going to do it anyway.

Because he is Anakin Skywalker, and he doesn't believe in *impossible*.

He extends his hands and for one long, long moment he merely strokes controls, feeling their shape under his fingers, listening to the shivers his soft touch brings to each remaining control surface of the disintegrating ship, allowing their resonances to join inside his head until they resolve into harmony like a Ferroan joy-harp virtuoso checking the tuning of his instrument.

And at the same time, he draws power from the Force. He gathers perception, and luck, and sucks into himself the instinctive, preconscious *what-will-happen-in-the-next-ten-seconds* intuition that has always been the core of his talent.

And then he begins.

On the downbeat, atmospheric drag fins deploy; as he tweaks their angles and cycles them in and out to slow the ship's descent without burning them off altogether, their contrabass roar takes on a punctuated rhythm like a heart that skips an occasional beat. The forward attitude thrusters, damaged in the ship-to-ship battle, now fire in random directions, but he can feel where they're taking him and he strokes them in sequence, making their song the theme of his impromptu concerto.

And the true inspiration, the sparkling grace note of genius that brings his masterpiece to life, is the soprano counterpoint: a syncopated sequence of exterior hatches in the outer hull sliding open and closed and open again, subtly altering the aerodynamics of the ship to give it just exactly the amount of sideslip or lift or yaw to bring the huge half cruiser into the approach cone of a pinpoint target an eighth of the planet away.

It is the Force that makes this possible, and more than the Force. Anakin has no interest in serene acceptance of what the Force will bring. Not here. Not now. Not with the lives of Palpatine and Obi-Wan at stake. It's just the opposite: he seizes upon the Force with a stark refusal to fail.

He *will* land this ship.

He *will* save his friends.

Between his will and the will of the Force, there is no contest.

PART TWO

SEDUCTION

The dark is generous, and it is patient.

It is the dark that seeds cruelty into justice, that drips contempt into compassion, that poisons love with grains of doubt.

The dark can be patient, because the slightest drop of rain will cause those seeds to sprout.

The rain will come, and the seeds will sprout, for the dark is the soil in which they grow, and it is the clouds above them, and it waits behind the star that gives them light.

The dark's patience is infinite.

Eventually, even stars burn out.

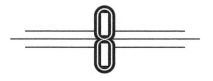

FAULT LINES

Mace Windu hung on to the corrugated hatch grip beside the gunship's open troop bay with one hand, squinting into the wind that whipped his overcloak behind him. His other hand shaded his eyes against the glare from one of the orbital mirrors that concentrated the capital planet's daylight. The mirror was slowly turning aside now, allowing a band of twilight to approach the gunship's destination.

That destination, a kilometer-thick landing platform in the planet's vast industrial zone, was marked with a steeply slanting tower of smoke and vapor that stretched from the planet's surface to the uppermost reaches of the atmosphere, a tower that only now was beginning to spread and coil from its tiny source point to a horizon-spanning smear across the stratospheric winds.

The gunship roared over the bottomless canyons of durasteel and permacrete that formed the landscape of Coruscant, arrowing straight for the industrial zone without regard for the rigid traffic laws that governed flight on the galactic planet; until martial law was officially lifted by the Senate, the darkening skies would be traveled only by Republic military craft, Jedi transports, and emergency vehicles.

The gunship qualified as all three.

Mace could see the ship now—what was left of it—resting on the scorched platform far ahead: a piece of a ship, a fragment, less than a third of what once had been the Trade Federation flagship, still burning despite the gouts of fire-suppression foam raining down on it from five different ships and the emergency-support clone troops who surrounded it on the platform.

Mace shook his head. Skywalker again. The chosen one.

Who else could have brought in this hulk? Who else could have even come close?

The gunship swung into a hot landing, repulsors howling; Mace hopped out before it could settle, and gave the pilot an open-palm gesture to signal him to wait. The pilot, faceless within his helmet, responded with a closed fist.

Though, of course, the pilot wasn't faceless at all. Under his armored helmet, that clone pilot had a face that Mace Windu remembered all too well.

That face would always remind him that he had once held Dooku within his grasp, and had let him slip away.

Across the platform, an escape pod hatch cycled open. Emergency crews scrambled with an escape slide, and a moment later the Supreme Chancellor, Obi-Wan Kenobi, and Anakin Skywalker were all on the deck beside the burning ship, closely followed by a somewhat battered R2 unit that lifted itself down on customized maneuvering rockets.

Mace strode swiftly out to meet them.

Palpatine's robes were scorched and tattered at the hem, and he seemed weak; he leaned a bit on Skywalker's shoulder as they moved away from the ship. On Skywalker's other side, Master Kenobi seemed a touch the worse for wear himself: caked with dust and leaking a trickle of blood from a scalp wound.

Skywalker, by contrast, looked every bit the HoloNet hero he was supposed to be. He seemed to tower over his companions, as though he had somehow gotten even taller in the months since Mace had seen him last. His hair was tousled, his color was high, and his walk still had the grounded grace of a natural fighter, but there was something new in his physicality: in the way he moved his head, perhaps, or the way the weight of Palpatine's arm on his shoulder seemed somehow to belong there . . . or something less definable. Some new ease, new confidence. An aura of inner power.

Presence.

Skywalker was not the same young man the Council had sent off to the Outer Rim five standard months ago.

"Chancellor," Mace said as he met them. "Are you well? Do you need medical attention?" He gestured over his shoulder at the waiting gunship. "I have a fully equipped field surgery—"

"No, no, no need," Palpatine said, rather faintly. "Thank you, Master Windu, but I am well. Quite well, thanks to these two."

Mace nodded. "Master Kenobi? Anakin?"

"Never better," Skywalker replied, looking as if he meant it, and Kenobi only shrugged, with a slight wince as he touched his scalp wound.

"Only a bump on the head. That field surgery must be needed elsewhere."

"It is." Mace looked grim. "We don't have even a preliminary estimate of civilian casualties."

He waved off the gunship, and it roared away toward the countless fires that painted red the approach of night.

"A shuttle is on its way. Chancellor, we'll have you on the Senate floor within the hour. The HoloNet has already been notified that you will want to make a statement."

"I will. I will, indeed." Palpatine touched Mace on the arm.

"You have always been of great value to me, Master Windu. Thank you."

"The Jedi are honored to serve the Senate, sir." There might have been the slightest emphasis on the word *Senate*. Mace remained expressionless as he subtly moved his arm away from the Chancellor's hand. He looked at Obi-Wan. "Is there anything else to report, Master Kenobi? What of General Grievous?"

"Count Dooku was there," Skywalker interjected. He had a look on his face that Mace couldn't decipher, proud yet wary— even unhappy. "He's dead now."

"Dead?" He looked from Anakin to Obi-Wan and back again. "Is this true? You killed Count *Dooku*?"

"My young friend is too modest; *he* killed Count Dooku." Smiling, Kenobi touched the lump on his head. "I was . . . taking a nap."

"But . . ." Mace blinked. Dooku was to the Separatists what Palpatine was to the Republic: the center of gravity binding together a spiral galaxy of special interests. With Dooku gone, the Confederacy of Independent Systems would no longer really be a confederacy at all. They'd fly to pieces within weeks.

Within *days*.

Mace said again, "But . . ."

And, in the end, he couldn't think of a *but*.

This was all so astonishing that he very nearly—almost, but not quite—cracked a smile.

"That is," he said, "the best news I've heard since . . ." He shook his head. "Since I can't remember. Anakin—how did you *do* it?"

Inexplicably, young Skywalker looked distinctly uncomfortable; that newly confident presence of his collapsed as suddenly as an overloaded deflector, and instead of meeting Mace's eyes, his gaze flicked to Palpatine. Somehow Mace didn't think this was modesty. He looked to the Chancellor as well, his elation sinking, becoming puzzlement tinged with suspicion.

"It was . . . entirely extraordinary," Palpatine said blandly, oblivious to Mace's narrowing stare. "I know next to nothing of swordplay, of course; to my amateur's eye, it seemed that Count Dooku may have been . . . a trace overconfident. Especially after having disposed of Master Kenobi so neatly."

Obi-Wan flushed, just a bit—and Anakin flushed considerably more deeply.

"Perhaps young Anakin was simply more . . . highly *motivated*," Palpatine said, turning a fond smile upon him. "After all, Dooku was fighting only to slay an enemy; Anakin was fighting to save—if I may presume the honor—a friend."

Mace's scowl darkened. Fine words. Perhaps even true words, but he still didn't like them.

No one on the Jedi Council had ever been comfortable with Skywalker's close relationship with the Chancellor—they'd had more than one conversation about it with Obi-Wan while Skywalker had still been his Padawan—and Mace was less than happy to hear Palpatine speaking for a young Jedi who seemed unprepared to speak for himself. He said, "I'm sure the Council will be very interested in your full report, Anakin," with just enough emphasis on *full* to get his point across.

Skywalker swallowed, and then, just as suddenly as it had collapsed, that aura of calm, centered confidence rebuilt itself around him. "Yes. Yes of course, Master Windu."

"And we must report that Grievous escaped," Obi-Wan said. "He is as cowardly as ever."

Mace accepted this news with a nod. "But he is only a military commander. Without Dooku to hold the coalition together, these so-called independent systems will splinter, and they know it." He looked straight into the Supreme Chancellor's eyes. "This is our best chance to sue for peace. We can end this war right now."

And while Palpatine answered, Mace Windu reached into the Force.

To Mace's Force perception, the world crystallized around them, becoming a gem of reality shot through with flaws and fault lines of possibility. This was Mace's particular gift: to see how people and situations fit together in the Force, to find the shear planes that can cause them to break in useful ways, and to intuit what sort of strike would best make the cut. Though he could not consistently determine the significance of the structures he perceived—the darkening cloud upon the Force that had risen with the rebirth of the Sith made that harder and harder with each passing day—the presence of shatterpoints was always clear.

Mace had supported the training of Anakin Skywalker, though it ran counter to millennia of Jedi tradition, because from the structure of fault lines in the Force around him, he had been able to intuit the truth of Qui-Gon Jinn's guess: that the young slave boy from Tatooine was in fact the prophesied chosen one, born to bring balance to the Force. He had argued for the elevation of Obi-Wan Kenobi to Mastership, and to give the training of the chosen one into the hands of this new, untested Master, because his unique perception had shown him powerful lines of destiny that bound their lives together, for good or ill. On the day of Palpatine's election to the Chancellorship, he had seen that Palpatine was himself a shatterpoint of unimaginable significance: a man upon whom might depend the fate of the Republic itself.

Now he saw the three men together, and the intricate lattice of fault lines and stress fractures that bound them each to the other was so staggeringly powerful that its structure was beyond calculation.

Anakin was somehow a pivot point, the fulcrum of a lever with Obi-Wan on one side, Palpatine on the other, and the galaxy in the balance, but the dark cloud on the Force prevented his perception from reaching into the future for so much as a hint of where this might lead. The balance was already so delicate that he could not guess the outcome of any given shift: the slightest tip in any direction would generate chaotic oscillation. Anything could happen.

Anything at all.

And the lattice of fault lines that bound all three of them to each other stank of the dark side.

He lifted his head and looked to the sky, picking out the dropping star of the Jedi shuttle as it swung toward them through the darkening afternoon.

"I'm afraid peace is out of the question while Grievous is at large," the Chancellor was saying sadly. "Dooku was the only check on Grievous's monstrous lust for slaughter; with Dooku gone, the general has been unleashed to rampage across the galaxy. I'm afraid that, far from being over, this war is about to get a very great deal *worse*."

"And what of the Sith?" Obi-Wan said. "Dooku's death should have at least begun the weakening of the darkness, but instead it feels stronger than ever. I fear Master Yoda's intuition is correct: that Dooku was merely the apprentice to the Sith Lord, not the Master."

Mace started walking toward the small-craft dock where the Jedi shuttle would land, and the others fell in with him.

"The Sith Lord, if one still exists, will reveal himself in time. They always do." He hoped Obi-Wan would take the hint and shut up about it; Mace had no desire to speak openly of the investigation in front of the Supreme Chancellor.

The less Palpatine knew, the better.

"A more interesting puzzle is Grievous," he said. "He had you at his mercy, Chancellor, and mercy is not numbered among his virtues. Though we all rejoice that he spared you, I cannot help but wonder why."

Palpatine spread his hands. "I can only assume the Separatists preferred to have me as a hostage rather than as a martyr. Though it is of course impossible to say; it may merely have been a whim of the general. He is notoriously erratic."

"Perhaps the Separatist leadership can restrain him, in exchange for certain . . ." Mace let his gaze drift casually to a point somewhere above the Chancellor's head. ". . . considerations."

"Absolutely not." Palpatine drew himself up, straightening his robes. "A negotiated peace would be a recognition of the CIS as the legitimate government of the rebellious systems—tantamount to losing the war! No, Master Windu, this war can end only one way. Unconditional surrender. And while Grievous lives, that will never happen."

"Very well," Mace said. "Then the Jedi will make the capture of General Grievous our particular task." He glanced at Anakin and Obi-Wan, then back to Palpatine. He leaned close to the Chancellor and his voice went low and final, with a buried intensity that hinted—just the slightest bit—of suspicion, and warning. "This war has gone on far too long already. We will find him, and this war *will* end."

"I have no doubt of it." Palpatine strolled along, seemingly oblivious. "But we should never underestimate the deviousness of the Separatists. It is possible that even the war itself has been only one further move," he said with elegant, understated precision, "in some greater game."

As the Jedi shuttle swung toward the Chancellor's private landing platform at the Senate Offices, Obi-Wan watched Anakin pretending not to stare out the window. On the platform was a small welcome-contingent of Senators, and Anakin was trying desperately to look as if he wasn't searching that little crowd hungrily for a particular face. The pretense was a waste of time; Anakin radiated excitement so powerfully in the Force that Obi-Wan could practically hear the thunder of his heartbeat.

Obi-Wan gave a silent sigh. He had entirely too good an idea whose face his former Padawan was so hoping to see.

When the shuttle touched down, Master Windu caught his eye from beyond Anakin's shoulder. The Korun Master made a nearly invisible gesture, to which Obi-Wan did not visibly respond; but when Palpatine and Anakin and R2 all debarked toward the crowd of well-wishers, Obi-Wan stayed behind.

Anakin stopped on the landing deck, looking back at Obi-Wan. "You coming?"

"I haven't the courage for politics," Obi-Wan said, showing his usual trace of a smile. "I'll brief the Council."

"Shouldn't I be there, too?"

"No need. This isn't the formal report. Besides—" Obi-Wan nodded toward the clot of HoloNet crews clogging the pedestrian gangway. "—someone has to be the poster boy."

Anakin looked pained. "Poster *man.*"

"Quite right, quite right," Obi-Wan said with a gentle chuckle. "Go meet your public, Poster Man."

"Wait a minute—this whole operation was *your* idea. You planned it. You led the rescue. It's your turn to take the bows."

"You won't get out of it that easily, my young friend. Without you, I wouldn't even have made it to the flagship. You killed Count Dooku, and single-handedly rescued the Chancellor . . . all while, I might be forgiven for adding, carrying some old broken-down Jedi Master unconscious on your back. Not to mention making a landing that will be the standard of Impossible in every flight manual for the next thousand years."

"Only because of your training, Master—"

"That's just an excuse. You're the hero. Go spend your glorious day surrounded by—" Obi-Wan allowed himself a slightly disparaging cough. "—politicians."

"Come on, Master—you *owe* me. And not just for saving your skin for the tenth time—"

"*Ninth* time. Cato Neimoidia doesn't count; it was your fault in the first place." Obi-Wan waved him off. "See you at the Outer Rim briefing in the morning."

"Well . . . all right. Just this once." Anakin laughed and waved, and then headed briskly off to catch up with Palpatine as the Chancellor waded into the Senators with the smooth-as-oiled-transparisteel ease of the lifelong politician.

The hatch cycled shut, the shuttle lifted off, and Obi-Wan's smile faded as he turned to Mace Windu. "You wanted to speak with me."

Windu moved close to Obi-Wan's position by the window, nodding out at the scene on the landing platform. "It's Anakin. I don't like his relationship with Palpatine."

"We've had this conversation before."

"There is something between them. Something new. I could see it in the Force." Mace's voice was flat and grim. "It felt powerful. And incredibly dangerous."

Obi-Wan spread his hands. "I trust Anakin with my life."

"I know you do. I only wish we could trust the Chancellor with Anakin's."

"Yes," Obi-Wan said, frowning. "Palpatine's policies are . . . sometimes questionable. But he dotes on Anakin like a kindly old uncle on his favorite nephew."

Mace stared out the window. "The Chancellor loves power. If he has any other passion, I have not seen it."

Obi-Wan shook his head with a trace of disbelief. "I recall that not so long ago, you were something of an admirer of his."

"Things," Mace Windu said grimly, "change."

Flying over a landscape pocked with smoldering wreckage where once tall buildings filled with living beings had gleamed in the sun, toward a Temple filled with memories of so many, many Jedi who would never return from this war, Obi-Wan could not disagree.

After a moment, he said, "What would you have me do?"

"I am not certain. You know my power; I cannot always interpret what I've seen. Be alert. Be mindful of Anakin, and be careful of Palpatine. He is not to be trusted, and his influence on Anakin is dangerous."

"But Anakin is the chosen one—"

"All the more reason to fear an outsider's influence. We have circumstantial evidence that traces Sidious to Palpatine's inner circle."

Suddenly Obi-Wan had difficulty breathing. "Are you certain?"

Mace shook his head. "Nothing is certain. But this raid—the capture of Palpatine had to be an inside job. And the timing . . . we were closing *in* on him, Master Kenobi! The information you and Anakin discovered—we had traced the Sith Lord to an abandoned factory in The Works, not far from where Anakin landed the cruiser. When the attack began, we were tracking him through the downlevel tunnels." Mace stared out the viewport at a vast residential complex that dominated the skyline to the west. "The trail led to the sub-basement of Five Hundred Republica."

Five Hundred Republica was the most exclusive address on the planet. Its inhabitants included only the incredibly wealthy or the incredibly powerful, from Raith Sienar of the Sienar Systems conglomerate to Palpatine himself. Obi-Wan could only say, "Oh."

"We have to face the possibility—the probability—that what Dooku told you on Geonosis was actually *true*. That the Senate is under the influence—under the control—of Darth Sidious. That it has been for *years*."

"Do you—" Obi-Wan had to swallow before he could go on. "Do you have any suspects?"

"Too many. All we know of Sidious is that he's bipedal, of roughly human conformation. Sate Pestage springs to mind. I wouldn't rule out Mas Amedda, either. The Sith Lord might even be hiding among the Red Guards. There's no way to know."

"Who's handling the questioning?" Obi-Wan asked. "I'd be happy to sit in; my perceptions are not so refined as some, but—"

Mace shook his head. "Interrogate the Supreme Chancellor's personal aides and advisors? Impossible."

"But—"

"Palpatine will never allow it. Though he hasn't said so . . ." Mace stared out the window. ". . . I'm not sure he even believes the Sith exist."

Obi-Wan blinked. "But—how can he—"

"Look at it from his point of view: the only real evidence we have is Dooku's word. And he's dead now."

"The Sith Lord on Naboo—the Zabrak who killed Qui-Gon—"

Mace shrugged. "Destroyed. As you know." He shook his head. "Relations with the Chancellor's Office are . . . difficult. I feel he has lost his trust in the Jedi; I have certainly lost my trust in him."

"But he doesn't have the authority to interfere with a Jedi investigation . . ." Obi-Wan frowned, suddenly uncertain. "Does he?"

"The Senate has surrendered so much power, it's hard to say where his authority stops."

"It's that bad?"

Mace's jaw locked. "The only reason Palpatine's not a suspect is because he *already* rules the galaxy."

"But we are closer than we have ever been to rooting out the Sith," Obi-Wan said slowly. "That can only be good news. I would think that Anakin's friendship with Palpatine could be of use to us in this—he has the kind of access to Palpatine that other Jedi might only dream of. Their friendship is an asset, not a danger."

"You can't tell him."

"I beg your pardon?"

"Of the whole Council, only Yoda and myself know how deep this actually goes. And now you. I have decided to share this with you because you are in the best situation to watch Anakin. Watch him. Nothing more."

"We—" Obi-Wan shook his head helplessly. "We don't keep secrets from each other."

"You must keep this one." Mace laced his fingers together and squeezed until his knuckles crackled like blasterfire. "Skywalker is arguably the most powerful Jedi alive, and he is still getting stronger. But he is not *stable*. You know it. We all do. It is why he cannot be given Mastership. We must keep him off the Council, despite his extraordinary gifts. And Jedi prophecy . . . is not absolute. The less he has to do with Palpatine, the better."

"But surely—" Obi-Wan stopped himself. He thought of how many times Anakin had violated orders. He thought of how unflinchingly loyal Anakin was to anyone he considered a friend. He thought of the danger Palpatine faced unknowingly, with a Sith Lord among his advisers . . .

Master Windu was right. This was a secret Anakin could not be trusted to keep.

"What *can* I tell him?"

"Tell him nothing. I sense the dark side around him. Around them both."

"As it is around us all," Obi-Wan reminded him. "The dark side touches all of us, Master Windu. Even you."

"I know that too well, Obi-Wan." For one second Obi-Wan saw something raw and haunted in the Korun Master's eyes. Mace turned away. "It is possible that we may have to . . . move against Palpatine."

"Move *against*—?"

"If he is truly under the control of a Sith Lord, it may be the only way."

Obi-Wan's whole body had gone numb. This didn't seem real. It was not possible that he was actually having this conversation.

"You haven't *been* here, Obi-Wan." Mace stared bleakly down at his hands. "You've been off fighting the war in the Outer Rim. You don't know what it's been like, dealing with all the petty squabbles and special interests and greedy, grasping fools in the Senate, and Palpatine's constant, cynical, ruthless maneuvering for power—he carves away chunks of our freedom and bandages the wounds with tiny scraps of security. And for what? Look at this planet, Obi-Wan! We have given up so much freedom—how secure do we *look?*"

Obi-Wan's heart clenched. This was not the Mace Windu he knew and admired; it was as though the darkness in the Force was so much thicker here on Coruscant that it had breathed poison into Mace's spirit—and perhaps was even breeding suspicion and dissension among the members of the Jedi Council.

The greatest danger from the darkness outside came when Jedi fed it with the darkness within.

He had feared he might find matters had deteriorated when he returned to Coruscant and the Temple; not even in his darkest dreams had he thought it would get this bad.

"Master Windu—Mace. We'll go to Yoda together," he said firmly. "And among the three of us we'll work something out. We will. You'll see."

"It may be too late already."

"It may be. And it may not be. We can only do what we can do, Mace. A very, very wise Jedi once said to me, *We don't have to win. All we have to do is fight.*"

Some of the lines erased themselves from the Korun Master's face then, and when he met Obi-Wan's eye there was a quirk at the corner of his mouth that might someday develop into a smile—a tired, sad smile, but a smile nonetheless. "I seem," he said slowly, "to have forgotten that particular Jedi. Thank you for reminding me."

"It was the least I could do," Obi-Wan said lightly, but a sad weight had gathered on his chest.

Things change, indeed.

Anakin's heart pounded in his throat, but he kept smiling, and nodding, and shaking hands—and trying desperately to work his way toward a familiar golden-domed protocol droid who hung back beyond the crowd of Senators, right arm lifted in a small, tentative wave at R2-D2.

She wasn't here. Why wasn't she here?

Something must have happened.

He *knew*, deep in his guts, that something had happened to her. An accident, or she was sick, or she'd been caught in one of the vast number of buildings hit by debris from the battle today . . . She might be trapped somewhere *right now*, might be wounded, might be *smothering*, calling out his name, might be feeling the approach of *flames*—

Stop it, he told himself. *She's not hurt.* If anything had happened to her, he would know. Even from the far side of the Outer Rim, he would know.

So why wasn't she here?

Had something . . .

He could barely breathe. He couldn't make himself even think it. He couldn't stop himself from thinking it.

Had something *changed*? For her?

In how she felt?

He managed to disengage himself from Tundra Dowmeia's clammy grip and insistent invitations to visit his family's deepwater estate on Mon Calamari; he slid past the Malastarian Senator Ask Aak with an apologetic shrug.

He had a different Senator on his mind.

R2 was wheeping and beeping and whistling intensely when Anakin finally struggled free of the mass of sweaty, grasping politicians; C-3PO had turned away dismissively. "It couldn't have been that bad. Don't exaggerate! You're hardly even dented."

R2's answering *feroo* sounded a little defensive. C-3PO sent a wisp of static through his vocabulator that sounded distinctly like a disapproving sniff. "On that point I agree; you're long overdue for a tune-up. And, if I may say so, a *bath*."

"Threepio—"

Anakin came up close beside the droid he had built in the back room of his mother's slave hovel on Tatooine: the droid who had been both project and friend through his painful childhood: the droid who now served the woman he loved . . .

Threepio had been with her all these months, had seen her every day, had *touched* her, perhaps even *today*—he could feel echoes of her resonating outward from his electroplated shell, and they left him breathless.

"Oh, Master Anakin!" Threepio exclaimed. "I am *very* glad to find you well! One does worry, when friends fall out of touch! Why, I was saying to the Senator, just the other day—or was it last week? Time seems to run together so; do you think you might have the opportunity to adjust my internal calendar settings while you're—"

"Threepio, have you *seen* her?" Anakin was trying so hard not to shout that his voice came out a strangled croak. "Where *is* she? Why isn't she *here*?"

"Oh, well, certainly, certainly. Officially, Senator Amidala is *extremely* busy," C-3PO said imperturbably. "She has been sequestered all day in the Naboo embassy, reviewing the new Security Act, preparing for tomorrow's debate—"

Anakin couldn't breathe. She wasn't *here*, hadn't come to meet him, over some *debate*?

The Senate. He *hated* the Senate. Hated everything about it.

A red haze gathered inside his head. Those self-righteous, narrow-minded, grubby little *squabblers* . . . He'd be doing the galaxy a *favor* if he were to go over there right *now* and just—

"Wait," he murmured, blinking. "Did you say, *officially?*"

"Oh, yes, Master Anakin." Threepio sounded entirely virtuous. "That is my *official* answer to all queries regarding the Senator's whereabouts. All afternoon."

The red haze evaporated, leaving only sunlight and dizzyingly fresh air.

Anakin smiled.

"And *un*officially?"

The protocol droid leaned close with an exaggeratedly conspiratorial whisper: "Unofficially, she's waiting in the hallway."

It felt like being struck by lightning. But in a good way. In the best way any man has ever felt since, roughly, the birth of the universe.

Threepio gave a slight nod at the other Senators and the HoloNet crews on the gangway. "She thought it best to avoid a, ah, *public* scene. And she wished for me to relate to you that she believes the *both* of you might . . . *avoid* a public *scene* . . . all *afternoon*. And perhaps all night, as well."

"Threepio!" Anakin blinked at him. He felt an irrational desire to giggle. "What exactly are you suggesting?"

"I'm sure I couldn't say, sir. I am only performing as per the Senator's instructions."

"You—" Anakin shook his head in wonder while his smile grew to a grin he thought might split open his cheeks. "You are amazing."

"Thank you, Master Anakin, though credit for that is due largely—" C-3PO made an elegantly gracious bow. "—to my creator."

Anakin could only go on grinning.

With that, the golden protocol droid laid an affectionate hand on R2's dome. "Come along, Artoo. I have found the most delightful body shop down in the Lipartian Way."

They moved away, whirring and clanking after the Senators who were already off among the HoloNet crews. Anakin's smile faded as he watched them go.

He felt a presence at his shoulder and turned to find Palpatine beside him with a warm smile and a soft word, as he always seemed to be when Anakin was troubled.

"What is it, Anakin?" the Chancellor asked kindly. "Something is disturbing you. I can tell."

Anakin shrugged and gave his head a dismissive shake, embarrassed. "It's nothing."

"Anakin, anything that might upset a man such as yourself is certainly *some*thing. Let me help."

"There's nothing you can do. It's just—" Anakin nodded after 3PO and R2. "I was just thinking that even after all I've done, See-Threepio is still the only person I know who calls me *Master.*"

"Ah. The Jedi Council." Palpatine slid an arm around Anakin's shoulders and gave him a comradely squeeze. "I believe I can be of some use to you in this problem after all."

"You can?"

"I should be very much surprised if I couldn't."

Palpatine's smile was still warm, but his eyes had gone distant.

"You may have noticed that I have a certain gift," he murmured, "for getting my way."

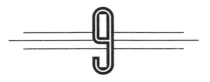

PADMÉ

From the shadow of a great pillar stretching up into the reddening afternoon that leaked through the vaulted roof of transparisteel over the Atrium of the Senate Office Building, she watched Senators clustering in through the archway from the Chancellor's landing platform, and then she saw the Chancellor himself and C-3PO and yes, that was *R2-D2!*—and so *he* could not be far behind . . . and only then did she finally find him among them, tall and straight, his hair radiation-bleached to golden streaks and on his lips a lively smile that opened her chest and unlocked her heart.

And she could breathe again.

Through the swirl of HoloNet reporters and the chatter of Senators and the gently comforting tones of Palpatine's most polished, reassuringly paternal voice, she did not move, not so much as to lift a hand or turn her head. She was silent, and still, only letting herself breathe, feeling the beat of her heart, and she could have stood there forever, in the shadows, and had her fondest dreams all fulfilled, simply by watching him be alive . . .

But when he moved away from the group, pacing in soft conversation with Bail Organa of Alderaan, and she heard Bail saying something about *the end of Count Dooku* and *the end of the war* and *finally an end to Palpatine's police-state tactics,* her breath caught again and she held it, because she knew the next thing she heard would be *his* voice.

"I wish that were so," he said, "but the fighting will continue until General Grievous is spare parts. The Chancellor is very clear on this, and I believe the Senate and the Jedi Council will both agree."

And beyond that, there was no hope she could be happier—until his eye found her silent, still shadow, and he straightened, and a new light broke over his golden face and he said, "Excuse me," to the Senator from Alderaan, and a moment later he came to her in the shadows and they were in each other's arms.

Their lips met, and the universe became, one last time, perfect.

───────

This is Padmé Amidala:

She is an astonishingly accomplished young woman, who in her short life has been already the youngest-ever elected Queen of her planet, a daring partisan guerrilla, and a measured, articulate, and persuasive voice of reason in the Republic Senate.

But she is, at this moment, none of these things.

She can still play at them—she pretends to be a Senator, she still wields the moral authority of a former Queen, and she is not shy about using her reputation for fierce physical courage to her advantage in political debate—but her inmost reality, the most fundamental, unbreakable core of her being, is something entirely different.

She is Anakin Skywalker's wife.

Yet *wife* is a word too weak to carry the truth of her; *wife* is such a small word, such a common word, a word that can come from a downturned mouth with so many petty, unpleasant echoes. For Padmé Amidala, saying *I am Anakin Skywalker's wife* is saying neither more nor less than *I am alive.*

Her life before Anakin belonged to someone else, some lesser being to be pitied, some poor impoverished spirit who could never suspect how profoundly life should be lived.

Her real life began the first time she looked into Anakin Skywalker's eyes and found in there not the uncritical worship of little Annie from Tatooine, but the direct, unashamed, smoldering passion of a powerful Jedi: a *young* man, to be sure, but every centimeter a *man*—a man whose legend was already growing within the Jedi Order and beyond. A man who knew exactly what he wanted and was honest enough to simply *ask* for it; a man strong enough to unroll his deepest feelings before her without fear and without shame. A man who had loved her for a decade, with faithful and patient heart, while he waited for the act of destiny he was sure would someday open her own heart to the fire in his.

But though she loves her husband without reservation, love does not blind her to his faults. She is older than he, and wise enough to understand him better than he does himself. He is not a perfect man: he is prideful, and moody, and quick to anger— but these faults only make her love him the more, for his every flaw is more than balanced by the greatness within him, his capacity for joy and cleansing laughter, his extraordinary generosity of spirit, his passionate devotion not only to her but also in the service of every living being.

He is a wild creature who has come gently to her hand, a vine tiger purring against her cheek. Every softness of his touch, every kind glance or loving word is a small miracle in itself. How can she not be grateful for such gifts?

This is why she will not allow their marriage to become public knowledge. Her husband *needs* to be a Jedi. Saving people is what he was born for; to take that away from him would cripple every good thing in his troubled heart.

Now she holds him in their infinite kiss with both arms tight around his neck, because there is a cold dread in the center of her heart that whispers this kiss is not infinite at all, that it's only a pause in the headlong rush of the universe, and when it ends, she will have to face the future.

And she is terrified.

Because while he has been away, everything has changed.

Today, here in the hallway of the Senate Office Building, she brings him news of a gift they have given each other—a gift of joy, and of terror. This gift is the edge of a knife that has already cut their past from their future.

For these long years they have held each other only in secret, only in moments stolen from the business of the Republic and the war; their love has been the perfect refuge, a long quiet after-noon, warm and sunny, sealed away from fear and doubt, from duty and from danger. But now she carries within her a planetary terminator that will end their warm afternoon forever and leave them blind in the oncoming night.

She is more, now, than Anakin Skywalker's wife.

She is the mother of Anakin Skywalker's unborn child.

⸻

After an all-too-brief eternity, the kiss finally ended.

She clung to him, just breathing in the presence of him after so long, murmuring love against his broad strong chest while he murmured love into the coils of her softly scented hair.

Some time later, she found words again. "Anakin, Anakin, oh my Anakin, I—I can't believe you're *home*. They told me . . ." She almost choked on the memory. "There were whispers . . . that you'd been *killed*. I couldn't—every day—"

"Never believe stories like that," he whispered. "Never. I will always come back to you, Padmé."

"I've lived a year for every hour you were away—"

"It's been a lifetime. Two."

She reached up to the burn-scar high on his cheek. "You were hurt . . ."

"Nothing serious," he said with half a smile. "Just an unfriendly reminder to keep up with my lightsaber practice."

"Five *months*." It was almost a moan. "Five months—how could they *do* that to us?"

He rested his cheek lightly on the crown of her head. "If the Chancellor hadn't been kidnapped, I'd still be out there. I'm almost—it's terrible to say it, but I'm *grateful*. I'm glad he was kidnapped. It's like it was all arranged just to bring me home again . . ."

His arms were so strong, and so warm, and his hand touched her hair in the softest caress, as though he was afraid she were as fragile as a dream, and he bent down for another kiss, a new kiss, a kiss that would wipe away every dark dream and all the days and hours and minutes of unbearable dread—

But only steps away, the main vault of the Atrium still held Senators and HoloNet crews, and the knowledge of the price Anakin would pay when their love became known made her turn her face aside, and put her hands on his chest to hold him away. "Anakin, not here. It's too risky."

"No, *here*! *Exactly* here." He drew her against him again, effortlessly overpowering her halfhearted resistance. "I'm tired of the deception. Of the sneaking and the lying. We have *nothing* to be ashamed of! We love each other, and we are married. Just like trillions of beings across the galaxy. This is something we should *shout*, not whisper—"

"No, Anakin. *Not* like all those others. They are not Jedi. We can't let our love force you out of the Order—"

"Force me out of the Order?" He smiled down at her fondly. "Was that a pun?"

"Anakin—" He could still make her angry without even trying. "*Listen* to me. We have a duty to the Republic. Both of us— but yours is now so much more important. You are the face of the Jedi, Anakin. Even after these years of war, many people still love the Jedi, and it's mostly because they love *you,* do you understand that? They love the *story* of you. You're like something out of a bedtime tale, the secret prince, hidden among the peasants, growing up without ever a clue of his special destiny— except for you it's all *true.* Sometimes I think that the only reason the people of the Republic still believe we can win the war is because *you're* fighting it for them—"

"And it always comes back to politics for you," Anakin said. His smile had gone now. "I'm barely even home, and you're already trying to talk me into going back to the war—"

"This isn't about politics, Anakin, it's about *you.*"

"Something has changed, hasn't it?" Thunder gathered in his voice. "I felt it, even outside. Something has changed."

She lowered her head. "Everything has changed."

"What is it? What?" He took her by the shoulders now, his hands hard and irresistibly powerful. "There's someone else. I can *feel* it in the Force! There is someone coming *between* us—"

"Not the way you think," she said. "Anakin, listen—"

"Who is it? *Who?*"

"*Stop* it. Anakin, *stop.* You'll hurt us."

His hands sprang open as though she had burned them. He took an unsteady step backward, his face suddenly ashen. "Padmé—I would never—I'm so sorry, I just—"

He leaned on the pillar and brought a hand weakly to his eyes. "The Hero With No Fear. What a joke . . . Padmé, I can't *lose* you. I *can't.* You're all I *live* for. Wait . . ." He lifted his head, frowning quizzically. "Did you say, *us?*"

She reached for him, and he came to meet her hand. Rising

tears burned her eyes, and her lip trembled. "I'm . . . Annie, I'm *pregnant* . . ."

She watched him as everything their child would mean cycled through his mind, and her heart caught when she saw first of all the wild, almost explosive joy that dawned over his face, because that meant that whatever he had gone through on the Outer Rim, he was still her Annie.

It meant that the war that had scarred his face had not scarred his spirit.

And she watched that joy fade as he began to understand that their marriage could not stay hidden much longer; that even the voluminous robes she wore could not conceal a pregnancy forever. That he would be cast out in disgrace from the Jedi Order. That she would be relieved of her post and recalled to Naboo. That the very celebrity that had made him so important to the war would turn against them both, making them the freshest possible meat for an entire galaxy full of scandalmongers.

And she watched him decide that he didn't care.

"That is," he said slowly, that wild spark returning to his eyes, ". . . *wonderful* . . . Padmé—that's *wonderful*. How long have you known?"

She shook her head. "What are we going to *do*?"

"We're going to be happy, that's what we're going to do. And we're going to be *together*. All *three* of us."

"But—"

"No." He laid a gentle finger on her lips, smiling down at her. "No buts. No worries. You worry too much as it is."

"I have to," she said, smiling through the tears in her eyes. "Because you never worry at all."

Anakin lurched upright in bed, gasping, staring blindly into alien darkness.

How she had *screamed* for him—how she had begged for him, how her strength had failed on that alien table, how at the last she could only whimper, *Anakin, I'm sorry. I love you. I love you*—thundered inside his head, blinding him to the contours of the night-shrouded room, deafening him to every sound save the turbohammer of his heart.

His hand of flesh found unfamiliar coils of sweat-damp silken sheets around his waist. Finally he remembered where he was.

He half turned, and she was with him, lying on her side, her glorious fall of hair fanned across her pillow, eyes closed, half a smile on her precious lips, and when he saw the long, slow rise and fall of her chest with the cycle of her breathing, he turned away and buried his face in his hands and sobbed.

The tears that ran between his fingers then were tears of gratitude.

She was alive, and she was with him.

In silence so deep he could hear the whirring of the electro-drivers in his mechanical hand, he disentangled himself from the sheets and got up.

Through the closet, a long curving sweep of stairs led to the veranda that overlooked Padmé's private landing deck. Leaning on the night-chilled rail, Anakin stared out upon the endless nightscape of Coruscant.

It was still burning.

Coruscant at night had always been an endless galaxy of light, shining from trillions of windows in billions of buildings that reached kilometers into the sky, with navigation lights and advertising and the infinite streams of speeders' running lights coursing the rivers of traffic lanes overhead. But tonight, local power outages had swallowed ragged swaths of the city into vast nebulae of darkness, broken only by the malignant red-dwarf glares of innumerable fires.

Anakin didn't know how long he stood there, staring. The city looked like he felt. Damaged. Broken in battle.

Stained with darkness.

And he'd rather look at the city than think about why he was out here looking at it in the first place.

She moved more quietly than the smoky breeze, but he felt her approach.

She took a place beside him at the railing and laid her soft human hand along the back of his hard mechanical one. And she simply stood with him, staring silently out across the city that had become her second home. Waiting patiently for him to tell her what was wrong. Trusting that he would.

He could feel her patience, and her trust, and he was so grateful for both that tears welled once more. He had to blink out at the burning night, and blink again, to keep those fresh tears from spilling over onto his cheeks. He put his flesh hand on top of hers and held it gently until he could let himself speak.

"It was a dream," he said finally.

She accepted this with a slow, serious nod. "Bad?"

"It was—like the ones I used to have." He couldn't look at her. "About my mother."

Again, a nod, but even slower, and more serious. "And?"

"And—" He looked down at her small, slim fingers, and he slipped his between them, clasping their two hands into a knot of prayer. "It was about you."

Now she turned aside, leaning once more upon the rail, staring out into the night, and in the slowly pulsing rose-glow of the distant fires she was more beautiful than he had ever seen her. "All right," she said softly. "It was about me."

Then she simply waited, still trusting.

When Anakin could finally make himself tell her, his voice was raw and hoarse as though he'd been shouting all day. "It was . . . about you *dying*," he said. "I couldn't stand it. I can't stand it."

He couldn't look at her. He looked at the city, at the deck, at the stars, and he found no place he could bear to see.

All he could do was close his eyes.

"You're going to die in childbirth."

"Oh," she said.

That was all.

She had only a few months left to live. They had only a few months left to love each other. She would never see their child. And all she said was, "Oh."

After a moment, the touch of her hand to his cheek brought his eyes open again, and he found her gazing up at him calmly. "And the baby?"

He shook his head. "I don't know."

She nodded and pulled away, drifting toward one of the veranda chairs. She lowered herself into it and stared down at her hands, clasped together in her lap.

He couldn't take it. He couldn't watch her be calm and accepting about her own death. He came to her side and knelt.

"It won't happen, Padmé. I won't let it. I could have saved my mother—a day earlier, an hour—I . . ." He bit down on the rising pain inside him, and spoke through clenched teeth. "This dream will *not* become real."

She nodded. "I didn't think it would."

He blinked. "You didn't?"

"This is Coruscant, Annie, not Tatooine. Women don't die in childbirth on *Coruscant*—not even the twilighters in the downlevels. And I have a top-flight medical droid, who assures me I am in perfect health. Your dream must have been . . . some kind of metaphor, or something."

"I—my dreams are *literal,* Padmé. I wouldn't know a metaphor if it *bit* me. And I couldn't see the place you were in— you might not even *be* on Coruscant . . ."

She looked away. "I had been thinking—about going somewhere . . . somewhere else. Having the baby in secret, to protect you. So you can stay in the Order."

"I don't *want* to stay in the Order!" He took her face between his palms so that she had to look into his eyes, so that she had to see how much he meant every word he said. "Don't protect me. I don't need it. We have to start thinking, right now, about how we can protect *you*. Because all I want is for us to be together."

"And we will be," she said. "But there must be more to your dream than death in childbirth. That doesn't make any sense."

"I know. But I can't begin to guess what it might be. It's too—I can't even think about it, Padmé. I'll go crazy. What are we going to do?"

She kissed the palm of his hand of flesh. "We're going to do what you told me, when I asked you the same question this afternoon. We're going to be happy together."

"But we—we can't just . . . *wait*. *I* can't. I have to *do* something."

"Of course you do." She smiled fondly. "That's who you are. That's what being a hero is. What about Obi-Wan?"

He frowned. "What about him?"

"You told me once that he is as wise as Yoda and as powerful as Mace Windu. Couldn't he help us?"

"No." Anakin's chest clenched like a fist squeezing his heart. "I can't—I'd have to *tell* him . . ."

"He's your best friend, Annie. He must suspect already."

"It's one thing to have him suspect. It's something else to shove it in his face. He's still on the Council. He'd *have* to report me. And . . ."

"And what? Is there something you haven't told me?"

He turned away. "I'm not sure he's on my side."

"*Your* side? Anakin, what are you saying?"

"He's on the Jedi Council, Padmé. I *know* my name has come up for Mastery—I'm more powerful than any Jedi Master alive. But someone is blocking me. Obi-Wan could tell me who, and why . . . but he *doesn't*. I'm not sure he even stands up for me with them."

"I can't believe that."

"It has nothing to do with believing," he murmured, softly bitter. "It's the truth."

"There must be some *reason,* then. Anakin, he's your best friend. He loves you."

"Maybe he does. But I don't think he trusts me." His eyes went as bleak as the empty night. "And I'm not sure we can trust him."

"Anakin!" She clutched at his arm. "What would make you *say* that?"

"*None* of them trust me, Padmé. None of them. You know what I feel, when they look at me?"

"Anakin—"

He turned to her, and everything in him ached. He wanted to cry and he wanted to rage and he wanted to make his rage a weapon that would cut himself free forever. "Fear," he said. "I feel their *fear.* And for *nothing.*"

He could show them something, though. He could show them a *reason* for their fear.

He could show them what he'd discovered within himself in the General's Quarters on *Invisible Hand.*

Something of it must have risen on his face, because he saw a flicker of doubt shadow her eyes, just for a second, just a flash, but still it burned into him like a lightsaber and he shuddered, and his shudder turned into a shiver that became shaking, and he gathered her to his chest and buried his face in her hair, and the strong sweet warmth of her cooled him, just enough.

"Padmé," he murmured, "oh, Padmé, I'm so sorry. Forget I said anything. None of that matters now. I'll be gone from the Order soon—because I will not let you go away to have our baby in some alien place. I will not let you face my dream alone. I *will* be there for you, Padmé. Always. No matter what."

"I know it, Annie. I know." She pulled gently away and looked up at him. Tears sparkled like red gems in the firelight.

Red as the synthetic bloodshine of Dooku's lightsaber.

He closed his eyes.

She said, "Come upstairs, Anakin. The night's getting cold. Come up to our bed."

"All right. All right." He found that he could breathe again, and his shaking had stilled. "Just—"

He put his arm around her shoulders so that he didn't have to meet her eyes. "Just don't say anything to Obi-Wan, all right?"

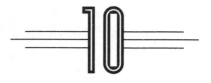

MASTERS

Obi-Wan sat beside Mace Windu while they watched Yoda scan the report. Here in Yoda's simple living space within the Jedi Temple, every softly curving pod chair and knurled organi-form table hummed with gentle, comforting power: the same warm strength that Obi-Wan remembered enfolding him even as an infant. These chambers had been Yoda's home for more than eight hundred years. Everything within them echoed with the harmonic resonance of Yoda's calm wisdom, tuned through centuries of his touch. To sit within Yoda's chambers was to inhale serenity; to Obi-Wan, this was a great gift in these troubled times.

But when Yoda looked at them through the translucent shimmer of the holoprojected report on the contents of the latest amendment to the Security Act, his eyes were anything but calm: they had gone narrow and cold, and his ears had flattened back along his skull.

"This report—from where does it come?"

"The Jedi still have friends in the Senate," Mace Windu replied in his grim monotone, "for now."

"When presented this amendment is, passed it will be?"

Mace nodded. "My source expects passage by acclamation. Overwhelming passage. Perhaps as early as this afternoon."

"The Chancellor's goal in this—unclear to me it is," Yoda said slowly. "Though nominally in command of the Council, the Senate may place him, the Jedi he cannot control. Moral, our authority has always been; much more than merely *legal*. Simply follow orders, Jedi do not!"

"I don't think he intends to control the Jedi," Mace said. "By placing the Jedi Council under the control of the Office of the Supreme Chancellor, this amendment will give him the constitutional authority to disband the Order itself."

"Surely you cannot believe this is his intention."

"*His* intention?" Mace said darkly. "Perhaps not. But *his* intentions are irrelevant; all that matters now is the intent of the Sith Lord who has our government in his grip. And the Jedi Order may be all that stands between him and galactic domination. What do you *think* he will do?"

"Authority to disband the Jedi, the Senate would never grant."

"The Senate will vote to grant exactly that. This afternoon."

"The implications of this, they must not comprehend!"

"It no longer matters what they comprehend," Mace said. "They know where the power is."

"But even disbanded, even without legal authority, still Jedi we would be. Jedi Knights served the Force long before there was a Galactic Republic, and serve it we will when this Republic is but dust."

"Master Yoda, that day may be coming sooner than any of us think. That day may be *today*." Mace shot a frustrated look at Obi-Wan, who picked up his cue smoothly.

"We don't know what the Sith Lord's plans may be," Obi-Wan said, "but we can be certain that Palpatine is not to be trusted. Not anymore. This draft resolution is not the product of some overzealous Senator; we may be sure Palpatine wrote it himself and passed it along to someone he controls—to make it look like the Senate is once more 'forcing him to reluctantly accept extra powers in the name of security.' We are afraid that they will continue to do so until one day he's 'forced to reluctantly accept' dictatorship for *life*."

"I am convinced this is the next step in a plot aimed directly at the heart of the Jedi," Mace said. "This is a move toward our destruction. The dark side of the Force surrounds the Chancellor."

Obi-Wan added, "As it has surrounded and cloaked the Separatists since even before the war began. If the Chancellor is being influenced through the dark side, this whole war may have been, from the beginning, a plot by the Sith to destroy the Jedi Order."

"Speculation!" Yoda thumped the floor with his gimer stick, making his hoverchair bob gently. "On theories such as these we cannot rely. *Proof* we need. Proof!"

"Proof may be a luxury we cannot afford." A dangerous light had entered Mace Windu's eyes. "We must be ready to *act*."

"Act?" Obi-Wan asked mildly.

"He cannot be allowed to move against the Order. He cannot be allowed to prolong the war needlessly. Too many Jedi have died already. He is dismantling the Republic itself! I have *seen* life outside the Republic; so have you, Obi-Wan. Slavery. Torture. Endless war."

Mace's face darkened with the same distant, haunted shadow Obi-Wan had seen him wear the day before. "I have seen it in Nar Shaddaa, and I saw it on Haruun Kal. I saw what it did to Depa, and to Sora Bulq. Whatever its flaws, the Republic is our sole hope for justice, and for peace. It is our only defense against the dark. Palpatine may be about to do what the Separatists cannot: bring down the Republic. If he tries, he must be removed from office."

"Removed?" Obi-Wan said. "You mean, *arrested*?"

Yoda shook his head. "To a dark place, this line of thought will lead us. Great care, we must take."

"The Republic *is* civilization. It's the only one we have." Mace looked deeply into Yoda's eyes, and into Obi-Wan's, and Obi-Wan could feel the heat in the Korun Master's gaze. "We must be prepared for radical action. It is our duty."

"But," Obi-Wan protested numbly, "you're talking about *treason . . .*"

"I'm not afraid of words, Obi-Wan! If it's treason, then so be it. I would do this right now, if I had the Council's support. The *real* treason," Mace said, "would be failure to *act.*"

"Such an act, destroy the Jedi Order it could," Yoda said. "Lost the trust of the public, we have already—"

"No disrespect, Master Yoda," Mace interrupted, "but that's a politician's argument. We can't let public opinion stop us from doing what's *right.*"

"*Convinced* it is right, I am *not,*" Yoda said severely. "Working behind the scenes we should be, to uncover Lord Sidious! To move against Palpatine while the Sith still exist—this may be part of the Sith plan *itself,* to turn the Senate and the public against the Jedi! So that we are not only disbanded, but *outlawed.*"

Mace was half out of his pod. "To *wait* gives the Sith the advantage—"

"Have the advantage *already,* they do!" Yoda jabbed at him with his gimer stick. "*Increase* their advantage we will, if in haste we act!"

"Masters, Masters, please," Obi-Wan said. He looked from one to the other and inclined his head respectfully. "Perhaps there is a middle way."

"Ah, of course: Kenobi the Negotiator." Mace Windu settled back into his seating pod. "I should have guessed. That is why you asked for this meeting, isn't it? To mediate our differences. If you can."

"So sure of your skills you are?" Yoda folded his fists around the head of his stick. "Easy to negotiate, this matter is not!"

Obi-Wan kept his head down. "It seems to me," he said carefully, "that Palpatine himself has given us an opening. He has said—both to you, Master Windu, and in the HoloNet address he gave following his rescue—that General Grievous is the true obstacle to peace. Let us forget about the rest of the Separatist leadership, for now. Let Nute Gunray and San Hill and the rest run wherever they like, while we put every available Jedi and all of our agents—the whole of Republic Intelligence, if we can—to work on locating Grievous himself. This will force the hand of the Sith Lord; he will know that Grievous cannot elude our full efforts for long, once we devote ourselves exclusively to his capture. It will draw Sidious out; he will have to make some sort of move, if he wishes the war to continue."

"If?" Mace said. "The war has been a Sith operation from the beginning, with Dooku on one side and Sidious on the other— it has always been a plot aimed at *us*. At the Jedi. To bleed us dry of our youngest and best. To make us into something we were never intended to be."

He shook his head bitterly. "I had the truth in my hands years ago—back on Haruun Kal, in the first months of the war. I had it, but I did not understand how right I was."

"Seen glimpses of this truth, we all have," Yoda said sadly. "Our arrogance it is, which has stopped us from fully opening our eyes."

"Until now," Obi-Wan put in gently. "We understand now the goal of the Sith Lord, we know his tactics, and we know where to look for him. His actions will reveal him. He cannot escape us. He *will* not escape us."

Yoda and Mace frowned at each other for one long moment, then both of them turned to Obi-Wan and inclined their heads in mirrors of his respectful bow.

"Seen to the heart of the matter, young Kenobi has."

Mace nodded. "Yoda and I will remain on Coruscant, monitoring Palpatine's advisers and lackeys; we'll move against Sidious the instant he is revealed. But who will capture Grievous? I have fought him blade-to-blade. He is more than a match for most Jedi."

"We'll worry about that once we find him," Obi-Wan said. A slight, wistful smile crept over his face. "If I listen hard enough, I can almost hear Qui-Gon reminding me that *until the possible becomes actual, it is only a distraction.*"

General Grievous stood wide-legged, hands folded behind him, as he stared out through the reinforced viewport at the towering sphere of the Geonosian Dreadnaught. The immense ship looked small, though, against the scale of the vast sinkhole that rose around it.

This was Utapau, a remote backworld on the fringe of the Outer Rim. At ground level—far above where Grievous stood now—the planet appeared to be a featureless ball of barren rock, scoured flat by endless hyperwinds. From orbit, though, its cities and factories and spaceports could be seen as the planet's rotation brought its cavernous sinkholes one at a time into view. These sinkholes were the size of inverted mountains, and every available square meter of their interior walls was packed with city. And every square meter of every city was under the guns of Separatist war droids, making sure that the Utapauns behaved themselves.

Utapau had no interest in the Clone Wars; it had never been a member of the Republic, and had carefully maintained a stance of quiet neutrality.

Right up until Grievous had conquered it.

Neutrality, in these times, was a joke; a planet was neutral only so long as neither the Republic nor the Confederacy wanted it. If Grievous could laugh, he would have.

The members of the Separatist leadership scurried across

the permacrete landing platform like the alley rats they were—scampering for the ship that would take them to the safety of the newly constructed base on Mustafar.

But one alley rat was missing from the scuttle.

Grievous shifted his gaze fractionally and found the reflection of Nute Gunray in the transparisteel. The Neimoidian viceroy stood dithering in the control center's doorway. Grievous regarded the reflection of the bulbous, cold-blooded eyes below the tall peaked miter.

"Gunray." He made no other motion. "Why are you still here?"

"Some things should be said privately, General." The viceroy's reflection cast glances either way along the hallway beyond the door. "I am disturbed by this new move. You told us that Utapau would be safe for us. Why is the Leadership Council being moved now to Mustafar?"

Grievous sighed. He had no time for lengthy explanations; he was expecting a secret transmission from Sidious himself. He could not take the transmission with Gunray in the room, nor could he follow his natural inclinations and boot the Neimoidian viceroy so high he'd burn up on reentry. Grievous still hoped, every day, that Lord Sidious would give him leave to smash the skulls of Gunray and his toady, Rune Haako. Repulsive sniveling grub-greedy scum, both of them. And the rest of the Separatist leadership was every bit as vile.

But for now, a pretense of cordiality had to be maintained.

"Utapau," Grievous said slowly, as though explaining to a child, "is a hostile planet under military occupation. It was never intended to be more than a stopgap, while the defenses of the base on Mustafar were completed. Now that they are, Mustafar is the most secure planet in the galaxy. The stronghold prepared for you can withstand the entire Republic Navy."

"It should," Gunray muttered. "Construction nearly bankrupted the Trade Federation!"

"Don't whine to me about money, Viceroy. I have no interest in it."

"You had better, General. It's my *money* that finances this entire war! It's my money that pays for that *body* you wear, and for those insanely expensive MagnaGuards of yours! It's my *money*—"

Grievous moved so swiftly that he seemed to teleport from the window to half a meter in front of Gunray. "How much use is your money," he said, flexing his hand of jointed duranium in the Neimoidian's face, "against *this*?"

Gunray flinched and backed away. "I was only—I have some concerns about your ability to keep us *safe*, General, that's all. I—we—the Trade Federation cannot work in a climate of fear. What about the *Jedi*?"

"Forget the Jedi. They do not enter into this equation."

"They will be entering into that *base* soon enough!"

"The base is secure. It can stand against a thousand Jedi. *Ten* thousand."

"Do you *hear* yourself? Are you *mad*?"

"What I am," Grievous replied evenly, "is unaccustomed to having my orders challenged."

"We are the Leadership Council! You cannot give *us* orders! *We* give the orders here!"

"Are you certain of that? Would you care to wager?" Grievous leaned close enough that he could see the reflection of his mask in Gunray's rose-colored eyes. "Shall we, say, bet your life on it?"

Gunray kept on backing away. "You tell us we'll be safe on Mustafar—but you *also* told us you would deliver Palpatine as a *hostage*, and *he* managed to escape your grip!"

"Be thankful, Viceroy," Grievous said, admiring the smooth flexion of his finger joints as though his hand were some species of exotic predator, "that you have not found *yourself* in my grip."

He went back to the viewport and reassumed his original position, legs wide, hands clasped behind his back. To look on the sickly pink in Gunray's pale green cheeks for one second longer was to risk forgetting his orders and splattering the viceroy's brains from here to Ord Mantell.

"Your ship is waiting."

His auditory sensors clearly picked up the slither of Gunray's sandals retreating along the corridor, and not a second too soon: his sensors were also registering the whine of the control center's holocomm warming up. He turned to face the disk, and when the enunciator chimed to indicate the incoming transmission, he pressed the ACCEPT key and knelt.

Head down, he could see only the scanned image of the hem of the great Lord's robes, but that was all he needed to see.

"Yes, Lord Sidious."

"Have you moved the Separatist Council to Mustafar?"

"Yes, Master." He risked a glance out the viewport. Most of the council had reached the starship. Gunray should be joining them any second; Grievous had seen firsthand how fast the viceroy could run, given proper motivation. "The ship will lift off within moments."

"Well done, my general. Now you must turn your hand to preparing our trap there on Utapau. The Jedi hunt you personally at last; you must be ready for their attack."

"Yes, Master."

"I am arranging matters to give you a second chance to do my bidding, Grievous. Expect that the Jedi sent to capture you will be Obi-Wan Kenobi."

"Kenobi?" Grievous's fists clenched hard enough that his carpal electrodrivers whined in protest. "And Skywalker?"

"I believe Skywalker will be . . . otherwise engaged."

Grievous dropped his head even lower. "I will not fail you again, my Master. Kenobi will die."

"See to it."

"Master? If I may trouble you with boldness—why did you

not let me kill Chancellor Palpatine? We may never get a better chance."

"The time was not yet ripe. Patience, my general. The end of the war is near, and victory is certain."

"Even with the loss of Count Dooku?"

"Dooku was not lost, he was sacrificed—a strategic sacrifice, as one offers up a piece in dejarik: to draw the opponent into a fatal blunder."

"I was never much the dejarik player, my Master. I prefer *real* war."

"And you shall have your fill, I promise you."

"This fatal blunder you speak of—if I may once again trouble you with boldness . . ."

"You will come to understand soon enough."

Grievous could hear the smile in his Master's voice.

"All will be clear, once you meet my new apprentice."

Anakin finger-combed his hair as he trotted out across the restricted landing deck atop the Temple ziggurat near the base of the High Council Tower. Far across the expanse of deck stood the Supreme Chancellor's shuttle. Anakin squinted at it, and at the two tall red-robed guards that stood flanking its open access ramp.

And coming toward him from the direction of the shuttle, shielding his eyes and leaning against the morning wind that whipped across the unprotected field—was that Obi-Wan?

"Finally," Anakin muttered. He'd scoured the Temple for his former Master; he'd nearly giving up hope of finding him when a passing Padawan had mentioned that he'd seen Obi-Wan on his way out to the landing deck to meet Palpatine's shuttle. He hoped Obi-Wan wouldn't notice he hadn't changed his clothes.

It wasn't like he could explain.

Though his secret couldn't last, he wasn't ready for it to come out just yet. He and Padmé had agreed last night that they would keep it as long as they could. He wasn't ready to leave the Jedi Order. Not while she was still in danger.

Padmé had said that his nightmare must be only a metaphor, but he knew better. He knew that Force prophecy was not absolute—but his had never been wrong. Not in the slightest detail. He had known as a boy that he would be chosen by the Jedi. He had known his adventures would span the galaxy. As a mere nine-year-old, long before he even understood what love was, he had looked upon Padmé Amidala's flawless face and seen there that she would love him, and that they would someday marry.

There had been no metaphor in his dreams of his mother. Screaming in pain. Tortured to death.

I knew you would come to me, Annie . . . I missed you so much.

He could have saved her.

Maybe.

It had always seemed so obvious to him—that if he had only returned to Tatooine a day earlier, an hour, he could have found his mother and she would still be alive. And yet—

And yet the great prophets of the Jedi had always taught that the gravest danger in trying to prevent a vision of the future from coming to pass is that in doing so, a Jedi can actually *bring* it to pass—as though if he'd run away in time to save his mother, he might have made himself somehow responsible for her death.

As though if he tried to save Padmé, he could end up—blankly impossible though it was—killing her *himself* . . .

But to do nothing . . . to simply wait for Padmé to die . . .

Could something be *more* than impossible?

When a Jedi had a question about the deepest subtleties of the Force, there was one source to whom he could always turn; and so, first thing that morning, without even taking time to stop by his own quarters for a change of clothing, Anakin had gone to Yoda for advice.

He'd been surprised by how graciously the ancient Jedi Master had invited him into his quarters, and by how patiently Yoda had listened to his stumbling attempts to explain his question without giving away his secret; Yoda had never made any attempt to conceal what had always seemed to Anakin to be a gruff disapproval of Anakin's very existence.

But this morning, despite clearly having other things on his mind—even Anakin's Force perceptions, far from the most subtle, had detected echoes of conflict and worry within the Master's chamber—Yoda had simply offered Anakin a place on one of the softly rounded pod seats and suggested that they meditate together.

He hadn't even asked for details.

Anakin had been so grateful—and so relieved, and so unexpectedly hopeful—that he'd found tears welling into his eyes, and some few minutes had been required for him to compose himself into proper Jedi serenity.

After a time, Yoda's eyes had slowly opened and the deep furrows on his ancient brow had deepened further. "Premonitions . . . premonitions . . . deep questions they are. Sense the future, once all Jedi could; now few alone have this skill. Visions . . . gifts from the Force, and curses. Signposts and snares. These visions of yours . . ."

"They are of pain," Anakin had said. "Of suffering."

He had barely been able to make himself add: "And death."

"In these troubled times, no surprise this is. Yourself you see, or someone you know?"

Anakin had not trusted himself to answer.

"Someone close to you?" Yoda had prompted gently.

"Yes," Anakin had replied, eyes turned away from Yoda's too-wise stare. Let him think he was talking about Obi-Wan. It was close enough.

Yoda's voice was still gentle, and understanding. "The fear of loss is a path to the dark side, young one."

"I won't let my visions come true, Master. I *won't*."

"Rejoice for those who transform into the Force. Mourn them not. Miss them not."

"Then why do we fight at all, Master? Why save *anybody*?"

"Speaking of *anybody*, we are not," Yoda had said sternly. "Speaking of you, and your vision, and your *fear*, we are. The shadow of greed, attachment is. What you fear to lose, train yourself to release. Let go of fear, and loss cannot harm you."

Which was when Anakin had realized Yoda wasn't going to be any help at all. The greatest sage of the Jedi Order had nothing better to offer him than more pious babble about Letting Things Pass Out Of His Life.

Like he hadn't heard that a million times already.

Easy for *him*—who had *Yoda* ever cared about? *Really* cared about? Of one thing Anakin was certain: the ancient Master had never been in love.

Or he would have known better than to expect Anakin to just fold his hands and close his eyes and settle in to *meditate* while what was left of Padmé's life evaporated like the ghost-mist of dew in a Tatooine winter dawn . . .

So all that had been left for him was to find some way to respectfully extricate himself.

And then go find Obi-Wan.

Because he wasn't about to give up. Not in this millennium.

The Jedi Temple was the greatest nexus of Force energy in the Republic; its ziggurat design focused the Force the way a lightsaber's gemstone focused its energy stream. With the thousands of Jedi and Padawans within it every day contemplating peace, seeking knowledge, and meditating on justice and surrender to the will of the Force, the Temple was a fountain of the light.

Just being on its rooftop landing deck sent a surge of power through Anakin's whole body; if the Force was ever to show him a way to change the dark future of his nightmares, it would do so here.

The Jedi Temple also contained the archives, the vast library that encompassed the Order's entire twenty-five millennia of existence: everything from the widest-ranging cosmographical surveys to the intimate journals of a billion Jedi Knights. It was there Anakin hoped to find everything that was known about prophetic dreams—and everything that was known about preventing these prophecies from coming to pass.

His only problem was that the deepest secrets of the greatest Masters of the Force were stored in restricted holocrons; since the Lorian Nod affair, some seventy standard years before, access to these holocrons was denied to all but Jedi Masters.

And he couldn't exactly explain to the archives Master why he wanted them.

But now here was Obi-Wan—Obi-Wan would help him, Anakin *knew* he would—if only Anakin could figure out the right way to ask . . .

While he was still hunting for words, Obi-Wan reached him. "You missed the report on the Outer Rim sieges."

"I—was held up," Anakin said. "I have no excuse."

That, at least, was true.

"Is Palpatine here?" Anakin asked. It was a convenient-enough way to change the subject. "Has something happened?"

"Quite the opposite," Obi-Wan said. "That shuttle did not bring the Chancellor. It is waiting to bring *you* to *him*."

"Waiting? For *me*?" Anakin frowned. Worries and lack of sleep had his head full of fog; he couldn't make this make sense. He patted his robes vacantly. "But—my beacon hasn't gone off. If the Council wanted me, why didn't they—"

"The Council," Obi-Wan said, "has not been consulted."

"I don't understand."

"Nor do I." Obi-Wan stepped close, nodding minutely back

toward the shuttle. "They simply arrived, some time ago. When the deck-duty Padawans questioned them, they said the Chancellor has requested your presence."

"Why wouldn't he go through the Council?"

"Perhaps he has some reason to believe," Obi-Wan said carefully, "that the Council might have resisted sending you. Perhaps he did not wish to reveal his reason for this summons. Relations between the Council and the Chancellor are . . . stressed."

A queasy knot began to tie itself behind Anakin's ribs. "Obi-Wan, what's going on? Something's wrong, isn't it? You know something, I can tell."

"Know? No: only suspect. Which is not at all the same thing."

Anakin remembered what he'd said to Padmé about exactly that last night. The queasy knot tightened. "And?"

"And that's why I am out here, Anakin. So I can talk to you. Privately. *Not* as a member of the Jedi Council—in fact, if the Council were to find out about this conversation . . . well, let's say, I'd rather they didn't."

"*What* conversation? I still don't know what's going on!"

"None of us does. Not really." Obi-Wan put a hand on Anakin's shoulder and frowned deeply into his eyes. "Anakin, you know I am your friend."

"Of course you are—"

"No. No *of courses*, Anakin. Nothing is *of course* anymore. I am your friend, and *as* your friend, I am asking you: be wary of Palpatine."

"What do you mean?"

"I know you are *his* friend. I am concerned that he may not be yours. Be careful of him, Anakin. And be careful of your own feelings."

"Careful? Don't you mean, *mindful?*"

Obi-Wan's frown deepened. "No. I don't. The Force grows ever darker around us, and we are all affected by it, even as we affect it. This is a dangerous time to be a Jedi. Please, Anakin—please be *careful*."

Anakin tried for his old rakish smile. "You worry too much."

"I *have* to—"

"—because I don't worry at all, right?" Anakin finished for him.

Obi-Wan's frown softened toward a smile. "How did you know I was going to say that?"

"You're wrong, you know." Anakin stared off through the morning haze toward the shuttle, past the shuttle—

Toward 500 Republica, and Padmé's apartment.

He said, "I worry plenty."

The ride to Palpatine's office was quietly tense. Anakin had tried making conversation with the two tall helmet-masked figures in the red robes, but they weren't exactly chatty.

Anakin's discomfort only increased when he arrived at Palpatine's office. He had been here so often that he didn't even really see it, most times: the deep red runner that matched the softly curving walls, the long comfortable couches, the huge arc of window behind Palpatine's desk—these were all so familiar that they were usually almost invisible, but today—

Today, with Obi-Wan's voice whispering *be wary of Palpatine* in the back of his head, everything looked different. New. And not in a good way.

Some indefinable gloom shrouded everything, as though the orbital mirrors that focused the light of Coruscant's distant sun into bright daylight had somehow been damaged, or smudged with the brown haze of smoke that still shrouded the cityscape. The light of the Chancellor's lampdisks seemed brighter than usual, almost harsh, but somehow that only deepened the gloom. He discovered now an odd, accidental echo of memory, a new harmonic resonance inside his head, when he looked at the curving view wall that threw into silhouette the Chancellor's single large chair.

Palpatine's office reminded him of the General's Quarters on *Invisible Hand*.

And it struck him as unaccountably sinister that the robes worn by the Chancellor's cadre of bodyguards were the exact color of Palpatine's carpet.

Palpatine himself stood at the view wall, hands clasped behind him, gazing out upon the smoke-hazed morning.

"Anakin." He must have seen Anakin's reflection in the curve of transparisteel; he had not moved. "Join me."

Anakin came up beside him, mirroring his stance. Endless cityscape stretched away before them. Here and there, the remains of shattered buildings still smoldered. Space lane traffic was beginning to return to normal, and rivers of gnat-like speeders and air taxis and repulsor buses crisscrossed the city. In the near distance, the vast dome of the Galactic Senate squatted like a gigantic gray mushroom sprung from the duracrete plain that was Republic Plaza. Farther, dim in the brown haze, he could pick out the quintuple spires that topped the ziggurat of the Jedi Temple.

"Do you see, Anakin?" Palpatine's voice was soft, hoarse with emotion. "Do you see what they have done to our magnificent city? This war *must* end. We cannot allow such . . . such . . ."

His voice trailed away, and he shook his head. Gently, Anakin laid a hand on Palpatine's shoulder, and a hint of frown fleeted over his face at how frail seemed the flesh and bone beneath the robe. "You know you have my best efforts, and those of every Jedi," he said.

Palpatine nodded, lowering his head. "I know I have yours, Anakin. The rest of the Jedi . . ." He sighed. He looked even more exhausted than he had yesterday. Perhaps he had passed a sleepless night as well.

"I have asked you here," he said slowly, "because I need your help on a matter of extreme delicacy. I hope I can depend upon your discretion, Anakin."

Anakin went still for a moment, then he very slowly lifted his hand from the Chancellor's shoulder.

Be wary of Palpatine

"As a Jedi, there are . . . limits . . . to my discretion, Chancellor."

"Oh, of course. Don't worry, my boy." A flash of his familiar fatherly smile forced its way into his eyes. "Anakin, in all the years we have been friends, have I ever asked you to do anything even the slightest bit against your conscience?"

"Well—"

"And I never will. I am very proud of your accomplishments as a Jedi, Anakin. You have won many battles the Jedi Council insisted to me were already lost—and you saved my *life*. It's frankly appalling that they still keep you off the Council yourself."

"My time will come . . . when I am older. And, I suppose, wiser." He didn't want to get into this with Palpatine; talking with the Chancellor like this—seriously, man-to-man—made him feel good, feel strong, despite Obi-Wan's warning. He certainly didn't want to start whining about being passed over for Mastery like some preadolescent Padawan who hadn't been chosen for a scramball team.

"Nonsense. Age is no measure of wisdom. They keep you off the Council because it is the last hold they have on you, Anakin; it is how they control you. Once you're a Master, as you deserve, how will they make you do their bidding?"

"Well . . ." Anakin gave him a half-sheepish smile. "They can't exactly *make* me, even now."

"I know, my boy. I know. That is precisely the point. You are not like them. You are younger. Stronger. *Better.* If they cannot control you now, what will happen once you are a Master in your own right? How will they keep your toes on their political line? You may become more powerful than all of them together. That is why they keep you down. They fear your power. They fear *you*."

Anakin looked down. This had struck a little close to the bone. "I have sensed . . . something like that."

"I have asked you here today, Anakin, because I have fears of my own." He turned, waiting, until Anakin met his eye, and on Palpatine's face was something approaching bleak despair. "I am coming to fear the Jedi themselves."

"Oh, Chancellor—" Anakin broke into a smile of disbelief. "There is no one more loyal than the Jedi, sir—surely, after all this time—"

But Palpatine had already turned away. He lowered himself into the chair behind his desk and kept his head down as though he was ashamed to say this directly to Anakin's face. "The Council keeps pushing for more control. More autonomy. They have lost all respect for the rule of law. They have become more concerned with avoiding the oversight of the Senate than with winning the war."

"With respect, sir, many on the Council would say the same of *you*." He thought of Obi-Wan, and he had to stop himself from wincing. Had he betrayed a confidence just now?

Or had Obi-Wan been doing the Council's bidding after all? . . . *Be wary of Palpatine,* he'd said, and *be careful of your feelings . . .*

Were these honest warnings, out of concern for him? Or had they been *calculated:* seeds of doubt planted to hedge Anakin away from the one man who really understood him?

The one man he could really trust . . .

"Oh, I have no doubt of it," Palpatine was saying. "Many of the Jedi on your Council would prefer I was out of office altogether—because they know I'm on to them, now. They're shrouded in secrecy, obsessed with covert action against mysteriously faceless enemies—"

"Well, the Sith are hardly faceless, are they? I mean, Dooku himself—"

"Was he truly a Lord of the Sith? Or was he just another in your string of fallen Jedi, posturing with a red lightsaber to intimidate you?"

"I . . ." Anakin frowned. How could he be sure? "But *Sidious* . . ."

"Ah, yes, the mysterious Lord Sidious. 'The *Sith infiltrator* in the *highest* levels of *government.*' Doesn't that sound a little overly familiar to you, Anakin? A little overly *convenient*? How do you know this Sidious even exists? How do you know he is not a *fiction*, a fiction created by the Jedi Council, to give them an excuse to harass their political enemies?"

"The Jedi are not political—"

"In a democracy, *everything* is political, Anakin. And everyone. This imaginary Sith Lord of theirs—even if he does exist, is he anyone to be feared? To be hunted down and exterminated without trial?"

"The Sith are the definition of evil—"

"Or so you have been trained to believe. I have been reading about the history of the Sith for some years now, Anakin. Ever since the Council saw fit to finally reveal to me their . . . *assertion* . . . that these millennium-dead sorcerers had supposedly sprung back to life. Not every tale about them is sequestered in your conveniently secret Temple archives. From what I have read, they were not so different from Jedi; seeking power, to be sure, but so does your Council."

"The dark side—"

"Oh, yes, yes, certainly, the dark side. Listen to me: if this 'Darth Sidious' of yours were to walk through *that* door right *now*—and I could somehow stop you from killing him on the spot—do you know what I would do?"

Palpatine rose, and his voice rose with him. "I would ask him to *sit down,* and I would ask him if he has any power he could use to *end this war!*"

"You would—you would—" Anakin couldn't quite make himself believe what he was hearing. The blood-red rug beneath his feet seemed to shift under him, and his head was starting to spin.

"And if he said he *did,* I'd bloody well offer him a *brandy* and *talk it out!*"

"You—Chancellor, you can't be *serious*—"

"Well, not entirely." Palpatine sighed, and shrugged, and lowered himself once more into his chair. "It's only an example, Anakin. I would do anything to return peace to the galaxy, do you understand? That's all I mean. After all—" He offered a tired, sadly ironic smile. "—what are the chances of an actual Sith Lord ever walking through that door?"

"I wouldn't know," Anakin said feelingly, "but I do know that you probably shouldn't use that . . . *example* . . . in front of the Jedi Council."

"Oh, yes." Palpatine chuckled. "Yes, quite right. They might take it as an excuse to accuse *me.*"

"I'm sure they'd never do *that*—"

"I am not. I am no longer sure they'll stop at anything, Anakin. That's actually the reason I asked you here today." He leaned forward intently, resting his elbows on the desk. "You may have heard that this afternoon, the Senate will call upon this office to assume direct control of the Jedi Council."

Anakin's frown deepened. "The Jedi will no longer report to the Senate?"

"They will report to me. Personally. The Senate is too unfocused to conduct this war; we've seen this for years. Now that this office will be the single authority to direct the prosecution of the war, we'll bring a quick end to things."

Anakin nodded. "I can see how that will help, sir, but the

Council probably won't. I can tell you that they are in no mood for further constitutional amendments."

"Yes, thank you, my friend. But in this case, I have no choice. This war must be won."

"Everyone agrees on that."

"I hope they do, my boy. I hope they do."

Inside his head, he heard the echo of Obi-Wan, murmuring *relations between the Council and the Chancellor are . . . stressed.* What had been going on, here in the capital?

Weren't they all on the same side?

"I can assure you," he said firmly, "that the Jedi are absolutely dedicated to the core values of the Republic."

One of Palpatine's eyebrows arched. "Their actions will speak more loudly than their words—as long as someone keeps an eye on them. And that, my boy, is exactly the favor I must ask of you."

"I don't understand."

"Anakin, I am asking you—as a personal favor to me, in respect for our long friendship—to accept a post as my personal representative on the Jedi Council."

Anakin blinked.

He blinked again.

He said, "Me?"

"Who else?" Palpatine spread his hands in a melancholy shrug. "You are the only Jedi I know, truly *know*, that I can trust. I *need* you, my boy. There is no one else who can do this job: to be the eyes and ears—and the voice—of the Republic on the Jedi Council."

"On the Council . . . ," Anakin murmured.

He could see himself seated in one of the low, curving chairs, opposite Mace Windu. Opposite *Yoda*. He might sit next to Ki-Adi-Mundi, or Plo Koon—or even beside Obi-Wan! And he could not quite ignore the quiet whisper, from down within the furnace doors that sealed his heart, that he was about to become the youngest Master in the twenty-five-thousand-year history of the Jedi Order . . .

But none of that really mattered.

Palpatine had somehow seen into his secret heart, and had chosen to offer him the one thing he most desired in all the galaxy. He didn't care about the Council, not really—that was a childish dream. He didn't need the Council. He didn't need recognition, and he didn't need respect. What he needed was the rank itself.

All that mattered was Mastery.

All that mattered was Padmé.

This was a gift beyond gifts: as a Master, he could access those forbidden holocrons in the restricted vault.

He could find a way to save her from his dream . . .

He shook himself back to the present. "I . . . am overwhelmed, sir. But the Council elects its own members. They will never accept this."

"I promise you they will," Palpatine murmured imperturbably. He swung his chair around to gaze out the window toward the distant spires of the Temple. "They need you more than they realize. All it will take is for someone to properly . . ."

He waved a hand expressively.

". . . *explain* it to them."

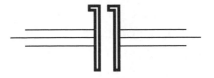

POLITICS

Orbital mirrors rotated, resolving the faint light of Coruscant's sun to erase the stars; fireships crosshatched the sky with contrails of chemical air scrubber, bleaching away the last reminders of the fires of days past; chill remnants of night slid down the High Council Tower of the Jedi Temple; and within the cloistered chamber itself, Obi-Wan was still trying to talk them out of it.

"Yes, of course I trust him," he said patiently. "We can always trust Anakin to do what he thinks is right. But we *can't* trust him to do what he's *told*. He can't be made to simply *obey*. Believe me: I've been trying for many years."

Conflicting currents of energy swirled and clashed in the Council Chamber. Traditionally, decisions of the Council were reached by quiet, mutual contemplation of the flow of the Force, until all the Council was of a single mind on the matter. But Obi-Wan knew of this tradition only by reputation, from tales in the archives and stories told by Masters whose tenure on the Council predated the return of the Sith. In the all-too-short years since Obi-Wan's own elevation, argument in this Chamber was more the rule than the exception.

"An unintentional opportunity, the Chancellor has given us," Yoda said gravely. "A window he has opened into the operations of his office. Fools we would be, to close our eyes."

"Then we should use someone else's eyes," Obi-Wan said. "Forgive me, Master Yoda, but you just don't know him the way I do. None of you does. He is *fiercely* loyal, and there is not a gram of deception in him. You've all seen it; it's one of the arguments that some of you, here in this room, have used against elevating him to Master: he *lacks true Jedi reserve,* that's what you've said. And by that we all mean that he wears his emotions like a HoloNet banner. How can you ask him to lie to a friend— to *spy* upon him?"

"That is why we must call upon a friend to ask him," said Agen Kolar in his gentle Zabrak baritone.

"You don't understand. Don't make him choose between me and Palpatine—"

"Why not?" asked the holopresence of Plo Koon from the bridge of *Courageous,* where he directed the Republic Navy strike force against the Separatist choke point in the Ywllandr system. *"Do you fear you would lose such a contest?"*

"You don't know how much Palpatine's friendship has meant to him over the years. You're asking him to use that friendship as a weapon! To stab his friend in the back. Don't you understand what this will cost him, even if Palpatine is entirely innocent? *Especially* if he's innocent. Their relationship will never be the same—"

"And that," Mace Windu said, "may be the best argument in favor of this plan. I have told you all what I have seen of the energy between Skywalker and the Supreme Chancellor. Anything that might distance young Skywalker from Palpatine's influence is worth the attempt."

Obi-Wan didn't need to reach into the Force to know that he would lose this argument. He inclined his head. "I will, of course, abide by the ruling of this Council."

"Doubt of that, none of us has." Yoda turned his green gaze on the other councilors. "But if to be done this is, decide we must how best to use him."

The holopresence of Ki-Adi-Mundi flickered in and out of focus as the Cerean Master leaned forward, folding his hands. *"I, too, have reservations on this matter, but it seems that in these desperate times, only desperate plans have hope of success. We have seen that young Skywalker has the power to battle a Sith Lord alone, if need be; he has proven that with Dooku. If he is indeed the chosen one, we must keep him in play against the Sith—keep him in a position to fulfill his destiny."*

"And even if the prophecy has been misread," Agen Kolar added, "Anakin is the one Jedi we can best hope would survive an encounter with a Sith Lord. So let us also use him to help us set our trap. In Council, let us emphasize that we are intensifying our search for Grievous. Anakin will certainly report this to the Chancellor's Office. Perhaps, as you say, that will draw Sidious into action."

"It may not be enough," Mace Windu said. "Let us take this one step farther—we should appear shorthanded, and weak, giving Sidious an opening to make a move he thinks will go unobserved. I'm thinking that perhaps we should let the Chancellor's Office know that Yoda and I have both been forced to take the field—"

"Too risky that is," Yoda said. "And too convenient. One of us only should go."

"Then it should be you, Master Yoda," Agen Kolar said. "It is your sensitivity to the broader currents of the Force that a Sith Lord has most reason to fear."

Obi-Wan felt the ripple of agreement flow through the Chamber, and Yoda nodded solemnly. "The Separatist attack on Kashyyyk, a compelling excuse will make. And good relations with the Wookiees I have; destroy the droid armies I can, and still be available to Coruscant, should Sidious take our bait."

"Agreed." Mace Windu looked around the half-empty Council Chamber with a deepening frown. "And one last touch. Let's let the Chancellor know, through Anakin, that our most cunning and insightful Master—and our most tenacious—is to lead the hunt for Grievous."

"So Sidious will need to act, and act fast, if the war is to be maintained," Plo Koon added approvingly.

Yoda nodded judiciously. "Agreed." Agen Kolar assented as well, and Ki-Adi-Mundi.

"This sounds like a good plan," Obi-Wan said. "But what Master do you have in mind?"

For a moment no one spoke, as though astonished he would ask such a question.

Only after a few seconds in which Obi-Wan looked from the faces of one Master to the next, puzzled by the expressions of gentle amusement each and every one of them wore, did it finally register that all of them were looking at *him*.

Bail Organa stopped cold in the middle of the Grand Concourse that ringed the Senate's Convocation Chamber. The torrent of multispecies foot traffic that streamed along the huge curving hall broke around him like a river around a boulder. He stared up in disbelief at one of the huge holoprojected Proclamation Boards; these had recently been installed above the concourse to keep the thousands of Senators up to the moment on news of the war, and on the Chancellor's latest executive orders.

His heart tripped, and he couldn't seem to make his eyes focus. He pushed his way through the press to a hardcopy stand and punched a quick code. When he had the flimsies in his hands, they still said the same thing.

He'd been expecting this day. Since yesterday, when the Senate had voted to give Palpatine control of the Jedi, he'd known it would come soon. He'd even started planning for it.

But that didn't make it any easier to bear.

He found his way to a public comm booth and keyed a privacy code. The transparisteel booth went opaque as stone, and a moment later a hand-sized image shimmered into existence above the small holodisk: a slender woman in floor-length white, with short, neatly clipped auburn hair and a clear, steadily intelligent gaze from her aquamarine eyes. *"Bail,"* she said. *"What's happened?"*

Bail's elegantly thin goatee pulled downward around his mouth. "Have you seen this morning's decree?"

"The Sector Governance Decree? Yes, I have—"

"It's time, Mon," he said grimly. "It's time to stop talking, and start *doing.* We have to bring in the Senate."

"I agree, but we must tread carefully. Have you thought about whom we should consult? Whom we can trust?"

"Not in detail. Giddean Danu springs to mind. I'm sure we can trust Fang Zar, too."

"Agreed. What about Iridik'k-stallu? Her hearts are in the right place. Or Chi Eekway."

Bail shook his head. "Maybe later. It'll take a few hours at least to figure out exactly where they stand. We need to start with Senators we *know* we can trust."

"All right. Then Terr Taneel would be my next choice. And, I think, Amidala of Naboo."

"Padmé?" Bail frowned. "I'm not sure."

"You know her better than I do, Bail, but to my mind she is exactly the type of Senator we need. She is intelligent, principled, extremely articulate, and she has the heart of a warrior."

"She is also a longtime associate of Palpatine," he reminded her. "He was her ambassador during her term as Queen of Naboo. How sure can you be that she will stand with us, and not with him?"

Senator Mon Mothma replied serenely, *"There's only one way to find out."*

By the time the doors to the Jedi Council Chamber finally swung open, Anakin was already angry.

If asked, he would have denied it, and would have thought he was telling the truth . . . but they had left him out here for so *long*, with nothing to do but stare through the soot-smudged curve of the High Council Tower's window ring at the scarred skyline of Galactic City—damaged in a battle *he* had won, by the way, *personally*. Almost *single-handedly*—and with nothing to think about except why it was taking them so long to reach such a simple decision . . .

Angry? Not at all. He was sure he wasn't angry. He kept telling himself he wasn't angry, and he made himself believe it.

Anakin walked into the Council Chamber, head lowered in a show of humility and respect. But down inside him, down around the nuclear shielding that banked his heart, he was hiding.

It wasn't anger he was hiding. His anger was only camouflage.

Behind his anger hid the dragon.

He remembered too well the first time he had entered this Chamber, the first time he had stood within a ring of Jedi Masters gathered to sit in judgment upon his fate. He remembered how Yoda's green stare had seen into his heart, had seen the cold worm of dread eating away at him, no matter how hard he'd tried to deny it: the awful fear he'd felt that he might never see his mother again.

He couldn't let them see what that worm had grown into.

He moved slowly into the center of the circle of brown-toned carpet, and turned toward the Senior Members.

Yoda was unreadable as always, his rumpled features composed in a mask of serene contemplation.

Mace Windu could have been carved from stone.

Ghost-images of Ki-Adi-Mundi and Plo Koon hovered a centimeter above their Council seats, maintained by the seats' internal holoprojectors. Agen Kolar sat alone, between the empty chairs belonging to Shaak Ti and Stass Allie.

Obi-Wan sat in the chair that once had belonged to Oppo Rancisis, looking pensive. Even worried.

"Anakin Skywalker." Master Windu's tone was so severe that the dragon inside Anakin coiled instinctively. "The Council has decided to comply with Chancellor Palpatine's directive, and with the instructions of the Senate that give him the unprecedented authority to command this Council. You are hereby granted a seat at the High Council of the Jedi, as the Chancellor's personal representative."

Anakin stood very still for a long moment, until he could be absolutely sure he had heard what he thought he'd heard.

Palpatine had been right. He seemed to be right about a lot of things, these days. In fact—now that Anakin came to think of it—he couldn't remember a single instance when the Supreme Chancellor had been wrong.

Finally, as it began to sink in upon him, as he gradually allowed himself to understand that the Council had finally decided to grant him his heart's desire, that they finally had recognized his accomplishments, his dedication, his *power*, he took a slow, deep breath.

"Thank you, Masters. You have my pledge that I will uphold the highest principles of the Jedi Order."

"Allow this appointment lightly, the Council does not." Yoda's ears curled forward at Anakin like accusing fingers. "Disturbing is this move by Chancellor Palpatine. On many levels."

They have become more concerned with avoiding the oversight of the Senate than they are with winning the war . . .

Anakin inclined his head. "I understand."

"I'm not sure you do." Mace Windu leaned forward, staring into Anakin's eyes with a measuring squint.

Anakin was barely paying attention; in his mind, he was already leaving the Council Chamber, riding the turbolift to the archives, demanding access to the restricted vault by authority of his new rank—

"You will attend the meetings of this Council," the Korun Master said, "but you will not be granted the rank and privileges of a Jedi Master."

"What?"

It was a small word, a simple word, an instinctive recoil from words that felt like punches, like stun blasts exploding inside his brain that left his head ringing and the room spinning around him—but even to his own ears, the voice that came from his lips didn't sound like his own. It was deeper, darker, clipped and oiled, resonating from the depths of his heart.

It didn't sound like him at all, and it smoked with fury.

"How dare you? How *dare* you?"

Anakin stood welded to the floor, motionless. He wasn't even truly aware of speaking. It was as if someone else were using his mouth—and now, finally, he recognized the voice.

It sounded like Dooku. But it was not Dooku's voice.

It was the voice of Dooku's destroyer.

"No Jedi in this room can match my power—no Jedi in the *galaxy*! You think you can deny Mastery to *me*?"

"The Chancellor's representative you are," Yoda said. "And it is as his representative you shall attend the Council. Sit in this Chamber you will, but no vote will you have. The Chancellor's views you shall present. His wishes. His ideas and directives. Not your own."

Up from the depths of his furnace heart came an answer so far transcending fury that it sounded cold as interstellar space. "This is an insult to me, and to the Chancellor. Do not imagine that it will be tolerated."

Mace Windu's eyes were as cold as the voice from Anakin's mouth. "Take your seat, young Skywalker."

Anakin matched his stare. *Perhaps I'll take yours.* His own voice, inside his head, had a hot black fire that smoked from the depths of his furnace heart. *You think you can stop me from saving my love? You think you can make me watch her die? Go ahead and Vaapad this, you—*

"Anakin," Obi-Wan said softly. He gestured to an empty seat beside him. "Please."

And something in Obi-Wan's gentle voice, in his simple, straightforward request, sent his anger slinking off ashamed, and Anakin found himself alone on the carpet in the middle of the Jedi Council, blinking.

He suddenly felt very young, and very foolish.

"Forgive me, Masters." His bow of contrition couldn't hide the blaze of embarrassment that climbed his cheeks.

The rest of the session passed in a haze; Ki-Adi-Mundi said something about no Republic world reporting any sign of Grievous, and Anakin felt a dull shock when the Council assigned the task of coordinating the search to Obi-Wan *alone*.

On top of everything else, now they were splitting up the *team?*

He was so numbly astonished by it all that he barely registered what they were saying about a droid landing on Kashyyyk—but he had to say *something*, he couldn't just *sit* here for his whole first meeting of the Council, Master or not—and he knew the Kashyyyk system almost as well as he knew the back alleys of Mos Espa. "I can handle it," he offered, suddenly brightening. "I could clear that planet in a day or two—"

"Skywalker, your assignment is *here*." Mace Windu's stare was hard as durasteel, and only a scrape short of openly hostile.

Then Yoda volunteered, and for some reason, the Council didn't even bother to vote.

"It is settled then," Mace said. "May the Force be with us all."

And as the holopresences of Plo Koon and Ki-Adi-Mundi winked out, as Obi-Wan and Agen Kolar rose and spoke together in tones softly grave, as Yoda and Mace Windu walked from the room, Anakin could only sit, sick at heart, stunned with helplessness.

Padmé—oh, Padmé, what are we going to do?

He didn't know. He didn't have a clue. But he knew one thing he *wasn't* going to do.

He wasn't going to give up.

Even with the Council against him—even with the whole *Order* against him—he would find a way.

He would save her.

Somehow.

"I am no happier than the rest of you about this," Padmé said, gesturing at the flimsiplast of the Sector Governance Decree on Bail Organa's desk. "But I've known Palpatine for years; he was my most trusted adviser. I'm not prepared to believe his intent is to dismantle the Senate."

"Why should he bother?" Mon Mothma countered. "As a practical matter—as of this morning—the Senate no longer exists."

Padmé looked from one grim face to another. Giddean Danu nodded his agreement. Terr Taneel kept her eyes down, pretending to be adjusting her robes. Fang Zar ran a hand over his unruly gray-streaked topknot.

Bail leaned forward. His eyes were hard as chips of stone. "Palpatine no longer has to worry about controlling the Senate. By placing his own lackeys as governors over every planet in the Republic, he controls our systems *directly*." He folded his hands, and squeezed them together until his knuckles hurt. "He's become a dictator. We *made* him a dictator."

And he's my husband's friend, and mentor, Padmé thought. *I shouldn't even be listening to this.*

"But what can we *do* about it?" Terr Taneel asked, still gazing down at her robe with a worried frown.

"That's what we asked you here to discuss," Mon Mothma told her calmly. "What we're going to do about it."

Fang Zar shifted uncomfortably. "I'm not sure I like where this is going."

"None of us likes where *anything* is going," Bail said, half rising. "That's exactly the point. We can't let a thousand years of democracy disappear without a fight!"

"A *fight?*" Padmé said. "I can't believe what I'm hearing— Bail, you sound like a Separatist!"

"I—" Bail sank back into his seat. "I apologize. That was not my intent. I asked you all here because of all the Senators in the galaxy, you four have been the most consistent—and *influential*— voices of reason and restraint, doing all you could to preserve our poor, tattered Constitution. We don't want to hurt the Republic. With your help, we hope to *save* it."

"It has become increasingly clear," Mon Mothma said, "that Palpatine has become an enemy of democracy. He must be stopped."

"The Senate gave him these powers," Padmé said. "The Senate can rein him in."

Giddean Danu sat forward. "I fear you underestimate just how deeply the Senate's corruption has taken hold. Who will vote against Palpatine now?"

"*I* will," Padmé said. She discovered that she meant it. "And I'll find others, too."

She'd have to. No matter how much it hurt Anakin. *Oh, my love, will you ever find a way to forgive me?*

"You do that," Bail said. "Make as much noise as you can— keep Palpatine watching what you're doing in the Senate. That should provide some cover while Mon Mothma and I begin building our organization—"

"Stop." Padmé rose. "It's better to leave some things unsaid. Right now, it's better I don't know anything about . . . anything."

Don't make me lie to my husband was her unspoken plea. She tried to convey it with her eyes. *Please, Bail. Don't make me lie to him. It will break his heart.*

Perhaps he saw something there; after a moment's indecision, he nodded. "Very well. Other matters can be left for other times. Until then, this meeting must remain absolutely secret. Even hinting at an effective opposition to Palpatine can be, as we've all seen, very dangerous. We must agree never to speak of these matters except among the people who are now in this room. We must bring no one into this secret without the agreement of each and every one of us."

"That includes even those closest to you," Mon Mothma added. "Even your families—to share anything of this will expose them to the same danger we all face. No one can be told. No one."

Padmé watched them all nod, and what could she do? What could she say? *You can keep your own secrets, but I'll have to tell my Jedi husband, who is Palpatine's beloved protégé . . .*

She sighed. "Yes. Yes: agreed."

And all she could think as the little group dispersed to their own offices was *Oh, Anakin—Anakin, I'm sorry . . .*

I'm so sorry.

Anakin was glad the vast vaulted Temple hallway was deserted save for him and Obi-Wan; he didn't have to keep his voice down.

"This is *outrageous.* How can they *do* this?"

"How can they not?" Obi-Wan countered. "It's your friendship with the Chancellor—the same friendship that got you a seat at the Council—that makes it impossible to grant you Mastery. In the Council's eyes, that would be the same as giving a vote to Palpatine himself!"

He waved this off. He didn't have time for the Council's political maneuvering—*Padmé* didn't have time. "I didn't ask for this. I don't *need* this. So if I wasn't friends with Palpatine I'd be a Master already, is that what you're saying?"

Obi-Wan looked pained. "I don't know."

"I have the power of any five Masters. Any *ten*. You know it, and so do they."

"Power alone is no credit to you—"

Anakin flung an arm back toward the Council Tower. "*They're* the ones who call me the chosen one! Chosen for what? To be a dupe in some slimy political game?"

Obi-Wan winced as if he'd been stung. "Didn't I warn you, Anakin? I told you of the . . . tension . . . between the Council and the Chancellor. I was very clear. Why didn't you *listen*? You walked right into it!"

"Like that ray shield trap." Anakin snorted. "Should I blame *this* on the dark side, too?"

"However it happened," Obi-Wan said, "you are in a very . . . delicate situation."

"*What* situation? Who cares about *me*? I'm no Master, I'm just a *kid*, right? Is that what it's about? Is Master Windu turning everyone against me because until I came along, he was the youngest Jedi ever named to the Council?"

"No one cares about that—"

"Sure they don't. Let me tell you something a smart *old* man said to me no so long ago: *Age is no measure of wisdom*. If it were, Yoda would be twenty times as wise as *you* are—"

"This has nothing to do with Master Yoda."

"That's right. It has to do with *me*. It has to do with them all being *against* me. They always *have* been—most of them didn't even want me to *be* a Jedi. And if they'd won out, where would they be right now? Who would have done the things I've done? Who would have saved Naboo? Who would have saved Kamino? Who would have killed Dooku, and rescued the Chancellor? Who would have come for you and Alpha after Ventress—"

"Yes, Anakin, yes. Of course. No one questions your accomplishments. It's your relationship to Palpatine that is the problem. And it is a very *serious* problem."

"I'm too close to him? Maybe I am. Maybe I should alienate a man who's been nothing but kind and generous to me ever since I first *came* to this planet! Maybe I should reject the only man who gives me the respect I *deserve*—"

"Anakin, stop. *Listen* to yourself. Your thoughts are of jealousy, and pride. These are dark thoughts, Anakin. Dangerous thoughts, in these dark times—you are focused on yourself when you need to focus on your service. Your outburst in the Council was an eloquent argument *against* granting you Mastery. How can you be a Jedi Master when you have not mastered yourself?"

Anakin passed his flesh hand over his eyes and drew a long, heavy breath. In a much lower, calmer, quieter tone, he said, "What do I have to do?"

Obi-Wan frowned. "I'm sorry?"

"They want something from me, don't they? That's what this is really about. That's what it's been about from the beginning. They won't give me my rank until I give them what they want."

"The Council does not operate that way, Anakin, and you know it."

Once you're a Master, as you deserve, how will they make you do their bidding?

"Yes, I know it. Sure I do," Anakin said. Suddenly he was tired. So incredibly tired. It hurt to talk. It hurt even to stand here. He was sick of the whole business. Why couldn't it just be *over*? "Tell me what they want."

Obi-Wan's eyes shifted, and the sick fatigue in Anakin's guts turned darker. How bad did it have to be to make Obi-Wan unable to look him in the eye?

"Anakin, look, I'm on your side," Obi-Wan said softly. He looked tired, too: he looked as tired and sick as Anakin felt. "I never wanted to see you put in this situation."

"What situation?"

Still Obi-Wan hesitated.

Anakin said, "Look, whatever it is, it's not getting any better while you're standing here working up the nerve to tell me. Come on, Obi-Wan. Let's have it."

Obi-Wan glanced around the empty hall as if he wanted to make sure they were still alone; Anakin had a feeling it was just an excuse to avoid facing him when he spoke.

"The Council," Obi-Wan said slowly, "approved your appointment because Palpatine trusts you. They want you to report on all his dealings. They have to know what he's up to."

"They want me to *spy* on the *Supreme Chancellor of the Republic?*" Anakin blinked numbly. No wonder Obi-Wan couldn't look him in the face. "Obi-Wan, that's *treason!*"

"We are at war, Anakin." Obi-Wan looked thoroughly miserable. "The Council is sworn to uphold the principles of the Republic through any means necessary. We *have* to. Especially when the greatest enemy of those principles seems to be the Chancellor himself!"

Anakin's eyes narrowed and turned hard. "Why didn't the Council give me this assignment while we were in session?"

"Because it's not for the record, Anakin. You must be able to understand why."

"What I understand," Anakin said grimly, "is that you are trying to turn me against Palpatine. You're trying to make me keep *secrets* from him—you want to make me *lie* to him. That's what this is *really* about."

"It *isn't,*" Obi-Wan insisted. He looked wounded. "It's about keeping an eye on who he deals with, and who deals with him."

"He's not a bad man, Obi-Wan—he's a *great* man, who's holding this Republic together with his bare *hands*—"

"By staying in office long after his term has expired. By gathering dictatorial powers—"

"The Senate *demanded* that he stay! They *pushed* those powers on him—"

"Don't be naïve. The Senate is so intimidated they give him anything he wants!"

"Then it's *their* fault, not his! They should have the guts to stand up to him!"

"That is what we're asking *you* to do, Anakin."

Anakin had no answer. Silence fell between them like a hammer.

He shook his head and looked down at the fist he had made of his mechanical hand.

Finally, he said, "He's my *friend*, Obi-Wan."

"Yes," Obi-Wan said softly. Sadly. "I know."

"If *he* asked me to spy on *you*, do you think I would do it?"

Now it was Obi-Wan's turn to fall silent.

"You know how kind he has been to me." Anakin's voice was hushed. "You know how he's looked after me, how he's done everything he could to help me. He's like *family*."

"The *Jedi* are your family—"

"No." Anakin turned on his former Master. "No, the Jedi are *your* family. The only one you've ever known. But I'm not *like* you—I had a mother who *loved* me—"

And a wife who loves me, he thought. *And soon a child who will love me, too.*

"Do you *remember* my mother? Do you remember what *happened* to her—?"

—because you didn't let me go to save her? he finished silently. *And the same will happen to Padmé, and the same will happen to our child.*

Within him, the dragon's cold whisper chewed at his strength. *All things die, Anakin Skywalker. Even stars burn out.*

"Anakin, yes. Of course. You know how sorry I am for your mother. Listen: we're not asking you to act against Palpatine. We're only asking you to . . . monitor his activities. You must believe me."

Obi-Wan stepped closer and put a hand on Anakin's arm. With a long, slowly indrawn breath, he seemed to reach some difficult decision. "Palpatine himself may be in danger," he said. "This may be the only way you can help him."

"What are you talking about?"

"I am not supposed to be telling you this. Please do not reveal we have had this conversation. To *anyone,* do you understand?"

Anakin said, "I can keep a secret."

"All right." Obi-Wan took another deep breath. "Master Windu traced Darth Sidious to Five Hundred Republica before Grievous's attack—we think that the Sith Lord is someone within Palpatine's closest circle of advisers. *That* is who we want you to spy on, do you understand?"

A fiction created by the Jedi Council . . . an excuse to harass their political enemies . . .

"If Palpatine is under the influence of a Sith Lord, he may be in the gravest danger. The only way we can help him is to find Sidious, and to stop him. What we are asking of you is *not* treason, Anakin—it may be the only way to save the Republic!"

If this Darth Sidious of yours were to walk through that door right now . . . I would ask him to sit down, and I would ask him if he has any power he could use to end this war

"So all you're really asking," Anakin said slowly, "is for me to help the Council find Darth Sidious."

"Yes." Obi-Wan looked relieved, incredibly relieved, as though some horrible chronic pain had suddenly and inexplicably eased. "Yes, that's it exactly."

Locked within the furnace of his heart, Anakin whispered an

echo—not quite an echo—slightly altered, just at the end: *I would ask him to sit down, and I would ask him if he has any power he could use*—

—*to save Padmé.*

The gunship streaked through the capital's sky.

Obi-Wan stared past Yoda and Mace Windu, out through the gunship's window at the vast deployment platform and the swarm of clones who were loading the assault cruiser at the far end.

"You weren't there," he said. "You didn't see his face. I think we have done a terrible thing."

"We don't always have the right answer," Mace Windu said. "Sometimes there *isn't* a right answer."

"Know how important your friendship with young Anakin is to you, I do." Yoda, too, stared out toward the stark angles of the assault cruiser being loaded for the counterinvasion of Kashyyyk; he stood leaning on his gimer stick as though he did not trust his legs. "Allow such attachments to pass out of one's life, a Jedi must."

Another man—even another Jedi—might have resented the rebuke, but Obi-Wan only sighed. "I suppose—he is the chosen one, after all. The prophecy says he was born to bring balance to the Force, but . . ."

The words trailed off. He couldn't remember what he'd been about to say. All he could remember was the look on Anakin's face.

"Yes. Always in motion, the future is." Yoda lifted his head and his eyes narrowed to thoughtful slits. "And the prophecy, misread it could have been."

Mace looked even grimmer than usual. "Since the fall of Darth Bane more than a millennium ago, there have been hundreds of thousands of Jedi—hundreds of thousands of Jedi feeding the light with each work of their hands, with each breath, with every beat of their hearts, bringing justice, building civil society, radiating peace, acting out of selfless love for all living things—and in all these thousand years, there have been only two Sith at any time. Only two. Jedi create light, but the Sith do not create darkness. They merely use the darkness that is always there. That has always been there. Greed and jealousy, aggression and lust and fear—these are all natural to sentient beings. The legacy of the jungle. Our inheritance from the dark."

"I'm sorry, Master Windu, but I'm not sure I follow you. Are you saying—to follow your metaphor—that the Jedi have cast too much light? From what I have seen these past years, the galaxy has not become all that bright a place."

"All I am saying is that we don't *know*. We don't even truly understand what it *means* to *bring balance to the Force*. We have no way of anticipating what this may involve."

"An infinite mystery is the Force," Yoda said softly. "The more we learn, the more we discover how much we do not know."

"So you both feel it, too," Obi-Wan said. The words hurt him. "You both can feel that we have turned some invisible corner."

"In motion, are the events of our time. Approach, the crisis does."

"Yes." Mace interlaced his fingers and squeezed until his knuckles popped. "But we're in a spice mine without a glow rod. If we stop walking, we'll never reach the light."

"And what if the light just isn't there?" Obi-Wan asked. "What if we get to the end of this tunnel and find only night?"

"Faith must we have. Trust in the will of the Force. What other choice is there?"

Obi-Wan accepted this with a nod, but still when he thought of Anakin, dread began to curdle below his heart. "I should have argued more strongly in Council today."

"You think Skywalker won't be able to handle this?" Mace Windu said. "I thought you had more confidence in his abilities."

"I trust him with my life," Obi-Wan said simply. "And that is precisely the problem."

The other two Jedi Masters watched him silently while he tried to summon the proper words.

"For Anakin," Obi-Wan said at length, "there is nothing more important than friendship. He is the most loyal man I have ever met—loyal beyond reason, in fact. Despite all I have tried to teach him about the sacrifices that are the heart of being a Jedi, he—he will never, I think, truly understand."

He looked over at Yoda. "Master Yoda, you and I have been close since I was a boy. An infant. Yet if ending this war one week sooner—one *day* sooner—were to require that I sacrifice your life, you know I would."

"As you should," Yoda said. "As I would yours, young Obi-Wan. As any Jedi would any other, in the cause of peace."

"Any Jedi," Obi-Wan said, "except Anakin."

Yoda and Mace exchanged glances, both thoughtfully grim. Obi-Wan guessed they were remembering the times Anakin had violated orders—the times he had put at risk entire operations, the lives of thousands, the control of whole planetary systems— to save a friend.

More than once, in fact, to save Obi-Wan.

"I think," Obi-Wan said carefully, "that abstractions like *peace* don't mean much to him. He's loyal to *people,* not to principles. And he expects loyalty in return. He will stop at nothing to save me, for example, because he thinks I would do the same for him."

Mace and Yoda gazed at him steadily, and Obi-Wan had to lower his head.

"Because," he admitted reluctantly, "he *knows* I would do the same for him."

"Understand exactly where your concern lies, I do not." Yoda's green eyes had gone softly sympathetic. "*Named* must your fear be, before banish it you can. Do you fear that perform his task, he cannot?"

"Oh, no. That's not it at all. I am firmly convinced that Anakin can do anything. Except betray a friend. What we have done to him today . . ."

"But that is what Jedi *are*," Mace Windu said. "That is what we have pledged ourselves to: selfless service—"

Obi-Wan turned to stare once more toward the assault ship that would carry Yoda and the clone battalions to Kashyyyk, but he could see only Anakin's face.

If he *asked me to spy on* you, *do you think I would do it?*

"Yes," he said slowly. "That's why I don't think he will ever trust us again."

He found his eyes turning unaccountably hot, and his vision swam with unshed tears.

"And I'm not entirely sure he should."

NOT FROM A JEDI

The sunset over Galactic City was stunning tonight: enough particulates from the fires remained in the capital planet's atmosphere to splinter the light of its distant blue-white sun into a prismatic smear across multilayered clouds.

Anakin barely noticed.

On the broad curving veranda that doubled as the landing deck for Padmé's apartment, he watched from the shadows as Padmé stepped out of her speeder and graciously accepted Captain Typho's good night. As Typho flew the vehicle off toward the immense residential tower's speeder park, she dismissed her two handmaidens and sent C-3PO on some busywork errand, then turned to lean on the veranda's balcony right where Anakin had leaned last night.

She gazed out on the sunset, but he gazed only at her.

This was all he needed. To be here, to be with her. To watch the sunset bring a blush to her ivory skin.

If not for his dreams, he'd withdraw from the Order today. Now. The Lost Twenty would be the Lost Twenty-One. Let the scandal come; it wouldn't destroy their lives. Not their real lives.

It would destroy only the lives they'd had before each other: those separate years that now meant nothing at all.

He said softly, "Beautiful, isn't it?"

She jumped as if he'd pricked her with a needle. "Anakin!"

"I'm sorry." He smiled fondly as he moved out from the shadows. "I didn't mean to startle you."

She held one hand pressed to her chest as though to keep her heart from leaping out. "No—no, it's all right. I just—Anakin, you shouldn't be out here. It's still *daylight*—"

"I couldn't wait, Padmé. I had to see you." He took her in his arms. "Tonight is *forever* from now—how am I supposed to live that long without you?"

Her hand went from her chest to his. "But we're in full view of a million people, and you're a very famous man. Let's go inside."

He drew her back from the edge of the veranda, but made no move to enter the apartment. "How are you feeling?"

Her smile was radiant as Tatooine's primary as she took his flesh hand and pressed it to the soft fullness of her belly. "He keeps kicking."

"He?" Anakin asked mildly. "I thought you'd ordered your medical droid not to spoil the surprise."

"Oh, I didn't get this from the Emdee. It's my . . ." Her smile went softly sly. ". . . motherly intuition."

He felt a sudden pulse against his palm and laughed. "Motherly intuition, huh? With a kick that hard? Definitely a girl."

She laid her head against his chest. "Anakin, let's go inside."

He nuzzled her gleaming coils of hair. "I can't stay. I'm on my way to meet with the Chancellor."

"Yes, I heard about your appointment to the Council. Anakin, I'm so proud of you."

He lifted his head, an instant scowl gathering on his forehead. Why did she have to bring that up?

"There's nothing to be proud of," he said. "This is just political maneuvering between the Council and the Chancellor. I
got caught in the middle, that's all."

"But to be on the Council, at your age—"

"They put me on the Council because they *had* to. Because
he told them to, once the Senate gave him control of the Jedi."
His voice lowered toward a growl. "And because they think they
can use me against him."

Padmé's eyes went oddly remote, and thoughtful. "*Against*
him," she echoed. "The Jedi don't trust him?"

"That doesn't mean much. They don't trust me, either."
Anakin's mouth compressed to a thin bitter line. "They'll give
me a chair in the Council Chamber, but that's as far as it will go.
They won't accept me as a Master."

Her gaze returned from that thoughtful distance, and she
smiled up at him. "Patience, my love. In time, they will recognize your ability."

"They already recognize my abilities. They *fear* my abilities,"
he said bitterly. "But this isn't even about that. Like I said: it's a
political game."

"Anakin—"

"I don't know what's happening to the Order, but whatever
it is, I don't like it." He shook his head. "This war is destroying
everything the Republic is supposed to stand for. I mean, what
are we fighting for, anyway? What about all this is worth saving?"

Padmé nodded sadly, disengaging from Anakin's arms and
drifting away. "Sometimes I wonder if we're on the wrong side."

"The wrong side?"

*You think everything I've accomplished has been for
nothing—?*

He frowned at her. "You can't mean that."

She turned from him, speaking to the vast airway beyond the
veranda's edge. "What if the democracy we're fighting for no

longer *exists?* What if the Republic itself has become the very evil we've been fighting to destroy?"

"Oh, this again." Anakin irritably waved off her words. "I've been hearing that garbage ever since Geonosis. I never thought I'd hear it from you."

"A few seconds ago you were saying almost the same thing!"

"Where would the Republic be without Palpatine?"

"I don't know," she said. "But I'm not sure it would be worse than where we are."

All the danger, all the suffering, all the killing, all my friends who gave their lives—?

All for nothing—?

He bit down on his temper. "Everybody complains about Palpatine having too much power, but nobody offers a better alternative. Who *should* be running the war? The *Senate?* You're in the Senate, you know those people—how many of them do *you* trust?"

"All I know is that things are going wrong here. Our government is headed in exactly the wrong direction. You know it, too—you just *said* so!"

"I didn't mean that. I just—I'm tired of this, that's all. This political garbage. Sometimes I'd rather just be back out on the front lines. At least out there, I know who the bad guys are."

"I'm becoming afraid," she replied in a bitter undertone, "that I might know who the bad guys are *here,* too."

His eyes narrowed. "You're starting to sound like a Separatist."

"Anakin, the whole galaxy knows now that Count Dooku is dead. This is the time we should be pursing a *diplomatic* resolution to the war—but instead the fighting is intensifying! Palpatine's your friend, he might listen to you. When you see him tonight, ask him, in the name of simple *decency,* to offer a cease-fire—"

His face went hard. "Is that an order?"

She blinked. "What?"

"Do *I* get any say in this?" He stalked toward her. "Does *my* opinion matter? What if I don't agree with you? What if I think Palpatine's way is the *right* way?"

"Anakin, hundreds of thousands of beings are dying every day!"

"It's a *war*, Padmé. We didn't *ask* for it, remember? You were *there*—maybe we should have 'pursued a diplomatic resolution' in that *beast* arena!"

"I was—" She shrank away from what she saw on his face, blinking harder, brows drawn together. "I was only *asking* . . ."

"Everyone is *only asking*. Everyone *wants* something from me. And *I'm* the bad guy if they don't *get* it!" He spun away from her, cloak whirling, and found himself at the veranda's edge, leaning on the rail. The durasteel piping groaned in his mechanical grip.

"I'm sick of this," he muttered. "I'm sick of all of it."

He didn't hear her come to him; the rush of aircars through the lanes below the veranda drowned her footsteps. He didn't see the hurt on her face, or the hint of tears in her eyes, but he could feel them, in the tentative softness of her touch when she stroked his arm, and he could hear them in her hesitant voice. "Anakin, what is it? What is it really?"

He shook his head. He couldn't look at her.

"Nothing that's your fault," he said. "Nothing you can help."

"Don't shut me out, Anakin. Let me try."

"You can't help me." He stared down through dozens of crisscross lanes of traffic, down toward the invisible bedrock of the planet. "I'm trying to help *you*."

He'd seen something in her eyes, when he'd mentioned the Council and Palpatine.

He'd seen it.

"What aren't you telling me?"

Her hand went still, and she did not answer.

"I can feel it, Padmé. I sense you're keeping a secret."

"Oh?" she said softly. Lightly. "That's funny, I was thinking the same about *you*."

He just kept staring down over the rail into the invisible distance below. She moved close to him, moved against him, her arm sliding around his shoulders, her cheek leaning lightly on his arm. "Why does it have to be like this? Why does there have to even be such a thing as war? Can't we just . . . go *back*? Even just to pretend. Let's pretend we're back at the lake on Naboo, just the two of us. When there was no war, no politics. No plotting. Just us. You and me, and love. That's all we need. You and me, and love."

Right now Anakin couldn't remember what that had been like.

"I have to go," he said. "The Chancellor is waiting."

Two masked, robed, silent Red Guards flanked the door to the Chancellor's private box at the Galaxies Opera. Anakin didn't need to speak; as he approached, one of them said, "You are expected," and opened the door.

The small round box had only a handful of seats, overlooking the spread of overdressed beings who filled every seat in the orchestra; on this opening night, it seemed everyone had forgotten there was a war on. Anakin barely gave a glance toward the immense sphere of shimmering water that rippled gently in the stage's artificial zero-g; he had no interest in ballet, Mon Calamari or otherwise.

In the dim semi-gloom, Palpatine sat with the speaker of the Senate, Mas Amedda, and his administrative aide, Sly Moore. Anakin stopped at the back of the box.

If I were the spy the Council wants me to be, I suppose I should be creeping up behind them so that I can listen in.

A spasm of distaste passed over his face; he took care to wipe it off before he spoke. "Chancellor. Sorry I'm late."

Palpatine turned toward him, and his face lit up. "Yes, Anakin! Don't worry. Come in, my boy, come in. Thank you for your report on the Council meeting this afternoon—it made most interesting reading. And now I have good news for you— Clone Intelligence has located General Grievous!"

"That's tremendous!" Anakin shook his head, wondering if Obi-Wan would be embarrassed to have been scooped by the clones. "He won't escape us again."

"I'm going to—Moore, take a note—I will direct the Council to give *you* this assignment, Anakin. Your gifts are wasted on Coruscant—you should be out in the field. You can attend Council meetings by holoconference."

Anakin frowned. "Thank you, sir, but the Council coordinates Jedi assignments."

"Of course, of course. Mustn't step on any Jedi toes, must we? They are so jealous of their political prerogatives. Still, I shall wonder at their collective wisdom if they choose someone else."

"As I said in my report, they've already assigned Obi-Wan to find Grievous." *Because they want to keep me here, where I am supposed to spy on you.*

"To find him, yes. But you are the best man to *apprehend* him—though of course the Jedi Council cannot always be trusted to do the right thing."

"They try. I—believe they try, sir."

"Do you still? Sit down." Palpatine looked at the other two beings in the box. "Leave us."

They rose and withdrew. Anakin took Mas Amedda's seat.

Palpatine gazed distractedly down at the graceful undulations of the Mon Calamari principal soloist for a long moment, frowning as though there was so much he wanted to say, he was unsure where to begin. Finally he sighed heavily and leaned close to Anakin.

"Anakin, I think you know by now that I cannot rely upon the Jedi Council. That is why I put you on it. If they have not yet tried to use you in their plot, they soon will."

Anakin kept his face carefully blank. "I'm not sure I understand."

"You must sense what I have come to suspect," Palpatine said grimly. "The Jedi Council is after more than independence from Senate oversight; I believe they intend to control the Republic itself."

"Chancellor—"

"I believe they are planning treason. They hope to overthrow my government, and replace me with someone weak enough that Jedi mind tricks can control his every word."

"I can't believe the Council—"

"Anakin, search your feelings. You do know, don't you?"

Anakin looked away. "I know they don't trust you . . ."

"Or the Senate. Or the Republic. Or democracy itself, for that matter. The Jedi Council is not *elected*. It selects its own members according to its own rules—a less generous man than I might say *whim*—and gives them authority backed by power. They rule the Jedi as they hope to rule the Republic: by fiat."

"I admit . . ." Anakin looked down at his hands. ". . . my faith in them has been . . . shaken."

"How? Have they approached you already? Have they ordered you to do something dishonest?" Palpatine's frown cleared into a gently wise smile that was oddly reminiscent of Yoda's. "They want you to spy on me, don't they?"

"I—"

"It's all right, Anakin. I have nothing to hide."

"I—don't know what to say . . ."

"Do you remember," Palpatine said, drawing away from Anakin so that he could lean back comfortably in his seat, "how as a young boy, when you first came to this planet, I tried to teach you the ins and outs of politics?"

Anakin smiled faintly. "I remember that I didn't much care for the lessons."

"For *any* lessons, as I recall. But it's a pity; you should have paid more attention. To understand politics is to understand the fundamental nature of thinking beings. Right now, you should remember one of my first teachings: all those who gain power are afraid to lose it."

"The Jedi use their power for *good*," Anakin said, a little too firmly.

"Good is a point of view, Anakin. And the Jedi concept of *good* is not the only valid one. Take your Dark Lords of the Sith, for example. From my reading, I have gathered that the Sith believed in justice and security every bit as much as the Jedi—"

"Jedi believe in justice and *peace*."

"In these troubled times, is there a difference?" Palpatine asked mildly. "The Jedi have not done a stellar job of bringing peace to the galaxy, you must agree. Who's to say the Sith might not have done better?"

"This is another of those arguments you probably shouldn't bring up in front of the Council, if you know what I mean," Anakin replied with a disbelieving smile.

"Oh, yes. Because the Sith would be a threat to the Jedi Order's *power*. Lesson one."

Anakin shook his head. "Because the Sith are *evil*."

"From a Jedi's point of view," Palpatine allowed. "*Evil* is a label we all put on those who threaten us, isn't it? Yet the Sith and the Jedi are similar in almost every way, including their quest for greater power."

"The Jedi's quest is for greater *understanding*," Anakin countered. "For greater knowledge of the Force—"

"Which brings with it greater power, does it not?"

"Well . . . yes." Anakin had to laugh. "I should know better than to argue with a politician."

"We're not arguing, Anakin. We're just talking." Palpatine shifted his weight, settling in comfortably. "Perhaps the real difference between the Jedi and the Sith lies only in their orientation; a Jedi gains power through understanding, and a Sith gains understanding through power. This is the true reason the Sith have always been more powerful than the Jedi. The Jedi fear the dark side so much they cut themselves off from the most important aspect of life: passion. Of any kind. They don't even allow themselves to love."

Except for me, Anakin thought. *But then, I've never been exactly the perfect Jedi.*

"The Sith do not fear the dark side. The Sith *have* no fear. They embrace the whole spectrum of experience, from the heights of transcendent joy to the depths of hatred and despair. Beings have these emotions for a reason, Anakin. That is why the Sith are more powerful: they are not afraid to *feel*."

"The Sith rely on passion for strength," Anakin said, "but when that passion runs dry, what's left?"

"Perhaps nothing. Perhaps a great deal. Perhaps it never runs dry at all. Who can say?"

"They think inward, only about themselves."

"And the Jedi don't?"

"The Jedi are selfless—we *erase* the self, to join with the flow of the Force. We care only about *others* . . ."

Palpatine again gave him that smile of gentle wisdom. "Or so you've been trained to believe. I hear the voice of Obi-Wan Kenobi in your answers, Anakin. What do you *really* think?"

Anakin suddenly found the ballet a great deal more interesting than Palpatine's face. "I . . . don't know anymore."

"It is said that if one could ever entirely comprehend a single grain of sand—really, truly understand *everything* about it—one would, at the same time, entirely comprehend the universe. Who's to say that a Sith, by looking inward, sees less than a Jedi does by looking out?"

"The Jedi—Jedi are *good*. That's the difference. I don't care *who* sees *what*."

"What the Jedi are," Palpatine said gently, "is a group of very powerful beings you consider to be your comrades. And you are loyal to your friends; I have known that for as long as I have known you, and I admire you for it. But are your friends loyal to *you*?"

Anakin shot him a sudden frown. "What do you mean?"

"Would a true friend ask you to do something that's wrong?"

"I'm not sure it's wrong," Anakin said. Obi-Wan might have been telling the truth. It was possible. They might only want to catch Sidious. They might really be trying to protect Palpatine.

They might.

Maybe.

"Have they asked you to break the Jedi Code? To violate the Constitution? To betray a friendship? To betray your own *values*?"

"Chancellor—"

"*Think*, Anakin! I have always tried to teach you to think— yes, yes, Jedi do not think, they *know*, but those stale answers aren't good enough now, in these changing times. Consider their motives. Keep your mind clear of assumptions. The fear of losing power is a weakness of both the Jedi and the Sith."

Anakin sank lower in his seat. Too much had happened in too short a time. Everything jumbled together in his head, and none of it seemed to make complete sense.

Except for what Palpatine said.

That made too *much* sense.

"This puts me in mind of an old legend," Palpatine murmured idly. "Anakin—are you familiar with *The Tragedy of Darth Plagueis the Wise*?"

Anakin shook his head.

"Ah, I thought not. It is not a story the Jedi would tell you.

It's a Sith legend, of a Dark Lord who had turned his sight inward so deeply that he had come to comprehend, and master, life itself. And—because the two are one, when seen clearly enough—death itself."

Anakin sat up. Was he actually hearing this? "He could keep someone safe from death?"

"According to the legend," Palpatine said, "he could directly influence the midi-chlorians to create life; with such knowledge, to maintain life in someone already living would seem a small matter, don't you agree?"

A universe of possibility blossomed inside Anakin's head. He murmured, "Stronger than *death* . . ."

"The dark side seems to be—from my reading—the pathway to many abilities some would consider unnatural."

Anakin couldn't seem to get his breath. "What happened to him?"

"Oh, well, it *is* a tragedy, after all, you know. Once he has gained this ultimate power, he has nothing to fear save losing it— that's why the Jedi Council brought him to mind, you know."

"But what *happened*?"

"Well, to safeguard his power's existence, he teaches the path toward it to his apprentice."

"And?"

"And his apprentice kills him in his sleep," Palpatine said with a careless shrug. "Plageuis never sees it coming. That's the tragic irony, you see: he can save anyone in the galaxy from death—except himself."

"What about the apprentice? What happens to *him*?"

"Oh, him. *He* goes on to become the greatest Dark Lord the Sith have ever known . . ."

"So," Anakin murmured, "it's only a tragedy for *Plagueis*— for the apprentice, the legend has a *happy* ending . . ."

"Oh, well, yes. Quite right. I'd never really thought of it that way—rather like what we were talking about earlier, isn't it?"

"What if," Anakin said slowly, almost not daring to speak the words, "it's not just a legend?"

"I'm sorry?"

"What if Darth Plagueis really *lived*—what if someone really *had* this power?"

"Oh, I am . . . rather certain . . . that Plagueis did indeed exist. And if someone actually had this power—well, he would indeed be one of the most powerful men in the galaxy, not to mention virtually immortal . . ."

"How would I *find* him?"

"I'm sure I couldn't say. You could ask your friends on the Jedi Council, I suppose—but of course, if they ever found him they'd kill him on the spot. Not as punishment for any crime, you understand. Innocence is irrelevant to the Jedi. They would kill him simply for being Sith, and his knowledge would die with him."

"I just—I have to—" Anakin found himself half out of his seat, fists clenched and trembling. He forced himself to relax and sit back down, and he took a deep breath. "You seem to know so much about this, I need you to tell me: would it be possible, possible at all, to learn this power?"

Palpatine shrugged, regarding him with that smile of gentle wisdom.

"Well, clearly," he said, "not from a Jedi."

For a long, long time after leaving the opera house, Anakin sat motionless in his idling speeder, eyes closed, resting his head against the edge of his mechanical hand. The speeder bobbed gently in the air-wakes of the passing traffic; he didn't feel it. Klaxons blared, rising and fading as angry pilots swerved around him; he didn't hear them.

Finally he sighed and lifted his head. He stroked a private code into the speeder's comm screen. After a moment the screen lit up with an image of Padmé's half-asleep face.

"Anakin—?" She rubbed her eyes, blinking. *"Where are you? What time is it?"*

"Padmé, I can't—" He stopped himself, huffing a sigh out through his nose. "Listen, Padmé, something's come up. I have to spend the night at the Temple."

"Oh . . . well, all right, Anakin. I'll miss you."

"I'll miss you, too." He swallowed. "I miss you already."

"We'll be together tomorrow?"

"Yes. And soon, for the rest of our lives. We'll never have to be apart again."

She nodded sleepily. *"Rest well, my love."*

"I'll do my best. You, too."

She blew him a kiss, and the screen went blank.

Anakin fired thrusters and slid the speeder expertly into traffic, angling toward the Jedi Temple, because that part—the part about spending the night at the Temple—was the part that wasn't a lie.

The lie was that he was going to rest. That he was going to even try. How could he rest when every time he closed his eyes he could see her screaming on the birthing table?

Now the Council's insult burned hotter than ever; he even had a name, a story, a place to start—but how could he explain to the archives Master why he needed to research a Sith legend of immortality?

Yet maybe he didn't need the archives after all.

The Temple was still the greatest nexus of Force energy on the planet, perhaps even the galaxy, and it was unquestionably the best place in the galaxy for intense, focused meditation. He had much he needed the Force to teach him, and a very short time to learn.

He would start by thinking inward.

Thinking about *himself* . . .

THE WILL OF THE FORCE

When her handmaiden Moteé awakened her with the word that C-3PO had announced a Jedi was waiting to see her, Padmé flew out of bed, threw on a robe, and hurried out to her living room, a smile breaking through her sleepiness like the dawn outside—

But it was Obi-Wan.

The Jedi Master had his back to her, hands clasped behind him as he drifted restlessly about the room, gazing with abstracted lack of interest at her collection of rare sculpture.

"Obi-Wan," she said breathlessly, "has—" She bit off the following *something happened to Anakin?* How would she explain why this was the first thing out of her mouth?

"—has See-Threepio offered you anything to drink?"

He turned to her, a frown clearing from his brow. "Senator," he said warmly. "So good to see you again. I apologize for the early hour, and yes, your protocol droid has been quite insistent on offering me refreshment." His frown began to regather. "But as you may guess, this is not a social call. I've come to speak with you about Anakin."

Her years in politics had trained her well; even as her heart lurched and a shrill *How much does he* know? echoed inside her head, her face remained only attentively blank.

A primary rule of Republic politics: tell as much truth as you can. Especially to a Jedi. "I was very happy to learn of his appointment to the Council."

"Yes. It is perhaps less than he deserves—though I'm afraid it may be more than he can handle. Has he been to see you?"

"Several times," she said evenly. "Something is wrong, isn't it?"

Obi-Wan tilted his head, and a hint of rueful smile showed through his beard. "You should have been a Jedi."

She managed a light laugh. "And you should never go into politics. You're not very good at hiding your feelings. What is it?"

"It's Anakin." With his pretense of cheer fading away, he seemed to age before her eyes. He looked very tired, and profoundly troubled. "May I sit?"

"Please." She waved him to the couch and lowered herself onto its edge beside him. "Is he in trouble again?"

"I certainly hope not. This is more . . . a personal matter." He shifted his weight uncomfortably. "He's been put in a difficult position as the Chancellor's representative, but I think there's more to it than that. We—had words, yesterday, and we parted badly."

Her heart shrank; he *must* know, and he'd come to confront her—to bring their whole lives crashing down around their ears. She ached for Anakin, but her face showed only polite curiosity.

"What were these words about?" she asked delicately.

"I'm afraid I can't tell you," he said with a vaguely apologetic frown. "Jedi business. You understand."

She inclined her head. "Of course."

"It's only that—well, I've been a bit worried about him. I was hoping he may have talked to you."

"Why would he talk to *me* about—" She favored him with her best friendly-but-skeptical smile. "—Jedi business?"

"Senator—Padmé. Please." He gazed into her eyes with nothing on his face but compassion and fatigued anxiety. "I am not blind, Padmé. Though I have tried to be, for Anakin's sake. And for yours."

"What do you mean?"

"Neither of you is very good at hiding feelings, either."

"Obi-Wan—"

"Anakin has loved you since the day you met, in that horrible junk shop on Tatooine. He's never even tried to hide it, though we do not speak of it. We . . . pretend that I don't know. And I was happy to, because it made him happy. *You* made him happy, when nothing else ever truly could." He sighed, his brows drawing together. "And you, Padmé, skilled as you are on the Senate floor, cannot hide the light that comes to your eyes when anyone so much as mentions his name."

"I—" She lurched to her feet. "I can't—Obi-Wan, don't make me talk about this . . ."

"I don't mean to hurt you, Padmé. Nor even to make you uncomfortable. I'm not here to interrogate you; I have no interest in the details of your relationship."

She turned away, walking just to be moving, barely conscious of passing through the door out onto the dawn-painted veranda. "Then why *are* you here?"

He followed her respectfully. "Anakin is under a great deal of pressure. He carries tremendous responsibilities for a man so young; when I was his age I still had some years to go as a Padawan. He is—changing. Quickly. And I have some anxiety about what he is changing into. It would be a . . . very great mistake . . . were he to leave the Jedi Order."

She blinked as though he'd slapped her. "Why—that seems . . . *unlikely,* doesn't it? What about this prophecy the Jedi put so much faith in? Isn't he the chosen one?"

"Very probably. But I have scanned this prophecy; it says

only that a chosen one will be born and bring balance to the Force; nowhere does it say he has to be a Jedi."

She blinked harder, fighting down a surge of desperate hope that left her breathless. "He doesn't *have* to—?"

"My Master, Qui-Gon Jinn, believed that it was the will of the Force that Anakin should be trained as a Jedi—and we all have a certain, oh, I suppose you could call it a Jedi-centric bias. It is a Jedi prophecy, after all."

"But the will of the Force—isn't that what Jedi follow?"

"Well, yes. But you must understand that not even the Jedi know all there is to be known about the Force; no mortal mind can. We speak of the *will of the Force* as someone ignorant of gravity might say it is the will of a river to flow to the ocean: it is a metaphor that describes our ignorance. The simple truth—if any truth is ever simple—is that we do not truly know what the will of the Force may be. We can *never* know. It is so far beyond our limited understanding that we can only surrender to its mystery."

"What does this have to do with Anakin?" She swallowed, but her voice stayed tight and thin. "And with me?"

"I fear that some of his current . . . difficulty . . . has to do with your relationship."

If you only knew how much, she thought. "What do you want me to do?"

He looked down. "I cannot tell you what to do, Padmé. I can only ask you to consider Anakin's best interests. You know the two of you can never be together while he remains in the Order."

A bleak chill settled into her chest. "Obi-Wan, I can't talk about this."

"Very well. But remember that the Jedi are his family. The Order gives his life *structure*. It gives him a direction. You know how . . . undisciplined he can be."

And that's why he is the only Jedi I could ever love . . . "Yes. Yes, of course."

"If his true path leads him away from the Jedi, so be it. But please, for both of your sakes, tread carefully. Be sure. Some decisions can never be reversed."

"Yes," she said slowly. Feelingly. "I know that too well."

He nodded as though he understood, though of course he did not understand at all. "We all do, these days."

A soft chiming came from within his robe. "Excuse me," he said, and turned aside, producing a comlink from an inner pocket. "Yes . . . ?"

A man's voice came thinly through the comlink, deep and clipped: *"We are calling the Council into special session. We've located General Grievous!"*

"Thank you, Master Windu," Obi-Wan said. "I'm on my way."

General Grievous? Her eyes went hot, and stung with sudden tears. And so they would take her Anakin away from her again.

She felt a stirring below her ribs. Away from *us,* she amended, and there was so much love and fear and joy and loss all swirling and clashing within her that she dared not speak. She only stared blindly out across the smog-shrouded cityscape as Obi-Wan came close to her shoulder.

"Padmé," he said softly. Gently. Almost regretfully. "I will not tell the Council of this. Any of it. I'm very sorry to burden you with this, and I—I hope I haven't upset you too much. We have all been friends for so long . . . and I hope we always will be."

"Thank you, Obi-Wan," she said faintly. She couldn't look at him. From the corner of her eye she saw him incline his head respectfully and turn to go.

For a moment she said nothing, but as his footsteps receded she said, "Obi-Wan?"

She heard him stop.

"You love him, too, don't you?"

When he didn't answer, she turned to look. He stood motionless, frowning, in the middle of the expanse of buff carpeting.

"You do. You love him."

He lowered his head. He looked very alone.

"Please do what you can to help him," he said, and left.

The holoscan of Utapau rotated silently in the center of the Jedi Council Chamber. Anakin had brought the holoprojector from the Chancellor's office; Obi-Wan wondered idly if the projector had been scanned for recording devices planted by the Chancellor to spy on their meeting, then dismissed the thought. In a sense, Anakin *was* the Chancellor's recording device.

And that's our fault, he thought.

The only Council members physically present, other than Obi-Wan and Anakin, were Mace Windu and Agen Kolar. The Council reached a quorum by the projected holopresences of Ki-Adi-Mundi, en route to Mygeeto, Plo Koon on Cato Neimoidia, and Yoda, who was about to make planetfall on Kashyyyk.

"Why Utapau?" Mace Windu was saying. "A neutral system, of little strategic significance, and virtually no planetary defense force—"

"Perhaps that is itself the reason," Agen Kolar offered. "Easily taken, and their sinkhole-based culture can hide a tremendous number of droids from long-range scans."

Ki-Adi-Mundi's frown wrinkled the whole length of his forehead. *"Our agents on Utapau have made no report of this."*

"They may be detained, or dead," Obi-Wan said.

Mace Windu leaned toward Anakin, scowling. "How could the Chancellor have come by this information when we know nothing about it?"

"Clone Intelligence intercepted a partial message in a diplomatic packet from the Chairman of Utapau," Anakin told him.

"We've only managed to verify its authenticity within the past hour."

Obi-Wan felt a frown crawl onto his forehead at the way Anakin now referred to the Chancellor's Office as *we* . . .

"Clone Intelligence," Mace said heavily, "reports to *us*."

"I beg your pardon, Master Windu, but that is no longer the case." Though Anakin's expression was perfectly solemn, Obi-Wan thought he could detect a hint of satisfaction in his young friend's voice. "I thought it had been already made clear. The constitutional amendment bringing the Jedi under the Chancellor's Office naturally includes troops commanded by Jedi. Palpatine is now Supreme Commander of the Grand Army of the Republic."

"Pointless it is, to squabble over jurisdiction," the image of Yoda said. *"Act on this, we must."*

"I believe we all agree on that," Anakin said briskly. "Let's move to the operational planning. The Chancellor has requested that I lead this mission, and so I—"

"The *Council* will decide this," Mace said sternly. "Not the Chancellor."

"Dangerous, Grievous is. To face him, steady minds are needed. Masters, we should send."

Perhaps of all the Council, only Obi-Wan could detect the shadow of disappointment and hurt that crept into Anakin's eyes. Obi-Wan understood perfectly, and could even sympathize: to take the field would have slipped Anakin out from under the pressures of what he saw as his conflicting duties.

"Given the strain on our current resources," Mace Windu said, "I recommend we send only one Jedi—Master Kenobi."

Which would leave Mace and Agen Kolar—both among the greatest bladesbeings the Jedi Order had ever produced—here on Coruscant in case Sidious did indeed take this opportunity to make a dramatic move. Not to mention Anakin, who was a brigade's worth of firepower in his own right.

Obi-Wan nodded. Perfectly logical. Everyone would agree.

Except Anakin. He leaned forward, red climbing his cheeks. "He wasn't so successful the *last* time he met Grievous!"

"Anakin—" Obi-Wan began.

"No offense, my Master. I am only stating a fact."

"Oh no, not at all. You're quite right. But I have a feel for how he fights now—and for how he runs away. I am certain I can catch him."

"Master—"

"And you, my young friend, have duties here on Coruscant. Extremely *important* duties, that require your *full attention*," Obi-Wan reminded him. "Am I being clear?"

Anakin didn't answer. He sank back into his chair and turned away.

"Obi-Wan, my choice is," Yoda said.

Ki-Adi-Mundi's image nodded. *"I concur. Let's put it to a vote."*

Mace Windu counted nods. "Six in favor."

He waited, looking at Anakin. "Further comment?"

Anakin only stared at the wall.

After a moment, Mace shrugged.

"It is unanimous."

Senator Chi Eekway accepted a tube of Aqualish hoi-broth from C-3PO's refreshment tray. "I am very grateful to be included here," she said, her dewlaps jiggling as she tilted her blue head in a gesture around Padmé's living room at the gathering of Senators. "I speak directly only for my own sector, of course, but I can tell you that many Senators are becoming very nervous indeed. You may not know that the new governors are arriving with full regiments of clone troops—what they call *security forces*. We all have begun to wonder if these regiments are intended to protect us from the Separatists . . . or to protect the governors from *us*."

Padmé looked up from the document reader in her hand. "I have . . . reliable information . . . that General Grievous has been located, and that the Jedi are already moving against his position. The war may be over in a matter of days."

"But what then?" Bail Organa leaned forward, elbows to knees, fingers laced together. "How to we make Palpatine with-draw his governors? How do we stop him from garrisoning troops in *all* our systems?"

"We don't have to *make* him do anything," Padmé said rea-sonably. "The Senate granted him executive powers only for the duration of the emergency—"

"Yet it is only Palpatine himself who has the authority to de-clare when the emergency is over," Bail countered. "How do we make him surrender power back to the Senate?"

Chi Eekway shifted backward. "There are many who are will-ing to do just that," she said. "Not just my own people. Many Senators. We are ready to *make* him surrender power."

Padmé snapped the document reader closed. She looked from Senator to Senator expressionlessly. "Would anyone care for further refreshment?"

"Senator Amidala," Eekway said, "I fear you don't understand—"

"Senator Eekway. Another hoi-broth?"

"No, that's—"

"Very well, then." She looked up at C-3PO. "Threepio, that will be all. Please tell Moteé and Ellé that they are dismissed for the day, then you are free to power down for a while."

"Thank you, Mistress," Threepio replied. "Though I must say, this discussion has been *most* stimu—"

"Threepio." Padmé's tone went a trace extra firm. "That will be *all*."

"Yes, Mistress. Of course. I quite understand." The droid turned stiffly and shuffled out of the room.

As soon as 3PO was safely out of earshot, Padmé brandished

the document reader as though it were a weapon. "This is a very dangerous step. We cannot let this turn into another war."

"That's the last thing any of us wants," Bail said with a disapproving look at Senator Eekway. "Alderaan has no armed forces; we don't even have a planetary defense system. A political solution is our only option."

"Which is the purpose of this petition," Mon Mothma said, laying her soft hand over Padmé's. "We're hoping that a show of solidarity within the Senate might stop Palpatine from further subverting the Constitution, that's all. With the signatures of a full two thousand Senators—"

"—we still have less than we need to stop his supermajority from amending the Constitution any way he happens to want," Padmé finished for her. She weighed the reader in her hand. "I am willing to present this to Palpatine, but I am losing faith in the Senate's readiness, or even ability, to rein him in. I think we should consult the Jedi."

Because I really think they can help, or because I just can't stand to lie to my husband? She couldn't say. She hoped that both were true, though she was sure only of the second.

Bana Breemu examined her long, elegantly manicured fingertips. "That," she said remotely, "would be dangerous."

Mon Mothma nodded. "We don't know where the Jedi stand in all this."

Padmé sat forward. "The Jedi aren't any happier with the situation than we are."

Senator Breemu's high-arched cheekbones made the look she gave Padmé appear even more distant and skeptical. "You seem . . . remarkably well informed about Jedi business, Senator Amidala."

Padmé felt herself flush, and she didn't trust herself to answer.

Giddean Danu shook his head, doubt plainly written across his dark face. "If we are to openly oppose the Chancellor, we need the support of the Jedi. We need their moral authority. Otherwise, what do we have?"

"The *moral authority* of the Jedi, such as it is," Bana Breemu said, "has been spent lavishly upon war; I fear they have none left for politics."

"*One* Jedi, then," Padmé offered to the others. *At least let me speak the truth to my love. At least. Please,* she pleaded with them silently. "There is one Jedi—one whom I truly know all of us can trust absolutely . . ."

Her voice trailed off into appalled silence when she realized that she wasn't talking about Anakin.

This had been all about him when she'd started—all about her love, her need to be open with him, the pain that keeping this secret stabbed her heart at each and every beat—but when the thought had turned to *trust,* when it became a question of someone she knew, truly and abolutely *knew,* she could trust—

She discovered that she was talking about Obi-Wan.

Anakin . . . Something was breaking inside her. *Oh, my love, what are they doing to us?*

Chi Eekway shook her head. "Patience, Senator."

Fang Zar unknotted his fingers from his raggedly bushy beard and shrugged. "Yes, we cannot block the Chancellor's supermajority—but we can show him that opposition to his methods is growing. Perhaps that alone might persuade him to moderate his tactics."

Bana Breemu went back to examining her fingertips. "When you present the Petition of the Two Thousand, many things may change."

"But," Giddean Danu said, "will they change for the better?"

Bail Organa and Mon Mothma exchanged glances that whispered of some shared secret. Bail said slowly, "Let us see what we can accomplish in the Senate before we involve the Jedi."

And as one after another of the Senators agreed, Padmé could only sit in silence. In mourning.

Grieving for the sudden death of an illusion.

Anakin—Anakin, I love you. If only—

But that *if only* would take her to a place she could not bear to go. In the end, she could only return to the thought she feared would echo within her for the rest of her life.

Anakin, I'm sorry.

The last of the hovertanks whirred up the ramp into the sky-shrouding wedge of the assault cruiser. It was followed by rank upon immaculately regimented rank of clone troopers, marshaled by battalions, marching in perfect synchrony.

Standing alongside Obi-Wan on the landing deck, Anakin watched them go.

He couldn't quite make himself believe he wasn't going along.

It wasn't that he really *wanted* to go with Obi-Wan to Utapau—even though it'd be a relief to pull out of the political quagmire that was sucking him down. But how could he leave Padmé now? He didn't even care anymore about being the Jedi to capture Grievous, though such a feat would almost certainly bring him his Mastery. He was no longer certain he needed to be a Master at all.

Through the long, black hours of meditation last night—meditation that was often indistinguishable from brooding—he had begun to sense a deeper truth within the Force: a submerged reality, lurking like a Sarlacc beneath the sunlit sands of Jedi training.

Somewhere down there was all the power he would ever need.

So no, it wasn't that he wanted to go. It was more, inexplicably, that he wanted Obi-Wan to *stay.*

There was a cold void in his chest that he was afraid would soon fill with regret, and grief.

Of course there was no chance at all that Obi-Wan wouldn't go; he'd be the last Jedi in the galaxy to defy an order of the

Council. Not for the first time, Anakin found himself wishing that Obi-Wan could be a little more like the late Qui-Gon. Though he'd known Qui-Gon for mere days, Anakin could almost see him right now, brow furrowing as he gently inclined his head over his shorter Padawan; he could almost hear his gentle baritone instructing Obi-Wan to *be mindful of the currents of the living Force: to do one's duty is not always to do right. Concern yourself with right action. Let duty take care of itself.*

But he couldn't say that. Though he'd passed his trials many months ago, to Obi-Wan he was still the learner, not the Master.

All he could say was, "I have a bad feeling about this."

Obi-Wan was frowning as he watched a clone deck crew load his blue-and-white starfighter onto the assault cruiser's flight deck. "I'm sorry, Anakin. Did you say something?"

"You're going to need me on this one, Master." And he could feel an unexpected truth there, too—if he *were* to go along, if he could somehow bring himself to forget about Padmé for a few days, if he could somehow get himself away from Palpatine and the Council and his meditations and politics and everything here on Coruscant that was dragging him this way and that way and sucking him under, if he could just tag along and play the *Kenobi and Skywalker* game for a few days, everything might still be all right.

If only.

"It may be nothing but a wild bantha chase," Obi-Wan said. "Your job here is much more important, Anakin."

"I know: the Sith." The word left a bitter taste in Anakin's mouth. The Council's manipulation had a rank stench of politics on it. "I just—" Anakin shrugged helplessly, looking away. "I don't like you going off without me like this. It's a bad idea to split up the team. I mean, look what happened *last* time."

"Don't remind me."

"You want to go spend another few months with somebody like Ventress? Or worse?"

"Anakin." Anakin could hear a gentle smile in Obi-Wan's voice. "Don't worry. I have enough clones to take three systems the size of Utapau's. I believe I should be able to handle the situation, even without your help."

Anakin had to answer his smile. "Well, there's always a first time."

Obi-Wan said, "We're not really splitting up, Anakin. We've worked on our own many times—like when you took Padmé to Naboo while I went to Kamino and Geonosis."

"And look how *that* turned out."

"All right, bad example," Obi-Wan admitted, his smile shading toward rueful. "Yet years later, here we all are: still alive, and still friends. My point, Anakin, is that even when we work separately, we work together. We have the same goals: end the war, and save the Republic from the Sith. As long as we're on the same side, everything will come out well in the end. I'm certain of it."

"Well . . ." Anakin sighed. "I suppose you could be right. You are, once in a while. Occasionally."

Obi-Wan chuckled and clapped him on the shoulder. "Farewell, old friend."

"Master, wait." Anakin turned to face him fully. He couldn't just stand here and let him walk away. Not now. He had to say *something* . . .

He had a sinking feeling he might not get another chance.

"Master . . . ," he said hesitantly, "I know I've . . . disappointed you in these past few days. I have been arrogant. I have . . . not been very appreciative of your training, and what's worse, of your friendship. I offer no excuse, Master. My frustration with the Council . . . I know that none of it is your fault, and I apologize. For all of it. Your friendship means everything to me."

Obi-Wan gripped Anakin's mechanical hand, and with his other he squeezed Anakin's arm above the joining of flesh and metal. "You are wise and strong, Anakin. You are a credit to the Jedi Order, and you have far surpassed my humble efforts at instruction."

Anakin felt his own smile turn melancholy. "Just the other day, you were saying that my power is no credit to me."

"I'm not speaking of your power, Anakin, but of your heart. The greatness in you is a greatness of spirit. Courage and generosity, compassion and commitment. These are your virtues," Obi-Wan said gently. "You have done great things, and I am very proud of you."

Anakin found he had nothing to say.

"Well." Obi-Wan looked down, chuckling, releasing Anakin's hand and arm. "I believe I hear General Grievous calling my name. Good-bye, old friend. May the Force be with you."

All Anakin could offer in return was a reflexive echo.

"May the Force be with you."

He stood, still and silent, and watched Obi-Wan walk away. Then he turned and slowly, head hanging, moved toward his speeder.

The Chancellor was waiting.

FREE FALL IN THE DARK

A chill wind scoured the Chancellor's private landing deck at the Senate Office Building. Anakin stood wrapped in his cloak, chin to his chest, staring down at the deck below his feet. He didn't feel the chill, or the wind. He didn't hear the whine of the Chancellor's private shuttle angling in for a landing, or smell the swirls of brown smog coiling along the wind.

What he saw were the faces of Senators who had stood on this deck to cheer for him; what he heard were exclamations of joy and congratulations when he returned their Supreme Chancellor to them unharmed. What he felt was a memory of hot pride at being the focus of so many eager HoloNet crews, anxious to get even the slightest glimpse of the man who had conquered Count Dooku.

How many days ago had that been? He couldn't remember. Not many. When you don't sleep, days smear together into a haze of fatigue so deep it becomes a physical pain. The Force could keep him upright, keep him moving, keep him thinking, but it could not give him rest. Not that he wanted rest. Rest might bring sleep.

What sleep might bring, he could not bear to know.

He remembered Obi-Wan telling him about some poet he'd once read—he couldn't remember the name, or the exact quote, but it was something about how there is no greater misery than to remember, with bitter regret, a day when you were happy . . .

How had everything gone so fast from so right to so wrong?

He couldn't even imagine.

Greasy dust swirled under the shuttle's repulsors as it settled to the deck. The hatch cycled open, and four of Palpatine's personal guards glided out, long robes catching the breeze in silken blood-colored ripples. They split into two pairs to flank the doors as the Chancellor emerged beside the tall, bulky form of Mas Amedda, the Speaker of the Senate. The Chagrian's horns tilted over Palpatine as they walked together, seemingly deep in conversation.

Anakin moved forward to meet them. "Chancellor," he said, bowing a greeting. "Lord Speaker."

Mas Amedda looked at Anakin with a curl to his blue lips that, on a human, would have signaled disgust; it was a Chagrian smile. "Greetings, Your Grace. I trust the day finds you well?"

Anakin's eyes felt as if they'd been dusted with sand. "Very well, Lord Speaker, thank you for asking."

Amedda turned back to Palpatine, and Anakin's polite smile faded to a twist of contempt. Maybe he was just overtired, but somehow, looking at the curlings of the Chagrian's naked head-tentacles as they twisted across his chest, he found himself hoping that Obi-Wan hadn't been lying to him about Sidious. He rather hoped that Mas Amedda might be a secret Sith, because something about the Speaker of the Senate was so revolting that Anakin could easily imagine just slicing his head in half . . .

It gradually dawned on Anakin that Palpatine was giving Mas Amedda the brush-off, and was sending the Redrobes with him.

Good. He wasn't in the mood to play games. By themselves, they could talk straight with each other. A little straight talk might be just what he needed. A little straight talk might burn through the fog of half-truths and subtle confusions that the Jedi Council had poured into his head.

"So, Anakin," Palpatine said as the others moved away, "did you see your friend off?"

Anakin nodded. "If I didn't hate Grievous so much, I'd almost feel sorry for him."

"Oh?" Palpatine appeared mildly interested. "Are Jedi allowed to hate?"

"Figure of speech," Anakin said, waving this off. "It doesn't matter how I feel about Grievous. Obi-Wan will soon have his head."

"Provided, of course," Palpatine murmured as he took Anakin's arm to guide him toward the entryway, "that the Council didn't make a mistake. I still believe Master Kenobi is not the Jedi for this job."

Anakin shrugged irritably. Why did everyone keep bringing up things he didn't want to talk about? "The Council was . . . very sure in its decision."

"Certainty is a fine thing," the Chancellor allowed. "Though it too often happens that those who are the most entirely certain are also the most entirely wrong. What will the Council do if Kenobi proves unable to apprehend Grievous without your help?"

"I'm sure I cannot say, sir. I imagine they will deal with that if and when it happens. The Jedi teach that anticipation is distraction."

"I am no philosopher, Anakin; in my work, anticipation is often my sole hope of success. I must anticipate the actions of my adversaries—and even those of my allies. Even—" He opened a hand toward Anakin, smiling. "—my friends. It is the only way I can be prepared to take advantage of opportunity . . . and conversely, to avoid disaster."

"But if a disaster comes about by the will of the Force—"

"I'm afraid I don't believe in the will of the Force," Palpatine said, his smile turning apologetic. "I believe it is *our* will that matters. I believe that everything good in our civilization has come about not by the blind action of some mystical field of energy, but by the focused will of *people:* lawmakers and warriors, inventors and engineers, struggling with every breath of their bodies to shape galactic culture. To improve the lives of all."

They stood now before the vaulted door to Palpatine's office. "Please come in, Anakin. Much as I enjoy a philosophical chat, that was not the reason I asked you to meet me. We have business to discuss, and I fear it may be very serious business indeed."

Anakin followed him through the outer chambers to Palpatine's intimate private office. He took up a respectful standing position opposite Palpatine's desk, but the Chancellor waved him to a chair. "Please, Anakin, make yourself comfortable. Some of this may be difficult for you to hear."

"Everything is, these days," Anakin muttered as he took a seat.

Palpatine didn't seem to hear. "It concerns Master Kenobi. My friends among the Senators have picked up some . . . disturbing rumors about him. Many in the Senate believe that Kenobi is not fit for this assignment."

Anakin frowned. "Are you serious?"

"I'm most serious, I'm afraid. It is a . . . complicated situation, Anakin. It seems there are some in the Senate who now regret having granted me emergency powers."

"There have been dissenters and naysayers since before Geonosis, sir. Why should it be cause for concern now? And how does it affect Obi-Wan?"

"I'm getting to that." Palpatine took a deep breath and swung his chair around so that he could gaze through his window of armored transparisteel onto the cityscape beyond. "The difference is that now, some of these Senators—actually a large number of them—seem to have given up on democracy. Unable to achieve their ends in the Senate, they are organizing into a cabal, preparing to remove me by . . . other means."

"You mean treason?" Anakin had enough Jedi discipline to force away his memory of using that word with Obi-Wan.

"I'm afraid so. The rumor is that the ringleaders of this group may have fallen victim to the . . . persuasive powers . . . of the Jedi Council, and are on their way to becoming accomplices in the Council's plot against the Republic."

"Sir, I—" Anakin shook his head. "This just seems . . . ridiculous."

"And it may be entirely false. Remember that these are only rumors. Entirely unconfirmed. Senate gossip is rarely accurate, but if this *is* true . . . we must be *prepared,* Anakin. I still have friends enough in the Senate to catch the scent of whatever this disloyal cabal is cooking up. And I have a very good idea of who the leaders are; in fact, my final meeting this afternoon is with a delegation representing the cabal. I would like you to be present for that as well."

"Me?" Couldn't everyone leave him alone for day? For even a few *hours?* "What for?"

"Your Jedi senses, Anakin. Your ability to read evil intent. I have no doubt these Senators will put some virtuous façade on their plotting; with your help, we will pierce that veil and discover the truth."

Anakin sighed, rubbing his stinging eyes. How could he let Palpatine down? "I'm willing to try, sir."

"We won't try, Anakin. We will *do.* After all, they are only Senators. Most of them couldn't hide what they're thinking from a brain-damaged blindworm, let alone the most powerful Jedi in the galaxy."

He leaned back in his chair and steepled his fingers pensively. "The Jedi Council, however, is another matter entirely. A secret society of antidemocratic beings who wield tremendous power, individually as well as collectively—how am I to trace the labyrinth of *their* plots? That's why I put you on the Council. If these rumors are true, you may be democracy's last hope."

Anakin let his chin sink once more to his chest, and his eyelids scraped shut. It seemed like he was always *somebody's* last hope.

Why did everyone always have to make their problems into *his* problems? Why couldn't people just let him be?

How was he supposed to deal with all this when Padmé could *die*?

He said slowly, eyes still closed, "You still haven't told me what this has to do with Obi-Wan."

"Ah, that—well, that is the difficult part. The *disturbing* part. It seems that Master Kenobi has been in contact with a certain Senator who is known to be among the leaders of this cabal. Apparently, very *close* contact. The rumor is that he was seen leaving this Senator's residence this very morning, at an . . . unseemly hour."

"Who?" Anakin opened his eyes and sat forward. "Who is this Senator? Let's go question *him*."

"I'm sorry, Anakin. But the Senator in question is, in fact, a *her*. A woman you know quite well, in fact."

"You—" He wasn't hearing this. He couldn't be. "You mean—"

Anakin choked on her name.

Palpatine gave him a look of melancholy sympathy. "I'm afraid so."

Anakin coughed his voice back to life. "That's *impossible*! I would *know*—she doesn't . . . she couldn't—"

"Sometimes the closest," Palpatine said sadly, "are those who cannot see."

Anakin sat back, stunned. He felt like he'd been punched in

the chest by a Gamorrean. By a *rancor*. His ears rang, and the room whirled around him.

"I would know," he repeated numbly. "I would know . . ."

"Don't take it too hard," Palpatine said. "It may be only idle gossip. All this may be only a figment of my overheated imagination; after all these years of war, I find myself inspecting every shadow that might hide an enemy. That is what I need from *you*, Anakin: I need you to find the truth. To set my mind at rest."

A distant smolder kindled under Anakin's breastbone, so faint as to be barely there at all, but even a hint of that fire gave Anakin the strength to throw himself to his feet.

"I can do that," he said.

The flame grew stronger now. Hotter. The numb fatigue that had dragged at his limbs began to burn away.

"Good, Anakin. I knew I could count on you."

"Always, sir. Always."

He turned to go. He would go to her. He would see her. He would get the truth. He would do it *now*. Right now. In the middle of the day. It didn't matter who might see him.

This was business.

"I know who my friends are," he said, and left.

He moved through Padmé's apartment like a shadow, like a ghost at a banquet. He touched nothing. He looked at everything.

He felt as if he'd never seen it before.

How could she do this to him?

Sometimes the closest are those who cannot see.

How *could* she?

How could *he*?

In the Force, the whole apartment stank of Obi-Wan.

His finger traced the curving back of her couch.

Here. Obi-Wan had sat here.

Anakin rounded the couch and settled into that same spot. His hand fell naturally to the seat beside him . . . and there he felt an echo of Padmé.

The dragon whispered, *That's a little close for casual conversation.*

This was a different kind of fear. Even colder. Even uglier.

Fear that Palpatine might be *right* . . .

The apartment's air still hummed with discord and worry, and there was a smell of oxidized spices and boiled seaweed—hoi-broth, that was it. Someone in the past few hours had been drinking hoi-broth in this room.

Padmé hated hoi-broth.

And Obi-Wan was allergic to it—once on a diplomatic mission to Ando, his violent reaction to a ceremonial toast had nearly triggered an intersystem incident.

So Padmé had been entertaining other visitors, too.

From a pocket on his equipment belt he pulled a flimsi of Palpatine's list of suspect Senators. He scanned down the list, looking for names of Senators he knew well enough that he might recognize the Force-echoes of their presence here. Many he'd never heard of; there were thousands of Senators, after all. But those he knew by reputation were the cream of the Senate: people like Terr Taneel, Fang Zar, Bail Organa, Garm Bel Iblis—

He began to think Palpatine *was* just imagining things after all. These beings were known to be incorruptible.

He frowned down at the flimsi. It was *possible* . . .

A Senator might carefully construct a reputation, appearing to all the galaxy as honest and upright and honorable, all the while holding the rotten truth of himself so absolutely secret that no one would sense his evil until he had so much power that it was too late to stop him . . .

It *was* possible.

But so many? Could they *all* have accomplished that?

Could Padmé?

Suspicion leaked back into his mind and gathered itself into so thick a cloud that he didn't sense her approach until she was already in the room.

"Anakin? What are you doing here? It's still the middle of the afternoon . . ."

He looked up to find her standing in the archway in full Senatorial regalia: heavy folds of burgundy robes and a coif like a starfighter's hyperdrive ring. Instead of a smile, instead of sunlight in her eyes, instead of the bell-clear joy with which she had always greeted him, her face was nearly expressionless: attentively blank.

Anakin called it her Politician Look, and he hated it.

"Waiting for you," he replied, a little unsteadily. "What are *you* doing here in the middle of the afternoon?"

"I have a very important meeting in two hours," she said stiffly. "I left a document reader here this morning—"

"This meeting—is it with the *Chancellor*?" Anakin's voice came out low and harsh. "Is it his *last meeting of the afternoon*?"

"Y-yes, yes it is." She frowned, blinking. "Anakin, what's—"

"I have to be there, too." He crumpled the flimsi and stuffed it back into his equipment belt. "I'm starting to look forward to it."

"Anakin, what is it?" She came toward him, one hand reaching for him. "What's wrong?"

He lurched to his feet. "Obi-Wan's been here, hasn't he?"

"He came by this morning." She stopped. Her hand slowly lowered back to her side. "Why?"

"What did you talk about?"

"Anakin, why are you acting like this?"

One long stride brought him to her. He towered over her. For one stretching second she looked very small, very insignificant, very much like some kind of bug that he could crush beneath his heel and just keep on walking.

"What did you *talk* about?"

She gazed steadily up at him, and on her face was only concern, shaded with growing hurt. "We talked about you."

"What *about* me?"

"He's worried about you, Anakin. He says you're under a lot of stress."

"And he's *not*?"

"The way you've been acting, since you got back—"

"*I'm* not the one doing the *acting*. I'm not the one doing the pretending! I'm not the one sneaking *in* here in the *morning*!"

"No," she said with a smile. She reached up to lay the palm of her hand along the line of his jaw. "That's usually when you're sneaking *out*."

Her touch unclenched his heart.

He half fell into a chair and pressed the edge of his flesh hand against his eyes.

When he could overcome his embarrassment enough to speak, he said softly, "I'm sorry, Padmé. I'm sorry. I know I've been . . . difficult to deal with. I just—I feel like I'm in free fall. Free fall in the dark. I don't know which way is up. I don't know where I'll be when I land. Or crash."

He frowned against his fingers, squeezing his eyes more tightly shut to make sure no tears leaked out. "I think it's going to be a crash."

She sat on the wide-rolled arm of his chair and laid her slim arm along his shoulders. "What has happened, my love? You've always been so sure of yourself. What's changed?"

"Nothing," he said. "Everything. I don't know. It's all so screwed up, I can't even tell you. The Council doesn't trust me, Palpatine doesn't trust the Council. They're plotting against each other and both sides are pressuring *me*, and—"

"Surely that's only your imagination, Anakin. The Jedi Council is the bedrock of the Republic."

"The bedrock of the Republic is *democracy*, Padmé—

something the Council doesn't much like when votes don't go their way. *All those who gain power are afraid to lose it*—that's something you should remember." He looked up at her. "You and your *friends* in the *Senate*."

She took this without a blink. "But Obi-Wan is on the Council; *he'd* never participate in anything the least bit underhanded—"

"You think so?"

Because it's not for the record, Anakin. You must be able to understand why.

He shook the memory away. "It doesn't matter. Obi-Wan's on his way to Utapau."

"What is this really about?"

"I don't *know*," he said helplessly. "I don't know *anything* anymore. All I know is, I'm not the Jedi I should be. I'm not the *man* I should be."

"You're the man for me," she said, leaning toward him to kiss his cheek, but he pulled away.

"You don't understand. *Nobody* understands. I'm one of the most powerful Jedi alive, but it's not enough. It'll *never* be enough, not until—"

His voice trailed away, and his eyes went distant, and his memory burned with an alien birthing table, and blood, and screams.

"Until what, my love?"

"Until I can *save* you," he murmured.

"Save me?"

"From my nightmares."

She smiled sadly. "Is that what's bothering you?"

"I won't lose you, Padmé. I can't." He sat forward and twisted to take both of her hands, small and soft and deceptively strong and beyond precious, between his own. "I am still learning, Padmé—I have found a key to truths deeper than the Jedi could ever teach me. I will become so powerful that I will keep you *safe*. Forever. I *will*."

"You don't need more power, Anakin." She gently extricated one of her hands and used it to draw him close. "I believe you can save me from anything, just as you are."

She pulled him to her and their lips met, and Anakin gave himself to the kiss, and while it lasted, he believed it, too.

A shroud of twilight lowered upon Galactic City.

Anakin stood at what a clone trooper would have called parade rest—a wide, balanced stance, feet parallel, hands clasped behind his back. He stood one pace behind and to the left of the chair where Palpatine sat, behind his broad desk in the small private office attached to his large public one.

On the other side of the desk stood the Senate delegation.

The way they had looked at him, when they had entered the office—the way their eyes still, even now, flicked to his, then away again before he could fully meet their gaze—the way none of them, not even Padmé, dared to ask why the Supreme Chancellor had a Jedi at his shoulder during what was supposed to be a private meeting . . . it seemed to him that they already guessed why he was here.

They were simply afraid to bring it up.

Now they couldn't be sure where the Jedi stood. The only thing that was clear was where Anakin stood—

Respectfully in attendance upon Supreme Chancellor Palpatine.

Anakin studied the Senators.

Fang Zar: face creased with old laugh lines, dressed in robes so simple they might almost be homespun, unruly brush of hair gathered into a tight topknot, and an even more unruly brush of beard that sprayed uncontrolled around his jaw. He had a gentle, almost simplistic way of speaking that could easily lead one to forget that he was one of the sharpest political minds in the Senate. Also, he was such a close friend of Garm Bel Iblis that the powerful Corellian Senator might as well have been present in person.

Anakin had watched him closely throughout the meeting. Fang Zar had something on his mind, that was certain—something that he did not seem willing to say.

Nee Alavar and Malé-Dee he could dismiss as threats; the two stood together—perhaps needing each other for moral support—and neither had said anything at all. And then, of course, there was Padmé.

Glowing in her Senatorial regalia, the painted perfection of her face luminous as all four of Coruscant's moons together, not a single hair out of place in her elaborate coif—

Speaking in her Politician Voice, and wearing her Politician Look.

Padmé did the talking. Anakin had a sickening suspicion that this was all her idea.

"We are not attempting to delegitimize your government," she was saying. "That's why we're here. If we were trying to organize an opposition—if we sought to impose our requests as demands—we would hardly bring them before you in this fashion. This petition has been signed by two thousand Senators, Chancellor. We ask only that you instruct your governors not to interfere with the legitimate business of the Senate, and that you open peace talks with the Separatists. We seek only to end the war, and bring peace and stability back to our homeworlds. Surely you can understand this."

"I understand a great many things," Palpatine said.

"This system of governors you have created is very troubling—it seems that you are imposing military controls even on loyalist systems."

"Your reservations are noted, Senator Amidala. I assure you that the Republic governors are intended only to make your systems safer—by coordinating planetary defense forces, and ensuring that neighboring systems mesh into cooperative units, and bringing production facilities up to speed in service to the war effort. That's all. They will in no way compete with the duties and prerogatives—with the power—of the Senate."

Something in the odd emphasis he put on the word *power* made Anakin think Palpatine was speaking more for Anakin's benefit than for Padmé's.

All those who gain power are afraid to lose it

"May I take it, then," Padmé said, "that there will be no further amendments to the Constitution?"

"My dear Senator, what has the Constitution to do with this? I thought we were discussing ending the war. Once the Separatists have been defeated, then we can start talking about the Constitution again. Must I remind you that the extraordinary powers granted to my office by the Senate are only in force for the duration of the emergency? Once the war ends, they expire automatically."

"And your governors? Will they 'expire,' too?"

"They are not *my* governors, my lady, they are the Republic's," Palpatine replied imperturbably. "The fate of their positions will be in the hands of the Senate, where it belongs."

Padmé did not seem reassured. "And peace talks? Will you offer a cease-fire? Have you even *tried* a diplomatic resolution to the war?"

"You must trust me to do the right thing," he said. "That is, after all, why I am here."

Fang Zar roused himself. "But surely—"

"I have said I will do what is *right*," Palpatine said, a testy edge sharpening his voice. He rose, drawing himself up to his full height, then inclining his head with an air of finality. "And that should be enough for your . . . committee."

His tone said: *Don't let the door crunch you on the way out.*

Padmé's mouth compressed into a thin, grim line. "On behalf of the Delegation of the Two Thousand," she said with tight-drawn formality, "I thank you, Chancellor."

"And I thank you, Senator Amidala, and your friends—" Palpatine lifted the document reader containing the petition. "—for bringing this to my attention."

The Senators turned reluctantly and began to file out. Padmé paused, just for a second, to meet Anakin's eyes with a gaze as clear as a slap on the mouth.

He stayed expressionless. Because in the end, no matter how much he wanted to, no matter how much it hurt . . . he couldn't quite make himself believe he was on her side.

DEATH ON UTAPAU

When constructing an effective Jedi trap—as opposed to the sort that results in nothing more than an embarrassingly brief entry in the Temple archives—there are several design features that one should include for best results.

The first is an irresistible bait. The commanding general of an outlaw nation, personally responsible for billions of deaths across the galaxy, is ideal.

The second is a remote, nearly inaccessible location, one that is easily taken and easily fortified, with a sharply restricted field of action. It should also, ideally, belong to someone else, preferably an enemy; the locations used for Jedi traps never survive the operation unscathed, and many don't survive it at all. An excellent choice would be an impoverished desert planet in the Outer Rim, with unwarlike natives, whose few cities are built in a cluster of sinkholes on a vast arid plateau. A city in a sinkhole is virtually a giant kill-jar; once a Jedi flies in, all one need do is seal the lid.

Third, since it is always a good idea to remain well out of reach when plotting against a Jedi's life—on the far side of the galaxy is considered best—one should have a reliable proxy to do the actual murder. The exemplar of a reliable proxy would be, for example, the most prolific living Jedi killer, backed up by a squad of advanced combat droids designed, built, and armed specifically to fight Jedi. Making one's proxy double as the bait is an impressively elegant stroke, if it can be managed, since it ensures that the Jedi victim will voluntarily place himself in contact with the Jedi killer—and will continue to do so even *after* he realizes the extent of the trap, out of a combination of devotion to duty and a not-entirely-unjustified arrogance.

The fourth element of an effective Jedi trap is a massively overwhelming force of combat troops who are willing to burn the whole planet, including themselves if necessary, to ensure that the Jedi in question does not escape.

A textbook example of the ideal Jedi trap is the one that waited on Utapau for Obi-Wan Kenobi.

As Obi-Wan sent his starfighter spiraling in toward a landing deck that protruded from the sheer sandstone wall of the biggest of Utapau's sinkhole-cities, he reviewed what he knew of the planet and its inhabitants.

There wasn't much.

He knew that despite its outward appearance, Utapau was not a true desert planet; there was water aplenty in an underground ocean that circled its globe. The erosive action of this buried ocean had undermined vast areas of its surface, and frequent groundquakes collapsed them into sinkholes large enough to land a *Victory*-class Star Destroyer, where civilization could thrive below reach of the relentless scouring hyperwinds on the surface. He knew that the planet had little in the way of high technology, and that their energy economy was based on wind power; the planet's limited interstellar trade had begun only a few decades before, when offworld water-mining companies had discovered that the waters of the world-ocean were rich in dissolved trace elements. He knew that the inhabitants were near-human, divided into two distinct species, the tall, lordly, slow-moving Utapauns, nicknamed Ancients for their astonishing longevity, and the stubby Utai, called Shorts, both for their stature and for their brief busy lives.

And he knew that Grievous was here.

How he knew, he could not say; so far as he could tell, his conviction had nothing to do with the Force. But within seconds of the *Vigilance*'s realspace reversion, he was sure. This was it. One way or another, this was the place his hunt for General Grievous would come to a close.

He felt it in his bones: Utapau was a planet for endings.

He was going in alone; Commander Cody and three battalions of troopers waited in rapid-deployment vehicles—LAAT/i's and *Jadthu*-class landers—just over the horizon. Obi-Wan's plan was to pinpoint Grievous's location, then keep the bio-droid general busy until the clones could attack; he would be a one-man diversionary force, holding the attention of what was sure to be thousands or tens of thousands of combat droids directed inward toward him and Grievous, to cover the approach of the clones. Two battalions would strike full-force, with the third in reserve, both to provide reinforcements and to cover possible escape routes.

"I can keep them distracted for quite some time," Obi-Wan had told Cody on the flight deck of *Vigilance*. "Just don't take too long."

"Come on, boss," Cody had said, smiling out of Jango Fett's face, "have I ever let you down?"

"Well—" Obi-Wan had said with a slim answering smile, "Cato Neimoidia, for starters . . ."

"That was Anakin's fault; *he* was the one who was late . . ."

"Oh? And who will you blame it on *this* time?" Obi-Wan had chuckled as he climbed into his starfighter's cockpit and strapped himself in. "Very well, then. I'll try not to destroy all the droids before you get there."

"I'm counting on you, boss. Don't let me down."

"Have I ever?"

"Well," Cody had said with a broad grin, "there *was* Cato Neimoidia . . ."

Obi-Wan's fighter bucked through coils of turbulence; the rim of the sinkhole caught enough of the hyperwinds above that the first few levels of city resided in a semipermanent hurricane. Whirling blades of wind-power turbines stuck out from the sinkhole's sides on generator pods so scoured by the fierce winds that they might themselves have been molded of liquid sandstone. He fought the fighter's controls to bring it down level after level until the wind had become a mere gale; even after reaching the landing deck in the depths of the sinkhole, R4-G9 had to extend the starfighter's docking claws to keep it from being blown, skidding, right off the deck.

A ribbed semitransparent canopy swung out to enfold the landing deck; once it had settled into place around him, the howl of winds dropped to silence and Obi-Wan popped the cockpit.

A pack of Utai was already scampering toward the starfighter, which stood alone on the deck; they carried a variety of tools and dragged equipment behind them, and Obi-Wan assumed they were some sort of ground crew. Behind them glided the stately form of an Utapaun in a heavy deck-length robe of deep scarlet that had a lapel collar so tall it concealed his vestigial ear-disks. The Utapaun's glabrous scalp glistened with a sheen of moisture, and he walked with a staff that reminded Obi-Wan vaguely of Yoda's beloved gimer stick.

That was quick, Obi-Wan thought. *Almost like they've been expecting me.*

"Greetings, young Jedi," the Utapaun said gravely in accented Basic. "I am Tion Medon, master of port administration for this place of peace. What business could bring a Jedi to our remote sanctuary?"

Obi-Wan sensed no malice in this being, and the Utapaun ra-diated a palpable aura of fear; Obi-Wan decided to tell the truth. "My business is the war," he said.

"There is no war here, unless you have brought it with you," Medon replied, a mask of serenity concealing what the Force told Obi-Wan was anxiety verging on panic.

"Very well, then," Obi-Wan said, playing along. "Please per-mit me to refuel here, and to use your city as a base to search the surrounding systems."

"For what do you search?"

"Even in the Outer Rim, you must have heard of General Grievous. It is he I seek, and his army of droids."

Tion Medon took another step closer and leaned down to bring his face near Obi-Wan's ear. "He is here!" Medon whis-pered urgently. "We are hostages—we are being watched!"

Obi-Wan nodded matter-of-factly. "Thank you, Master Medon," he said in a thoroughly ordinary voice. "I am grateful for your hospitality, and will depart as soon as your crew refuels my starfighter."

"Listen to me, young Jedi!" Medon's whisper became even more intense. "You must depart in *truth!* I was *ordered* to reveal their presence—this is a trap!"

"Of course it is," Obi-Wan said equably.

"The tenth level—thousands of war droids—*tens* of thou-sands!"

"Have your people seek shelter." Obi-Wan turned casually and scanned upward, counting levels. On the tenth, his eye found a spiny spheroid of metal: a Dreadnaught-sized structure that clearly had not been there for long—its gleaming surface had not yet been scoured to matte by the sand in the constant winds. He nodded absently and spoke softly, as though to him-self. "Geenine, take my starfighter back to the *Vigilance*. Instruct Commander Cody to inform Jedi Command on Coruscant that

I have made contact with General Grievous. I am engaging now. Cody is to attack in full force, as planned."

The astromech beeped acknowledgment from its forward socket, and Obi-Wan turned once more to Tion Medon. "Tell them I promised to file a report with Republic Intelligence. Tell them I really only wanted fuel enough to leave immediately."

"But—but what will you *do*?"

"If you have warriors," Obi-Wan said gravely, "now is the time."

In the holocomm center of Jedi Command, within the heart of the Temple on Coruscant, Anakin watched a life-sized holoscan of Clone Commander Cody report that Obi-Wan had made contact with General Grievous.

"We are beginning our supporting attack as ordered. And—if I may say so, sirs—from my experience working with General Kenobi, I have a suspicion that Grievous does not have long to live."

If I were there with *him*, Anakin thought, *it'd be more than a suspicion. Obi-Wan, be* careful—

"Thank you, Commander." Mace Windu's face did not betray the slightest hint of the mingled dread and anticipation Anakin was sure he must be feeling; while Anakin himself felt ready to burst, Windu looked calm as a stone. "Keep us apprised of your progress. May the Force be with you, and with Master Kenobi."

"I'm sure it will be, sir. Cody out."

The holoscan flickered to nothingness. Mace Windu turned brief but seemingly significant glances upon the other two Masters in attendance, both holoscans themselves: Ki-Adi-Mundi from the fortified command center on Mygeeto, and from a guerrilla outpost on Kashyyyk, Yoda.

Then he turned to Anakin. "Take this report to the Chancellor."

"Of course I will, Master."

"And take careful note of his reaction. We will need a full account."

"Master?"

"What he says, Anakin. Who he calls. What he does. Everything. Even his facial expressions. It's very important."

"I don't understand—"

"You don't have to. Just do it."

"Master—"

"Anakin, do I have to remind you that you are still a Jedi? You are still subject to the orders of this Council."

"Yes, Master Windu. Yes, I am," he said, and left.

Once Skywalker was gone, Mace Windu found himself in a chair, staring at the doorway through which the young Jedi Knight had left. "Now we shall see," he murmured. "At last. The waters will begin to clear."

Though he shared the command center with the holoscans of two other Jedi Masters, Mace wasn't talking to them. He spoke to the grim, clouded future inside his head.

"Have you considered," Ki-Adi-Mundi said carefully, from faraway Mygeeto, *"that if Palpatine refuses to surrender power, removing him is only a first step?"*

Mace looked at the blue ghost of the Cerean Master. "I am not a politician. Removing a tyrant is enough for me."

"But it will not be enough for the Republic," Ki-Adi-Mundi countered sadly. *"Palpatine's dictatorship has been legitimized— and can be legalized, even enshrined in a revised Constitution—by the supermajority he controls in the Senate."*

The grim future inside Mace's head turned even darker. The Cerean was right.

"Filled with corruption, the Senate is," Yoda agreed from Kashyyyk. *"Controlled, they must be, until replaced the corrupted Senators can be, with Senators honest and—"*

"Do you *hear* us?" Mace lowered his head into his hands. "How have we come to this? Arresting a Chancellor. Taking over the *Senate*—! It's as though Dooku was *right*—to save the Republic, we'll have to destroy it . . ."

Yoda lifted his head, and his eyes slitted as though he struggled with some inner pain. *"Hold on to hope we must; our true enemy, Palpatine is not, nor the Senate; the true enemy is instead the Sith Lord Sidious, who controls them both. Once destroyed Sidious is . . . all these other concerns, less dire they will instantly become."*

"Yes." Mace Windu rose, and moved to the window, hands folded behind his back. "Yes, that is true."

Indigo gloom gathered among the towers outside.

"And we have put the chosen one in play against the last Lord of the Sith," he said. "In that, we must place our faith, and our hopes for the future of the Republic."

The landing deck canopy parted, and the blue-and-white Jedi starfighter blasted upward into the gale. From deep shadows at the rear of the deck, Obi-Wan watched it go.

"I suppose I am committed, now," he murmured.

Through electrobinoculars produced from his equipment belt, he examined that suspiciously shiny spheroid high above on the tenth level. The spray of spines had to be droid-control antennas. That's where Grievous would be: at the nerve center of his army.

"Then that's where I should be, too." He looked around, frowning. "Never an air taxi when you need one . . ."

The reclosing of the deck canopy quieted the howl of the wind outside, and now from deeper within the city Obi-Wan could hear a ragged choir of hoarsely bellowing cries that had the resonance of large animals—they reminded him of something . . .

Suubatars, that was it—they sounded vaguely like the calls of the suubatars he and Anakin had ridden on one of their last missions before the war, back when biggest worry Obi-Wan had had was how to keep his promise to Qui-Gon . . .

But he had no time for nostalgia. He could practically hear Qui-Gon reminding him to focus on the now, and give himself over to the living Force.

So he did.

Mere moments of following the cries through the shadows of deserted hallways carved into the sandstone brought Obi-Wan in sight of an immense, circular arena-like area, where a ring of balcony was joined to a flat lower level by spokes of broad, corrugated ramps; the ceiling above was hung with yellowish lamp-rods that cast a light the same color as the sunbeams striking through an arc of wide oval archways open to the interior of the sinkhole outside. The winds that whistled through those wide archways also went a long way toward cutting the eye-watering reptile-den stench down from overpowering to merely nauseating.

Squatting, lying, and milling aimlessly about the lower level were a dozen or so large lizard-like beasts that looked like the product of some mad geneticist's cross of Tatooine krayt dragons with Haruun Kal ankkoxen: four meters tall at the shoulder, long crooked legs that ended in five-clawed feet clearly designed for scaling rocky cliffs, ten meters of powerful tail ridged with spines and tipped with a horn-bladed mace, a flexible neck leading up to an armor-plated head that sported an impressive cowl of spines of its own—they looked fearsome enough that Obi-Wan might have thought them some sort of dangerous wild predators or vicious watchbeasts, were it not for the docile way they tolerated the team of Utai wranglers who walked among them, hosing them down, scraping muck from their scales, and letting them take bundles of greens from their hands.

Not far from where Obi-Wan stood, several large racks were hung with an array of high-backed saddles in various styles and degrees of ornamentation, very much indeed like those the Alwari of Ansion had strapped to their suubatars.

Now he *really* missed Anakin . . .

Anakin disliked living mounts almost as much as Obi-Wan hated to fly. Obi-Wan had long suspected that it was Anakin's gift with machines that worked against him with suubatar or dewback or bantha; he could never get entirely comfortable riding anything with a mind of its own. He could vividly imagine Anakin's complaints as he climbed into one of these saddles.

It seemed an awfully long time since Obi-Wan had had an opportunity to tease Anakin a bit.

With a sigh, he brought himself back to business. Moving out of the shadows, he walked down one of the corrugated ramps and made a slight, almost imperceptible hand gesture in the direction of the nearest of the Utai dragonmount wranglers. "I need transportation."

The Short's bulging eyes went distant and a bit glassy, and he responded with a string of burbling glottal hoots that had a decidedly affirmative tone.

Obi-Wan made another gesture. "Get me a saddle."

With another string of affirmative burbles, the Short waddled off.

While he waited for his saddle, Obi-Wan examined the dragonmounts. He passed up the largest, and the one most heavily muscled; he skipped over the leanest built-for-speed beast, and didn't even approach the one with the fiercest gleam in its eye. He didn't actually pay attention to outward signs of strength or health or personality; he was using his hands and eyes and ears purely as focusing channels for the Force. He didn't know what he was looking for, but he trusted that he would recognize it when he found it.

Qui-Gon, he reflected with an inward smile, would approve.

Finally he came to a dragonmount with a clear, steady gleam in its round yellow eyes, and small, close-set scales that felt warm and dry. It neither shied back from his hand nor bent submissively to his touch, but only returned his searching gaze with calm, thoughtful intelligence. Through the Force, he felt in the beast an unshakable commitment to obedience and care for its rider: an almost Jedi-like devotion to service as the ultimate duty.

This was why Obi-Wan would always prefer a living mount. A speeder is incapable of caring if it crashes.

"This one," he said. "I'll take this one."

The Short had returned with a plain, sturdily functional saddle; as he and the other wranglers undertook the complicated task of tacking up the dragonmount, he nodded at the beast and said, "Boga."

"Ah," Obi-Wan said. "Thank you."

He took a sheaf of greens from a nearby bin and offered them to the dragonmount. The great beast bent its head, its wickedly hooked beak delicately withdrew the greens from Obi-Wan's hand, and it chewed them with fastidious thoroughness.

"Good girl, Boga. Erm—" Obi-Wan frowned at the Short. "—she *is* a *she,* isn't she?"

The wrangler frowned back. "Warool noggaggllo?" he said, shrugging, which Obi-Wan took to mean *I have no idea what you're saying to me.*

"Very well, then," Obi-Wan said with an answering shrug. "*She* you will have to be, then, Boga. Unless you care to tell me otherwise."

Boga made no objection.

He swung himself up into the saddle and the dragonmount rose, arching her powerful back in a feline stretch that lifted Obi-Wan more than four meters off the floor. Obi-Wan looked down at the Utai wranglers. "I cannot pay you. As compensation, I can only offer the freedom of your planet; I hope that will suffice."

Without waiting for a reply that he would not have understood anyway, Obi-Wan touched Boga on the neck. Boga reared straight up and raked the air with her hooked foreclaws as though she were shredding an imaginary hailfire droid, then gathered herself and leapt to the ring-balcony in a single bound. Obi-Wan didn't need to use the long, hook-tipped goad strapped in a holster alongside the saddle; nor did he do more than lightly hold the reins in one hand. Boga seemed to understand exactly where he wanted to go.

The dragonmount slipped sinuously through one of the wide oval apertures into the open air of the sinkhole, then turned and seized the sandstone with those hooked claws to carry Obi-Wan straight up the sheer wall.

Level after level they climbed. The city looked and felt deserted. Nothing moved save the shadows of clouds crossing the sinkhole's mouth far, far above; even the wind-power turbines had been locked down.

The first sign of life he saw came on the tenth level itself; a handful of other dragonmounts lay basking in the midday sun, not far from the durasteel barnacle of the droid-control center. Obi-Wan rode Boga right up to the control center's open archway, then jumped down from the saddle.

The archway led into a towering vaulted hall, its durasteel decking bare of furnishing. Deep within the shadows that gathered in the hall stood a cluster of five figures. Their faces were the color of bleached bone. Or ivory armorplast.

They looked like they might, just possibly, be waiting for him.

Obi-Wan nodded to himself.

"You'd best find your way home, girl," he said, patting Boga's scaled neck. "One way or another, I doubt I'll have further need of your assistance."

Boga gave a soft, almost regretful honk of acknowledgment, then bent a sharper curve into her long flexible neck to place her beak gently against Obi-Wan's chest.

"It's all right, Boga. I thank you for your help, but to stay here will be dangerous. This area is about to become a free-fire zone. Please. Go home."

The dragonmount honked again and moved back, and Obi-Wan stepped from the sun into the shadow.

A wave-front of cool passed over him with the shade's embrace. He walked without haste, without urgency. The Force layered connections upon connections, and brought them all to life within him: the chill deck plates beneath his boots, and the stone beneath those, and far below that the smooth lightless currents of the world-ocean. He became the turbulent swirl of wind whistling through the towering vaulted hall; he became the sunlight outside and the shadow within. His human heart in its cage of bone echoed the beat of an alien one in a casket of armorplast, and his mind whirred with the electronic signal cascades that passed for thought in Jedi-killer droids.

And when the Force layered into his consciousness the awareness of the structure of the great hall itself, he became aware, without surprise and without distress, that the entire expanse of vaulted ceiling above his head was actually a storage hive.

Filled with combat droids.

Which made him also aware, again without surprise and without distress, that he would very likely die here.

Contemplation of death brought only one slight sting of regret, and more than a bit of puzzlement. Until this very moment, he had never realized he'd always expected, for no discernible reason—

That when he died, Anakin would be with him.

How curious, he thought, and then he turned his mind to business.

Anakin had a feeling Master Windu was going to be disappointed.

Palpatine had hardly reacted at all.

The Supreme Chancellor of the Republic sat at the small desk in his private office, staring distractedly at an abstract twist of neuranium that Anakin had always assumed was supposed to be some kind of sculpture, and merely sighed, as though he had matters of much greater importance on his mind.

"I'm sorry, sir," Anakin said, shifting his weight in front of Palpatine's desk. "Perhaps you didn't hear me. Obi-Wan has made contact with General Grievous. His attack is already under way—they're fighting *right now,* sir!"

"Yes, yes, of course, Anakin. Yes, quite." Palpatine still looked as if he was barely paying attention. "I entirely understand your concern for your friend. Let us hope he is up to the task."

"It's not just concern for Obi-Wan, sir; taking General Grievous will be the final victory for the Republic—!"

"Will it?" He turned to Anakin, and a distinctly troubled frown chased the distraction from his face. "I'm afraid, my boy, that our situation is a great deal more grave than even I had feared. Perhaps you should sit down."

Anakin didn't move. "What do you mean?"

"Grievous is no longer the real enemy. Even the Clone Wars themselves are now only . . . a distraction."

"What?"

"The Council is about to make its move," Palpatine said, grim and certain. "If we don't stop them, by this time tomorrow the Jedi may very well have taken over the Republic."

Anakin burst into astonished laughter. "But sir—please, you can't possibly *believe* that—"

"Anakin, I *know.* I will be the first to be arrested—the first to be *executed*—but I will be far from the last."

Anakin could only shake his head in disbelief. "Sir, I know that the Council and you have . . . disagreements, but—"

"This is far beyond any personal dispute between me and the members of the Council. This is a plot *generations* in the

making—a plot to take over the Republic itself. Anakin, *think*—
you know they don't trust you. They never have. You know they
have been keeping things from you. You know they have made
plans behind your back—you know that even your great friend
Obi-Wan has not told you what their true intentions are . . . It's
because you're not *like* them, Anakin—you're a *man*, not just
a Jedi."

Anakin's head drew down toward his shoulders as though he
found himself under enemy fire. "I don't—they wouldn't—"

"Ask yourself: why did they send you to me with this news?
Why? Why not simply notify me through normal channels?"

*And take careful note of his reaction. We will need a full ac-
count*

"Sir, I—ah—"

"No need to fumble for an explanation," he said gently.
"You've already as much as admitted they've ordered you to spy
upon me. Don't you understand that anything you tell them
tonight—whatever it may be—will be used as an excuse to order
my execution?"

"That's impossible—" Anakin sought desperately for an argument. "The Senate—the Senate would never allow it—"

"The Senate will be powerless to stop it. I told you this is
bigger than any personal dislike between the Council and myself.
I am only one man, Anakin. My authority is granted by the Senate; it is the Senate that is the true government of the Republic.
Killing me is nothing; to control the Republic, the Jedi will have
to take over the Senate *first*."

"But the Jedi—the Jedi *serve* the Senate—!"

"Do they?" Palpatine asked mildly. "Or do they serve certain
Senators?"

"This is all—I'm sorry, Chancellor, please, you have to
understand how this *sounds* . . ."

"Here—" The Chancellor rummaged around within his desk

for a moment, then brought forth a document reader. "Do you know what this is?"

Anakin recognized the seal Padmé had placed on it. "Yes, sir—that's the Petition of the Two Thousand—"

"*No,* Anakin! No!" Palpatine slammed the document reader on his desktop hard enough to make Anakin jump. "It is a roll of *traitors.*"

Anakin went absolutely still. "What?"

"There are, now, only two kinds of Senators in our government, Anakin. Those whose names are on this so-called *petition,*" Palpatine said, "and those whom the Jedi are about to *arrest.*"

Anakin could only stare.

He couldn't argue. He couldn't even make himself disbelieve.

He had only one thought.

Padmé . . . ?

How much trouble was she in?

"Didn't I *warn* you, Anakin? Didn't I tell you what Obi-Wan was up to? Why do you think he was meeting with the leaders of this . . . delegation . . . behind your *back?*"

"But—but, sir, please, surely, all they asked for is an end to the war. It's what the Jedi want, too. I mean, it's what we *all* want, isn't it? Isn't it?"

"Perhaps. Though *how* that end comes about may be the single most important thing about the war. More important, even, than who wins."

Oh, Padmé, Anakin moaned inside his head. *Padmé, what have you gotten yourself into?*

"Their . . . sincerity . . . may be much to be admired," Palpatine said. "Or it would be, were it not that there was much more to that meeting than met the eye."

Anakin frowned. "What do you mean?"

"Their . . . petition . . . was nothing of the sort. It was, in fact, a not-so-veiled *threat*." Palpatine sighed regretfully. "It was a show of force, Anakin. A demonstration of the political power the Jedi will be able to muster in support of their rebellion."

Anakin blinked. "But—but surely—" he stammered, rounding Palpatine's desk, "surely Senator *Amidala,* at least, can be trusted . . ."

"I understand how badly you need to believe that," the Chancellor said. "But Senator Amidala is hiding something. Surely you sensed it."

"If she is—" Anakin swayed; the floor seemed to be tilting under his feet like the deck of *Invisible Hand*. "Even if she *is,*" he said, his voice flat, overcontrolled, "it doesn't mean that what she is hiding is treason."

Palpatine's brows drew together. "I'm surprised your Jedi insights are not more sensitive to such things."

"I simply don't sense betrayal in Senator Amidala," Anakin insisted.

Palpatine leaned back in his chair, steepling his fingers, studying Anakin skeptically. "Yes, you do," he said after a moment. "Though you don't want to admit it. Perhaps it is because neither you nor she yet understands that by betraying me, she is also betraying *you*."

"She couldn't—" Anakin pressed a hand to his forehead; his dizziness was getting worse. When had he last eaten? He couldn't remember. It might have been before the last time he'd slept. "She could *never* . . ."

"Of course she could," Palpatine said. "That is the nature of politics, my boy. Don't take it too personally. It doesn't mean the two of you can't be happy together."

"What—?" The room seemed to darken around him. "What do you mean?"

"Please, Anakin. Are we not past the point of playing childish games with one another? I *know,* do you understand? I have *always* known. I have pretended ignorance only to spare you discomfort."

Anakin had to lean on the desk. "What—what do you know?"

"Anakin, Padmé was my Queen; I was her ambassador to the Senate. Naboo is my *home.* You of all people know how I value loyalty and friendship; do you think I have no friends among the civil clergy in Theed? Your secret ceremony has never *been* secret. Not from me, at any rate. I have always been very happy for you both."

"You—" Words whirled through Anakin's mind, and none of them made sense. "But if she's going to *betray* us—"

"*That,* my boy," Palpatine said, "is entirely up to *you.*"

The fog inside Anakin's head seemed to solidify into a long, dark tunnel. The point of light at the end was Palpatine's face. "I don't—I don't understand . . ."

"Oh yes, that's very clear." The Chancellor's voice seemed to be coming from very far away. "Please sit, my boy. You're looking rather unwell. May I offer you something to drink?"

"I—no. No, I'm all right." Anakin sank gratefully into a dangerously comfortable chair. "I'm just—a little tired, that's all."

"Not sleeping well?"

"No." Anakin offered an exhausted chuckle. "I haven't been sleeping well for a few years, now."

"I quite understand, my boy. Quite." Palpatine rose and rounded his desk, sitting casually on its front edge. "Anakin, we must stop pretending. The final crisis is approaching, and our only hope to survive it is to be completely, absolutely, ruthlessly honest with each other. And with ourselves. You must understand that what is at stake here is nothing less than the fate of the galaxy."

"I don't know—"

"Don't be afraid, Anakin. What is said between us here need never pass beyond these walls. Anakin, *think:* think how hard it has been to hold all your secrets inside. Have you ever needed to keep a secret from *me*?"

He ticked his fingers one by one. "I have kept the secret of your marriage all these years. The slaughter at the Tusken camp, you shared with me. I was there when you executed Count Dooku. And I know where you got the power to defeat him. You see? You have never needed to *pretend* with me, the way you must with your Jedi comrades. Do you understand that you need never hide *anything* from me? That I accept you exactly as you are?"

He spread his hands as though offering a hug. "Share with me the truth. Your absolute truth. Let yourself *out*, Anakin."

"I—" Anakin shook his head. How many times had he dreamed of not having to pretend to be the perfect Jedi? But what else could he be? "I wouldn't even know how to begin."

"It's quite simple, in the end: tell me what you want."

Anakin squinted up at him. "I don't understand."

"Of course you don't." The last of the sunset haloed his ice-white hair and threw his face into shadow. "You've been trained to never think about that. The Jedi never ask what *you* want. They simply *tell* you what you're *supposed* to want. They never give you a choice at all. That's why they take their students—their *victims*—at an age so young that choice is meaningless. By the time a Padawan is old enough to *choose*, he has been so indoctrinated—so *brainwashed*—that he is incapable of even considering the question. But you're different, Anakin. You had a real life, outside the Jedi Temple. You can break through the fog of lies the Jedi have pumped into your brain. I ask you again: what do you want?"

"I still don't understand."

"I am offering you . . . anything," Palpatine said. "Ask, and it is yours. A glass of water? It's yours. A bag full of Corusca gems? Yours. Look out the window behind me, Anakin. Pick something, and it's yours."

"Is this some kind of joke?"

"The time for jokes is past, Anakin. I have never been more serious." Within the shadow that cloaked Palpatine's face, Anakin could only just see the twin gleams of the Chancellor's eyes. "Pick something. Anything."

"All right . . ." Shrugging, frowning, still not understanding, Anakin looked out the window, looking for the most ridiculously expensive thing he could spot. "How about one of those new SoroSuub custom speeders—"

"Done."

"Are you serious? You know how much one of those costs? You could practically outfit a *battle* cruiser—"

"Would you prefer a battle cruiser?"

Anakin went still. A cold void opened in his chest. In a small, cautious voice, he said, "How about the Senatorial Apartments?"

"A private apartment?"

Anakin shook his head, staring up at the twin gleams in the darkness on Palpatine's face. "The whole building."

Palpatine did not so much as blink. "Done."

"It's privately owned—"

"Not anymore."

"You can't just—"

"Yes, I can. It's yours. Is there anything else? Name it."

Anakin gazed blankly out into the gathering darkness. Stars began to shimmer through the haze of twilight. A constellation he recognized hung above the spires of the Jedi Temple.

"All right," Anakin said softly. "Corellia. I'll take Corellia."

"The planet, or the whole system?"

Anakin stared.

"Anakin?"

"I just—" He shook his head blankly. "I can't figure out if you're kidding, or completely insane."

"I am neither, Anakin. I am trying to impress upon you a fundamental truth of our relationship. A fundamental truth of *yourself*."

"What if I really *wanted* the Corellian system? The whole Five Brothers—*all* of it?"

"Then it would be yours. You can have the whole sector, if you like." The twin gleams within the shadow sharpened. "Do you understand, now? I will give you *anything you want.*"

The concept left him dizzy. "What if I wanted—what if I went along with Padmé and her friends? What if I want the *war* to *end?*"

"Would tomorrow be too soon?"

"How—" Anakin couldn't seem to get his breath. "How can you do that?"

"Right now, we are only discussing *what. How* is a different issue; we'll come to that presently."

Anakin sank deeper into the chair while he let everything sink deeper into his brain. If only his head would stop spinning—why did Palpatine have to start all this *now?*

This would all be easier to comprehend if the nightmares of Padmé didn't keep screaming inside his head.

"And in exchange?" he asked, finally. "What do *I* have to do?"

"You have to do what you *want.*"

"What I want?"

"Yes, Anakin. Yes. Exactly that. Only that. Do the one thing that the Jedi fear most: make up your *own* mind. Follow your own *conscience.* Do what *you* think is right. I know that you have been longing for a life greater than that of an ordinary Jedi. *Commit* to that life. I know you burn for greater power than any Jedi can wield; give yourself *permission* to *gain* that power, and allow yourself license to *use* it. You have dreamed of leaving the Jedi Order, having a family of your own—one that is based on *love,* not on enforced rules of self-denial."

"I—can't . . . I can't just . . . *leave* . . ."

"But you can."

Anakin couldn't breathe.

He couldn't blink.

He sat frozen. Even thought was impossible.

"You can have every one of your dreams. Turn aside from the lies of the Jedi, and follow the truth of yourself. Leave them. Join me on the path of true power. Be my friend, Anakin. Be my student. My apprentice."

Anakin's vision tunneled again, but this time there was no light at the far end. He pulled back his hand, and it was shaking as he brought it up to support his face.

"I'm sorry," he said. "I'm sorry, but—but as much as I want those things—as much as I care for you, sir—I can't. I just can't. Not yet. Because there's only one thing I *really* want, right now. Everything else will just have to wait."

"I know what you truly want," the shadow said. "I have only been waiting for you to admit it to yourself." A hand—a human hand, warm with compassion—settled onto his shoulder. "Listen to me: *I can help you save her.*"

"You—"

Anakin blinked blindly.

"How can *you* help?"

"Do you remember that myth I told you of, *The Tragedy of Darth Plagueis the Wise?*" the shadow whispered.

The myth—

. . . directly influence the midi-chlorians to create life; with such knowledge, to maintain life in someone already living would seem a small matter . . .

"Yes," Anakin said. "Yes, I remember."

The shadow leaned so close that it seemed to fill the world.

"Anakin, it's no mere myth."

Anakin swallowed.

"Darth Plagueis was real."

Anakin could force out only a strangled whisper. "*Real . . . ?*"

"Darth Plagueis was my Master. He taught me the key to his power," the shadow said, dryly matter-of-fact, "before I killed him."

Without understanding how he had moved, without even intending to move, without any transition of realization or dawning understanding, Anakin found himself on his feet. A blue bar of sizzling energy terminated a centimeter from Palpatine's chin, its glow casting red-edged shadows up his face and across the ceiling.

Only gradually did Anakin come to understand that this was his lightsaber, and that it was in his hand.

"You," he said. Suddenly he was neither dizzy nor tired.

Suddenly everything made sense.

"It's *you*. It's *been* you all *along*!"

In the clean blue light of his blade he stared into the face of a man whose features were as familiar to him as his own, but now seemed as alien as an extragalactic comet—because now he finally understood that those familiar features were only a mask.

He had never seen this man's real face.

"I should *kill* you," he said. "I *will* kill you!"

Palpatine gave him that wise, kindly-uncle smile Anakin had been seeing since the age of nine. "For what?"

"You're a *Sith Lord*!"

"I am," he said simply. "I am also your friend."

The blue bar of energy wavered, just a bit.

"I am also the man who has always been here for you. I am the man you have never needed to lie to. I am the man who wants nothing from you but that you follow your conscience. If that conscience requires you to commit murder, simply over a . . . philosophical difference . . . I will not resist."

His hands opened, still at his sides. "Anakin, when I told you that you can have anything you want, did you think I was excluding my life?"

The floor seemed to soften beneath Anakin's feet, and the room started to swirl darkness and ooze confusion. "You—you won't even *fight*—?"

"Fight you?" In the blue glow that cast shadows up from Palpatine's chin, the Chancellor looked astonished that he would suggest such a thing. "But what will happen when you kill me? What will happen to the Republic?" His tone was gently reasonable. "What will happen to Padmé?"

"Padmé . . ."

Her name was a gasp of anguish.

"When I die," Palpatine said with the air of a man reminding a child of something he ought to already know, "my knowledge dies with me."

The sizzling blade trembled.

"Unless, that is, I have the opportunity to teach it . . . to my apprentice . . ."

His vision swam.

"I . . ." A whisper of naked pain, and despair. "I don't know what to *do* . . ."

Palpatine gazed upon him, loving and gentle as he had ever been, though only a whisker shy of a lightsaber's terminal curve.

And what if this face was *not* a mask? What if the true face of the Sith was exactly what he saw before him: a man who had cared for him, had helped him, had been his loyal friend when he'd thought he had no other?

What *then*?

"Anakin," Palpatine said kindly, "let's talk."

The four bodyguard droids spread out in a shallow arc between Obi-Wan and Grievous, raising their electrostaffs. Obi-Wan stopped a respectful distance away; he still carried bruises from one of those electrostaffs, and he felt no particular urge to add to his collection.

"General Grievous," he said, "you're under arrest."

The bio-droid general stalked toward him, passing through his screen of bodyguards without the slightest hint of reluctance. "Kenobi. Don't tell me, let me guess: this is the part where you give me the chance to surrender."

"It can be," Obi-Wan allowed equably. "Or, if you like, it can be the part where I dismantle your exoskeleton and ship you back to Coruscant in a cargo hopper."

"I'll take option three." Grievous lifted his hand, and the bodyguards moved to box Obi-Wan between them. "That's the one where I watch you die."

Another gesture, and the droids in the ceiling hive came to life.

They uncoiled from their sockets heads-downward, with a rising chorus of whirring and buzzing and clicking that thickened until Obi-Wan might as well have stumbled into a colony of Corellian raptor-wasps. They began to drop free of the ceiling, first only a few, then many, like the opening drops of a summer cloudburst; finally they fell in a downpour that shook the stone-mounted durasteel of the deck and left Obi-Wan's ears ringing. Hundreds of them landed and rolled to standing; as many more stayed attached to the overhead hive, hanging upside down by their magnapeds, weapons trained so that Obi-Wan now stood at the focus of a dome of blasters.

Through it all, Obi-Wan never moved.

"I'm sorry, was I not clear?" he said. "There is no *option three*."

Grievous shook his head. "Do you never tire of this pathetic banter?"

"I rarely tire at all," Obi-Wan said mildly, "and I have no better way to pass the time while I wait for you to either decide to surrender, or choose to die."

"That choice was made long before I ever met *you*." Grievous turned away. "Kill him."

Instantly the box of bodyguards around Obi-Wan filled with crackling electrostaffs whipping faster than the human eye could see—which was less troublesome than it might have been, for that box was already empty of Jedi.

The Force had let him collapse as though he'd suddenly fainted, then it brought his lightsaber from his belt to his hand and ignited it while he turned his fall into a roll; that roll carried his lightsaber through a crisp arc that severed the leg of one of the bodyguards, and as the Force brought Obi-Wan back to his feet, the Force also nudged the crippled bodyguard to topple sideways into the path of the blade and sent it clanging to the floor in two smoking, sparking pieces.

One down.

The remaining three pressed the attack, but more cautiously; their weapons were longer than his, and they struck from beyond the reach of his blade. He gave way before them, his defensive velocities barely keeping their crackling discharge blades at bay.

Three MagnaGuards, each with a double-ended weapon that generated an energy field impervious to lightsabers, each with reflexes that operated near lightspeed, each with hypersophisticated heuristic combat algorithms that enabled it to learn from experience and adapt its tactics instantly to any situation, were certainly beyond Obi-Wan's ability to defeat, but it was not Obi-Wan who would defeat them; Obi-Wan wasn't even fighting. He was only a vessel, emptied of self. The Force, shaped by his skill and guided by his clarity of mind, fought through him.

In the Force, he felt their destruction: it was somewhere above and behind him, and only seconds away.

He went to meet it with a backflipping leap that the Force used to lift him neatly to an empty droid socket in the ceiling hive. The MagnaGuards sprang after him but he was gone by the time they arrived, leaping higher into the maze of girders and cables and room-sized cargo containers that was the control center's superstructure.

Here, said the Force within him, and Obi-Wan stopped, balancing on a girder, frowning back at the oncoming killer droids that leapt from beam to beam below him like malevolent durasteel primates. Though he could feel its close approach, he had no idea from where their destruction might come . . . until the Force showed him a support beam within reach of his blade and whispered, *Now.*

His blade flicked out and the durasteel beam parted, freshcut edges glowing white hot, and a great hulk of ship-sized cargo container that the beam had been supporting tore free of its other supports with shrieks of anguished metal and crashed down upon all three MagnaGuards with the finality of a meteor strike.

Two, three, and four.

Oh, thought Obi-Wan with detached approval. *That worked out rather well.*

Only ten thousand to go. Give or take.

An instant later the Force had him hurtling through a storm of blasterfire as every combat droid in the control center opened up on him at once.

Letting go of intention, letting go of desire, letting go of life, Obi-Wan fixed his entire attention on a thread of the Force that pulled him toward Grievous: not where Grievous was, but where Grievous would be when Obi-Wan got there . . .

Leaping girder to girder, slashing cables on which to swing through swarms of ricocheting particle beams, blade flickering so fast it became a deflector shield that splattered blaster bolts in all directions, his presence alone became a weapon: as he spun and whirled through the control center's superstructure, the blasts of particle cannons from power droids destroyed equipment and shattered girders and unleashed a torrent of red-hot debris that crashed to the deck, crushing droids on all sides. By the time he flipped down through the air to land catfooted on the deck once more, nearly half the droids between him and Grievous had been destroyed by their own not-so-friendly fire.

He cut his way into the mob of remaining troops as smoothly as if it were no more than a canebrake near some sunlit beach; his steady pace left behind a trail of smoking slices of droid.

"Keep *firing*!" Grievous roared to the spider droids that flanked him. *"Blast him!"*

Obi-Wan felt the massive shoulder cannon of a spider droid track him, and he felt it fire a bolt as powerful as a proton grenade, and he let the Force nudge him into a leap that carried him just far enough toward the fringe of the bolt's blast radius so that instead of shattering his bones it merely gave him a very strong, very hot *push*—

—that sent him whirling over the rest of the droids to land directly in front of Grievous.

A single slash of his lightsaber amputated the shoulder cannon of one power droid and continued into a spinning Force-assisted kick that brought his boot heel to the point of the other power droid's duranium chin, snapping the droid's head back hard enough to sever its cervical sensor cables. Blind and deaf, the power droid could only continue to obey its last order; it staggered in a wild circle, its convulsively firing cannon blasting random holes in droids and walls alike, until Obi-Wan deactivated it with a precise thrust that burned a thumb-sized hole through its thoracic braincase.

"General," Obi-Wan said with blandly polite smile as though unexpectedly greeting, on the street, someone he privately disliked. "My offer is still open."

Droid guns throughout the control center fell silent; Obi-Wan stood so close to Grievous that the general was in the line of fire.

Grievous threw back his cloak imperiously. "Do you believe that I would surrender to you *now*?"

"I am still willing to take you alive." Obi-Wan's nod took in the smoking, sparking wreckage that filled the control center. "So far, no one has been hurt."

Grievous tilted his head so that he could squint down into Obi-Wan's face. "I have *thousands* of troops. You cannot defeat them all."

"I don't have to."

"This is *your* chance to surrender, General Kenobi." Grievous swept a duranium hand toward the sinkhole-city behind him. "Pau City is in my grip; lay down your blade, or I will *squeeze* . . . until this entire sinkhole brims over with innocent blood."

"That's not what it's about to brim with," Obi-Wan said. "You should pay more attention to the weather."

Yellow eyes narrowed behind a mask of armorplast. "What?"

"Have a look outside." He pointed his lightsaber toward the archway. "It's about to start raining clones."

Grievous said again, turning to look, "What?"

A shadow had passed over the sun as though one of the towering thunderheads on the horizon had caught a stray current in the hyperwinds and settled above Pau City. But it wasn't a cloud.

It was the *Vigilance*.

While twilight enfolded the sinkhole, over the bright desert above assault craft skimmed the dunes in a tightening ring centered on the city. Hailfire droids rolled out from caves in the wind-scoured mesas, unleashing firestorms of missiles toward the oncoming craft for exactly 2.5 seconds apiece, which was how long it took for the *Vigilance*'s sensor operators to transfer data to its turbolaser batteries.

Thunderbolts roared down through the atmosphere, and hailfire droids disintegrated. Pinpoint counterfire from the bubble turrets of LAAT/i's met missiles in blossoming fireballs that were ripped to shreds of smoke as the oncoming craft blasted through them.

LAAT/i's streaked over the rim of the sinkhole and spiraled

downward with all guns blazing, crabbing outward to keep their forward batteries raking on the sinkhole's wall, while at the rim above, *Jadthu*-class armored landers hovered with bay doors wide, trailing sprays of polyplast cables like immense ice-white tassels that looped all the way to the ocean mouths that gaped at the lowest level of the city. Down those tassels, rappelling so fast they seemed to be simply falling, came endless streams of armored troopers, already firing on the combat droids that marched out to meet them.

Streamers of cables brushed the outer balcony of the control center, and down them slid white-armored troopers, each with one hand on his mechanized line-brake and the other full of DC-15 blaster rifle on full auto, spraying continuous chains of packeted particle beams. Droids wheeled and dropped and leapt into the air and burst to fragments. Surviving droids opened up on the clones as though grateful for something to shoot at, blasting holes in armor, cooking flesh with superheated steam from deep-tissue hits, blowing some troopers entirely off their cables to tumble toward a messy final landing ten levels below.

When the survivors of the first wave of clones hit the deck, the next wave was right behind them.

Grievous turned back to Obi-Wan. He lowered his head like an angry bantha, yellow glare fixed on the Jedi Master. "To the death, then."

Obi-Wan sighed. "If you insist."

The bio-droid general cast back his cloak, revealing the four lightsabers pocketed there. He stepped back, spreading wide his duranium arms. "You will not be the first Jedi I have killed, nor will you be the last."

Obi-Wan's only reply was to subtly shift the angle of his lightsaber up and forward.

The general's wide-spread arms now *split* along their lengths, dividing in half—even his *hands* split in half—

Now he had *four* arms. And four hands.

And each hand took a lightsaber as his cloak dropped to the floor.

They snarled to life and Grievous spun all four of them in a flourishing velocity so fast and so seamlessly integrated that he seemed to stand within a pulsing sphere of blue and green energy.

"Come on, then, Kenobi! Come for me!" he said. "I have been trained in your Jedi arts by Lord Tyranus himself!"

"Do you mean Count Dooku? What a curious coincidence," Obi-Wan said with a deceptively pleasant smile. "I trained the man who killed him."

With a convulsive snarl, Grievous lunged.

The sphere of blue lightsaber energy around him bulged toward Obi-Wan and opened like a mouth to bite him in half. Obi-Wan stood his ground, his blade still.

Chain-lightning teeth closed upon him.

This is how it feels to be Anakin Skywalker, right now:

You don't remember putting away your lightsaber.

You don't remember moving from Palpatine's private office to his larger public one; you don't remember collapsing in the chair where you now sit, nor do you remember drinking water from the half-empty glass that you find in your mechanical hand.

You remember only that the last man in the galaxy you still thought you could trust has been lying to you since the day you met.

And you're not even angry about it.

Only stunned.

"After all, Anakin, you are the last man who has a right to be angry at someone for keeping a secret. What else was I to do?"

Palpatine sits in his familiar tall oval chair behind his familiar desk; the lampdisks are full on, the office eerily bright.

Ordinary.

As though this is merely another one of your friendly conversations, the casual evening chats you've enjoyed together for so many years.

As though nothing has happened.

As though nothing has changed.

"Corruption had made the Republic a cancer in the body of the galaxy, and no one could burn it out; not the judicials, not the Senate, not even the Jedi Order itself. I was the only man strong and skilled enough for this task; I was the only man who dared even *attempt* it. Without my small deception, how should I have cured the Republic? Had I revealed myself to you, or to anyone else, the Jedi would have hunted me down and murdered me without trial—very much as you nearly did, only a moment ago."

You can't argue. Words are beyond you.

He rises, moving around his desk, taking one of the small chairs and drawing it close to yours.

"If only you could know how I have longed to tell you, Anakin. All these years—since the very day we met, my boy. I have watched over you, waiting as you grew in strength and wisdom, biding my time until now, today, when you are finally ready to understand who you truly are, and your true place in the history of the galaxy."

Numb words blur from your numb lips. "The chosen one . . ."

"Exactly, my boy. *Exactly.* You *are* the chosen one." He leans toward you, eyes clear. Steady. Utterly honest. "Chosen by *me.*"

He turns a hand toward the panorama of light-sprayed cityscape through window behind his desk. "Look out there, Anakin. A trillion beings on this planet alone—in the galaxy as a whole, uncounted quadrillions—and of them all, I have chosen *you*, Anakin Skywalker, to be the heir to my power. To all that I am."

"But that's not . . . that's not the prophecy. That's not the prophecy of the chosen one . . ."

"Is this such a problem for you? Is not your quest to find a way to *overturn* prophecy?" Palpatine leaned close, smiling, warm and kindly. "Anakin, do you think the Sith did not know of this prophecy? Do you think we would simply sleep while it came to *pass*?"

"You mean—"

"This is what you must understand. This Jedi submission to fate . . . this is not the way of the Sith, Anakin. This is not my way. This is not your way. It has never been. It need never be."

You're drowning.

"I am not . . . ," you hear yourself say, ". . . on your side. I am not *evil*."

"Who said anything about evil? I am bringing peace to the galaxy. Is that evil? I am offering you the power to save Padmé. Is that evil? Have I attacked you? Drugged you? Are you being tortured? My boy, I am *asking* you. I am asking you to *do the right thing*. Turn your back on treason. On all those who would harm the Republic. I'm asking you to do exactly what you have sworn to do: bring peace and justice to the galaxy. And save Padmé, of course—haven't you sworn to protect *her*, too . . . ?"

"I—but—I—" Words will not fit themselves into the answers you need. If only Obi-Wan were here—Obi-Wan would know what to say. What to do.

Obi-Wan could handle this.

Rght now, you know you can't.

"I—I'll turn you over to the Jedi Council—*they'll* know what to do—"

"I'm sure they will. They are already planning to overthrow the Republic; you'll give them exactly the excuse they're looking for. And when they come to execute me, will that be justice? Will they be bringing *peace*?"

"They won't—they *wouldn't*—!"

"Well, of course I hope you're correct, Anakin. You'll forgive me if I don't share your blind loyalty to your comrades. I suppose it does indeed come down, in the end, to a question of loyalty," he said thoughtfully. "That's what you must ask yourself, my boy. Whether your loyalty is to the Jedi, or to the Republic."

"It's not—it's not *like* that—"

Palpatine lifted his shoulders. "Perhaps not. Perhaps it's simply a question of whether you love Obi-Wan Kenobi more than you love your wife."

There is no more searching for words.

There are no longer words at all.

"Take your time. Meditate on it. I will still be here when you decide."

Inside your head, there is only fire. Around your heart, the dragon whispers that all things die.

This is how it feels to be Anakin Skywalker, right now.

——————

There is an understated elegance in Obi-Wan Kenobi's lightsaber technique, one that is quite unlike the feel one might get from the other great swordsbeings of the Jedi Order. He lacks entirely the flash, the pure bold *élan* of an Anakin Skywalker; there is nowhere in him the penumbral ferocity of a Mace Windu or a Depa Billaba nor the stylish grace of a Shaak Ti or a Dooku, and he is nothing resembling the whirlwind of destruction that Yoda can become.

He is simplicity itself.

That is his power.

Before Obi-Wan had left Coruscant, Mace Windu had told him of facing Grievous in single combat atop a mag-lev train during the general's daring raid to capture Palpatine. Mace had told him how the computers slaved to Grievous's brain had apparently analyzed even Mace's unconventionally lethal Vaapad and had been able to respond in kind after a single exchange.

"He must have been trained by Count Dooku," Mace had said, "so you can expect Makashi as well; given the number of Jedi he has fought and slain, you must expect that he can attack in any style, or all of them. In fact, Obi-Wan, I believe that of all living Jedi, you have the best chance to defeat him."

This pronouncement had startled Obi-Wan, and he had protested. After all, the only form in which he was truly even proficient was Soresu, which was the most common lightsaber form in the Jedi Order. Founded upon the basic deflection principles all Padawans were taught—to enable them to protect themselves from blaster bolts—Soresu was very simple, and so restrained and defense-oriented that it was very nearly downright passive.

"But surely, Master Windu," Obi-Wan had said, "you, with the power of Vaapad—or Yoda's mastery of Ataro—"

Mace Windu had almost smiled. "I created Vaapad to answer my weakness: it channels my own darkness into a weapon of the light. Master Yoda's Ataro is also an answer to weakness: the limitations of reach and mobility imposed by his stature and his age. But for you? What weakness does Soresu answer?"

Blinking, Obi-Wan had been forced to admit he'd never actually thought of it that way.

"That is so like you, Master Kenobi," the Korun Master had said, shaking his head. "I am called a great swordsman because I invented a lethal style; but who is greater, the creator of a killing form—or the master of the classic form?"

"I'm very flattered that you would consider me a master, but really—"

"Not a master. *The* master," Mace had said. "Be who you are, and Grievous will never defeat you."

So now, facing the tornado of annihilating energy that is Grievous's attack, Obi-Wan simply is who he is.

───────

The electrodrivers powering Grievous's mechanical arms let each of the four attack thrice in a single second; integrated by combat algorithms in the bio-droid's electronic network of peripheral processors, each of the twelve strikes per second came from a different angle with different speed and intensity, an unpredictably broken rhythm of slashes, chops, and stabs of which every single one could take Obi-Wan's life.

Not one touched him.

After all, he had often walked unscathed through hornet-swarms of blasterfire, defended only by the Force's direction of his blade; countering twelve blows per second was only difficult, not impossible. His blade wove an intricate web of angles and curves, never truly fast but always just fast enough, each motion of his lightsaber subtly interfering with three or four or eight of the general's strikes, the rest sizzling past him, his precise, minimal shifts of weight and stance slipping them by centimeters.

Grievous, snarling fury, ramped up the intensity and velocity of his attacks—sixteen per second, eighteen—until finally, at twenty strikes per second, he overloaded Obi-Wan's defense.

So Obi-Wan used his defense to attack.

A subtle shift in the angle of a single parry brought Obi-Wan's blade in contact not with the blade of the oncoming lightsaber, but with the handgrip.

—*slice*—

The blade winked out of existence a hairbreadth before it would have burned through Obi-Wan's forehead. Half the severed lightsaber skittered away, along with the duranium thumb and first finger of the hand that had held it.

Grievous paused, eyes pulsing wide, then drawing narrow. He lifted his maimed hand and stared at the white-hot stumps that held now only half a useless lightsaber.

Obi-Wan smiled at him.

Grievous lunged.

Obi-Wan parried.

Pieces of lightsabers bounced on the durasteel deck.

Grievous looked down at the blade-sliced hunks of metal that were all he had left in his hands, then up at Obi-Wan's shining sky-colored blade, then down at his hands again, and then he seemed to suddenly remember that he had an urgent appointment somewhere else.

Anywhere else.

Obi-Wan stepped toward him, but a shock from the Force made him leap back just as a scarlet HE bolt struck the floor right where he'd been about to place his foot. Obi-Wan rode the explosion, flipping in the air to land upright between a pair of super battle droids that were busily firing upon the flank of a squad of clone troopers, which they continued to do until they found themselves falling in pieces to the deck.

Obi-Wan spun.

In the chaos of exploding droids and dying men, Grievous was nowhere to be seen.

Obi-Wan waved his lightsaber at the clones. "The general!" he shouted. "Which way?"

One trooper circled his arm as though throwing a proton grenade back toward the archway where Obi-Wan had first entered. He followed the gesture and saw, for an instant in the sunshadow of the *Vigilance* outside, the back curves of twin bladed rings—ganged together to make a wheel the size of a starfighter—rolling swiftly off along the sinkhole rim.

General Grievous was very good at running away.

"Not this time," Obi-Wan muttered, and cut a path through

the tangled mob of droids all the way to the arch in a single sustained surge, reaching the open air just in time to see the blade-wheeler turn; it was an open ring with a pilot's chair inside, and in the pilot's chair sat Grievous, who lifted one of his bodyguards' electrostaffs in a sardonic wave as he took the scooter straight out over the edge. Four claw-footed arms deployed, digging into the rock to carry him down the side of the sinkhole, angling away at a steep slant.

"Blast." Obi-Wan looked around. Still no air taxis. Not that he had any real interest in flying through the storm of battle that raged throughout the interior of the sinkhole, but there was certainly no way he could catch Grievous on foot . . .

From around the corner of an interior tunnel, he heard a resonant *honnnnk!* as though a nearby bantha had swallowed an air horn.

He said, "Boga?"

The beaked face of the dragonmount slowly extended around the interior angle of the tunnel.

"Boga! Come here, girl! We have a general to catch."

Boga fixed him with a reproachful glare. *"Honnnnnk."*

"Oh, very well." Obi-Wan rolled his eyes. "I was wrong; you were right. Can we please *go* now?"

The remaining fifteen meters of dragonmount hove into view and came trotting out to meet him. Obi-Wan sprang to the saddle, and Boga leapt to the sinkhole's rim in a single bound. Her huge head swung low, searching, until Obi-Wan spotted Grievous's blade-wheeler racing away toward the landing decks below.

"*There,* girl—that's him! Go!"

Boga gathered herself and sprang to the rim of the next level down, poised for an instant to get her bearings, then leapt again down into the firestorm that Pau City had become. Obi-Wan spun his blade in a continuous whirl to either side of the dragonmount's back, disintegrating shrapnel and slapping away stray blasterfire. They plummeted through the sinkhole-city, gaining tens of meters on Grievous with every leap.

On one of the landing decks, the canopy was lifting and parting to show a small, ultrafast armored shuttle of the type favored by the famously nervous Neimoidian executives of the Trade Federation. Grievous's wheeler sprayed a fan of white-hot sparks as it tore across the landing deck; the bio-droid whipped the wheeler sideways, laying it down for a skidding halt that showered the shuttle with molten durasteel.

But before he could clamber out of the pilot's chair, several metric tons of Jedi-bearing dragonmount landed on the shuttle's roof, crouched and threatening and hissing venomously down at him.

"I hope you have another vehicle, General!" Obi-Wan waved his lightsaber toward the shuttle's twin rear thrusters. "I believe there's some damage to your sublights!"

"You're insane! There's no—"

Obi-Wan shrugged. "Show him, Boga."

The dragonmount dutifully pointed out the damage with two whistling strikes of her massive tail-mace—*wham* and *wham* again—which crumpled the shuttle's thruster tubes into crimped-shut knots of metal.

Obi-Wan beckoned. "Let's settle this, shall we?"

Grievous's answer was a shriek of tortured gyros that wrenched the wheeler upright, and a metal-on-metal scream of blades ripping into deck plates that sent it shooting straight toward the sinkhole wall—and, with the claw-arms to help, straight *up* it.

Obi-Wan sighed. "Didn't we just *come* from there?"

Boga coiled herself and sprang for the wall, and the chase was on once more.

They raced through the battle, clawing up walls, shooting through tunnels, skidding and leaping, sprinting where the way was clear and screeching into high-powered serpentines where it was not, whipping around knots of droids and bounding over troopers. Boga ran straight up the side of a clone hovertank and sprang from its turret directly between the high-slanting ring-wheels of a hailfire, and a swipe of Obi-Wan's blade left the droid crippled behind them. Native troops had taken the field: Utapaun dragonriders armed with sparking power lances charged along causeways, spearing droids on every side. Grievous ran right over anything in his path, the blades of his wheeler shredding droid and trooper and dragon alike; behind him, Obi-Wan's lightsaber caught and returned blaster bolts in a spray that shattered any droid unwise enough to fire on him. A few stray bolts he batted into the speeding wheeler ahead, but without visible effect.

"Fine," he muttered. "Let's try this from a little *closer.*"

Boga gained steadily. Grievous's vehicle had the edge in raw speed, but Boga could out-turn it and could make instant leaps at astonishing angles; the dragonmount also had an uncanny instinct for where the general might be heading, as well as a seemingly infinite knowledge of useful shortcuts through side tunnels, along sheer walls, and over chasms studded with locked-down wind turbines. Grievous tried once to block Obi-Wan's pursuit by screeching out onto a huge pod that held a whole bank of wind turbines and knocking the blade-brakes off them with quick blows of the electrostaff, letting the razor-edged blades spin freely in the constant gale, but Obi-Wan merely brought Boga alongside the turbines and stuck his lightsaber into their whirl. Sliced-free chunks of carboceramic blade shrieked through the air and shattered on the stone on all sides, and with a curse Grievous kicked his vehicle into motion again.

The wheeler roared into a tunnel that seemed to lead straight into the rock of the plateau. The tunnel was jammed with groundcars and dragonmounts and wheelers and jetsters and all manner of other vehicles and every kind of beast that might bear or draw the vast numbers of Utapauns and Utai fleeing the battle. Grievous blasted right into them, blade-wheel chewing through groundcars and splashing the tunnel walls with chunks of shredded lizard; Boga raced along the walls above the traffic, sometimes even galloping on the ceiling with claws gouging chunks from the rock.

With a burst of sustained effort that strangled her *honnnk*ing to thin gasps for air, Boga finally pulled alongside Grievous. Obi-Wan leaned forward, stretching out with his lightsaber, barely able to reach the wheeler's back curve, and carved away an arc of the wheeler's blade-tread, making the vehicle buck and skid; Grievous answered with a thrust of his electrostaff that crackled lightning against Boga's extended neck. The great beast jerked sideways, honking fearfully and whipping her head as though the burn was a biting creature she could shake off her flank.

"One more leap, Boga!" Obi-Wan shouted, pressing himself along the dragonmount's shoulder. "Bring me even with him!"

The dragonmount complied without hesitation, and when Grievous thrust again, Obi-Wan's free hand flashed out and seized the staff below its discharge blade, holding it clear of Boga's vulnerable flesh. Grievous yanked on the staff, nearly pulling Obi-Wan out of the saddle, then jabbed it back at him, discharge blade sparking in his face—

With a sigh, Obi-Wan realized he needed both hands.

He dropped his lightsaber.

As his deactivated handgrip skittered and bounced along the tunnel behind him, he reflected that it was just as well Anakin wasn't there after all; he'd have never heard the end of it.

He got his other hand on the staff just as Grievous jerked the wheeler sideways, half laying it down to angle for a small side tunnel just ahead. Obi-Wan hung on grimly. Through the Force he could feel Boga's exhaustion, the buildup of anaerobic breakdown products turning the dragonmount's mighty legs to cloth. An open archway showed daylight ahead. Boga barely made the turn, and they raced side by side along the empty darkened way, joined by the spark-spitting rod of the electrostaff.

As they cleared the archway to a small, concealed landing deck deep in a private sinkhole, Obi-Wan leapt from the saddle, yanking on the staff to swing both his boots hard into the side of Grievous's duranium skull. The wheeler's internal gyros screamed at the sudden impact and shift of balance. Their shrieks cycled up to bursts of smoke and fragments of metal as their catastrophic failure sent the wheeler tumbling in a white-hot cascade of sparks.

Dropping the staff, Obi-Wan leapt again, the Force lifting him free of the crash.

Grievous's electronic reflexes sent him out of the pilot's chair in the opposite direction.

The wheeler flipped over the edge of the landing deck and into the shadowy abyss of the sinkhole. It trailed smoke all the way down to a distant, delayed, and very final crash.

The electrostaff had rolled away, coming to rest against the landing jack of a small Techno Union starfighter that stood on the deck a few meters behind Obi-Wan. Behind Grievous, the archway back into the tunnel system was filled with a panting, exhausted, but still dangerously angry dragonmount.

Obi-Wan looked at Grievous.

Grievous looked at Obi-Wan.

There was no longer any need for words between them.

Obi-Wan simply stood, centered in the Force, waiting for Grievous to make his move.

A concealed compartment in the general's right thigh sprang open, and a mechanical arm delivered a slim hold-out blaster to his hand. He brought it up and fired so fast that his arm blurred to invisiblity.

Obi-Wan . . . reached.

The electrostaff flipped into the air between them, one discharge blade catching the bolt. The impact sent the staff whirling—

Right into Obi-Wan's hand.

There came one instant's pause, while they looked into each other's eyes and shared an intimate understanding that their relationship had reached its end.

Obi-Wan charged.

Grievous backed away, unleashing a stream of blaster bolts as fast as his half a forefinger could pull the trigger.

Obi-Wan spun the staff, catching every bolt, not even slowing down, and when he reached Grievous he slapped the blaster out of his hand with a crack of the staff that sent blue lightning scaling up the general's arm.

His following strike was a stiff stab into Grievous's jointed stomach armor that sent the general staggering back. Obi-Wan hit him again in the same place, denting the armorplast plate, cracking the joint where it met the larger, thicker plates of his chest as Grievous flailed for balance, but when he spun the staff for his next strike the general's flailing arm flailed itself against the middle of the staff and his other hand found it as well and he seized it, yanking himself upright against Obi-Wan's grip, his metal skull-face coming within a centimeter of the Jedi Master's nose.

He snarled, "Do you think I am foolish enough to arm my bodyguards with weapons that can actually *hurt* me?"

Instead of waiting for an answer he spun, heaving Obi-Wan right off the deck with effortless strength, whipping up him over his head to slam him to the deck with killing power; Obi-Wan could only let go of the staff and allow the Force to angle his fall into a stumbling roll. Grievous sprang after him, swinging the electrostaff and slamming it across Obi-Wan's flank before the Jedi Master could recover his balance. The impact sent Obi-Wan tumbling sideways and the electroburst discharge set his robe on fire. Grievous stayed right with him, attacking before Obi-Wan could even realize exactly what was happening, attacking faster than thought—

But Obi-Wan didn't need to think. The Force was with him, and he *knew*.

When Grievous spun the staff overhand, discharge blade sizzling down at Obi-Wan's head for the killing blow, Obi-Wan went to the inside.

He met Grievous chest-to-chest, his upraised hand blocking the general's wrist; Grievous snarled something incoherent and bore down on the Jedi Master's block with all his weight, driving the blade closer and closer to Obi-Wan's face—

But Obi-Wan's arm had the Force to give it strength, and the general's arm only had the innate crystalline intermolecular structure of duranium alloy.

Grievous's forearm bent like a cheap spoon.

While the general stared in disbelief at his mangled arm, Obi-Wan had been working the fingers of his free hand around the lower edge of Grievous's dented, joint-loose stomach plate.

Grievous looked down. "What?"

Obi-Wan slammed the elbow of his blocking arm into the general's clavicle while he yanked as hard as he could on the stomach plate, and it ripped free in his hand. Behind it hung a translucent sac of synthskin containing a tangle of green and gray organs.

The true body of the alien inside the droid.

Grievous howled and dropped the staff to seize Obi-Wan with his three remaining arms. He lifted the Jedi Master over his head again and hurled him tumbling over the landing deck toward the precipice above the gloom-shrouded drop. Reaching into the Force, Obi-Wan was able to connect with the stone itself as if he were anchored to it with a cable tether; instead of hurtling over the edge he slammed down onto the rock hard enough to crush all breath from his lungs.

Grievous picked up the staff again and charged.

Obi-Wan still couldn't breathe. He had no hope of rising to meet the general's attack.

All he could do was extend a hand.

As the bio-droid loomed over him, electrostaff raised for the kill, the hold-out blaster flipped from the deck into Obi-Wan's palm, and with no hesitation, no second thoughts, not even the faintest pause to savor his victory, he pulled the trigger.

The bolt ripped into the synthskin sac.

Grievous's guts exploded in a foul-smelling shower the color of a dead swamp. Energy chained up his spine and a mist of vaporized brain burst out both sides of his skull and sent his face spinning off the precipice.

The electrostaff hit the deck, followed shortly by the general's knees.

Then by what was left of his head.

Obi-Wan lay on his back, staring at the circle of cloudless sky above the sinkhole while he gasped air back into into his spasming lungs. He barely managed to roll over far enough to smother the flames on his robe, then fell back.

And simply enjoyed being alive.

Much too short a time later—long before he was actually ready to get up—a shadow fell across him, accompanied by the smell of overheated lizard and an admonitory *honnnk.*

"Yes, Boga, you're right," Obi-Wan agreed reluctantly. Slowly, painfully, he pushed himself to his feet.

He picked up the electrostaff, and paused for one last glance at the remains of the bio-droid general.

"So . . ." He summoned a condemnation among the most offensive in his vocabulary. ". . . *uncivilized.*"

He triggered his comlink, and directed Cody to report to Jedi Command on Coruscant that Grievous had been destroyed.

"Will do, General," said the tiny holoscan of the clone commander. *"And congratulations. I knew you could do it."*

Apparently everyone did, Obi-Wan thought, *except Grievous, and me . . .*

"General? We do still have a little problem out here. About ten thousand heavily armed little problems, actually."

"On my way. Kenobi out."

Obi-Wan sighed and clambered painfully onto the dragon-mount's saddle.

"All right, girl," he said. "Let's go win *that* battle, too."

As has been said, the textbook example of a Jedi trap is the one that was set on Utapau, for Obi-Wan Kenobi.

It worked perfectly.

The final element essential to the creation of a truly effective Jedi trap is a certain coldness of mind—a detachment, if you will, from any desire for a particular outcome.

The best way to arrange matters is to create a win–win situation.

For example, one might use as one's proxy a creature that not only is expendable, but would eventually have to be killed anyway. Thus, if one's proxy fails and is destroyed, it's no loss—in fact, the targeted Jedi has actually done one a favor, by taking care of a bit of dirty work one would otherwise have to do one-self.

And the final stroke of perfection is to organize the Jedi trap so that by walking into it at all, the Jedi has already lost.

That is to say, a Jedi trap works best when one's true goal is merely to make sure that the Jedi in question spends some hours or days off somewhere on the far side of the galaxy. So that he won't be around to interfere with one's *real* plans.

So that by the time he can return, it will be already too late.

REVELATION

Mace Windu stood in the darkened comm center of Jedi Command, facing a life-sized holoscan of Yoda, projected from a concealed Wookiee comm center in the heart of a wroshyr tree on Kashyyyk.

"Minutes ago," Mace said, "we received confirmation from Utapau: Kenobi was successful. Grievous is dead."

"Time it is to execute our plan."

"I will personally deliver the news of Grievous's death." Mace flexed his hands. "It will be up to the Chancellor to cede his emergency powers back over to the Senate."

"Forget not the existence of Sidious. Anticipate your action, he may. Masters will be necessary, if the Lord of the Sith you must face."

"I have chosen four of our best. Master Tiin, Master Kolar, and Master Fisto are all here, in the Temple. They are preparing already."

"What about Skywalker? The chosen one."

"Too much of a risk," Mace replied. "I am the fourth."

With a slow purse of the lips and an even slower nod, Yoda

said, *"On watch you have been too long, my Padawan. Rest you must."*

"I will, Master. When the Republic is safe once more." Mace straightened. "We are waiting only for your vote."

"Very well, then. Have my vote, you do. May the Force be with you."

"And with you, Master."

But he spoke to empty air; the holoscan had already flickered to nonexistence.

Mace lowered his head and stood in the darkness and the silence.

The door of the comm center shot open, spilling yellow glare into the gloom and limning the silhouette of a man half collapsed against the frame.

"Master . . ." The voice was a hoarse half whisper. "Master Windu . . . ?"

"Skywalker?" Mace was at his side in an instant. "What's wrong? Are you hurt?"

Anakin took Mace's arm in a grip of desperate strength, and used it like a crutch to haul himself upright.

"Obi-Wan . . . ," he said faintly. "I need to talk to *Obi-Wan*—!"

"Obi-Wan is operational on Utapau; he has destroyed General Grievous. We are leaving now to tell the Chancellor, and to see to it that he steps down as he has promised—"

"Steps—steps *down*—" Anakin's voice had a sharply bitter edge. "You have no *idea* . . ."

"Anakin—? What's wrong?"

"Listen to me—*you have to listen to me*—" Anakin sagged against him, shaking; Mace wrapped his arms around the young Jedi and guided him into the nearest chair. "You can't—please, Master Windu, give me your word, promise me it'll be an *arrest*, promise you're not going to *hurt* him—"

"Skywalker—Anakin. You must try to answer. Have you been attacked? Are you injured? You have to tell me what's wrong!"

Anakin collapsed forward, face into his hands.

Mace reached into the Force, opening the eye of his special gift of perception—

What he found there froze his blood.

The tangled web of fault lines in the Force he had seen connecting Anakin to Obi-Wan and to Palpatine was no more; in their place was a single spider-knot that sang with power enough to crack the planet. Anakin Skywalker no longer had shatterpoints. He *was* a shatterpoint.

The shatterpoint.

Everything depended on him.

Everything.

Mace said slowly, with the same sort of deliberate care he would use in examining an unknown type of bomb that might have the power to destroy the universe itself, "Anakin, look at me."

Skywalker raised his head.

"Are you hurt? Do you need—"

Mace frowned. Anakin's eyes were raw, and red, and his face looked swollen. For a long time he didn't know if Anakin would answer, if he *could* answer, if he could even speak at all; the young Jedi seemed to be struggling with something inside himself, as though he fought desperately against the birth of a monster hatching within his chest.

But in the Force, there was no *as though;* there was no *seemed to be.* In the Force, Mace could feel the monster inside Anakin Skywalker, a *real* monster, *too* real, one that was eating him alive from the inside out.

Fear.

This was the wound Anakin had taken. This was the hurt that had him shaking and stammering and too weak to stand. Some black fear had hatched like fever wasps inside the young Knight's brain, and it was killing him.

Finally, after what seemed forever, Anakin opened his blood-raw eyes.

"Master Windu . . ." He spoke slowly, painfully, as though each word ripped away a raw hunk of his own flesh. "I have . . . bad news."

Mace stared at him.

"Bad news?" he repeated blankly.

What news could be bad enough to make a Jedi like Anakin Skywalker collapse? What *news* could make Anakin Skywalker look like the stars had gone out?

Then, in nine simple words, Anakin told him.

This is the moment that defines Mace Windu.

Not his countless victories in battle, nor the numberless battles his diplomacy has avoided. Not his penetrating intellect, or his talents with the Force, or his unmatched skills with the lightsaber. Not his dedication to the Jedi Order, or his devotion to the Republic that he serves.

But this.

Right here.

Right now.

Because Mace, too, has an *attachment*. Mace has a secret love.

Mace Windu loves the Republic.

Many of his students quote him to students of their own: *"Jedi do not fight for peace. That's only a slogan, and is as misleading as slogans always are. Jedi fight for* civilization, *because only* civilization *creates* peace.*"*

For Mace Windu, for all his life, for all the lives of a thousand years of Jedi before him, true civilization has had only one true name: the Republic.

He has given his life in the service of his love. He has taken lives in its service, and lost the lives of innocents. He has seen beings that he cares for maimed, and killed, and sometimes worse: sometimes so broken by the horror of the struggle that their only answer was to commit horrors greater still.

And because of that love now, here, in this instant, Anakin Skywalker has nine words for him that shred his heart, burn its pieces, and feed him its smoking ashes.

Palpatine is Sidious. The Chancellor is the Sith Lord.

He doesn't even hear the words, not really; their true meaning is too large for his mind gather in all at once.

They mean that all he's done, and all that has been done to him—

That all the Order has accomplished, all it has suffered—

All the Galaxy *itself* has gone through, all the years of suffering and slaughter, the death of entire *planets*—

Has all been for nothing.

Because it was all done to save the Republic.

Which was already gone.

Which had already fallen.

The corpse of which had been defended only by a Jedi Order that was now under the command of a Dark Lord of the Sith.

Mace Windu's entire existence has become crystal so shot-through with flaws that the hammer of those nine words has crushed him to sand.

But because he is Mace Windu, he takes this blow without a change of expression.

Because he is Mace Windu, within a second the man of sand is stone once more: pure Jedi Master, weighing coldly the risk of facing the last Dark Lord of the Sith without the chosen one—

Against the risk of facing the last Dark Lord of the Sith with a chosen one eaten alive by fear.

And because he is Mace Windu, the choice is no choice at all.

"Anakin, wait in the Council Chamber until we get back."

"Wh—what? Master—"

"That's an *order,* Anakin."

"But—but—but the *Chancellor*—" Anakin says desperately, clutching at the Jedi Master's hand. "What are you going to *do?*"

And it is the true measure of Mace Windu that, even now, he still is telling the truth when he says, "Only as much as I have to."

———

In the virtual nonspace of the HoloNet, two Jedi Masters meet.

One is ancient, tiny, with skin of green leather and old wisdom in his eyes, standing in a Kashyyyk cave hollowed from the trunk of a vast wroshyr tree; the other is tall and fierce, seated before a holodisk in Coruscant's Jedi Temple.

To each other, they are blue ghosts, given existence by scanning lasers. Though they are light-years apart, they are of one mind; it hardly matters who says what.

Now they know the truth.

For more than a decade, the Republic has been in the hands of the Sith.

Now, together, blue ghost to blue ghost, they decide to take it back.

PART THREE

APOCALYPSE

The dark is generous, and it is patient, and it always wins.

It always wins because it is everywhere.

It is in the wood that burns in your hearth, and in the kettle on the fire; it is under your chair and under your table and under the sheets on your bed. Walk in the midday sun and the dark is with you, attached to the soles of your feet.

The brightest light casts the darkest shadow.

THE FACE OF THE DARK

Depowered lampdisks were rings of ghostly gray floating in the gloom. The shimmering jewelscape of Coruscant haloed the knife-edged shadow of the chair.

This was the office of the Chancellor.

Within the chair's shadow sat another shadow: deeper, darker, formless and impenetrable, an abyssal umbra so profound that it drained light from the room around it.

And from the city. And the planet.

And the galaxy.

The shadow waited. It had told the boy it would. It was looking forward to keeping its word.

For a change.

Night held the Jedi Temple.

On its rooftop landing deck, thin yellow light spilled in a stretching rectangle through a shuttle's hatchway, reflecting upward onto the faces of three Jedi Masters.

"I'd feel better if Yoda were here." This Master was a Nautiloid, tall and broad-shouldered, his glabrous scalp-tentacles restrained by loops of embossed leather. "Or even Kenobi. On Ord Cestus, Obi-Wan and I—"

"Yoda is pinned down on Kashyyyk, and Kenobi is out of contact on Utapau. The Dark Lord has revealed himself, and we dare not hesitate. Think not of *if,* Master Fisto; this duty has fallen to us. We will suffice." This Master was an Iktotchi, shorter and slimmer than the first. Two long horns curved downward from his forehead to below his chin. One had been amputated after being shattered in battle a few months before. Bacta had accelereated its regrowth, and the once maimed horn was now a match to the other. "We will suffice," he repeated. "We will have to."

"Peace," said the third Master, a Zabrak. Dew had gathered on his array of blunt vestigial skull-spines, glistening very like sweat. He gestured toward a Temple door that had cycled open. "Windu is coming."

Clouds had swept in with the twilight, and now a thin drizzling rain began to fall. The approaching Master walked with his shaven head lowered, his hands tucked within his sleeves.

"Master Ti and Gate Master Jurokk will direct the Temple's defense," he said as he reached the others. "We are shutting down all nav beacons and signal lights, we have armed the older Padawans, and all blast doors are sealed and code-locked." His gaze swept the Masters. "It's time to go."

"And Skywalker?" The Zabrak Master cocked his head as though he felt a distant disturbance in the Force. "What of the chosen one?"

"I have sent him to the Council Chamber until our return." Mace Windu turned a grim stare upon the High Council Tower, squinting against the thickening rain. His hands withdrew from his sleeves. One of them held his lightsaber.

"He has done his duty, Masters. Now we shall do ours."

He walked between them into the shuttle.

The other three Masters shared a significant silence, then

Agen Kolar nodded to himself and entered; Saesee Tiin stroked his regrown horn, and followed.

"I'd *still* feel better if Yoda were here . . . ," Kit Fisto muttered, and then went in as well.

Once the hatch had sealed behind him, the Jedi Temple belonged entirely to the night.

Alone in the Chamber of the Jedi Council, Anakin Skywalker wrestled with his dragon.

He was losing.

He paced the Chamber in blind arcs, stumbling among the chairs. He could not feel currents of the Force around him; he could not feel echoes of Jedi Masters in these ancient seats.

He had never dreamed there was this much pain in the universe.

Physical pain he could have handled even without his Jedi mental skills; he'd always been tough. At four years old he'd been able to take the worst beating Watto would deliver without so much as making a sound.

Nothing had prepared him for this.

He wanted to rip open his chest with his bare hands and claw out his heart.

"What have I *done?*" The question started as a low moan but grew to a howl he could no longer lock behind his teeth. *"What have I done?"*

He knew the answer: he had done his duty.

And now he couldn't imagine why.

When I die, Palpatine had said, so calmly, so warmly, so reasonably, *my knowledge dies with me . . .*

Everywhere he looked, he saw only the face of the woman he loved beyond love: the woman for whom he channeled through his body all the love that had ever existed in the galaxy. In the universe.

He didn't care what she had done. He didn't care about conspiracies or cabals or secret pacts. Treason meant nothing to him now. She was everything that had ever been loved by anyone, and he was watching her die.

His agony somehow became an invisible hand, stretching out through the Force, a hand that found her, far away, alone in her apartment in the dark, a hand that felt the silken softness of her skin and the sleek coils of her hair, a hand that dissolved into a field of pure energy, of pure *feeling* that reached *inside* her—

And now he felt her, really *felt* her in the Force, as though she could have been some kind of Jedi, too, but more than that: he felt a bond, a connection, deeper and more intimate than he'd ever had before with anyone, even Obi-Wan; for a precious eternal instant he *was* her . . . he was the beat of her heart and he was the motion of her lips and he was her soft words as though she spoke a prayer to the stars—

I love you, Anakin. I am yours, in life, and in death, wherever you go, whatever you do, we will always be one. Never doubt me, my love. I am yours.

—and her purity and her passion and the truth of her love flowed into him and through him and every atom of him screamed to the Force *how can I let her die?*

The Force had no answer for him.

The dragon, on the other hand, did.

All things die, Anakin Skywalker. Even stars burn out.

And no matter how hard he tried to summon it, no wisdom of Yoda's, no teaching of Obi-Wan's, not one scrap of Jedi lore came to him that could choke the dragon down.

But there *was* an answer; he'd heard it just the other night.

With such knowledge, to maintain life in someone already living would seem a small matter, don't you agree?

Anakin stopped. His agony evaporated.

Palpatine was right.

It *was* simple.

All he had to do was decide what he wanted.

The Coruscant nightfall was spreading through the galaxy.

The darkness in the Force was no hindrance to the shadow in the Chancellor's office; it *was* the darkness. Wherever darkness dwelled, the shadow could send perception.

In the night, the shadow felt the boy's anguish, and it was good. The shadow felt the grim determination of four Jedi Masters approaching by air.

This, too, was good.

As a Jedi shuttle settled to the landing deck outside, the shadow sent its mind into the far deeper night within one of the several pieces of sculpture that graced the office: an abstract twist of solid neuranium, so heavy that the office floor had been specially reinforced to bear its weight, so dense that more sensitive species might, from very close range, actually percieve the tiny warping of the fabric of space–time that was its gravitation.

Neuranium of more than roughly a millimeter thick is impervious to sensors; the standard security scans undergone by all equipment and furniture to enter the Senate Office Building had shown nothing at all. If anyone had thought to use an advanced gravimetric detector, however, they might have discovered that one smallish section of the sculpture massed slightly less than it should have, given that the manifest that had accompanied it, when it was brought from Naboo among the then-ambassador's personal effects, clearly stated that it was a single piece of solid-forged neuranium.

The manifest was a lie. The sculpture was not entirely solid, and not all of it was neuranium.

Within a long, slim, rod-shaped cavity around which the sculpture had been forged rested a device that had lain, waiting, in absolute darkness—darkness beyond darkness—for decades.

Waiting for night to fall on the Republic.

The shadow felt Jedi Masters stride the vast echoic emptiness of the vaulted halls outside. It could practically hear the cadence of their boot heels on the Alderaanian marble.

The darkness within the sculpture whispered of the shape and the feel and every intimate resonance of the device it cradled. With a twist of its will, the shadow triggered the device.

The neuranium got warm.

A small round spot, smaller than the circle a human child might make of thumb and forefinger, turned the color of old blood.

Then fresh blood.

Then open flame.

Finally a spear of scarlet energy lanced free, painting the office with the color of stars seen through the smoke of burning planets.

The spear of energy lengthened, drawing with it out from the darkness the device, then the scarlet blade shrank away and the device slid itself within the softer darkness of a sleeve.

As shouts of the Force scattered Redrobes beyond the office's outer doors, the shadow gestured and lampdisks ignited. Another shout of the Force burst open the inner door to the private office. As Jedi stormed in, a final flick of the shadow's will triggered a recording device concealed within the desk.

Audio only.

"Why, Master Windu," said the shadow. "What a pleasant surprise."

Shaak Ti felt him coming before she could see him. The infra- and ultrasound-sensitive cavities in the tall, curving montrals to either side of her head gave her a sense analogous to touch: the texture of his approaching footsteps was ragged as old sacking. As he rounded the corner to the landing deck door, his breathing felt like a pile of gravel and his heartbeat was spiking like a Zabrak's head.

He didn't look good, either; he was deathly pale, even for a human, and his eyes were raw.

"Anakin," she said warmly. Perhaps a friendly word was what he needed; she doubted he'd gotten many from Mace Windu. "Thank you for what you have done. The Jedi Order is in your debt—the whole galaxy, as well."

"Shaak Ti. Get out of my way."

Shaky as he looked, there was nothing unsteady in his voice: it was deeper than she remembered, more mature, and it carried undertones of authority that she had never heard before.

And she was not blind to the fact he had neglected to call her *Master.*

She put forth a hand, offering calming energies through the Force. "The Temple is sealed, Anakin. The door is code-locked."

"And you're in the way of the pad."

She stepped aside, allowing him to the pad; she had no reason to keep him here against his will. He punched the code hungrily. "If Palpatine retaliates," she said reasonably, "is not your place here, to help with our defense?"

"I'm the *chosen one.* My place is *there.*" His breathing roughened, and he looked as if he was getting even sicker. "I have to be there. That's the prophecy, isn't it? *I have to be there*—"

"Anakin, why? The Masters are the best of the Order. What can you possibly do?"

The door slid open.

"I'm the chosen one," he repeated. "Prophecy can't be changed. I'll do—"

He looked at her with eyes that were dying, and a spasm of unendurable pain passed over his face. Shaak Ti reached for him—he should be in the infirmary, not heading toward what might be a savage battle—but he lurched away from her hand.

"I'll do what I'm *supposed* to do," he said, and sprinted into the night and the rain.

[*the following is a transcript of an audio recording presented before the Galactic Senate on the afternoon of the*

*first Empire Day; identities of all speakers verified and con-
firmed by voiceprint analysis*]

PALPATINE: Why, Master Windu. What a pleasant surprise.

MACE WINDU: Hardly a surprise, Chancellor. And it
will be pleasant for neither of us.

PALPATINE: I'm sorry? Master Fisto, hello. Master
Kolar, greetings. I trust you are well. Master Tiin—I see
your horn has regrown; I'm very glad. What brings four
Jedi Masters to my office at this hour?

MACE WINDU: We know who you are. What you are.
We are here to take you into custody.

PALPATINE: I beg your pardon? What I am? When last
I checked, I was Supreme Chancellor of the Republic you
are sworn to serve. I hope I misunderstand what you
mean by *custody*, Master Windu. It smacks of treason.

MACE WINDU: You're under arrest.

PALPATINE: Really, Master Windu, you cannot be serious. On what charge?

MACE WINDU: You're a Sith Lord!

PALPATINE: Am I? Even if true, that's hardly a crime.
My philosophical outlook is a personal matter. In fact—
the last time I read the Constitution, anyway—we have
very strict laws against this type of persecution. So I ask
you again: what is my alleged crime? How do you expect
to justify your mutiny before the Senate? Or do you intend to arrest the Senate as well?

MACE WINDU: We're not here to argue with you.

PALPATINE: No, you're here to imprison me without trial. Without even the pretense of legality. So this is the plan, at last: the Jedi are taking over the Republic.

MACE WINDU: Come with us. Now.

PALPATINE: I shall do no such thing. If you intend to murder me, you can do so right here.

MACE WINDU: Don't try to resist.

[*sounds that have been identified by frequency resonances to be the ignition of several lightsabers*]

PALPATINE: Resist? How could I possibly resist? This is *murder*, you Jedi traitors! How can *I* be any threat to you? Master Tiin—you're the telepath. What am I thinking right now?

[*sounds of scuffle*]

KIT FISTO: Saesee—

AGEN KOLAR: [*garbled; possibly "It doesn't hurt"(?)*]

[*sounds of scuffle*]

PALPATINE: Help! Help! Security—*someone*! Help me! *Murder! Treason!*

[*recording ends*]

A fountain of amethyst energy burst from Mace Windu's fist. "Don't try to resist."

The song of his blade was echoed by green fire from the hands of Kit Fisto, Agen Kolar, and Saesee Tiin. Kolar and Tiin closed on Palpatine, blocking the path to the door. Shadows dripped and oozed color, weaving and coiling up office walls, slipping over chairs, spreading along the floor.

"Resist? How could I possibly resist?" Still seated at the desk, Palpatine shook an empty fist helplessly, the perfect image of a tired, frightened old man. "This is *murder*, you Jedi traitors! How can *I* be any threat to you?"

He turned desperately to Saesee Tiin. "Master Tiin—you're the telepath. What am I thinking right now?"

Tiin frowned and cocked his head. His blade dipped. A smear of red-flashing darkness hurtled from behind the desk.

Saesee Tiin's head bounced when it hit the floor.

Smoke curled from the neck, and from the twin stumps of the horns, severed just below the chin.

Kit Fisto gasped, "Saesee!"

The headless corpse, still standing, twisted as its knees buckled, and a thin sigh escaped from its trachea as it folded to the floor.

"It doesn't . . ." Agen Kolar swayed.

His emerald blade shrank away, and the handgrip tumbled from his opening fingers. A small, neat hole in the middle of his forehead leaked smoke, showing light from the back of his head.

". . . hurt . . ."

He pitched forward onto his face, and lay still.

Palpatine stood at the doorway, but the door stayed shut. From his right hand extended a blade the color of fire.

The door locked itself at his back.

"Help! Help!" Palpatine cried like a man in desperate fear for his life. "Security—*someone*! Help me! *Murder! Treason!*"

Then he smiled.

He held one finger to his lips, and, astonishingly, he winked.

In the blank second that followed, while Mace Windu and Kit Fisto could do no more than angle their lightsabers to guard, Palpatine swiftly stepped over the bodies back toward his desk, reversed his blade, and drove it in a swift, surgically precise stab down through his desktop.

"That's enough of *that*."

He let it burn its way free through the front, then he turned, lifting his weapon, appearing to study it as one might study the face of a beloved friend one has long thought dead. Power gathered around him until the Force shimmered with darkness.

"If you only knew," he said softly, perhaps speaking to the Jedi Masters, or perhaps to himself, or perhaps even to the scarlet blade lifted now as though in mocking salute, "how long I have been waiting for this . . ."

Anakin's speeder shrieked through the rain, dodging forked bolts of lightning that shot up from towers into the clouds, slicing across traffic lanes, screaming past spacescrapers so fast that his shock-wake cracked windows as he passed.

He didn't understand why people didn't just get out of his way. He didn't understand how the trillion beings who jammed Galactic City could go about their trivial business as though the universe hadn't changed. How could they think they counted for anything, compared with him?

How could they think they still mattered?

Their blind lives meant nothing now. None of them. Because ahead, on the vast cliff face of the Senate Office Building, one window spat lightning into the rain to echo the lightning of the storm outside—but this lightning was the color of clashing lightsabers.

Green fans, sheets of purple—

And crimson flame.

He was too late.

The green fire faded and winked out; now the lightning was only purple and red.

His repulsorlifts howled as he heeled the speeder up onto its side, skidding through wind-shear turbulence to bring it to a bobbing halt outside the window of Palpatine's private office. A blast of lightning hit the spire of 500 Republica, only a kilometer away, and its white burst flared off the window, flash-blinding him; he blinked furiously, slapping at his eyes in frustration.

The colorless glare inside his eyes faded slowly, bringing into focus a jumble of bodies on the floor of Palpatine's private office.

Bodies in Jedi robes.

On Palpatine's desk lay the head of Kit Fisto, faceup, scalp-tentacles unbound in a squid-tangle across the ebonite. His lidless eyes stared blindly at the ceiling. Anakin remembered him in the arena at Geonosis, effortlessly carving his way through wave after wave of combat droids, on his lips a gently humorous smile as though the horrific battle were only some friendly jest. His severed head wore that same smile.

Maybe he thought death was funny, too.

Anakin's own blade sang blue as it slashed through the window and he dived through the gap. He rolled to his feet among a litter of bodies and sprinted through a shattered door along the small private corridor and through a doorway that flashed and flared with energy-scatter.

Anakin skidded to a stop.

Within the public office of the Supreme Chancellor of the Galactic Republic, a last Jedi Master battled alone, blade-to-blade, against a living shadow.

Sinking into Vaapad, Mace Windu fought for his life.

More than his life: each whirl of blade and whipcrack of lightning was a strike in defense of democracy, of justice and peace, of the rights of ordinary beings to live their own lives in their own ways.

He was fighting for the Republic that he loved.

Vaapad, the seventh form of lightsaber combat, takes its name from a notoriously dangerous predator native to the moons of Sarapin: a vaapad attacks its prey with whipping strikes of its blindingly fast tentacles. Most have at least seven. It is not uncommon for them to have as many as twelve; the largest ever killed had twenty-three. With a vaapad, one never knew how many tentacles it had until it was dead: they move too fast to count. Almost too fast to see.

So did Mace's blade.

Vaapad is as aggressive and powerful as its namesake, but its power comes at great risk: immersion in Vaapad opens the gates that restrain one's inner darkness. To use Vaapad, a Jedi must allow himself to *enjoy* the fight; he must give himself over to the thrill of battle. The rush of *winning*. Vaapad is a path that leads through the penumbra of the dark side.

Mace Windu created this style, and he was its only living master.

This was Vaapad's ultimate test.

Anakin blinked and rubbed his eyes again. Maybe he was still a bit flash-blind—the Korun Master seemed to be fading in and out of existence, half swallowed by a thickening black haze in which danced a meter-long bar of sunfire. Mace pressed back the darkness with a relentless straight-ahead march; his own blade, that distinctive amethyst blaze that had been the final sight of so many evil beings across the galaxy, made a haze of its own: an oblate sphere of purple fire within which there seemed to be dozens of swords slashing in all directions at once.

The shadow he fought, that blur of speed—could that be *Palpatine?*

Their blades flared and flashed, crashing together with bursts of fire, weaving nets of killing energy in exchanges so fast that Anakin could not truly see them—

But he could feel them in the Force.

The Force itself roiled and burst and crashed around them, boiling with power and lightspeed ricochets of lethal intent.

And it was darkening.

Anakin could feel how the Force fed upon the shadow's murderous exaltation; he could feel fury spray into the Force though some poisonous abscess had crested in both their hearts.

There was no Jedi restraint here.

Mace Windu was cutting loose.

Mace was deep in it now: submerged in Vaapad, swallowed by it, he no longer truly existed as an independent being.

Vaapad is a channel for darkness, and that darkness flowed both ways. He accepted the furious speed of the Sith Lord, drew the shadow's rage and power into his inmost center—

And let it fountain out again.

He reflected the fury upon its source as a lightsaber redirects a blaster bolt.

There was a time when Mace Windu had feared the power of the dark; there was a time when he had feared the darkness in himself. But the Clone Wars had given him a gift of understanding: on a world called Haruun Kal, he had faced his darkness and had learned that the power of darkness is not to be feared.

He had learned that it is fear that gives the darkness power.

He was not afraid. The darkness had no power over him. But—

Neither did he have power over it.

Vaapad made him an open channel, half of a superconducting loop completed by the shadow; they became a standing wave of battle that expanded into every cubic centimeter of the Chancellor's office. There was no scrap of carpet nor shred of chair that might not at any second disintegrate in flares of red or purple; lampstands became brief shields, sliced into segments that whirled through the air; couches became terrain to be climbed for advantage or overleapt in retreat. But there was still only the cycle of power, the endless loop, no wound taken on either side, not even the possibility of fatigue.

Impasse.

Which might have gone on forever, if Vaapad were Mace's only gift.

The fighting was effortless for him now; he let his body handle it without the intervention of his mind. While his blade spun and crackled, while his feet slid and his weight shifted and his shoulders turned in precise curves of their own direction, his mind slid along the circuit of dark power, tracing it back to its limitless source.

Feeling for its shatterpoint.

He found a knot of fault lines in the shadow's future; he chose the largest fracture and followed it back to the here and the now—

And it led him, astonishingly, to a man standing frozen in the slashed-open doorway. Mace had no need to look; the presence in the Force was familiar, and was as uplifting as sunlight breaking through a thunderhead.

The chosen one was here.

Mace disengaged from the shadow's blade and leapt for the window; he slashed away the transparisteel with a single flourish.

His instant's distraction cost him: a dark surge of the Force nearly blew him right out of the gap he had just cut. Only a desperate Force-push of his own altered his path enough that he slammed into a stanchion instead of plunging half a kilometer from the ledge outside. He bounced off and the Force cleared his head and once again he gave himself to Vaapad.

He could feel the end of this battle approaching, and so could the blur of Sith he faced; in the Force, the shadow had become a pulsar of fear. Easily, almost effortlessly, he turned the shadow's fear into a weapon: he angled the battle to bring them both out onto the window ledge.

Out in the wind. Out with the lightning. Out on a rain-slicked ledge above a half-kilometer drop.

Out where the shadow's fear made it hesitate. Out where the shadow's fear turned some of its Force-powered speed into a Force-powered grip on the slippery permacrete.

Out where Mace could flick his blade in one precise arc and slash the shadow's lightsaber in half.

One piece flipped back in through the cut-open window. The other tumbled from opening fingers, bounced on the ledge, and fell through the rain toward the distant alleys below.

Now the shadow was only Palpatine: old and shrunken, thinning hair bleached white by time and care, face lined with exhaustion.

"For all your power, you are no Jedi. All you are, my lord," Mace said evenly, staring past his blade, "is under arrest."

"Do you see, Anakin? Do you?" Palpatine's voice once again had the broken cadence of a frightened old man's. "Didn't I warn you of the Jedi and their treason?"

"Save your twisted words, my lord. There are no politicians here. The Sith will never regain control of the Republic. It's over. You've lost." Mace leveled his blade. "You lost for the same reason the Sith always lose: defeated by your own fear."

Palpatine lifted his head.

His eyes smoked with hate.

"Fool," he said.

He lifted his arms, his robes of office spreading wide into raptor's wings, his hands hooking into talons.

"*Fool!*" His voice was a shout of thunder. "Do you think the fear you feel is *mine?*"

Lighting blasted the clouds above, and lightning blasted from Palpatine's hands, and Mace didn't have time to comprehend what Palpatine was talking about; he had time only to slip back into Vaapad and angle his blade to catch the forking arcs of pure, dazzling hatred that clawed toward him.

Because Vaapad is more than a fighting style. It is a state of mind: a channel for darkness. Power passed into him and out again without touching him.

And the circuit completed itself: the lightning reflected back to its source.

Palpatine staggered, snarling, but the blistering energy that poured from his hands only intensified.

He fed the power with his pain.

"Anakin!" Mace called. His voice sounded distant, blurred, as if it came from the bottom of a well. "Anakin, help me! This is your chance!"

He felt Anakin's leap from the office floor to the ledge, felt his approach behind—

And Palpatine was not afraid.

Mace could feel it: he wasn't worried at all.

"Destroy this traitor," the Chancellor said, his voice raised over the howl of writhing energy that joined his hands to Mace's blade. "This was never an arrest. It's an *assassination!*"

That was when Mace finally understood. He had it. The key to final victory. Palpatine's shatterpoint. The absolute shatterpoint of the Sith.

The shatterpoint of the dark side itself.

Mace thought, blankly astonished, *Palpatine trusts Anakin Skywalker . . .*

Now Anakin was at Mace's shoulder. Palpatine still made no move to defend himself from Skywalker; instead he ramped up the lightning bursting from his hands, bending the fountain of Mace's blade back toward the Korun Master's face.

Palpatine's eyes glowed with power, casting a yellow glare that burned back the rain from around them. "He is a traitor, Anakin. Destroy him."

"You're the chosen one, Anakin," Mace said, his voice going thin with strain. This was beyond Vaapad; he had no strength left to fight against his own blade. "Take him. It's your *destiny.*"

Skywalker echoed him faintly. "Destiny . . ."

"Help me! I can't hold on any longer!" The yellow glare from Palpatine's eyes spread outward through his flesh. His skin flowed like oil, as though the muscle beneath was burning away, as though even the bones of his skull were softening, were bending and bulging, deforming from the heat and pressure of his electric hatred. "He is *killing* me, Anakin—! Please, Anaa*ahhh*—"

Mace's blade bent so close to his face that he was choking on ozone. "Anakin, he's too *strong* for me—"

"*Ahhh*—" Palpatine's roar above above the endless blast of lightning became a fading moan of despair.

The lightning swallowed itself, leaving only the night and the rain, and an old man crumpled to his knees on a slippery ledge.

"I . . . can't. I give up. I . . . I am too weak, in the end. Too old, and too weak. Don't kill me, Master Jedi. Please. I surrender."

Victory flooded through Mace's aching body. He lifted his blade. "You Sith *disease*—"

"*Wait*—" Skywalker seized his lightsaber arm with desperate strength. "Don't kill him—you can't just *kill* him, Master—"

"Yes, I can," Mace said, grim and certain. "I have to."

"You came to *arrest* him. He has to stand *trial*—"

"A trial would be a joke. He controls the courts. He controls the Senate—"

"So are you going to kill all *them,* too? Like he *said* you would?"

Mace yanked his arm free. "He's too dangerous to be left alive. If you could have taken *Dooku* alive, would you have?"

Skywalker's face swept itself clean of emotion. "That was *different*—"

Mace turned toward the cringing, beaten Sith Lord. "You can explain the difference after he's dead."

He raised his lightsaber.

"*I* need him *alive!*" Skywalker shouted. "I need him to save *Padmé!*"

Mace thought blankly, *Why?* And moved his lightsaber toward the fallen Chancellor.

Before he could follow through on his stroke, a sudden arc of blue plasma sheared through his wrist and his hand tumbled away with his lightsaber still in it and Palpatine roared back to his feet and lightning speared from the Sith Lord's hands and without his blade to catch it, the power of Palpatine's hate struck him full-on.

He had been so intent on Palpatine's shatterpoint that he'd never thought to look for Anakin's.

Dark lightning blasted away his universe.

He fell forever.

Anakin Skywalker knelt in the rain.

He was looking at a hand. The hand had brown skin. The hand held a lightsaber. The hand had a charred oval of tissue where it should have been attached to an arm.

"What have I done?"

Was it his voice? It must have been. Because it was his question.

"What have I done?"

Another hand, a warm and human hand, laid itself softly on his shoulder.

"You're following your destiny, Anakin," said a familiar gentle voice. "The Jedi are traitors. You saved the Republic from their treachery. You can see that, can't you?"

"You were right," Anakin heard himself saying. "Why didn't I know?"

"You couldn't have. They cloaked themselves in deception, my boy. Because they feared your power, they could never trust you."

Anakin stared at the hand, but he no longer saw it. "Obi-Wan—Obi-Wan trusts me . . ."

"Not enough to tell you of their plot."

Treason echoed in his memory.

. . . this is not an assignment for the record . . .

That warm and human hand gave his shoulder a warm and human squeeze. "I do not fear your power, Anakin, I *embrace* it. You are the greatest of the Jedi. You can be the greatest of the Sith. I believe that, Anakin. I believe in *you. I* trust you. I *trust* you. I trust *you.*"

Anakin looked from the dead hand on the ledge to the living one on his shoulder, then up to the face of the man who stood above him, and what he saw there choked him like an invisible fist crushing his throat.

The hand on his shoulder was human.

The face . . . wasn't.

The eyes were a cold and feral yellow, and they gleamed like those of a predator lurking beyond a fringe of firelight; the bone around those feral eyes had swollen and melted and flowed like durasteel spilled from a fusion smelter, and the flesh that blanketed it had gone corpse-gray and coarse as rotten synthplast.

Stunned with horror, stunned with revulsion, Anakin could only stare at the creature. At the shadow.

Looking into the face of the darkness, he saw his future.

"Now come inside," the darkness said.

After a moment, he did.

Anakin stood just within the office. Motionless.

Palpatine examined the damage to his face in a broad expanse of wall mirror. Anakin couldn't tell if his expression might be revulsion, or if this were merely the new shape of his features. Palpatine lifted one tentative hand to the misshapen horror that he now saw in the mirror, then simply shrugged.

"And so the mask becomes the man," he sighed with a hint of philosophical melancholy. "I shall miss the face of Palpatine, I think; but for our purpose, the face of Sidious will serve. Yes, it will serve."

He gestured, and a hidden compartment opened in the office's ceiling above his desk. A voluminous robe of heavy black-on-black brocade floated downward from it; Anakin felt the current in the Force that carried the robe to Palpatine's hand.

He remembered playing a Force game with a shuura fruit, sitting across a long table from Padmé in the retreat by the lake on Naboo. He remembered telling her how grumpy Obi-Wan would be to see him use the Force so casually.

Palaptine seemed to catch his thought; he gave a yellow side-long glance as the robe settled onto his shoulders.

"You must learn to cast off the petty restraints that the Jedi have tried to place upon your power," he said. "Anakin, it's time. I need you to help me restore order to the galaxy."

Anakin didn't respond.

Sidious said, "Join me. Pledge yourself to the Sith. Become my apprentice."

A wave of tingling started at the base of Anakin's skull and spread over his whole body in a slow-motion shockwave.

"I—I can't."

"Of course you can."

Anakin shook his head and found that the rest of him threatened to begin shaking as well. "I—came to save your life, sir. Not to betray my friends—"

Sidious snorted. "*What* friends?"

Anakin could find no answer.

"And do you think that task is finished, my boy?" Sidious seated himself on the corner of the desk, hands folded in his lap, the way he always had when offering Anakin fatherly advice; the misshapen mask of his face made the familiarity of his posture into something horrible. "Do you think that killing one traitor will end treason? Do you think the Jedi will ever stop until I am dead?"

Anakin stared at his hands. The left one was shaking. He hid it behind him.

"It's them or me, Anakin. Or perhaps I should put it more plainly: It's them or *Padmé*."

Anakin made his right hand—his black-gloved hand of durasteel and electrodrivers—into a fist.

"It's just—it's not . . . easy, that's all. I have—I've been a Jedi for so long—"

Sidious offered an appalling smile. "There is a place within you, my boy, a place as briskly clean as ice on a mountaintop, cool and remote. Find that high place, and look down within yourself; breathe that clean, icy air as you regard your guilt and shame. Do not deny them; observe them. Take your horror in your hands and look at it. Examine it as a phenomenon. Smell it. Taste it. Come to know it as only you can, for it is yours, and it is precious."

As the shadow beside him spoke, its words became true. From a remote, frozen distance that was at the same time more extravagantly, hotly intimate than he could have ever dreamed, Anakin handled his emotions. He dissected them. He reassembled them and pulled them apart again. He still felt them—if anything, they burned hotter than before—but they no longer had the power to cloud his mind.

"You have found it, my boy: I can feel you there. That cold distance—that mountaintop within yourself—that is the first key to the power of the Sith."

Anakin opened his eyes and turned his gaze fully upon the grotesque features of Darth Sidious.

He didn't even blink.

As he looked upon that mask of corruption, the revulsion he felt was real, and it was powerful, and it was—

Interesting.

Anakin lifted his hand of durasteel and electrodrivers and cupped it, staring into its palm as though he held there the fear that had haunted his dreams for his whole life, and it was no larger than the piece of shuura he'd once stolen from Padmé's plate.

On the mountain peak within himself, he weighed Padmé's life against the Jedi Order.

It was no contest.

He said, "Yes."

"Yes to what, my boy?"

"Yes, I want your knowledge."

"Good. Good!"

"I want your power. I want the power to stop death."

"That power only my Master truly achieved, but together we will find it. The Force is strong with you, my boy. You can do *anything*."

"The Jedi betrayed you," Anakin said. "The Jedi betrayed both of us."

"As you say. Are you ready?"

"I am," he said, and meant it. "I give myself to you. I pledge myself to the ways of the Sith. Take me as your apprentice. Teach me. Lead me. Be my Master."

Sidious raised the hood of his robe and draped it to shadow the ruin of his face.

"Kneel before me, Anakin Skywalker."

Anakin dropped to one knee. He lowered his head.

"It is your will to join your destiny forever with the Order of the Sith Lords?"

There was no hesitation. "Yes."

Darth Sidious laid a pale hand on Anakin's brow. "Then it is done. You are now one with the Order of the Dark Lords of the Sith. From this day forward, the truth of you, my apprentice, now and forevermore, will be Darth . . ."

A pause; a questioning in the Force—

An answer, dark as the gap between galaxies—

He heard Sidious say it: his new name.

Vader.

A pair of syllables that meant *him*.

Vader, he said to himself. *Vader*.

"Thank you, my Master."

"Every single Jedi, including your friend Obi-Wan Kenobi, have been revealed as enemies of the Republic now. You understand that, don't you?"

"Yes, my Master."

"The Jedi are relentless. If they are not destroyed to the last being, there will be civil war without end. To sterilize the Jedi Temple will be your first task. Do what must be done, Lord Vader."

"I always have, my Master."

"Do not hesitate. Show no mercy. Leave no living creature behind. Only then will you be strong enough with the dark side to save Padmé."

"What of the other Jedi?"

"Leave them to me. After you have finished at the Temple, your second task will be the Separatist leadership, in their 'secret bunker' on Mustafar. When you have killed them all, the Sith will rule the galaxy once more, and we shall have peace. Forever.

"Rise, Darth Vader."

The Sith Lord who once had been a Jedi hero called Anakin Skywalker stood, drawing himself up to his full height, but he looked not outward upon his new Master, nor upon the planet-city beyond, nor out into the galaxy that they would soon rule. He instead turned his gaze inward: he unlocked the furnace gate within his heart and stepped forth to regard with new eyes the cold freezing dread of the dead-star dragon that had haunted his life.

I am Darth Vader, he said within himself.

The dragon tried again to whisper of failure, and weakness, and inevitable death, but with one hand the Sith Lord caught it, crushed away its voice; it tried to rise then, to coil and rear and strike, but the Sith Lord laid his other hand upon it and broke its power with a single effortless twist.

I am Darth Vader, he repeated as he ground the dragon's corpse to dust beneath his mental heel, as he watched the dragon's dust and ashes scatter before the blast from his furnace heart, *and you—*

You are nothing at all.

He had become, finally, what they all called him.

The Hero With No Fear.

Gate Master Jurokk sprinted through the empty vaulted hallway, clattering echoes of his footsteps making him sound like a platoon. The main doors of the Temple were slowly swinging inward in answer to the code key punched into the outside lockpad.

The Gate Master had seen him on the monitor.

Anakin Skywalker.

Alone.

The huge doors creaked inward; as soon as they were wide enough for the Gate Master to pass, he slipped through.

Anakin stood in the night outside, shoulders hunched, head down against the rain.

"Anakin!" he gasped, running up to the young man. "Anakin, what happened? Where are the Masters?"

Anakin looked at him as though he wasn't sure who the Gate Master was. "Where is Shaak Ti?"

"In the meditation chambers—we felt something happen in the Force, something awful. She's searching the Force in deep meditation, trying to get some feel for what's going on . . ."

His words trailed away. Anakin didn't seem to be listening.

"Something *has* happened, hasn't it?"

Jurokk looked past him now. The night beyond the Temple was full of clones. Battalions of them. Brigades.

Thousands.

"Anakin," he said slowly, "what's going on? Something's happened. Something horrible. How bad *is* it—?"

The last thing Jurokk felt was the emitter of a lightsaber

against the soft flesh beneath his jaw; the last thing he heard, as blue plasma chewed upward through his head and burst from the top of his skull and burned away his life, was Anakin Skywalker's melancholy reply.

"You have no idea . . ."

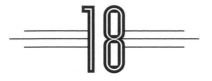

ORDER SIXTY-SIX

Pau City was a cauldron of battle.

From his observation post just off the landing ramp of the command lander on the tenth level, Clone Commander Cody swept the sinkhole with his electrobinoculars. The droid-control center lay in ruins only a few meters away, but the Separatists had learned the lesson of Naboo; their next-generation combat droids were equipped with sophisticated self-motivators that kicked in automatically when control signals were cut off, delivering a program of standing orders.

Standing Order Number One was, apparently, Kill Everything That Moves.

And they were doing a good job of it, too.

Half the city was rubble, and the rest was a firestorm of droids and clones and Utapaun dragon cavalry, and just when Commander Cody was thinking how he really wished they had a Jedi or two around right now, several metric tons of dragon-mount hurtled from the sky and hit the roof of the command lander hard enough to buckle the deck beneath it.

Not that it did the ship any harm; *Jadthu*-class landers are basically flying bunkers, and this particular one was triple-armored and equipped with internal shock buffers and inertial dampeners powerful enough for a fleet corvette, to protect the sophisticated command-and-control equipment inside.

Cody looked up at the dragonmount, and at its rider. "General Kenobi," he said. "Glad you could join us."

"Commander Cody," the Jedi Master said with a nod. He was still scanning the battle around them. "Did you contact Coruscant with the news of the general's death?"

The clone commander snapped to attention and delivered a crisp salute. "As ordered, sir. Erm, sir?"

Kenobi looked down at him.

"Are you all right, sir? You're a bit of a mess."

The Jedi Master wiped away some of the dust and gore that smeared his face with the sleeve of his robe—which was charred, and only left a blacker smear across his cheek. "Ah. Well, yes. It has been a . . . stressful day." He waved out at Pau City. "But we still have a battle to win."

"Then I suppose you'll be wanting this," Cody said, holding up the lightsaber his men had recovered from a traffic tunnel. "I believe you dropped it, sir."

"Ah. Ah, yes."

The weapon floated gently up to Kenobi's hand, and when he smiled down at the clone commander again, Cody could swear the Jedi Master was blushing, just a bit. "No, ah, need to mention this to, erm, Anakin, is there, Cody?"

Cody grinned. "Is that an order, sir?"

Kenobi shook his head, chuckling tiredly. "Let's go. You'll have noticed I *did* manage to leave a few droids for you . . ."

"Yes, sir." A silent buzzing vibration came from a compartment concealed within his armor. Cody frowned. "Go on ahead, General. We'll be right behind you."

That concealed compartment held a secure comlink, which was frequency-locked to a channel reserved for the commander in chief.

Kenobi nodded and spoke to his mount, and the great beast overleapt the clone commander on its way down into the battle.

Cody withdrew the comlink from his armor and triggered it.

A holoscan appeared on the palm of his gauntlet: a hooded man.

"It is time," the holoscan said. *"Execute Order Sixty-Six."*

Cody responded as he had been trained since before he'd even awakened in his crèche-school. "It will be done, my lord."

The holoscan vanished. Cody stuck the comlink back into its concealed recess and frowned down toward where Kenobi rode his dragonmount into selflessly heroic battle.

Cody was a clone. He would execute the order faithfully, without hesitation or regret. But he was also human enough to mutter glumly, "Would it have been too much to ask for the order to have come through *before* I gave him back the bloody *lightsaber* . . . ?"

The order is given once. Its wave-front spreads to clone commanders on Kashyyyk and Felucia, Mygeeto and Tellanroaeg and every battlefront, every military installation, every hospital and rehab center and spaceport cantina in the galaxy.

Except for Coruscant.

On Coruscant, Order Sixty-Six is already being executed.

Dawn crept across Galactic City. Fingers of morning brought a rose-colored glow to the wind-smeared upper reach of a vast twisting cone of smoke.

Bail Organa was a man not given to profanity, but when he caught a glimpse of the source of that smoke from the pilot's chair of his speeder, the curse it brought to his lips would have made a Corellian dockhand blush.

He stabbed a code that canceled his speeder's programmed route toward the Senate Office Building, then grabbed the yoke and kicked the craft into a twisting dive that shot him through half a dozen crisscrossing streams of air traffic.

He triggered his speeder's comm. "Antilles!"

The answer from the captain of his personal crew was instant. *"Yes, my lord?"*

"Route an alert to SER," he ordered. "The Jedi Temple is on fire!"

"Yes, sir. We know. Senate Emergency Response has announced a state of martial law, and the Temple is under lockdown. There's been some kind of Jedi rebellion."

"What are you talking about? That's impossible. Why aren't there fireships onstation?"

"I don't have any details, my lord; we only know what SER is telling us."

"Look, I'm right on top of it. I'm going down there to find out what's happening."

"My lord, I wouldn't recommend it—"

"I won't take any chances." Bail hauled the control yoke to slew the speeder toward the broad landing deck on the roof of the Temple ziggurat. "Speaking of not taking chances, Captain: order the duty crew onto the *Tantive* and get her engines warm. I've got a bad feeling about this."

"Sir?"

"Just do it."

Bail set the speeder down only a few meters from the deck entrance and hopped out. A squad of clone troopers stood in the open doorway. Smoke billowed out from the hallway behind them.

One of the troopers lifted a hand as Bail approached. "Don't worry, sir, everything is under control here."

"Under control? Where are the SER teams? What is the *army* doing here?"

"I'm sorry, I can't talk about that, sir."

"Has there been some kind of attack on the Temple?"

"I'm sorry, I can't talk about that, sir."

"Listen to me, Sergeant, I am a Senator of the Galactic Republic," Bail said, improvising, "and I am late for a meeting with the Jedi Council—"

"The Jedi Council is not in session, sir."

"Maybe you should let me see for myself."

The four clones moved together to block his path. "I'm sorry, sir. Entry is forbidden."

"I am a *Senator*—"

"Yes, sir." The clone sergeant snapped his DC-15 to his shoulder, and Bail, blinking, found himself staring into its blackened muzzle from close enough to kiss it. "And it is time for you to leave, sir."

"When you put it that way . . ." Bail backed off, lifting his hands. "Yes, all right, I'm going."

A burst of blasterfire ripped through the smoke and scattered into the dawn outside. Bail stared with an open mouth as a Jedi flashed out of nowhere and started cutting down clones. No: not a Jedi.

A boy.

A child, no more than ten years old, swinging a lightsaber whose blade was almost as long as he was tall. More blasterfire came from inside, and a whole platoon of clones came pelting toward the landing deck, and the ten-year-old was hit, and hit again, and then just shot to rags among the bodies of the troopers he'd killed, and Bail started backing away, faster now, and in the middle of it all, a clone wearing the colors of a commander came out of the smoke and pointed at Bail Organa.

"No witnesses," the commmander said. "Kill him."

Bail ran.

He dived through a hail of blasterfire, hit the deck, and rolled under his speeder to the opposite side. He grabbed on to its pilot's-side door and swung his leg onto a tail fin, using the vehicle's body as cover while he stabbed the keys to reinitialize its autorouter. Clones charged toward him, firing as they came.

His speeder heeled over and blasted away.

Bail pulled himself inside as the speeder curved up into the congested traffic lanes. He was white as flimsiplast, and his hands were shaking so badly he could barely activate his comm.

"Antilles! Organa to Antilles. Come in, Captain!"

"Antilles here, my lord."

"It's worse than I thought. Far worse than you've heard. Send someone to Chance Palp—no, strike that. Go yourself. Take five men and go to the spaceport. I know at least one Jedi ship is on the ground there; Saesee Tiin brought in *Sharp Spiral* late last night. I need you to steal his homing beacon."

"What? His beacon? Why?"

"No time to explain. Get the beacon and meet me at the *Tantive*. We're leaving the planet."

He stared back at the vast column of smoke that boiled from the Jedi Temple.

"While we still can."

Order Sixty-Six is the climax of the Clone Wars.

Not the end—the Clone Wars will end some few hours from now, when a coded signal, sent by Nute Gunray from the secret Separatist bunker on Mustafar, deactivates every combat droid in the galaxy at once—but the climax.

It's not a thrilling climax; it's not the culmination of an epic struggle. Just the opposite, in fact. The Clone Wars were never an epic struggle. They were never intended to be.

What is happening right now is why the Clone Wars were fought in the first place. It is their reason for existence. The

Clone Wars have always been, in and of themselves, from their very inception, the revenge of the Sith.

They were irresistible bait. They took place in remote locations, on planets that belonged, primarily, to "somebody else." They were fought by expendable proxies. And they were constructed as a win–win situation.

The Clone Wars were the perfect Jedi trap.

By fighting at all, the Jedi lost.

With the Jedi Order overextended, spread thin across the galaxy, each Jedi is alone, surrounded only by whatever clone troops he, she, or it commands. War itself pours darkness into the Force, deepening the cloud that limits Jedi perception. And the clones have no malice, no hatred, not the slightest ill intent that might give warning. They are only following orders.

In this case, Order Sixty-Six.

Hold-out blasters appear in clone hands. ARC-170s drop back onto the tails of Jedi starfighters. AT-STs swivel their guns. Turrets on hovertanks swung silently.

Clones open fire, and Jedi die.

All across the galaxy. All at once.

Jedi die.

Kenobi never saw it coming.

Cody had coordinated the heavy-weapons operators from five different companies spread over an arc of three different levels of the sinkhole-city. He'd served under Kenobi in more than a dozen operations since the beginning of the Outer Rim sieges, and he had a very clear and unsentimental estimate of just how hard to kill the unassuming Jedi Master was. He wasn't taking any chances.

He raised his comlink. "Execute."

On that order, T-21 muzzles swung, shoulder-fired torps locked on, and proton grenade launchers angled to precisely calibrated elevations.

"Fire."

They did.

Kenobi, his dragonmount, and all five of the destroyer droids he'd been fighting vanished in a fireball that for an instant outshone Utapau's sun.

Visual polarizers in Cody's helmet cut the glare by 78 percent; his vision cleared in plenty of time to see shreds of dragonmount and twisted hunks of droid raining into the ocean mouth at the bottom of the sinkhole.

Cody scowled and keyed his comlink. "Looks like the lizard took the worst of it. Deploy the seekers. All of them."

He stared down into the boil of the ocean mouth.

"I want to see the body."

C-3PO paused in the midst of dusting the Tarka-Null original on its display pedestal near his mistress's bedroom view wall, and used the electrostatic tissue to briefly polish his own photoreceptors. The astromech in the green Jedi starfighter docking with the veranda below—could that be R2-D2?

Well, this should be interesting.

Senator Amidala had spent the better part of these predawn hours simply staring over the city, toward the plume of smoke that rose from the Jedi Temple; now, at last, she might get some answers.

He might, too. R2-D2 was far from the sort of sparkling conversationalist with whom C-3PO preferred to associate, but the little astromech had a positive gift for jacking himself into the motherboards of the most volatile situations . . .

The cockpit popped open, and inevitably the Jedi within was revealed to be Anakin Skywalker. In watching Master Anakin climb down from the starfighter's cockpit, 3PO's photoreceptors captured data that unexpectedly activated his threat-aversion subroutines. "Oh," he said faintly, clutching at his power core. "Oh, I don't like the looks of *this* at all . . ."

He dropped the electrostatic tissue and shuffled as quickly as he could to the bedroom door. "My lady," he called to Senator Amidala, where she stood by the broad window. "On the veranda. A Jedi starfighter," he forced out. "Has docked, my lady."

She blinked, then rushed toward the bedroom door.

C-3PO shuffled along behind her and slipped out through the open door, making a wide circle around the humans, who were engaged in one of those inexplicable embraces they seemed so fond of.

Reaching the starfighter, he said, "Artoo, are you all right? What is going on?"

The astromech squeaked and beeped; C-3PO's autotranslator interpreted: NOBODY TELLS ME ANYTHING.

"Of course not. You don't keep up your end of the conversation."

A whirring squeal: SOMETHING'S WRONG. THE FACTORS DON'T BALANCE.

"You can't possibly be more confused than I am."

YOU'RE RIGHT. *NOBODY* CAN BE MORE CONFUSED THAN YOU ARE.

"Oh, very funny. Hush now—what was that?"

The Senator was sitting now, leaning distractedly on one of the tasteful, elegant bistro tables that dotted the veranda, while Master Anakin stood above her. "I think—he's saying something about a *rebellion*—that the Jedi have tried to overthrow the Republic! And—oh, my goodness. Mace Windu has tried to assassinate Chancellor Palpatine! Can he be *serious?*"

I DON'T KNOW. ANAKIN DOESN'T TALK TO ME ANYMORE.

C-3PO shook his cranial assembly helplessly. "How can Master Windu be an assassin? He has such impeccable manners."

LIKE I TOLD YOU: THE FACTORS DON'T ADD UP.

"I've been hearing the most awful rumors—they're saying the government is going to *banish* us—banish *droids,* can you imagine?"

DON'T BELIEVE EVERYTHING YOU HEAR.

"Shh. Not so loud!"

I'M ONLY SAYING THAT WE DON'T KNOW THE TRUTH.

"Of course we don't." C-3PO sighed. "And we likely never will."

"What about Obi-Wan?"

She looked stricken. Pale and terrified.

It made him love her more.

He shook his head. "Many of the Jedi have been killed."

"But . . ." She stared out at the rivers of traffic crosshatching the sky. "Are you *sure?* It seems so . . . *unbelievable* . . ."

"I was there, Padmé. It's all true."

"But . . . but how could *Obi-Wan* be involved in something like that?"

He said, "We may never know."

"Outlawed . . . ," she murmured. "What happens now?"

"All Jedi are required to surrender themselves immediately," he said. "Those who resist . . . are being dealt with."

"Anakin—they're your *family*—"

"They're traitors. *You're* my family. You and the baby."

"How can *all* of them be traitors—?"

"They're not the only ones. There were Senators in this as well."

Now, finally, she looked at him, and fear shone from her eyes.

He smiled.

"Don't worry. I won't let anything happen to you."

"To *me?*"

"You need to distance yourself from your . . . friends . . . in the Senate, Padmé. It's very important to avoid even the appearance of disloyalty."

"Anakin—you sound like you're *threatening* me . . ."

"This is a dangerous time," he said. "We are all judged by the company we keep."

"But—I've opposed the war, I opposed Palpatine's emergency powers—I publicly called him a *threat to democracy!*"

"That's all behind us now."

"*What* is? What I've done? Or democracy?"

"Padmé—"

Her chin came up, and her eyes hardened. "Am I under suspicion?"

"Palpatine and I have discussed you already. You're in the clear, so long as you avoid . . . inappropriate associations."

"How am I *in the clear?*"

"Because you're with *me*. Because I *say* you are."

She stared at him as if she'd never seen him before. "You told him."

"He knew."

"Anakin—"

"There's no more need for secrets, Padmé. Don't you see? *I'm not a Jedi anymore.* There *aren't* any Jedi. There's just *me*."

He reached for her hand. She let him take it. "And you, and our child."

"Then we can *go*, can't we?" Her hard stare melted to naked appeal. "We can leave this planet. Go somewhere we can be *together*—somewhere *safe*."

"We'll be together *here*," he said. "You *are* safe. I have *made* you safe."

"Safe," she echoed bitterly, pulling her hand away. "As long as Palpatine doesn't change his mind."

The hand she had pulled from his grasp was trembling.

"The Separatist leadership is in hiding on Mustafar. I'm on my way to deal with them right now."

"*Deal* with them?" The corners of her mouth drew down. "Like the Jedi are being *dealt with*?"

"This is an important mission. I'm going to end the war."

She looked away. "You're going alone?"

"Have faith, my love," he said.

She shook her head helplessly, and a pair of tears spilled from her eyes. He touched them with his mechanical hand; the fingertips of his black glove glistened in the dawn.

Two liquid gems, indescribably precious—because they were *his*. He had earned them. As he had earned *her*; as he had earned the child she bore.

He had paid for them with innocent blood.

"I love you," he said. "This won't take long. Wait for me."

Fresh tears streamed onto her ivory cheeks, and she threw herself into his arms. "Always, Anakin. Forever. Come back to me, my love—my *life*. Come back to me."

He smiled down on her. "You say that like I'm already gone."

Icy salt water shocked Obi-Wan back to full consciousness. He hung in absolute blackness; there was no telling how far underwater he might be, nor even which direction might be up. His lungs were choked, half full of water, but he didn't panic or even particularly worry; mostly, he was vaguely pleased to discover that even in his semiconscious fall, he'd managed to hang on to his lightsaber.

He clipped it back to his belt by feel, and—using only a minor exercise of Jedi discipline to suppress convulsive coughing—he contracted his diaphragm, forcing as much water from his lungs as he could. He took from his equipment belt his rebreather, and a small compressed-air canister intended for use in an emergency, when the breathable environment was not adequate to sustain his life.

Obi-Wan was fairly certain that his current situation qualified as an emergency.

He remembered . . .

Boga's wrenching leap, twisting in the air, the shock of impacts, multiple detonations blasting both of them farther and farther out from the sinkhole wall . . .

Using her massive body to shield Obi-Wan from his own troops.

Boga had *known*, somehow . . . the dragonmount had known what Obi-Wan had been incapable of even suspecting, and without hesitation she'd given her life to save her rider.

I suppose that makes me more than her rider, Obi-Wan thought as he discarded the canister and got his rebreather snugged into place. *I suppose that makes me her friend.*

It certainly made her mine.

He let grief take him for a moment; grief not for the death of a noble beast, but for how little time Obi-Wan had had to appreciate the gift of his friend's service.

But even grief is an attachment, and Obi-Wan let it flow out of his life.

Good-bye, my friend.

He didn't try to swim; he seemed to be hanging motionless, suspended in infinite night. He relaxed, regulated his breathing, and let the water take him whither it would.

C-3PO barely had time to wish his little friend good luck and remind him to stay alert as Master Anakin brushed past him and climbed into the starfighter's cockpit, then fired the engine and blasted off, taking R2-D2 goodness knows where—probably to some preposterously horrible alien planet and into a perfectly ridiculous amount of danger—with never a thought how his loyal *droid* might feel about being *dragged* across the galaxy without so much as a by-your-leave . . .

Really, what *had* happened to that young man's manners?

He turned to Senator Amidala and saw that she was crying. "Is there anything I can do, my lady?"

She didn't even turn his way. "No, thank you, Threepio."

"A snack, perhaps?"

She shook her head.

"A glass of water?"

"No."

All he could do was stand there. "I feel so *helpless* . . ."

She nodded, looking away again, up at the fading spark of her husband's starfighter.

"I know, Threepio," she said. "We all do."

In the underground shiplift beneath the Senate Office Building, Bail Organa was scowling as he boarded *Tantive IV*. When Captain Antilles met him at the top of the landing ramp, Bail nodded backward at the scarlet-clad figures posted around the accessways. "Since when do Redrobes guard Senate ships?"

Antilles shook his head. "I don't know, sir. I have a feeling there are some Senators whom Palpatine doesn't want leaving the planet."

Bail nodded. "Thank the Force I'm not one of them. Yet. Did you get the beacon?"

"Yes, sir. No one even tried to stop us. The clones at Chance Palp seemed confused—like they're not quite sure who's in charge."

"That'll change soon. Too soon. We'll *all* know who's in charge," Bail said grimly. "Prepare to raise ship."

"Back to Alderaan, sir?"

Bail shook his head. "Kashyyyk. There's no way to know if any Jedi have lived through this—but if I had to bet on one, my money'd be on Yoda."

Some undefinable time later, Obi-Wan felt his head and shoulders breach the surface of the lightless ocean. He unclipped his lightsaber and raised it over his head. In its blue glow he could see that he had come up in a large grotto; holding the lightsaber high, he tucked away his rebreather and sidestroked across the current to a rock outcropping that was rugged enough to offer handholds. He pulled himself out of the water.

The walls of the grotto above the waterline were pocked with openings; after inspecting the mouths of several caves, Obi-Wan came upon one where he felt a faint breath of moving air. It had a distinctly unpleasant smell—it reminded him more than a bit of the dragonmount pen—but when he doused his lightsaber for a moment and listened very closely, he could hear a faint rumble that might have been distant wheels and repulsorlifts passing over sandstone—and what was that? An air horn? Or possibly a very disturbed dragon . . . at any rate, this seemed to be the appropriate path.

He had walked only a few hundred meters before the gloom ahead of him was pierced by the white glare of high-intensity searchlights. He let his blade shrink away and pressed himself into a deep, narrow crack as a pair of seeker droids floated past.

Apparently Cody hadn't given up yet.

Their searchlights illuminated—and, apparently, awakened— some sort of immense amphibian cousin of a dragonmount; it blinked sleepily at them as it lifted its slickly glistening starfighter-sized head.

Oh, Obi-Wan thought. *That explains the smell.*

He breathed into the Force a suggestion that these small bobbing spheroids of circuitry and durasteel were actually, contrary to smell and appearance, some unexpected variety of immortally delicious confection sent down from the heavens by the kindly gods of Huge Slimy Cave-Monsters.

The Huge Slimy Cave-Monster in question promptly opened jaws that could engulf a bantha and snapped one of the seekers from the air, chewing it to slivers with every evidence of satisfaction. The second seeker emitted a startled and thoroughly alarmed *wheeepwheepwheep* and shot away into the darkness, with the creature in hot pursuit.

Reigniting his lightsaber and moving cautiously back out into the cavern, Obi-Wan came upon a nest of what must have been infant Huge Slimy Cave-Monsters; picking his way around it as they lunged and snapped and squalled at him, he reflected absently that people who thought all babies were cute should really get out more.

Obi-Wan walked, and occasionally climbed or slid or had to leap, and walked some more.

Soon the darkness in the cavern gave way to the pale glow of Utapaun traffic lighting, and Obi-Wan found himself standing in a smallish side tunnel off a major thoroughfare. This was clearly little traveled, though; the sandy dust on its floor was so thick it was practically a beach. In fact, he could clearly see the tracks of the last vehicle to pass this way.

Broad parallel tracks pocked with divots: a blade-wheeler.

And beside them stretched long splay-clawed prints of a running dragon.

Obi-Wan blinked in mild astonishment. He had never entirely grown accustomed to the way the Force always came through for him—but neither was he reluctant to accept its gifts. Frowning thoughtfully, he followed the tracks a short distance around a curve, until the tunnel gave way to the small landing platform.

Grievous's starfighter was still there. As were the remains of Grievous.

Apparently not even the local rock-vultures could stomach him.

Tantive IV swept through the Kashyyyk system on silent running; this was still a combat zone. Captain Antilles wouldn't even risk standard scans, because they could so easily be detected and backtraced by Separatist forces.

And the Separatists weren't the only ones Antilles was worried about.

"There's the signal again, sir. Whoops. Wait, I'll get it back." Antilles fiddled some more with the controls on the beacon. "Blasted thing," he muttered. "What, you can't calibrate it without using the Force?"

Bail stared through the forward view wall. Kashyyyk was only a tiny green disk two hundred thousand kilometers away. "Do you have a vector?"

"Roughly, sir. It seems to be on an orbital tangent, headed outsystem."

"I think we can risk a scan. Tight beam."

"Very well, sir."

Antilles gave the necessary orders, and moments later the scan tech reported that the object they'd picked up seemed to be some sort of escape pod. "It's not a Republic model, sir—wait, here comes the database—"

The scan tech frowned at his screen. "It's . . . Wookiee, sir. That doesn't make any sense. Why would a Wookiee escape pod be *outbound* from *Kashyyyk?*"

"Interesting." Bail didn't yet allow himself to hope. "Lifesigns?"

"Yes—well, maybe . . . this reading doesn't make any . . ." The scan tech could only shrug. "I'm not sure, sir. Whatever it is, it's no Wookiee, that's for sure . . ."

For the first time all day, Bail Organa allowed himself to smile. "Captain Antilles?"

The captain saluted crisply. "On our way, sir."

Obi-Wan took General Grievous's starfighter screaming out of the atmosphere so fast he popped the gravity well and made jump before the *Vigilance* could even scramble its fighters. He reverted to realspace well beyond the system, kicked the starfighter to a new vector, and jumped again. A few more jumps of random direction and duration left him deep in interstellar space.

"You know," he said to himself, "integral hyperspace capability is rather useful in a starfighter; why don't *we* have it yet?"

While the starfighter's nav system whirred and chunked its way through recalculating his position, he punched codes to gang his Jedi comlink into the starfighter's system.

Instead of a holoscan, the comlink generated an audio signal—an accelerating series of beeps.

Obi-Wan knew that signal. Every Jedi did. It was the recall code.

It was being broadcast on every channel by every HoloNet repeater. It was supposed to mean that the war was over. It was supposed to mean that the Council had ordered all Jedi to return to the Temple immediately.

Obi-Wan suspected it actually meant what had happened on Utapau was far from an isolated incident.

He keyed the comlink for audio. He took a deep breath.

"Emergency Code Nine Thirteen," he said, and waited.

The starfighter's comm system cycled through every response frequency.

He waited some more.

"Emergency Code Nine Thirteen. This is Obi-Wan Kenobi. Repeat: Emergency Code Nine Thirteen. Are there any Jedi out there?"

He waited. His heart thumped heavily.

"Any Jedi, please respond. This is Obi-Wan Kenobi declaring a Nine Thirteen Emergency."

He tried to ignore the small, still voice inside his head that whispered he might just be the only one out here.

He might just be the only one, period.

He started punching coordinates for a single jump that would bring him close enough to pick up a signal directly from Coruscant when a burst of fuzz came over his comlink. A quick glance confirmed the frequency: a Jedi channel.

"Please repeat," Obi-Wan said. "I'm locking onto your signal. Please repeat."

The fuzz became a spray of blue laser, which gradually resolved into a fuzzy figure of a tall, slim human with dark hair and an elegant goatee. *"Master Kenobi? Are you all right? Have you been wounded?"*

"Senator Organa!" Obi-Wan exclaimed with profound relief. "No, I'm not wounded—but I'm certainly *not* all right. I need help. My clones turned on me. I barely escaped with my life!"

"There have been ambushes all over the galaxy."

Obi-Wan lowered his head, offering a silent wish to the Force that the victims might find peace within it.

"Have you had contact with any other survivors?"

"Only one," the Alderaanian Senator said grimly. *"Lock onto my coordinates. He's waiting for you."*

A curve of knuckle, skinned, black scab corrugated with dirt and leaking red—

The fringe of fray at the cuff of a beige sleeve, dark, crusted with splatter from the death of a general—

The tawny swirl of grain in wine-dark tabletop of polished Alderaanian kriin—

These were what Obi-Wan Kenobi could look at without starting to shake.

The walls of the small conference room on *Tantive IV* were too featureless to hold his attention; to look at a wall allowed his mind to wander . . .

And the shaking began.

The shaking got worse when he met the ancient green stare of the tiny alien seated across the table from him, for that wrinkled leather skin and those tufts of withered hair were his earliest memory, and they reminded Obi-Wan of the friends who had died today.

The shaking got worse still when he turned to the other being in the room, because he wore politician's robes that reminded Obi-Wan of the enemy who yet lived.

The deception. The death of Jedi Masters he had admired, of Jedi Knights who had been his friends. The death of his oath to Qui-Gon.

The death of Anakin.

Anakin must have fallen along with Mace and Agen, Saesee and Kit; fallen along with the Temple.

Along with the Order itself.

Ashes.

Ashes and dust.

Twenty-five thousand years wiped from existence in a single day.

All the dreams. All the promises.

All the *children* . . .

"We took them from their *homes*." Obi-Wan fought to stay in his chair; the pain inside him demanded motion. It became wave after wave of tremors. "We *promised* their *families*—"

"Control yourself, you must; still Jedi, you are!"

"Yes, Master Yoda." That scab on his knuckle—focused on that, he could suppress the shaking. "Yes, we are Jedi. But what if we're the *last*?"

"If the last we are, unchanged our duty is." Yoda settled his chin onto hands folded over the head of his gimer stick. He looked every day of his nearly nine hundred years. "While one Jedi lives, survive the Order does. Resist the darkness with every breath, we must."

He lifted his head and the stick angled to poke Obi-Wan in the shin. "Especially the darkness in *ourselves*, young one. Of the dark side, despair is."

The simple truth of this called to him. Even despair is attachment: it is a grip clenched upon pain.

Slowly, very slowly, Obi-Wan Kenobi remembered what it was to be a Jedi.

He leaned back in his chair and covered his face with both hands, inhaling a thin stream of air between his palms; into himself with the air he brought pain and guilt and remorse, and as he exhaled, they trailed away and vanished in the air.

He breathed out his whole life.

Everything he had done, everything he had been, friends and enemies, dreams and hopes and fears.

Empty, he found clarity. Scrubbed clean, the Force shone through him. He sat up and nodded to Yoda.

"Yes," he said. "We may be the last. But what if we're *not?*"

Green leather brows drew together over lambent eyes. "The Temple beacon."

"Yes. Any surviving Jedi might still obey the recall, and be killed."

Bail Organa looked from one Jedi to the other, frowning. "What are you saying?"

"I'm saying," Obi-Wan replied, "that we have to go back to Coruscant."

"It's too dangerous," the Senator said instantly. "The whole planet is a *trap*—"

"Yes. We have a—ah . . ."

The loss of Anakin stabbed him.

Then he let that go, too.

"*I* have," he corrected himself, "a policy on traps . . ."

THE FACE OF THE SITH

Mustafar burned with lava streaming from volcanoes of glittering obsidian.

At the fringe of its gravity well, a spray of prismatic starlight warped a starfighter into existence. Declamping from its hyperdrive ring, the starfighter streaked into an atmosphere choked with dense smoke and cinders.

The starfighter followed a preprogrammed course toward the planet's lone installation, an automated lava mine built originally by the Techno Union to draw precious metals from the continuous rivers of burning stone. Upgraded with the finest mechanized defenses that money could buy, the settlement had become the final redoubt of the leaders of the Confederacy of Independent Systems. It was absolutely impenetrable.

Unless one had its deactivation codes.

Which was how the starfighter could land without causing the installation's defenses to so much as stir.

The habitable areas of the settlement were spread among towers that looked like poisonous toadstools sprung from the bank of a river of fire. The main control center squatted atop the largest, beside the small landing deck where the starfighter had alit. It was from this control center, less than an hour before, that a coded command had been transmitted over every HoloNet repeater in the galaxy.

At that signal, every combat droid in every army on every planet marched back to its transport, resocketed itself, and turned itself off. The Clone Wars were over.

Almost.

There was a final detail.

A dark-cloaked figure swung down from the cockpit of the starfighter.

Bail Organa strode onto the *Tantive*'s shuttle deck to find Obi-Wan and Yoda gazing dubiously at the tiny cockpit of Obi-Wan's starfighter. "I suppose," Obi-Wan was saying reluctantly, "if you don't mind riding on my lap . . ."

"That may not be necessary," Bail said. "I've just been summoned back to Coruscant by Mas Amedda; Palpatine has called the Senate into Extraordinary Session. Attendance is required."

"Ah." Obi-Wan's mouth turned downward. "It's clear what this will be about."

"I am," Bail said slowly, "concerned it might be a trap."

"Unlikely this is." Yoda hobbled toward him. "Unknown, is the purpose of your sudden departure from the capital; dead, young Obi-Wan and I are both presumed to be."

"And Palpatine won't be moving against the Senate as a whole," Obi-Wan added. "At least, not yet; he'll need the illusion of democracy to keep the individual star systems in line. He won't risk a general uprising."

Bail nodded. "In that case—" He took a deep breath. "—perhaps I can offer Your Graces a lift?"

Inside the control center of the Separatist bunker on Mustafar . . .

Wat Tambor was adjusting the gas mix inside his armor—

Poggle the Lesser was massaging his fleshy lip-tendrils—

Shu Mai was fiddling with the brass binding that restrained her hair into the stylish curving horn that rose behind her head—

San Hill was stretching his bodystocking, which had begun to ride up in the crotch—

Rune Haako was shifting his weight nervously from foot to foot—

While Nute Gunray spoke to the holopresence of Darth Sidious.

"The plan has gone exactly as you promised, my lord," Gunray said. "This is a glorious day for the galaxy!"

"Yes, indeed. Thanks, in great part, to you, Viceroy, and to your associates of the Techno Union and the IBC. And, of course, Archduke Poggle. You have all performed magnificently. Have your droid armies completed shutdown?"

"Yes, my lord. Nearly an hour ago."

"Excellent! You will be handsomely rewarded. Has my new apprentice, Darth Vader, arrived?"

"His ship touched down only a moment ago."

"Good, good," the holoscan of the cloaked man said pleasantly. *"I have left your reward in his hands. He will take care of you."*

The door cycled open.

A tall cloaked figure, slim but broad-shouldered, face shadowed by a heavy hood, stood in the doorway.

San Hill beat the others to the greeting. "Welcome, Lord Vader!" His elongated legs almost tangled with each other in his rush to shake the hand of the Sith Lord. "On behalf of the leadership of the Confederacy of Independent Systems, let me be the first to—"

"Very well. You will be the first."

The cloaked figure stepped inside and made a gesture with a

black-gloved hand. Blast doors slammed across every exit. The control panel exploded in a shower of sparking wires.

The cloaked figure threw back its hood.

San Hill recoiled, hands flapping like panicked birds sewn to his wrists.

He had time to gasp, "You're—you're *Anakin Skywalker!*" before a fountain of blue-white plasma burned into his chest, curving through a loop that charred all three of his hearts.

The Separatist leadership watched in frozen horror as the corpse of the head of the InterGalactic Banking Clan collapsed like a depowered protocol droid.

"The resemblance," Darth Vader said, "is deceptive."

The Senate Guard blinked, then straightened and smoothed the drape of his robe. He risked a glance at his partner, who flanked the opposite side of the door.

Had they really just gotten as lucky as he thought they had?

Were this Senator and his aides really walking right out of the turbolift with a couple of as-yet-uncaptured *Jedi?*

Wow. Promotions all around.

The guard tried not to stare at the two Jedi, and did his best to sound professional. "Welcome back, Senator. May I see your clearance?"

An identichip was produced without hesitation: Bail Organa, senior Senator from Alderaan.

"Thank you. You may proceed." The guard handed back the identichip. He was rather pleased with how steady and business-like he sounded. "We will take custody of the Jedi."

Then the taller of the two Jedi murmured gently that it would be better if he and his counterpart were to stay with the Senator, and really, he seemed like such a reasonable fellow, and it was such a good idea—after all, the Grand Convocation Chamber of the Galactic Senate was so secure there was really no way for a Jedi to cause any trouble for anyone and they could just as easily be apprehended on their way out, and the guard didn't want to seem like an unreasonable fellow himself, and so he found himself nodding and agreeing that yes, indeed, it would be better if the Jedi stayed with the Senator.

And everyone was so reasonable and agreeable that it seemed perfectly reasonable and agreeable to the guard that the Jedi and the Senator, instead of staying together as they'd said, made low-voiced *Force-be-with-you* farewells; it never occurred to the guard to object even when the Senator entered the Convocation Chamber and the two Jedi headed off for . . . well, apparently, somewhere else.

All eight members of Decoy Squad Five were deployed at a downlevel loading dock, where supplies that Jedi could not grow in their own Temple gardens had been delivered daily.

Not anymore.

This deep in Coruscant's downlevels, the sun never shone; the only illumination came from antiquated glow globes, their faded light yellow as ancient parchment, that only darkened the shadows around. In those shadows lived the dregs of the galaxy, squatters and scavengers, madmen and fugitives from the justice above. Parts of Coruscant's downlevels could be worse than Nar Shaddaa.

The men of Decoy Squad Five would have been alert on any post. They were bred to be. Here, though, they were in a combat zone, where their lives and their missions depended on their perceptions, and on how fast their blasters could come out from inside those Jedi-style robes.

So when a ragged, drooling hunchback lurched out of the gloom nearby, a bundle cradled in his arms, Decoy Squad Five took it for granted that he was a threat. Blasters appeared with miraculous speed. "Halt. Identify yourself."

"No, no, no, Yer Graces, oh, no, I'm bein' here to *help*, y'see,

I'm on *yerr* side!" The hunchback slurped drool back into his slack lips as he lurched toward them. "Lookit I got here, I mean, *lookit*—'sa Jedi *babby*, ennit?"

The sergeant of the squad squinted at the bundle in the hunchback's arms. "A Jedi baby?"

"Oooh, sher. Sher, Yer Grace. Jedi babby, sher azzell iddiz! Come from outcher Temple, dinnit? Lookit!"

The hunchback was now close enough that the sergeant could see what he carried in his filthy bundle. It *was* a baby. Sort of. It was the ugliest baby the sergeant had ever seen, alien or not, wizened and shriveled like a worn-out purse of moldly leather, with great pop eyes and a toothless idiot's grin.

The sergeant frowned skeptically. "Anyone could grab some deformed kid and claim it's anything they want. How do you know it's a Jedi?"

The baby said, "My lightsaber, the first clue would be, hmm?"

A burning blade of green slanted across the sergeant's face so close he could smell the ozone, and the hunchback wasn't a hunchback anymore: he now held a lightsaber the color of a summmer sky, and he said in a clipped, educated Coruscanti accent, "Please don't try to resist. No one has to get hurt."

The men of Decoy Squad Five disagreed.

Six seconds later, all eight of them were dead.

Yoda looked up at Obi-Wan. "To hide the bodies, no point there is."

Obi-Wan nodded agreement. "These are clones; an abandoned post is as much a giveaway as a pile of corpses. Let's get to that beacon."

Bail slipped into the rear of the Naboo delegation's Senate pod as Palpatine thundered from the podium, "These Jedi murderers left me *scarred*, left me *deformed*, but they could not scar my *integrity*! They could not deform my *resolve*! The remaining traitors will be hunted down, rooted out wherever they may hide, and brought to justice, dead or alive! All collaborators will suffer the same fate. Those who protect the enemy *are* the enemy! Now is the time! Now we will strike back! Now we will *destroy* the *destroyers! Death to the enemies of democracy!*"

The Senate roared.

Amidala didn't even glance at Bail as he slid into a seat beside her. On the opposite side, Representative Binks nodded at him, but said nothing, blinking solemnly. Bail frowned; if even the irrepressible Jar Jar was worried, this looked to be even worse than he'd expected. And he had expected it to be very, very bad.

He touched Amidala's arm softly. "It's all a lie. You know that, don't you?"

She stared frozenly toward the podium. Her eyes glistened with unshed tears. "I don't know *what* I know. Not anymore. Where have you been?"

"I was . . . held up." As she once had told him, some things were better left unsaid.

"He's been presenting evidence all afternoon," she said in a flat, affectless monotone. "Not just the assassination attempt. The Jedi were about to overthrow the Senate."

"It's a lie," he said again.

In the center of the Grand Convocation Chamber, Palpatine leaned upon the Chancellor's Podium as though he drew strength from the Great Seal on its front. "This has been the most trying of times, but we have passed the test. The war is *over!*"

The Senate roared.

"The Separatists have been utterly defeated, and the *Republic will stand!* United! United and *free!*"

The Senate roared.

"The Jedi Rebellion was our final test—it was the last gasp of the forces of darkness! Now we have left that darkness behind us forever, and a new day has begun! It is *morning* in the Republic!"

The Senate roared.

Padmé stared without blinking. "Here it comes," she said numbly.

Bail shook his head. "Here what comes?"

"You'll see."

"Never again will we be divided! Never again will sector turn against sector, planet turn against planet, *sibling* turn against *sibling*! We are one nation, *indivisible*!"

The Senate roared.

"To ensure that we will always stand together, that we will always speak with a single voice and act with a single hand, the Republic must change. We must *evolve*. We must *grow*. We have become an empire in fact; let us become an Empire in name as well! We *are* the first *Galactic Empire*!"

The Senate went wild.

"What are they doing?" Bail said. "Do they understand what they're *cheering* for?"

Padmé shook her head.

"We are an Empire," Palpatine went on, "that will continue to be ruled by this august body! We are an Empire that will never return to the political maneuvering and corruption that have wounded us so deeply; we are an Empire that will be directed by a *single* sovereign, chosen for *life*!"

The Senate went wilder.

"We are an Empire ruled by the *majority*! An Empire ruled by a new Constitution! An Empire of *laws*, not of politicians! An Empire devoted to the preservation of a just society. Of a *safe* and *secure* society! We are an Empire that will *stand ten thousand years*!"

The roar of the Senate took on a continuous boiling roll like the inside of a permanent thunderstorm.

"We will celebrate the anniversary of this day as *Empire Day*. For the sake of our *children*. For our children's children! For the next ten thousand years! Safety! Security! Justice and peace!"

The Senate went berserk.

"Say it with me! Safety, Security, Justice, and Peace! Safety, Security, Justice, and Peace!"

The Senate took up the chant, louder and louder until it seemed the whole galaxy roared along.

Bail couldn't hear Padmé over the din, but he could read her lips.

So this is how liberty dies, she was saying to herself. *With cheering, and applause.*

"We can't let this happen!" Bail lurched to his feet. "I have to get to my pod—we can still enter a motion—"

"No." Her hand seized his arm with astonishing strength, and for the first time since he'd arrived, she looked straight into his eyes. "No, Bail, you can't enter a motion. You *can't.* Fang Zar has already been arrested, and Tundra Dowmeia, and it won't be long until the entire Delegation of the Two Thousand are declared enemies of the state. You stayed off that list for good reason; don't add your name by what you do today."

"But I can't just stand by and *watch*—"

"You're right. You can't just watch. You have to vote *for* him."

"What?"

"Bail, it's the only way. It's the only hope you have of remaining in a position to do *anyone* any good. Vote for Palpatine. Vote for the Empire. Make Mon Mothma vote for him, too. Be good little Senators. Mind your manners and keep your heads down. And keep doing . . . all those things we can't talk about. All those things I can't know. *Promise* me, Bail."

"Padmé, what you're talking about—what we're *not* talking about—it could take *twenty years*! Are you under suspicion? What are you going to do?"

"Don't worry about me," she said distantly. "I don't know I'll live that long."

Within the Separatist leadership bunker's control center were dozens of combat droids. There were armed and armored guards. There were automated defense systems.

There were screams, and tears, and pleas for mercy.

None of them mattered.

The Sith had come to Mustafar.

Poggle the Lesser, Archduke of Geonosis, scrambled like an animal through a litter of severed arms and legs and heads, both metal and flesh, whimpering, fluttering his ancient gauzy wings until a bar of lightning flash-burned his own head free of his neck.

Shu Mai, president and CEO of the Commerce Guild, looked up from her knees, hands clasped before her, tears streaming down her shriveled cheeks. "We were promised a *reward*," she gasped. "A h—h—*handsome* reward—"

"I am your reward," the Sith Lord said. "You don't find me handsome?"

"Please!" she screeched through her sobbing. *"Pleee—"*

The blue-white blade cut into and out from her skull, and her corpse swayed. A negligent flip of the wrist slashed through her column of neck rings. Her brain-burned head tumbled to the floor.

The only sound, then, was a panicky stutter of footfalls as Wat Tambor and the two Neimoidians scampered along a hallway toward a nearby conference room.

The Sith Lord was in no hurry to pursue. All the exits from the control center were blast-shielded, and they were sealed, and he had destroyed the controls.

The conference room was, as the expression goes, a dead end.

Thousands of clone troops swarmed the Jedi Temple.

Multiple battalions on each level were not just an occupying force, but engaged in the long, painstaking process of preparing dead bodies for positive identification. The Jedi dead were to be tallied against the rolls maintained in the Temple archives; the clone dead would be cross-checked with regimental rosters. All the dead had to be accounted for.

This was turning out to be somewhat more complicated than the clone officers had expected. Though the fighting had ended hours ago, troopers kept turning up missing. Usually small patrolling squads—five troopers or less—that still made random sweeps through the Temple hallways, checking every door and window, every desk and every closet.

Sometimes when those closets were opened, what was found inside was five dead clones.

And there were disturbing reports as well; officers coordinating the sweeps recorded a string of sightings of movement—usually a flash of robe disappearing around a corner, caught in a trooper's peripheral vision—that on investigation seemed to have been only imagination, or hallucination. There were also multiple reports of inexplicable sounds coming from out-of-the-way areas that turned out to be deserted.

Though clone troopers were schooled from even before awakening in their Kaminoan crèche-schools to be ruthlessly pragmatic, materialistic, and completely impervious to superstition, some of them began to suspect that the Temple might be haunted.

In the vast misty gloom of the Room of a Thousand Fountains, one of the clones on the cleanup squad caught a glimpse of someone moving beyond a stand of Hylaian marsh bamboo. "Halt!" he shouted. "You there! Don't move!"

The shadowy figure darted off into the gloom, and the clone turned to his squad brothers. "Come on! Whatever that was, we can't let it get away!"

Clones pelted off into the mist. Behind them, at the spill of bodies they'd been working on, fog and gloom gave birth to a pair of Jedi Masters.

Obi-Wan stepped over white-armored bodies to kneel beside blaster-burned corpses of children. Tears flowed freely down tracks that hadn't had a chance to dry since he'd first entered the Temple. "Not even the younglings survived. It looks like they made a stand here."

Yoda's face creased with ancient sadness. "Or trying to flee they were, with some turning back to slow the pursuit."

Obi-Wan turned to another body, an older one, a Jedi fully mature and beyond. Grief punched a gasp from his chest. "Master Yoda—it's the *Troll* . . ."

Yoda looked over and nodded bleakly. "Abandon his young students, Cin Drallig would not."

Obi-Wan sank to his knees beside the fallen Jedi. "He was my lightsaber instructor . . ."

"And his, was I," Yoda said. "Cripple us, grief will, if let it we do."

"I know. But . . . it's one thing to know a friend is dead, Master Yoda. It's another to find his *body* . . ."

"Yes." Yoda moved closer. With his gimer stick, he pointed at a bloodless gash in Drallig's shoulder that had cloven deep into his chest. "Yes, it is. See this, do you? This wound, no blaster could make."

An icy void opened in Obi-Wan's heart. It swallowed his pain and his grief, leaving behind a precariously empty calm.

He whispered, "A *lightsaber*?"

"Business with the recall beacon, have we still." Yoda pointed with his stick at figures winding toward them among the trees and pools. "Returning, the clones are."

Obi-Wan rose. "I will learn who did this."

"Learn?"

Yoda shook his head sadly.

"Know already, you do," he said, and hobbled off into the gloom.

Darth Vader left nothing living behind when he walked from the main room of the control center.

Casually, carelessly, he strolled along the hallway, scoring the durasteel wall with the tip of his blade, enjoying the sizzle of disintegrating metal as he had savored the smoke of charred alien flesh.

The conference room door was closed. A barrier so paltry would be an insult to the blade; a black-gloved hand made a fist. The door crumpled and fell.

The Sith Lord stepped over it.

The conference room was walled with transparisteel. Beyond, obsidian mountains rained fire upon the land. Rivers of lava embraced the settlement.

Rune Haako, aide and confidential secretary to the viceroy of the Trade Federation, tripped over a chair as he stumbled back. He fell to the floor, shaking like a grub in a frying pan, trying to scrabble beneath the table.

"Stop!" he cried. "Enough! We *surrender*, do you understand? You can't just *kill* us—"

The Sith Lord smiled. "Can't I?"

"We're unarmed! We surrender! Please—please, you're a *Jedi*!"

"You fought a war to destroy the Jedi." Vader stood above the shivering Neimoidian, smiling down upon him, then fed him half a meter of plasma. "Congratulations on your success."

The Sith Lord stepped over Haako's corpse to where Wat Tambor clawed uselessly at the transparisteel wall with his armored gauntlets. The head of the Techno Union turned at his approach, cringing, arms lifted to shield his faceplate from the flames in the dragon's eyes. "Please, I'll give you *anything. Anything you want!*"

The blade flashed twice; Tambor's arms fell to the floor, followed by his head.

"Thank you."

Darth Vader turned to the last living leader of the Confederacy of Independent Systems.

Nute Gunray, viceroy of the Trade Federation, stood trembling in an alcove, blood-tinged tears streaming down his green-mottled cheeks. "The war . . . ," he whimpered. "The war is *over*—Lord Sidious *promised*—he promised we would be left in *peace* . . ."

"His transmission was garbled." The blade came up. "He promised you would be left in *pieces*."

In the main holocomm center of the Jedi Temple, high atop the central spire, Obi-Wan used the Force to reach deep within the shell of the recall beacon's mechanism, subtly altering the pulse calibration to flip the signal from *come home* to *run and hide*. Done without any visible alteration, it would take the troopers quite a while to detect the recalibration, and longer still to reset it. This was all that could be done for any surviving Jedi: a warning, to give them a fighting chance.

Obi-Wan turned from the recall beacon to the internal security scans. He had to find out exactly what he was warning them against.

"Do this not," Yoda said. "Leave we must, before discovered we are."

"I have to *see* it," Obi-Wan said grimly. "Like I said downstairs: knowing is one thing. Seeing is another."

"Seeing will only cause you pain."

"Then it is pain that I have earned. I won't hide from it." He keyed a code that brought up a holoscan of the Room of a Thousand Fountains. "I am not afraid."

Yoda's eyes narrowed to green-gold slits. "You should be."

Stone-faced, Obi-Wan watched younglings run into the

room, fleeing a storm of blasterfire; he watched Cin Drallig and a pair of teenage Padawans—was that Whie, the boy Yoda had brought to Vjun?—backing into the scene, blades whirling, cutting down the advancing clone troopers with deflected bolts.

He watched a lightsaber blade flick into the shot, cutting down first one Padawan, then the other. He watched the brisk stride of a caped figure who hacked through Drallig's shoulder, then stood aside as the old Troll fell dying to let the rest of the clones blast the children to shreds.

Obi-Wan's expression never flickered.

He opened himself to what he was about to see; he was prepared, and centered, and trusting in the Force, and yet . . .

Then the caped man turned to meet a cloaked figure behind him, and he was—

He was—

Obi-Wan, staring, wished that he had the strength to rip his eyes out of his head.

But even blind, he would see this forever.

He would see his friend, his student, his brother, turn and kneel in front of a black-cloaked Lord of the Sith.

His head rang with a silent scream.

"The traitors have been destroyed, Lord Sidious. And the archives are secured. Our ancient holocrons are again in the hands of the Sith."

"Good . . . good . . . Together, we shall master every secret of the Force." The Sith Lord purred like a contented rancor. *"You have done well, my new apprentice. Do you feel your power growing?"*

"Yes, my Master."

"Lord Vader, your skills are unmatched by any Sith before you. Go forth, my boy. Go forth, and bring peace to our Empire."

Fumbling nervelessly, Obi-Wan somehow managed to shut down the holoscan. He leaned on the console, but his arms would not support him; they buckled and he twisted to the floor.

He huddled against the console, blind with pain.

Yoda was as sympathetic as the root of a wroshyr tree. "Warned, you were."

Obi-Wan said, "I should have let them *shoot* me . . ."

"What?"

"No. That was already too late—it was already too late at Geonosis. The Zabrak, on Naboo—I should have died *there* . . . before I ever *brought* him here—"

"*Stop* this, you will!" Yoda gave him a stick-jab in the ribs sharp enough to straighten him up. "*Make* a Jedi fall, one cannot; beyond even Lord Sidious, this is. *Chose* this, Skywalker did."

Obi-Wan lowered his head. "And I'm afraid I might know why."

"Why? *Why* matters not. There is no *why*. There is only a Lord of the Sith, and his apprentice. Two Sith." Yoda leaned close. "And two Jedi."

Obi-Wan nodded, but he still couldn't meet the gaze of the ancient Master. "I'll take Palpatine."

"Strong enough to face Lord Sidious, you will never be. Die you will, and painfully."

"Don't make me kill Anakin," he said. "He's like my *brother*, Master."

"The boy you trained, gone he is—twisted by the dark side. Consumed by Darth Vader. Out of this misery, you must put him. To visit our new Emperor, *my* job will be."

Now Obi-Wan did face him. "Palpatine faced Mace and Agen and Kit and Saesee—four of the greatest swordsmen our Order has ever produced. By *himself*. Even both of us together wouldn't have a chance."

"True," Yoda said. "But both of us apart, a chance we might *create* . . ."

CHIAROSCURO

C-3PO identified the craft docking on the veranda as a DC0052 Intergalactic Speeder; to be on the safe side, he left the security curtain engaged.

In these troubled times, safety outweighed courtesy, even for him.

A cloaked and hooded human male emerged from the DC0052 and approached the veil of energy. C-3PO moved to meet him. "Hello, may I help you?"

The human lifted his hands to his hood; instead of taking it down, he folded it back far enough that C-3PO could register the distinctive relationship of eyes, nose, mouth, and beard.

"Master Kenobi!" C-3PO had long ago been given detailed and quite specific instructions on the procedure for dealing with the unexpected arrival of furtive Jedi.

He instantly deactivated the security curtain and beckoned. "Come inside, quickly. You may be seen."

As C-3PO swiftly ushered him into the sitting room, Master Kenobi asked, "Has Anakin been here?"

"Yes," C-3PO said reluctantly. "He arrived shortly after he and the army saved the Republic from the Jedi Rebellion—"

He cut himself off when he noticed that Master Kenobi suddenly looked fully prepared to dismantle him bolt by bolt. Perhaps he should not have been so quick to let the Jedi in.

Wasn't he some sort of outlaw, now?

"I, ah, I should—" C-3PO stammered, backing away. "I'll just go get the Senator, shall I? She's been lying down—after the Grand Convocation this morning, she didn't feel entirely well, and so—"

The Senator appeared at the top of the curving stairway, belting a soft robe over her dressing gown, and C-3PO decided his most appropriate course of action would be to discreetly withdraw.

But not too far; if Master Kenobi was up to mischief, C-3PO had to be in a position to alert Captain Typho and the security staff on the spot.

Senator Amidala certainly didn't seem inclined to *treat* Master Kenobi as a dangerous outlaw . . .

Quite the contrary, in fact: she seemed to have fallen into his arms, and her voice was thoroughly choked with emotion as she expressed a possibly inappropriate level of joy at finding the Jedi still alive.

There followed some discussion that C-3PO didn't entirely understand; it was political information entirely outside his programming, having to do with Master Anakin, and the Republic having fallen, whatever that meant, and with something called a Sith Lord, and Chancellor Palpatine, and the dark side of the Force, and really, he couldn't make sense of any of it. The only parts he clearly understood had to do with the Jedi Order being outlawed and all but wiped out (that news had been all over the Lipartian Way this morning) and the not-altogether-unexpected revelation that Master Kenobi had come here seeking Master Anakin. They *were* partners, after all (though despite all their years together, Master Anakin's recent behavior made it sadly clear that Master Kenobi's lovely manners had entirely failed to rub off).

"When was the last time you saw him? Do you know where he is?"

C-3PO's photoreceptors registered the Senator's flush as she lowered her eyes and said, "No."

Three years running the household of a career politician stopped C-3PO from popping back out and reminding the Senator that Master Anakin had told her just yesterday he was on his way to Mustafar; he knew very well that the Senator's memory failed only when she decided it should.

"Padmé, you must help me," Master Kenobi said. "Anakin must be found. He must be stopped."

"How can you *say* that?" She pulled back from him and turned away, folding her arms over the curve of her belly. "He's just won the war!"

"The war was never the Republic against the Separatists. It was Palpatine against the Jedi. We lost. The rest of it was just play-acting."

"It was real enough for everyone who *died*!"

"Yes." Now it was Master Kenobi's turn to lower his eyes. "Including the children at the Temple."

"What?"

"They were *murdered*, Padmé. I saw it." He took her shoulders and turned her back to face him. "They were murdered by *Anakin*."

"It's a *lie*—" She pushed him away forcefully enough that C-3PO nearly triggered the security alert then and there, but Master Kenobi only regarded her with an expression that matched C-3PO's internal recognition files of sadness and pity. "He could *never* . . . he could never . . . not my Anakin . . ."

Master Kenobi's voice was soft and slow. "He must be found."

Her reply was even softer; C-3PO's aural sensor barely recorded it at all.

"You've decided to kill him."

Master Kenobi said gravely, "He has become a very great threat."

At this, the Senator's medical condition seemed to finally overcome her; her knees buckled, and Master Kenobi was forced to catch her and help her onto the sofa. Apparently Master Kenobi knew somewhat more about human physiology than did C-3PO; though his photoreceptors hadn't been dark to the ongoing changes in Senator Amidala's contour, C-3PO had no idea what they might signify.

At any rate, Master Kenobi seemed to comprehend the situation instantly. He settled her comfortably onto the sofa and stood frowning down at her.

"Anakin is the father, isn't he?"

The Senator looked away. Her eyes were leaking again.

The Jedi Master said, hushed, "I'm very sorry, Padmé. If it could be different . . ."

"Go away, Obi-Wan. I won't help you. I can't." She turned her face away. "I won't help you kill him."

Master Kenobi said again, "I'm very sorry," and left.

C-3PO tentatively returned to the sitting room, intending to inquire after the Senator's health, but before he could access a sufficiently delicate phrase to open the discussion, the Senator said softly, "Threepio? Do you know what this is?"

She lifted toward him the pendant that hung from the cord of jerba leather she always wore around her neck.

"Why, yes, my lady," the protocol droid replied, bemused but happy, as always, to be of service. "It's a snippet of japor. Younglings on Tatooine carve tribal runes into them to make amulets; they are supposed by superstitious folk to bring good fortune and protect one from harm, and sometimes are thought to be love charms. I must say, my lady, I'm quite surprised *you've* forgotten, seeing as how you've worn that one ever since it was given to you so many years ago by Master An—"

"I hadn't forgotten what it was, Threepio," she said distantly.

"Thank you. I was . . . reminding myself of the boy who gave it to me."

"My lady?" If she hadn't forgotten, why would she ask? Before C-3PO could phrase a properly courteous interrogative, she said, "Contact Captain Typho. Have him ready my skiff."

"My lady? Are you going somewhere?"

"*We* are," she said. "We're going to Mustafar."

From the shadows beneath the mirror-polished skiff's landing ramp, Obi-Wan Kenobi watched Captain Typho try to talk her out of it.

"My lady," the Naboo security chief protested, "at least let me come *with* you—"

"Thank you, Captain, but there's no need," Padmé said distantly. "The war's over, and . . . this is a *personal* errand. And, Captain? It must *remain* personal, do you understand? You know nothing of my leaving, nor where I am bound, nor when I can be expected to return."

"As you wish, my lady," Typho said with a reluctant bow. "But I *strongly* disagree with this decision."

"I'll be fine, Captain. After all, I have Threepio to look after me."

Obi-Wan could clearly hear the droid's murmured "Oh, dear."

After Typho finally climbed into his speeder and took off, Padmé and her droid boarded the skiff. She wasted no time at all; the skiff's repulsorlifts engaged before the landing ramp had even retracted.

Obi-Wan had to jump for it.

He swung inside just as the hatch sealed itself and the gleaming starship leapt for the sky.

Darth Vader stood on the command bridge of the Mustafar control center, hand of durasteel clasping hand of flesh behind him, and gazed up through the transparisteel view wall at the galaxy he would one day rule.

He paid no attention to the litter of corpses around his feet.

He could feel his power growing, indeed. He had the measure of his "Master" already; not long after Palpatine shared the secret of Darth Plagueis's discovery, their relationship would undergo a sudden . . . transformation.

A fatal transformation.

Everything was proceeding according to plan.

And yet . . .

He couldn't shake a certain creeping sensation . . . a kind of cold, slimy ooze that slithered up the veins of his legs and spread clammy tendrils through his guts . . .

Almost as though he was still *afraid* . . .

She will die, you know, the dragon whispered.

He shook himself, scowling. Impossible. He was Darth Vader. Fear had no power over him. He had destroyed his fear.

All things die.

Yet it was as though when he had crushed the dragon under his boot, the dragon had sunk venomed fangs into his heel.

Now its poison chilled him to the bone.

Even stars burn out.

He shook himself again and strode toward the holocomm. He would talk to his Master.

Palpatine had always helped him keep the dragon down.

A comlink chimed.

Yoda opened his eyes in the darkness.

"Yes, Master Kenobi?"

"We're landing now. Are you in position?"

"I am."

A moment of silence.

"Master Yoda . . . if we don't see each other again—"

"Think not of *after*, Obi-Wan. Always now, even eternity will be."

Another moment of silence.

Longer.

"May the Force be with you."

"It is. And may the Force be with you, young Obi-Wan."

The transmission ended.

Yoda rose.

A gesture opened the grating of the vent shaft where he had waited in meditation, revealing the vast conic well that was the Grand Convocation Chamber of the Galactic Senate. It was sometimes called the Senate Arena.

Today, this nickname would be particularly apt.

Yoda stretched blood back into his green flesh.

This was his time.

Nine hundred years of study and training, of teaching and of meditation, all now focused, and refined, and resolved into this single moment; the sole purpose of his vast span of existence had been to prepare him to enter the heart of night and bring his light against the darkness.

He adjusted the angle of his blade against his belt.

He draped his robe across his shoulders.

With reverence, with gratitude, without fear, and without anger, Yoda went forth to war.

A silvery flash outside caught Darth Vader's eye, as though an elegantly curved mirror swung through the smoke and cinders, picking up the shine of white-hot lava. From one knee, he could look right through the holoscan of his Master while he continued his report.

He was no longer afraid; he was too busy pretending to be respectful.

"The Separatist leadership is no more, my Master."

"It is finished, then." The image offered a translucent mock-

ery of a smile. *"You have restored peace and justice to the galaxy, Lord Vader."*

"That is my sole ambition. Master."

The image tilted its head, its smile twisting without transition to a scowl. *"Lord Vader—I sense a disturbance in the Force. You may be in danger."*

He glanced at the mirror flash outside; he knew that ship. *In danger of being kissed to death, perhaps . . .*

"How should I be in danger, Master?"

"I cannot say. But the danger is real; be mindful."

Be mindful, be mindful, he thought with a mental sneer. *Is that the best you can do? I could get that much from Obi-Wan . . .*

"I will, my Master. Thank you."

The image faded.

He got to his feet, and now the sneer was on his lips and in his eyes. "You're the one who should be *mindful,* my 'Master.' I *am* a disturbance in the Force."

Outside, the sleek skiff settled to the deck. He spent a moment reassembling his Anakin Skywalker face: he let Anakin Skywalker's love flow through him, let Anakin Skywalker's glad smile come to his lips, let Anakin Skywalker's youthful energy bring a joyous bounce to his step as he trotted to the entrance over the mess of corpses and severed body parts.

He'd meet her outside, and he'd keep her outside. He had a feeling she wouldn't approve of the way he had . . . redecorated . . . the control center.

And after all, he thought with a mental shrug, *there's no arguing taste . . .*

The holding office of the Supreme Chancellor of the Republic comprised the nether vertex of the Senate Arena; it was little more than a circular preparations area, a green room, where guests of the Chancellor might be entertained before entering the Senate Podium—the circular pod on its immense hydraulic pillar, which contained controls that coordinated the movement of floating Senate delegation pods—and rising into the focal point of the chamber above.

Above that podium, the vast holopresence of a kneeling Sith bowed before a shadow that stood below. Guards in scarlet flanked the shadow; a Chagrian toady cringed nearby.

"But the danger is real; be mindful."

"I will, my Master. Thank you."

The holopresence faded, and where its huge translucency had knelt was now revealed another presence, a physical presence, tiny and aged, clad in robes and leaning on a twist of wood. But his physical presence was an illusion; the truth of him could be seen only in the Force.

In the Force, he was a fountain of light.

"Pity your new disciple I do; so lately an apprentice, so soon without a Master."

"Why, Master Yoda, what a delightful surprise! Welcome!" The voice of the shadow hummed with anticipation. "Let me be the first to wish you Happy Empire Day!"

"Find it happy, you will not. Nor will the murderer you call Vader."

"Ah." The shadow stepped closer to the light. "So *that* is the threat I felt. Who is it, if I may ask? Who have you sent to kill him?"

"Enough it is that you know your *own* destroyer."

"Oh, pish, Master Yoda. It wouldn't be Kenobi, would it? *Please* say it's Kenobi—Lord Vader gets such a thrill from killing people who care for him . . ."

Behind the shadow, some meters away, Mas Amedda—the Chagrian toady who was Speaker of the Galactic Senate—heard a whisper in Palpatine's voice. *Flee.*

He did.

Neither light nor shadow gave his exit a glance.

"So easily slain, Obi-Wan is not."

"Neither are you, apparently; but that is about to change." The shadow took another step, and another.

A lightsaber appeared, green as sunlight in a forest. "The test of that, today will be."

"Even a fraction of the dark side is more power than your Jedi arrogance can conceive; living in the light, you have never seen the depth of the darkness."

The shadow spread arms that made its sleeves into black wings.

"Until now."

Lightning speared from outstretched hands, and the battle was on.

Padmé stumbled down the landing ramp into Anakin's arms.

Her eyes were raw and numb; once inside the ship, her emotional control had finally shattered and she had sobbed the whole way there, crying from relentless mind-shredding dread, and so her lips were swollen and her whole body shook and she was just so *grateful,* so incredibly grateful, that again she flooded with fresh tears: grateful that he was alive, grateful that he'd come bounding across the landing deck to meet her, that he was still strong and beautiful, that his arms still were warm around her and his lips were soft against her hair.

"Anakin, my *Anakin* . . ." She shivered against his chest. "I've been so *frightened* . . ."

"Shh. Shh, it's all right." He stroked her hair until her trembling began to fade, then he cupped her chin and gently raised her face to look into his eyes. "You never need to worry about me. Didn't you understand? No one can hurt me. No one will ever hurt either of us."

"It wasn't that, my love, it was—oh, Anakin, he said such terrible things about you!"

He smiled down at her. "About me? Who would want to say bad things about me?" He chuckled. "Who would dare?"

"Obi-Wan." She smeared tears from her cheeks. "He said—he told me you turned to the dark side, that you murdered Jedi . . . even *younglings* . . ."

Just having gotten the words out made her feel better; now all she had to do was rest in his arms while he held her and hugged her and promised her he would never do anything like any of that, and she started half a smile aimed up toward his eyes—

But instead of the light of love in his eyes, she saw only reflections of lava.

He didn't say, *I could never turn to the dark side.*

He didn't say, *Murder younglings? Me? That's just crazy.*

He said, "Obi-Wan's *alive?*"

His voice had dropped an octave, and had gone colder than the chills that were spreading from the base of her spine.

"Y-yes—he, he said he was looking for you . . ."

"Did you tell him where I am?"

"*No,* Anakin! He wants to *kill* you. I didn't tell him *anything*—I wouldn't!"

"Too bad."

"Anakin, what—"

"He's a traitor, Padmé. He's an enemy of the state. He has to die."

"Stop it," she said. "Stop *talking* like that . . . you're frightening me!"

"You're not the one who needs to be afraid."

"It's like—it's like—" Tears brimmed again. "I don't even know who you *are* anymore . . ."

"I'm the man who *loves* you," he said, but he said it through clenched teeth. "I'm the man who would do *anything* to protect you. *Everything* I have done, I have done for *you.*"

"Anakin . . ." Horror squeezed her voice down to a whisper: small, and fragile, and very young. ". . . what *have* you done?"

And she prayed that he wouldn't actually answer.

"What I have done is bring *peace* to the Republic."

"The Republic is *dead*," she whispered. "You killed it. You and Palpatine."

"It needed to die."

New tears started, but they didn't matter; she'd never have enough tears for this. "Anakin, can't we just . . . *go*? Please. Let's leave. Together. Today. Now. Before you—before something happens—"

"Nothing will happen. Nothing *can* happen. *Let* Palpatine call himself Emperor. Let him. He can do the dirty work, all the messy, brutal oppression it'll take to unite the galaxy forever— unite it *against* him. He'll make himself into the most hated man in history. And when the time is right, we'll throw him *down*—"

"Anakin, stop—"

"Don't you see? We'll be *heroes*. The whole galaxy will *love* us, and we will *rule. Together.*"

"Please stop—Anakin, please, stop, I can't *stand* it . . ."

He wasn't listening to her. He wasn't looking at her. He was looking past her shoulder.

Feral joy burned from his eyes, and his face was no longer human.

"You . . ."

From behind her, calmly precise, with that clipped Coruscanti accent: "Padmé. Move away from him."

"Obi-Wan?" She whirled, and he was on the landing ramp, still and sad. *"No!"*

"You," growled a voice that should have been her love's. "You *brought* him here . . ."

She turned back, and now he *was* looking at her.

His eyes were full of flame.

"Anakin?"

"Padmé, move *away*." There was an urgency in Obi-Wan's voice that sounded closer to fear than Padmé had ever heard from him. "He's not who you think he is. He *will* harm you."

Anakin's lips peeled off his teeth. "I would thank you for this, if it were a gift of love."

Trembling, shaking her head, she began to back away. "No, Anakin—no . . ."

"Palpatine was right. Sometimes it is the closest who cannot see. I loved you too much, Padmé."

He made a fist, and she couldn't breathe.

"I loved you too much to *see* you! To see what you *are*!"

A veil of red descended on the world. She clawed at her throat, but there was nothing there her hands could touch.

"Let her go, Anakin."

His answer was a predator's snarl, over the body of its prey. "You will not take her from me!"

She wanted to scream, to beg, to howl, *No, Anakin, I'm sorry! I'm sorry . . . I love you . . .*, but her locked throat strangled the truth inside her head, and the world-veil of red smoked toward black.

"Let her go!"

"Never!"

The ground fell away beneath her, and then a white flash of impact blasted her into night.

In the Senate Arena, lightning forked from the hands of a Sith, and bent away from the gesture of a Jedi to shock Redrobes into unconsciousness.

Then there were only the two of them.

Their clash transcended the personal; when new lightning blazed, it was not Palpatine burning Yoda with his hate, it was the Lord of all Sith scorching the Master of all Jedi into a smoldering huddle of clothing and green flesh.

A thousand years of hidden Sith exulted in their victory.

"Your time is *over*! The *Sith* rule the galaxy! Now and *forever*!"

And it was the whole of the Jedi Order that rocketed from its huddle, making of its own body a weapon to blast the Sith to the ground.

"At an end your rule is, and not short enough it was, I must say."

There appeared a blade the color of life.

From the shadow of a black wing, a small weapon—a hold-out, an easily concealed backup, a tiny bit of treachery expressing the core of Sith mastery—slid into a withered hand and spat a flame-colored blade of its own.

When those blades met, it was more than Yoda against Palpatine, more the millennia of Sith against the legions of Jedi; this was the expression of the fundamental conflict of the universe itself.

Light against dark.

Winner take all.

Obi-Wan knelt beside Padmé's unconscious body, where she lay limp and broken in the smoky dusk. He felt for a pulse. It was thin, and erratic. "Anakin—Anakin, what have you *done?*"

In the Force, Anakin burned like a fusion torch. "You turned her against me."

Obi-Wan looked at the best friend he had ever had. "You did that yourself," he said sadly.

"I'll give you a chance, Obi-Wan. For old times' sake. Walk away."

"If only I could."

"Go some place out of the way. Retire. Meditate. That's what you like, isn't it? You don't have to fight for peace anymore. Peace is *here*. My Empire *is* peace."

"*Your* Empire? It will *never* have peace. It was founded on treachery and innocent blood."

"Don't make me kill you, Obi-Wan. If you are not with me, you are against me."

"Only Sith deal in absolutes, Anakin. The truth is never black and white." He rose, spreading empty hands. "Let me take Padmé to a medcenter. She's hurt, Anakin. She needs medical attention."

"She stays."

"Anakin—"

"*You* don't get to take her *anywhere*. You don't get to *touch* her. She's *mine,* do you understand? It's *your* fault, *all* of it—you made her *betray me!*"

"Anakin—"

Anakin's hand sprouted a bar of blue plasma.

Obi-Wan sighed.

He brought out his own lighstaber and angled it before him. "Then I will do what I must."

"You'll try," Anakin said, and leapt.

Obi-Wan met him in the air.

Blue blades crossed, and the volcano above echoed their lightning with a shout of fire.

C-3PO cautiously poked his head around the rim of the skiff's hatch.

Though his threat-avoidance subroutines were in full screaming overload, and all he really wanted to be doing was finding some nice dark closet in which to fold himself and power down until this was all over—preferably an *armored* closet, with a door that locked from the inside, or could be welded shut (he wasn't particular on that point)—he found himself nonetheless creeping down the skiff's landing ramp into what appeared to be a perfectly appalling rain of molten *lava* and burning *cinders* . . .

Which was an entirely ridiculous thing for any sensible droid to be doing, but he kept going because he hadn't liked the sound of those conversations at all.

Not one little bit.

He couldn't be entirely certain what the disagreement

among the humans was concerned with, but one element had been entirely clear.

She's hurt, Anakin . . . she needs medical attention . . .

He shuffled out into the swirling smoke. Burning rocks clattered around him. The Senator was nowhere to be seen, and even if he could find her, he had no idea how he could get her back to her ship—he certainly had not been designed for transporting anything heavier than a tray of cocktails; after all, weight-bearing capability was what *cargo* droids were for—but through the volcano's roar and the gusts of wind, his sonoreceptors picked up a familiar *ferooo-wheep peroo,* which his autotranslation protocol converted to DON'T WORRY. YOU'LL BE ALL RIGHT.

"Artoo?" C-3PO called. "Artoo, are you out here?"

A few steps more and C-3PO could see the little astromech: he'd tangled his manipulator arm in the Senator's clothing and was dragging her across the landing deck. "Artoo! Stop that this instant! You'll damage her!"

R2-D2's dome swiveled to bring his photoreceptor to bear on the nervous protocol droid. WHAT EXACTLY DO YOU SUGGEST? it whistled.

"Well . . . oh, all right. We'll do it together."

There came a turning point in the clash of the light against the dark.

It did not come from a flash of lightning or slash of energy blade, though there were these in plenty; it did not come from a flying kick or a surgically precise punch, though these were traded, too.

It came as the battle shifted from the holding office to the great Chancellor's Podium; it came as the hydraulic lift beneath the Podium raised it on its tower of durasteel a hundred meters and more, so that it became a laserpoint of battle flaring at the focus of the vast emptiness of the Senate Arena; it came as the

Force and the podium's controls ripped delegation pods free of the curving walls and made of them hammers, battering rams, catapult stones crashing and crushing against each other in a rolling thunder-roar that echoed the Senate's cheers for the galaxy's new Emperor.

It came when the avatar of light resolved into the lineage of the Jedi; when the lineage of the Jedi refined into one single Jedi.

It came when Yoda found himself alone against the dark.

In that lightning-speared tornado of feet and fists and blades and bashing machines, his vision finally pierced the darkness that had clouded the Force.

Finally, he saw the truth.

This truth: that he, the avatar of light, Supreme Master of the Jedi Order, the fiercest, most implacable, most devastatingly powerful foe the darkness had ever known . . .

just—

didn't—

have it.

He'd never had it. He had lost before he started.

He had lost before he was born.

The Sith had changed. The Sith had grown, had adapted, had invested a thousand years' intensive study into every aspect of not only the Force but Jedi lore itself, in preparation for exactly this day. The Sith had remade themselves.

They had become *new.*

While the Jedi—

The Jedi had spent that same millennium training to refight the *last* war.

The new Sith could not be destroyed with a lightsaber; they could not be burned away by any torch of the Force. The brighter his light, the darker their shadow. How could one win a war against the dark, when war itself had become the dark's own weapon?

He knew, at that instant, that this insight held the hope of the galaxy. But if he fell here, that hope would die with him.

Hmmm, Yoda thought. *A problem this is . . .*

Blade-to-blade, they were identical. After thousands of hours in lightsaber sparring, they knew each other better than brothers, more intimately than lovers; they were complementary halves of a single warrior.

In every exchange, Obi-Wan gave ground. It was his way. And he knew that to strike Anakin down would burn his own heart to ash.

Exchanges flashed. Leaps were sideslipped or met with flying kicks; ankle sweeps skipped over and punches parried. The door of the control center fell in pieces, and then they were inside among the bodies. Consoles exploded in fountains of white-hot sparks as they ripped free of their moorings and hurtled through the air. Dead hands spasmed on triggers and blaster bolts sizzled through impossibly intricate lattices of ricochet.

Obi-Wan barely caught some and flipped them at Anakin: a desperation move. Anything to distract him; anything to slow him down. Easily, contemptuously, Anakin sent them back, and the bolts flared between their blades until their galvening faded and the particles of the packeted beams dispersed into radioactive fog.

"Don't make me destroy you, Obi-Wan." Anakin's voice had gone deeper than a well and bleak as the obsidian cliffs. "You're no match for the power of the dark side."

"I've heard that before," Obi-Wan said through his teeth, parrying madly, "but I never thought I'd hear it from *you.*"

A roar of the Force blasted Obi-Wan back into a wall, smashing breath from his lungs, leaving him swaying, half stunned. Anakin stepped over bodies and lifted his blade for the kill.

Obi-Wan had only one trick left, one that wouldn't work twice—

But it was a very good trick.

It had, after all, worked rather splendidly on Grievous . . .

He twitched one finger, reaching through the Force to reverse the polarity of the electrodrivers in Anakin's mechanical hand.

Durasteel fingers sprang open, and a lightsaber tumbled free.

Obi-Wan reached. Anakin's lightsaber twisted in the air and flipped into his hand. He poised both blades in a cross before him. "The flaw of power is arrogance."

"You hesitate," Anakin said. "The flaw of *compassion*—"

"It's not compassion," Obi-Wan said sadly. "It's reverence for life. Even yours. It's respect for the man you were."

He sighed. "It's regret for the man you should have been."

Anakin roared and flew at him, using both the Force and his body to crash Obi-Wan back into the wall once more. His hands seized Obi-Wan's wrists with impossible strength, forcing his arms wide. "I am so *sick* of your *lectures!*"

Dark power bore down with his grip.

Obi-Wan felt the bones of his forearms bending, beginning to feather toward the greenstick fractures that would come before the final breaks.

Oh, he thought. *Oh, this is bad.*

The end came with astonishing suddenness.

The shadow could feel how much it cost the little green freak to bend back his lightnings into the cage of energy that enclosed them both; the creature had reached the limits of his strength. The shadow released its power for an instant, long enough only to whirl away through the air and alight upon one of the delegation pods as it flew past, and the creature leapt to follow—

Half a second too slow.

The shadow unleashed its lightning while the creature was still in the air, and the little green freak took its full power. The shock blasted him backward to crash against the podium, and he fell.

He fell a long way.

The base of the Arena was a hundred meters below, littered with twisted scraps and jags of metal from the pods destroyed in the battle, and as the little green freak fell, finally, above, the victorious shadow became once again only Palpatine: a very old, very tired man, gasping for air as he leaned on the pod's rail.

Old he might have been, but there was nothing wrong with his eyesight; he scanned the wreckage below, and he did not see a body.

He flicked a finger, and in the Chancellor's Podium a dozen meters away, a switch tripped and sirens sounded throughout the enormous building; another surge of the Force sent his pod streaking in a downward spiral to the holding office at the base of the Podium tower. Clone troops were already swarming into it.

"It was Yoda," he said as he swung out of the pod. "Another assassination attempt. Find him and kill him. If you have to, blow up the building."

He didn't have time to direct the search personally. The Force hummed a warning in his bones: Lord Vader was in danger.

Mortal danger.

Clones scattered. He stopped one officer. "You. Call the shuttle dock and tell them I'm on my way. Have my ship warmed and ready."

The officer saluted, and Palpatine, with vigor that surprised even himself, ran.

With the help of the Force, Yoda sprinted along the service accessway below the Arena faster than a human being could run; he sliced conduits as he passed, filling the accessway behind him with coils of high-voltage cables, twisting and spitting lightning. Every few dozen meters, he paused just long enough to slash a hole in the accessway's wall; once his pursuers got past the cables, they would have to divide their forces to search each of his possible exits.

But he knew they could afford to; there were thousands of them.

He pulled his comlink from inside his robe without slowing down; the Force whispered a set of coordinates and he spoke them into the link. "Delay not," he added. "Swiftly closing is the pursuit. Failed I have, and kill me they will."

The Convocation Center of the Galactic Senate was a drum-mounted dome more than a kilometer in diameter; even with the aid of the Force, Yoda was breathing hard by the time he reached its edge. He cut through the floor beneath him and dropped down into another accessway, this one used for maintenance on the huge lighting system that shone downward onto Republic Plaza through transparisteel panels that floored the underside of the huge dome's rim. He cut into the lightwell; the reflected wattage nearly blinded him to the vertiginous drop below the transparisteel on which he stood.

Without hesitation he cut through that as well and dived headlong into the night.

Catching the nether edges of his long cloak to use as an improvised airfoil, he let the Force guide him in a soaring free fall away from the Convocation Center; he was too small to trigger its automated defense perimeter, but the open-cockpit speeder toward which he fell would get blasted from the sky if it deviated one meter inward from its curving course.

He released his robe so that it flapped upward, making a sort of drogue that righted him in the air so that he fell feetfirst into the speeder's passenger seat beside Bail Organa.

While Yoda strapped himself in, the Senator from Alderaan pulled the rented speeder through a turn that would have impressed Anakin Skywalker, and shot away toward the nearest intersection of Coruscant's congested skyways.

Yoda's eyes squeezed closed.

"Master Yoda? Are you wounded?"

"Only my pride," Yoda said, and meant it, though Bail could not possibly understand how deep that wound went, nor how it bled. "Only my pride."

With Anakin's grip on his wrists bending his arms near to breaking, forcing both their lightsabers down in a slow but unstoppable arc, Obi-Wan let go.

Of everything.

His hopes. His fears. His obligation to the Jedi, his promise to Qui-Gon, his failure with Anakin.

And their lightsabers.

Startled, Anakin instinctively shifted his Force grip, releasing one wrist to reach for his blade; in that instant Obi-Wan twisted free of his other hand and with the Force caught up his own blade, reversing it along his forearm so that his swift parry of Anakin's thundering overhand not only blocked the strike but directed both blades to slice through the wall against which he stood. He slid Anakin's following thrust through the wall on the opposite side, guiding both blades again up and over his head in a circular sweep so that he could use the power of Anakin's next chop to drive himself backward through the wall, outside into the smoke and the falling cinders.

Anakin followed, constantly attacking; Obi-Wan again gave ground, retreating along a narrow balcony high above the black-sand shoreline of a lake of fire.

Mustafar hummed with death behind his back, only a moment away, somewhere out there among the rivers of molten rock. Obi-Wan let Anakin drive him toward it.

It was a place, he decided, they should reach together.

Anakin forced him back and back, slamming his blade down with strength that seemed to flow from the volcano overhead. He spun and whirled and sliced razor-sharp shards of steel from the wall and shot them at Obi-Wan with the full heat of his fury. He slashed through a control panel along the walkway, and the ray shield that had held back the lava storm vanished.

Fire rained around them.

Obi-Wan backed to the end of the balcony; behind him was only a power conduit no thicker than his arm, connecting it to the main collection plant of the old lava mine, over a riverbed that flowed with white-hot molten stone. Obi-Wan stepped backward onto the conduit without hesitation, his balance flawless as he parried chop after chop.

Anakin came on.

Out on the tightrope of power conduit, their blades blurred even faster than before. They chopped and slashed and parried and blocked. Lava bombs thundered to the ground below, shedding drops of burning stone that scorched their robes. Smoke shrouded the planet's star, and now the only light came from the hell-glow of the lava below them and from their blades themselves. Flares of energy crackled and spat.

This was not Sith against Jedi. This was not light against dark or good against evil; it had nothing to do with duty or philosophy, religion or morals.

It was Anakin against Obi-Wan.

Personally.

Just the two of them, and the damage they had done to each other.

Obi-Wan backflipped from the conduit to a coupling nexus of the main collection plant; when Anakin flew in pursuit, Obi-Wan leapt again. They spun and whirled throughout its levels, up its stairs, and across its platforms; they battled out onto the collection panels over which the cascades of lava poured, and Obi-Wan, out on the edge of the collection panel, hunching under a curve of durasteel that splashed aside gouts of lava, deflecting Force blasts and countering strikes from this creature of rage that had been his best friend, suddenly comprehended an unexpectedly profound truth.

The man he faced was everything Obi-Wan had devoted his life to destroying: Murderer. Traitor. Fallen Jedi. Lord of the Sith. And here, and now, despite it all . . .

Obi-Wan still loved him.

Yoda had said it, flat-out: *Allow such attachments to pass out of one's life, a Jedi must,* but Obi-Wan had never let himself understand. He had argued for Anakin, made excuses, covered for him again and again and again; all the while this attachment he denied even feeling had blinded him to the dark path his best friend walked.

Obi-Wan knew there was, in the end, only one answer for attachment . . .

He let it go.

The lake of fire, no longer held back by the ray shield, chewed away the shore on which the plant stood, and the whole massive structure broke loose, sending both warriors skidding, scrabbling desperately for handholds down tilting durasteel slopes that were rapidly becoming cliffs; they hung from scraps of cable as the plant's superstructure floated out into the lava, sinking slowly as its lower levels melted and burned away.

Anakin kicked off from the toppling superstructure, swinging through a wide arc over the lava's boil. Obi-Wan shoved out and met him there, holding the cable with one hand and the Force, angling his blade high. Anakin flicked a Shien whipcrack at his knees. Obi-Wan yanked his legs high and slashed through the cable above Anakin's hand, and Anakin fell.

Pockets of gas boiled to the surface of the lava, gouting flame like arms reaching to gather him in.

But Anakin's momentum had already swung back toward the dissolving wreck of the collection plant, and the Force carried him within reach of another cable. Obi-Wan whipped his legs around his cable, altering its arc to bring him within reach of the one from which Anakin now dangled, but Anakin was on to this game now, and he swung cable-to-cable ahead of Obi-Wan's advance, using the Force to carry himself higher and higher, forcing Obi-Wan to counter by doing the same; on this terrain, altitude was everything.

Simultaneous surges of the Force carried them both spinning up off the cables to the slant of the toppling superstructure's crane deck. Obi-Wan barely got his feet on the metal before Anakin pounced on him and they stood almost toe-to-toe, blades whirling and crashing on all sides, while around them the collection plant's maintenance droids still tinkered mindlessly away at the doomed machinery, as they would continue to do until lava closed over them and they melted to their constituent molecules and dissolved into the flow.

A roar louder even than the volcano's eruption came from the river ahead; metal began to shriek and stretch. The river dropped away in a vertical sheet of fire that vanished into boiling clouds of smoke and gases.

The whole collection plant was being carried, inexorably, out over a vast lava-fall.

Obi-Wan decided he didn't really want to see what was at the bottom.

He turned Anakin's blade aside with a two-handed block and landed a solid kick that knocked the two apart. Before Anakin could recover his balance, Obi-Wan took a running leap that became a graceful dive headlong off the crane deck. He hurtled down past level after level, and only a few tens of meters above the lava itself the Force called a dangling cable to his hand, turning his dive into a swing that carried him high and far, to the very limit of the cable.

And he let it go.

As though jumping from a swing in the Temple playrooms,

his velocity sent him flying up and out over a catenary arc that shot him toward the river's shore.

Toward. Not quite *to*.

But the Force had led him here, and again it had not betrayed him: below, humming along a few meters above the lava river, came a big, slow old repulsorlift platform, carrying droids and equipment out toward a collection plant that its programming was not sophisticated enough to realize was about to be destroyed.

Obi-Wan flipped in the air and let the Force bring him to a catfooted landing. An adder-quick stab of his lightsaber disabled the platform's guidance system, and Obi-Wan was able to direct it back toward the shore with a simple shift of his weight.

He turned to watch as the collection plant shrieked like the damned in a Corellian hell, crumbling over the brink of the falls until it vanished into invisible destruction.

Obi-Wan lowered his head. "Good-bye, old friend."

But the Force whispered a warning, and Obi-Wan lifted his head in time to see Anakin come hurtling toward him out from the boil of smoke above the falls, perched on a tiny repulsorlift droid. The little droid was vastly swifter than Obi-Wan's logy old cargo platform, and Anakin was easily able to swing around Obi-Wan and cut him off from the shore. Obi-Wan shifted weight one way, then another, but Anakin's droid was nimble as a sand panther; there was no way around, and this close to the lava, the heat was intense enough to crisp Obi-Wan's hair.

"This is the end for you, Master," he said. "I wish it were otherwise."

"Yes, Anakin, so do I," Obi-Wan said as he sprinted into a leaping dive, making a spear of his blade.

Anakin leaned aside and deflected the thrust almost contemptuously; he missed a cut at Obi-Wan's legs as the Jedi Master flew past him.

Obi-Wan turned his dive into a forward roll that left him barely teetering on the rim of a low cliff, just above the soft black sand of the riverbank. Anakin snarled a curse as he realized he'd been suckered, and leapt off his droid at Obi-Wan's back—

Half a second too slow.

Obi-Wan's whirl to parry didn't meet Anakin's blade. It met his knee. Then his other knee.

And while Anakin was still in the air, burned-off lower legs only starting their topple down the cliff, Obi-Wan's recovery to guard brought his blade through Anakin's left arm above the elbow. He stepped back as Anakin fell.

Anakin dropped his lightsaber, clawing at the edge of the cliff with his mechanical hand, but his grip was too powerful for the lava bank and it crumbled, and he slid down onto the black sand. His severed legs and his severed arm rolled into the lava below him and burned to ash in sudden bursts of scarlet flame.

The same color, Obi-Wan observed distantly, as a Sith blade.

Anakin scrabbled at the soft black sand, but struggling only made him slip farther. The sand itself was hot enough that digging his durasteel fingers into it burned off his glove, and his robes began to smolder.

Obi-Wan picked up Anakin's lightsaber. He lifted his own as well, weighing them in his hands. Anakin had based his design upon Obi-Wan's. So similar they were.

So differently they had been used.

"Obi-Wan . . . ?"

He looked down. Flame licked the fringes of Anakin's robe, and his long hair had blackened, and was beginning to char.

"You were the chosen one! It was said you would destroy the Sith, not join them. It was you who would bring balance to the Force, not leave it in darkness. You were my brother, Anakin," said Obi-Wan Kenobi. "I loved you, but I could not save you."

A flash of metal through the sky, and Obi-Wan felt the darkness closing in around them both. He knew that ship: the Chancellor's shuttle. Now, he supposed, the *Emperor*'s shuttle.

Yoda had failed. He might have died.

He might have left Obi-Wan alone: the last Jedi.

Below his feet, Darth Vader burst into flame.

"I *hate* you," he screamed.

Obi-Wan looked down. It would be a mercy to kill him.

He was not feeling merciful.

He was feeling calm, and clear, and he knew that to climb down to that black beach might cost him more time than he had.

Another Sith Lord approached.

In the end, there was only one choice. It was a choice he had made many years before, when he had passed his trials of Jedi Knighthood, and sworn himself to the Jedi forever. In the end, he was still Obi-Wan Kenobi, and he was still a Jedi, and he would not murder a helpless man.

He would leave it to the will of the Force.

He turned and walked away.

After a moment, he began to run.

He began to run because he realized, if he was fast enough, there was one thing he still could do for Anakin. He still could do honor to the memory of the man he had loved, and to the vanished Order they both had served.

At the landing deck, C-3PO stood on the skiff's landing ramp, waving frantically. "Master Kenobi! Please hurry!"

"Where's Padmé?"

"Already inside, sir, but she is badly hurt."

Obi-Wan ran up the ramp to the skiff's cockpit and fired the engines. As the Chancellor's shuttle curved in toward the landing deck, the sleek mirror-finished skiff streaked for the stars.

Obi-Wan never looked back.

A NEW JEDI ORDER

A Naboo skiff reverted to realspace and flashed toward an alien medical installation in the asteroid belt of Polis Massa.

Tantive IV reentered reality only moments behind.

And on Mustafar, below the red thunder of a volcano, a Sith Lord had already snatched from sand of black glass the charred torso and head of what once had been a man, and had already leapt for the cliffbank above with effortless strength, and had already roared to his clones to *bring the medical capsule immediately!*

The Sith Lord lowered the limbless man tenderly to the cool ground above, and laid his hand across the cracked and blackened mess that once had been his brow, and he set his will upon him.

Live, Lord Vader. Live, my apprentice.

Live.

Beyond the transparent crystal of the observation dome on the airless crags of Polis Massa, the galaxy wheeled in a spray of hard, cold pinpricks through the veil of infinite night.

Beneath that dome sat Yoda. He did not look at the stars.

He sat a very long time.

Even after nearly nine hundred years, the road to self-knowledge was rugged enough to leave him bruised and bleeding.

He spoke softly, but not to himself.

Though no one was with him, he was not alone.

"My failure, this was. Failed the Jedi, I did."

He spoke to the Force.

And the Force answered him. *Do not blame yourself, my old friend.*

As it sometimes had these past thirteen years, when the Force spoke to him, it spoke in the voice of Qui-Gon Jinn.

"Too old I was," Yoda said. "Too rigid. Too arrogant to see that the old way is not the *only* way. These Jedi, I trained to become the Jedi who had trained me, long centuries ago—but those ancient Jedi, of a different time they were. Changed, has the galaxy. Changed, the Order did not—because *let* it change, *I* did not."

More easily said than done, my friend.

"An infinite mystery is the Force." Yoda lifted his head and turned his gaze out into the wheel of stars. "Much to learn, there still is."

And you will have time to learn it.

"Infinite knowledge . . ." Yoda shook his head. "Infinite time, does that require."

With my help, you can learn to join with the Force, yet retain consciousness. You can join your light to it forever. Perhaps, in time, even your physical self.

Yoda did not move. "Eternal life . . ."

The ultimate goal of the Sith, yet they can never achieve it; it comes only by the release of self, not the exaltation of self. It comes through compassion, not greed. Love is the answer to the darkness.

"Become one with the Force, yet influence still to have . . ." Yoda mused. "A power greater than all, it is."

It cannot be granted; it can only be taught. It is yours to learn, if you wish it.

Slowly, Yoda nodded. "A very great Jedi Master you have become, Qui-Gon Jinn. A very great Jedi Master you always were, but too blind I was to see it."

He rose, and folded his hands before him, and inclined his head in the Jedi bow of respect.

The bow of the student, in the presence of the Master.

"Your apprentice, I gratefully become."

He was well into his first lesson when the hatch cycled open behind him. He turned.

In the corridor beyond stood Bail Organa. He looked stricken.

"Obi-Wan is asking for you at the surgical theater," he said. "It's Padmé. She's dying."

Obi-Wan sat beside her, holding one cold, still hand in both of his. "Don't give up, Padmé."

"Is it . . ." Her eyes rolled blindly. "It's a girl. Anakin thinks it's a girl."

"We don't know yet. In a minute . . . you have to stay *with* us."

Below the opaque tent that shrouded her from chest down, a pair of surgical droids assisted with her labor. A general medical droid fussed and tinkered among the clutter of scanners and equipment.

"If it's . . . a girl—oh, oh, oh *no* . . ."

Obi-Wan cast an appeal toward the medical droid. "Can't you do something?"

"All organic damage has been repaired." The droid checked another readout. "This systemic failure cannot be explained."

Not physically, Obi-Wan thought. He squeezed her hand as though he could keep life within her body by simple pressure. "Padmé, you *have* to hold on."

"If it's a girl . . . ," she gasped, "name her Leia . . ."

One of the surgical droids circled out from behind the tent, cradling in its padded arms a tiny infant, already swabbed clean and breathing, but without even the hint of tears.

The droid announced softly, "It's a boy."

Padmé reached for him with her trembling free hand, but she had no strength to take him; she could only touch her fingers to the baby's forehead.

She smiled weakly. *"Luke . . ."*

The other droid now rounded the tent as well, with another clean, quietly solemn infant. ". . . and a girl."

But she had already fallen back against her pillow.

"Padmé, you have twins," Obi-Wan said desperately. "They *need* you—please hang on . . ."

"Anakin . . ."

"Anakin . . . isn't here, Padmé," he said, though he didn't think she could hear.

"Anakin, I'm sorry. I'm so sorry . . . Anakin, please, I *love* you . . ."

In the Force, Obi-Wan felt Yoda's approach, and he looked up to see the ancient Master beside Bail Organa, both staring the same grave question down through the surgical theater's observation panel.

The only answer Obi-Wan had was a helpless shake of his head.

Padmé reached across with her free hand, with the hand she had laid upon the brow of her firstborn son, and pressed something into Obi-Wan's palm.

For a moment, her eyes cleared, and she knew him.

"Obi-Wan . . . there . . . is still good in him. I know there is . . . still . . ."

Her voice faded to an empty sigh, and she sagged back against the pillow. Half a dozen different scanners buzzed with conflicting alarm tones, and the medical droids shooed him from the room.

He stood in the hall outside, looking down at what she had pressed into his hand. It was a pendant of some kind, an amulet, unfamiliar sigils carved into some sort of organic material, strung on a loop of leather. In the Force, he could feel traces of the touch of her skin.

When Yoda and Bail came for him, he was still standing there, staring at it.

"She put this in my hand—" For what seemed the dozenth time this day, he found himself blinking back tears. "—and I don't even know what it is."

"Precious to her, it must have been," Yoda said slowly. "Buried with her, perhaps it should be."

Obi-Wan looked down at the simple, child-like symbols carved into it, and felt from it in the Force soaring echoes of transcendent love, and the bleak, black despair of unendurable heartbreak.

"Yes," he said. "Yes. Perhaps that would be best."

Around a conference table on *Tantive IV,* Bail Organa, Obi-Wan Kenobi, and Yoda met to decide the fate of the galaxy.

"To Naboo, send her body . . ." Yoda stretched his head high, as though tasting a current in the Force. "Pregnant, she must still appear. Hidden, safe, the children must be kept. Foundation of the new Jedi Order, they will be."

"We should split them up," Obi-Wan said. "Even if the Sith find one, the other may survive. I can take the boy, Master Yoda, and you take the girl. We can hide them away, keep them safe— train them as Anakin *should* have been trained—"

"No." The ancient Master lowered his head again, closing his eyes, resting his chin on his hands that were folded over the head of his stick.

Obi-Wan looked uncertain. "But how are they to learn the self-discipline a Jedi needs? How are they to master skills of the Force?"

"Jedi training, the sole source of self-discipline is not. When right is the time for skills to be taught, to us the living Force will bring them. Until then, wait we will, and watch, and learn."

"I can . . ." Bail Organa stopped, flushing slightly. "I'm sorry to interrupt, Masters; I know little about the Force, but I do know something of love. The Queen and I—well, we've always talked of adopting a girl. If you have no objection, I would like to take Leia to Alderaan, and raise her as our daughter. She would be loved with us."

Yoda and Obi-Wan exchanged a look. Yoda tilted his head. "No happier fate could any child ask for. With our blessing, and that of the Force, let Leia be your child."

Bail stood, a little jerkily, as though he simply could no longer keep his seat. His flush had turned from embarrassment to pure uncomplicated joy. "Thank you, Masters—I don't know what else to say. Thank you, that's all. What of the boy?"

"Cliegg Lars still lives on Tatooine, I think—and Anakin's stepbrother . . . Owen, that's it, and his wife, Beru, still work the moisture farm outside Mos Eisley . . ."

"As close to kinfolk as the boy can come," Yoda said approvingly. "But Tatooine, not like Alderaan it is—deep in the Outer Rim, a wild and dangerous planet."

"Anakin survived it," Obi-Wan said. "Luke can, too. And I can—well, I could take him there, and watch over him. Protect him from the worst of the planet's dangers, until he can learn to protect himself."

"Like a father you wish to be, young Obi-Wan?"

"More an . . . eccentric old uncle, I think. It is a part I can play very well. To keep watch over Anakin's son—" Obi-Wan sighed, finally allowing his face to register a suggestion of his old gentle smile. "I can't imagine a better way to spend the rest of my life."

"Settled it is, then. To Tatooine, you will take him."

Bail moved toward the door. "If you'll excuse me, Masters, I have to call the Queen . . ." He stopped in the doorway, looking back. "Master Yoda, do you think Padmé's twins will be able to defeat Palpatine?"

"Strong the Force runs, in the Skywalker line. Only hope, we can. Until the time is right, disappear we will."

Bail nodded. "And I must do the same—metaphorically, at least. You may hear . . . disturbing things . . . about what I do in the Senate. I must appear to support the new Empire, and my comrades with me. It was . . . Padmé's wish, and she was a shrewder political mind than I'll ever be. Please trust that what we do is only a cover for our true task. We will never betray the legacy of the Jedi. I will never surrender the Republic to the Sith."

"Trust in this, we always will. Go now; for happy news, your Queen is waiting."

Bail Organa bowed, and vanished into the corridor.

When Obi-Wan moved to follow, Yoda's gimer stick barred his way. "A moment, Master Kenobi. In your solitude on Tatooine, training I have for you. I and my new Master."

Obi-Wan blinked. "Your new Master?"

"Yes." Yoda smiled up at him. "And your *old* one . . ."

C-3PO shuffled along the starship's hallway beside R2-D2, following Senator Organa who had, by all accounts, inherited them both. "I'm certain I can't say why she malfunctioned," he was telling the little astromech. "Organics are so terribly complicated, you know."

Ahead, the Senator was met by a man whose uniform, C-3PO's conformation-recognition algorithm informed him, indicated he was a captain in the Royal Alderaan Civil Fleet.

"I'm placing these droids in your care," the Senator said. "Have them cleaned, polished, and refitted with the best of everything; they will belong to my new daughter."

"How lovely!" C-3PO exclaimed. "His daughter is the child of Master Anakin and Senator Amidala," he explained to R2-D2. "I can hardly wait to tell her all about her parents! I'm sure she will be *very* proud—"

"Oh, and the protocol droid?" Senator Organa said thoughtfully. "Have its mind wiped."

The captain saluted.

"Oh," said C-3PO. "Oh, dear."

In the newly renamed Emperor Palpatine Surgical Reconstruction Center on Coruscant, a hypersophisticated prototype Ubrikkian DD-13 surgical droid moved away from the project that it and an enhanced FX-6 medical droid had spent many days rebuilding.

It beckoned to a dark-robed shadow that stood at the edge of the pool of high-intensity light. "My lord, the construction is finished. He lives."

"Good. Good."

The shadow flowed into the pool of light as though the overhead illuminators had malfunctioned.

Droids stepped back as it came to the rim of the surgical table.

On the table was strapped the very first patient of the EmPal SuRecon Center.

To some eyes, it might have been a pieced-together hybrid of droid and human, encased in a life-support shell of gleaming black, managed by a thoracic processor that winked pale color against the shadow's cloak. To some eyes, its jointed limbs might have looked ungainly, clumsy, even monstrous; the featureless curves of black that served it for eyes might have appeared inhuman, and the underthrust grillwork of its vocabulator might have suggested the jaws of a saurian predator built of polished blast armor, but to the shadow—

It was *glorious*.

A magnificent jewel box, created both to protect and to exhibit the greatest treasure of the Sith.

Terrifying.

Mesmerizing.

Perfect.

The table slowly rotated to vertical, and the shadow leaned close.

"Lord Vader? Lord Vader, can you hear me?"

⸺

This is how it feels to be Anakin Skywalker, forever:

The first dawn of light in your universe brings pain.

The light burns you. It will always burn you. Part of you will always lie upon black glass sand beside a lake of fire while flames chew upon your flesh.

You can hear yourself breathing. It comes hard, and harsh, and it scrapes nerves already raw, but you cannot stop it. You can never stop it. You cannot even slow it down.

You don't even have lungs anymore.

Mechanisms hardwired into your chest breathe for you. They will pump oxygen into your bloodstream forever.

Lord Vader? Lord Vader, can you hear me?

And you can't, not in the way you once did. Sensors in the shell that prisons your head trickle meaning directly into your brain.

You open your scorched-pale eyes; optical sensors integrate light and shadow into a hideous simulacrum of the world around you.

Or perhaps the simulacrum is perfect, and it is the world that is hideous.

Padmé? Are you here? Are you all right? you try to say, but another voice speaks for you, out from the vocabulator that serves you for burned-away lips and tongue and throat.

"Padmé? Are you here? Are you all right?"

I'm very sorry, Lord Vader. I'm afraid she died. It seems in your anger, you killed her.

This burns hotter than the lava had.

"No . . . no, it is not *possible!*"

You loved her. You will always love her. You could never will her death.

Never.

But you remember . . .

You remember *all* of it.

You remember the dragon that you brought Vader forth from your heart to slay. You remember the cold venom in Vader's blood. You remember the furnace of Vader's fury, and the black hatred of seizing her throat to silence her lying mouth—

And there is one blazing moment in which you finally understand that there was no dragon. That there was no Vader. That there was only you. Only Anakin Skywalker.

That it was all you. Is you.

Only you.

You did it.

You killed her.

You killed her because, finally, when you *could* have saved her, when you could have gone *away* with her, when you could have been thinking about *her*, you were thinking about *yourself*. . .

It is in this blazing moment that you finally understand the trap of the dark side, the final cruelty of the Sith—

Because now your *self* is all you will ever have.

And you rage and scream and reach through the Force to crush the shadow who has destroyed you, but you are so far less now than what you were, you are more than half machine, you are like a painter gone blind, a composer gone deaf, you can remember where the power was but the power you can touch is only a memory, and so with all your world-destroying fury it is only droids around you that implode, and equipment, and the table on which you were strapped shatters, and in the end, you cannot touch the shadow.

In the end, you do not even want to.

In the end, the shadow is all you have left.

Because the shadow understands you, the shadow forgives you, the shadow gathers you unto itself—

And within your furnace heart, you burn in your own flame.

This is how it feels to be Anakin Skywalker.

Forever . . .

The long night has begun.

Huge solemn crowds line Palace Plaza in Theed, the capital of Naboo, as six beautiful white gualaars draw a flower-draped open casket bearing the remains of a beloved Senator through the Triumphal Arch, her fingers finally and forever clasping a snippet of japor, one that had been carved long ago by the hand of a nine-year-old boy from an obscure desert planet in the far Outer Rim . . .

On the jungle planet of Dagobah, a Jedi Master inspects the unfamiliar swamp of his exile . . .

From the bridge of a Star Destroyer, two Sith Lords stand with a sector governor named Tarkin, and survey the growing skeleton of a spherical battle station the size of a moon . . .

But even in the deepest night, there are some who dream of dawn.

On Alderaan, the Prince Consort delivers a baby girl into the loving arms of his Queen.

And on Tatooine, a Jedi Master brings an infant boy to the homestead of Owen and Beru Lars—

Then he rides his eopie off into the Jundland Wastes, toward the setting suns.

The dark is generous, and it is patient, and it always wins—but in the heart of its strength lies weakness: one lone candle is enough to hold it back.

Love is more than a candle.

Love can ignite the stars.

If you enjoyed *STAR WARS: REVENGE OF THE SITH,*

and would like to read what happened just prior to the events
of the movie,

the story is told in *STAR WARS: LABYRINTH OF EVIL*

by James Luceno

Available now at bookstores everywhere.